STACKED LIES

Also by Andrew Gruse

Zack Stack Series

Stacked Case

Andrew Gruse

STACKED LIES

To my mother; March 3rd, 2018 was a shitty day.

May you rest in peace.

The world has not been the same without you and I guarantee Heaven has not been the same since you arrived!

We miss you

vi

STACKED LIES

Chapter 1

The crowd assembled for the rally; a U.S. Senator was about to speak. A new candidate for President of the United States, it was time to inspire his base. Julie Fletcher, an investigative reporter, hired by the Senator to pen a biography on the Senator checked her cell phone for messages. She stood in the front row of the makeshift seating at the outdoor park with a clear view of the stage.

Better for her to keep an eye on the Senator and how the crowd reacts to his message, the chief of staff said to her. *It's important to document the energy and emotion that the Senator brings to the masses. That will be key in getting him elected.* That was her directive today.

Julie wanted to see her fiancé, Zack Stack. She hadn't seen him in six weeks. Today he returned from Europe after the exile by Lieutenant Ted Barnes following the Indiana incident. She promised to pick him up at the airport and told the Senator's staff, but the rally took precedence. *We need you to capture this moment,* they said.

"Hey, you must be someone important to get these seats," came a familiar voice from beside her.

Julie looked to her left and smiled at the tall, slender police Lieutenant. He dressed in plain clothes, though he wore a blue Police emblazoned vest. "Hi, Lieutenant," she said.

"Julie, I told you to call me Ted. Only Zack has to call me Lieutenant," he said. "How are you?"

"I'm good, how about you? Looks like you got a little sun lately?" Julie noted the red on his cheeks and nose.

Barnes smiled. "Spent the weekend at the beach. Forgot to put on sunscreen," he said.

Julie laughed. "If I don't put on sunscreen I burn. Look like bacon."

Barnes laughed. "Hear from Zack yet?"

"His plane was supposed to land thirty minutes ago. I was his ride."

"Oh," Ted grimaced. "Until Senator Blowhard called for this impromptu campaign rally?" He shook his head. "This idiot is going to get himself killed. There is no way we had enough time to secure this area." Barnes shook his head. "What is he thinking with an outdoor event? Complete narcissist."

Julie smiled. "You don't like him, either, huh? Zack can't stand him."

"Great minds think alike, Jules," Ted smiled. His cell phone rang. "Barnes, go." He listened, nodded and hung up.

"What is it?"

"Accident on 95. Inside city limits. A couple of bodies thrown from an Escalade I guess. Not pretty."

"Do you have to go?"

Barnes shrugged. "No, but I don't want to be here. I think you can handle this." He put his hand on her shoulder. "Hey, after this freak show, get Zack and let's meet later for dinner. I haven't seen him in four months."

"You sent him away, remember?"

Ted smiled. "Have him call me." Ted turned and rushed off.

Julie looked around; the crowd swelled. The time drew near, and she checked the seat next to her where she placed her bag. The front pointed at the podium.

Now let's get this damn thing going!

Key dignitaries and select people in the Senator's campaign assembled on the stage and talked while they took their places. The murmur in the crowd increased to an excited chatter. To the state of Maryland and the city of Baltimore, this Senator was their hero.

Julie knew the tallest hurdle for the Senator was his popularity outside the I95 Beltway. His campaign was a longshot, and some wondered why he would enter the fray of a presidential campaign.

Julie rechecked her phone. *Zack said he'd text as soon as he landed. He can't be mad at me. Getting a cab instead of me picking him up isn't the end of the world. Besides, I'm getting paid for this, and we need the money. A wedding isn't cheap. Where are you, Zack? He and Dre are probably at a bar already.*

The rally began. A woman took to the podium and asked the people to sit. *Time to focus. How are people responding?* The female host talked, and the people clapped. She introduced the next speaker, a state representative, an excellent lifelong friend of the Senator, she said, and the man took the podium amongst a roar of cheering.

Julie watched the people. They filled with excitement and hope. The state representative spoke, and Julie let herself feel what the people felt: Oh, the vision, the future, it was all going to be great as long as the next man is elected. Not even this beautiful sunny day is as bright as the future under the guidance of the Next President of the United States, the state rep said. Julie rolled her eyes.

The state representative then introduced the man of the hour: United States Senator from Maryland, Michael Rosler. The people roared and clapped and whistled. The electricity in the air was palpable. Julie saw tears flow from the eyes of several women in the crowd. *Their hero.*

Julie knew why the people loved Rosler. He was charming, charismatic, handsome, and articulate. She understood how his spell would capture the hearts of people. He already captured Maryland. The rest of the country was next. Rosler shook hands of the men on stage and hugged the females. He waved to the crowd, and every time he did the crowd exploded into another chorus of applause. Rosler got back to the podium and took it all in. Julie smiled. *This is what he loves most: adoration.*

The people didn't want to stop. They wanted Rosler to know they loved him. They *needed* him to know. Their hero stood on stage. They heard his pitch before: the promises he told, the changes he'd make, the problems Rosler alone could fix. Julie watched the mesmerized people. It was cult-like.

Rosler finally got his silence. The people sat. Julie made sure her backpack didn't budge and knew this was Rosler's favorite moment: *hearing himself speak, even better than hearing people praise him.* He thanked Sam Polzinski, the state representative and who Rosler said would be the next great Senator representing Maryland. The applause ignited again. Rosler silenced them.

"This is an important time for us. For all of us," Rosler paused for effect. He stared at the crowd, passion in his voice, on his face, his posture.

"For it is exactly this moment in time, that we all must make a choice, a choice for the future of this Great Country," and then he paused.

Julie heard a sickening thud; a woman screamed. Julie saw a young female on the stage slump and fall over motionless. Another scream. Blood exploded out of the back of the state representative's head, his body collapsed to the stage, and Rosler keeled to his left and fell to the floor of the stage.

It's gunfire!

THE SENATOR IS WOUNDED! Someone yelled, then pandemonium.

People panicked, screamed, ran in all directions. The police helped people to cover. Julie dove to the ground, her eyes on Rosler. His security team surrounded him and rushed his body off the stage. Julie saw two men in black suits rush towards her; Rosler's private security. They grabbed her as she grabbed her bag.

Police sirens blared, blue and white lights flashed as Julie fell into the back seat of a black Tahoe, the door slammed, and the vehicle sped away. Helicopters circled the area above. Two black Tahoe's raced through the crowd, oblivious to anyone or anything blocking the path. Police escorted the Tahoe's. Inside the Tahoe, Julie listened. Everyone talked at once; orders barked, demanded. The hospital wasn't far. *Get the trauma team ready!*

Julie sat silently in the back seat. *How did I end up in the middle of this?* She closed her eyes. *Why would anyone want to kill Michael Rosler?*

CHAPTER 2

J ulie waited in the emergency room wait-area; Rosler's private security told her to stay put, and guards closely monitored the entrance and exit doors. No one got inside that didn't belong.

The crowded area swarmed with police, critical people on Rosler's staff, his private security and a lot of press. Reporters stood in every nook and cranny of the waiting area and outside the doors with a live camera feed on them, each saying the same thing: *The only news we have is that the senator was wounded, it's believed near his chest and doctors are working on him right now.*

The shooter was still at large; the reporters used terms like senseless, madman, assassination attempt, and all asked why. Then, they would say words like courageous, survivor, and fighter to describe the senator. To Julie, the sound inside the waiting area surpassed the noise after the shooting. The commotion seemed just as chaotic.

She clutched her bag and sat away from the reporters. Julie didn't want anyone to talk to her, to ask what she saw, to speculate why. That's all she heard: speculation. *Why would anyone want to kill Michael Rosler?*

Then, she saw Lieutenant Barnes walk into the emergency room. He had two plain-clothes detectives with him along with two patrolmen. They stopped and talked to a man in Rosler's security. Julie recognized the man: second in charge. The head of security was likely with Rosler.

Lieutenant Barnes was in control and instructed the patrolmen and two detectives. The four men disappeared with the private security man. Barnes looked about the emergency room and saw Julie. The recognition on his face relieved Julie. A familiar face amidst the chaos.

Barnes fought through the crowd, blew off two reporters and reached Julie. She stood, and he put a hand on her arm. "Hey, are you ok?"

Julie nodded. "I'm fine. What is going on? This is crazy," she said.

"I don't know. But, I'm in charge of this investigation, so I better find out," Barnes told her.

"Good. You owe me a story by the way."

He laughed. "We'll see. What are you still doing here?"

"They won't let me leave. Said until the situation is secure and the threat subdued, all campaign staff is to remain on site."

"Oh bullshit," Barnes said. "That's ridiculous. There's no threat here and whoever tried to kill Rosler certainly isn't going to go after you. Come on."

He took her arm, and they fought their way through the thick crowd.

"What happened on 95?"

"You didn't hear?"

"Hear what?"

A reporter jammed a microphone into Barnes' face and asked for a statement. Barnes brushed it aside and forced his way past the horde, a hand firmly on Julie's arm to pull her along.

"Ted, hear what? What's going on?"

"Zack and Dre were involved," he said. Julie stopped. Ted stopped and looked at her. "It wasn't an accident. It looks like someone grabbed them at the airport. Shots were fired."

Julie's face turned white. Her mouth dropped, and tears filled her eyes. "And Zack?"

"I thought you knew. I'm sorry, Jules. He's here somewhere."

"What?"

"He's alive, that's all I know. I wasn't able to get to him before the ambulance took him away. Dre's fine."

"Oh my God!" She covered her mouth. "I should have been there."

"Dre said they were targeted. Whoever picked them up was waiting for them," Ted said.

"What? How did they know? Who are they?"

Ted shook his head. "Don't know. Not surprisingly, Zack and Dre killed all three. No leads on that. I want to know how the hell anyone knew Zack was arriving today. Anyway, he's somewhere upstairs. This is not how I envisioned this day turning out."

"I need to see him," Julie said.

"So do I."

The order to remain was firm, Julie knew it. She looked across the room and on the other side of the waiting room, three men in black suits, Rosler's private security, interrogated a member of the entourage. Julie remembered seeing the person in the front row four seats away. The men took the woman's phone and purse and searched it.

"Ted, I need a favor," she said softly.

"What?"

"They won't search you, right?" He shook his head. "Take my bag and get it out of here. Ok?"

She handed him the bag below her waist, out of sight from onlookers.

"Don't ask questions, Ted. Please get it out of here and don't let anyone search it, Ok?"

Ted exhaled and nodded. "This sounds like you and Zack." He pretended to look at his watch. "Consider it done." He tucked the bag under his arm. "Do I have to worry about doing time for this?"

Julie smiled. "No. Thank you, Ted. I'll get it from you as soon as they let me out of here."

The three security suits moved their way from one person to another and then saw Julie.

"Miss Fletcher, may we have a word with you?"

Julie moved closer to Lieutenant Barnes. She waited for them to speak but said nothing.

One of the men nodded and smiled. "Miss Fletcher, you know what happened today. Two people killed, and the Senator is wounded. As part of the private investigation," he looked at Barnes but continued, "we are asking the people who were there for their phones and any electronic equipment they had."

"Why?" Barnes asked.

"Sir," the man looked at the badge Ted eagerly displayed, "Lieutenant, today's event we explicitly told everyone no recording devices of any sort were to be held or used, for security sake," he said. "But there were reports some people did possibly record the event, and we need those recordings."

"Well, I don't have any. I wasn't there," Ted said.

The men looked at Julie. "I don't have anything," she said.

"Miss Fletcher, you were seen carrying a bag."

"I was," she said.

"We need to see it."

"It isn't here," she said. "You guys grabbed me before I could grab it off the chair."

One of the men looked at the bag tucked under Ted's arm. "Miss, is that your bag?" He pointed to it.

"No," Julie said. "I told you, it's at the park. It's probably in possession of some homeless person right now. Probably using my credit cards for alcohol and selling my stuff for drug money. Thanks a lot, by the way."

The men looked at Julie then to Barnes. "Sir, can we look inside that bag?"

"No," Ted said plainly. "It's police business, and I'm the police. I'm in charge of the investigation of the assassination attempt on your boss. If you come across any of those recordings, I'd like to see them myself."

"So you're not going to look inside that bag?"

"This bag is mine. It's none of your business, and if you want to look inside, you're going to have to look down the barrel of my .357 first." Ted stared down the men. "Your problem is elsewhere, gentlemen. It isn't here."

The men looked at each other, then at Ted, but left after an awkward moment. Ted looked at Julie. "I'm getting out of here right now. They want whatever you have inside here. You better stay," he said.

"No, take me with. I need to see Zack," Julie said.

Ted shook his head. "You want to draw any more suspicion to yourself, then let's go. But my guess is you don't. Be a good girl and play along. Do you have your phone?"

"It's in the bag."

Ted handed her one of his. "Here, it's my personal cell. Call my work number when you can leave. I'll get you home."

"What about Zack?"

Ted frowned and shrugged. "Stay low. Don't cause trouble." He winked and walked away.

Julie sat down along a wall near a window. She watched the security complete their interrogation of every person in the room. Julie, nervous and anxious, played with her fingers as she sat.

* * * * * *

At a hallway at the end of the room, the head of the security, Pete Kilgas, stopped by one of his men. "How did it go?"

"Good. No one had anything. No pictures, no video or recordings."

"What about Fletcher, the reporter?"

The man shook his head. "She claimed she left her bag at the park."

Kilgas looked across the room and saw her. "Bullshit. Where is it?"

"I think she gave it to the BPD Lieutenant in charge of the investigation."

Kilgas shook his head. "Damnit. Oh well. I doubt she was recording anything. And even if she was, it won't show anything."

"What do you want us to do?"

"Keep her here. Her boyfriend Stack is upstairs. I don't want her going anywhere near him. If she asks, make up some security crap. Say there was a credible threat of the shooter still looking for the senator. I don't care. Just keep her here along with everyone else. Let's keep a lid on any information until I say, got it?"

The boss saw Julie and looked one more time at the attractive sandy-blonde haired female. No matter how she looked, she was beautiful, and he understood why the Senator chose her to write his biography.

She was nervous and agitated. Frazzled, he thought and wondered why. *Seeing two people killed and a Senator shot would frazzle anyone. Stack is a lucky*

9

man. She is a hottie. Smart, too. Better keep an eye on her. He walked down the hallway and entered the room where the medical staff attended to the Senator, his boss. His boss was smiling and flirting with the nurses. *This is going to come back and bite me in the ass.*

CHAPTER 3

Lieutenant Ted Barnes found the room on the third floor, far away from the commotion surrounding the emergency room. The door was open, and there was the patient with a nurse standing alongside the bed chatting away with him while she checked his pulse. They didn't see Barnes enter, so he stood quietly in the doorway.

"So are you going to tell me what happened?" The nurse asked.

"Bad luck, I guess," the patient answered. "But I'm fine so go tell the doctor I'm fine so I can get out of here."

The nurse shook her head and put a stethoscope to his chest. "Take a deep breath." He did. "Again." He did. "Does that hurt?"

"Yes."

"It should." She smiled. "I'm not stupid. I know what happened."

"Tell me then because I don't know what happened."

"You were lucky. And judging by the other side of your ribcage, you were shot there recently, too."

"Yeah, that was an oversight on my part."

"And you're not a cop or a drug dealer or anything like that?"

"Nope, just an ordinary guy."

"Being a regular gunshot victim is not ordinary."

He smiled and winked. "Ok, so maybe I'm extraordinary."

"Ha-Ha, very funny." She turned to a computer terminal and entered data from her examination.

"By the way, I was shot in the ribs so why did they have to take off my clothes? I mean, I go to the dentist, and they don't make me strip for an X-Ray."

"Maybe I just wanted to see you with your clothes off," she smiled at him.

"I hope it was good for you."

"Did you hear me complain?"

"I didn't hear anything," the patient said.

Barnes smiled and entered the room with a clearing of his throat.

"Lieutenant Ted Barnes," the man said with a smile, "fancy seeing you here. Lieutenant meet my nurse, Stefani Oakley," he said.

Barnes greeted her and looked her up and down. Dark hair, shoulder length she wore in a ponytail, big brown eyes, wide bright smile, smooth white skin and a lovely figure. Even in the light green nurse scrubs, he could see her curves. Very attractive and she seemed to like flirting with the man on the table.

"How's our patient?"

"Zack? Pain in my butt, but he's fine," she said. She looked at Zack and winked.

"Zack Stack, a pain in the butt?" Barnes laughed. "Welcome to my world, Stefani. Trust me, he's typically ornery, obstinate, and a major pain in the butt. He sounds perfectly normal today."

Stefani laughed. "Today was normal? What does he do for a living?"

Barnes shook his head. "Causes me trouble," he said. He looked at Zack. "Stack, how are you feeling?"

"I'll give you three guesses, and the first two don't count and the third rhymes with 'I just got shot.' How would you feel?"

Ted looked at Stefani. "See what I mean?" He walked to the bed. "You were either lucky or smart," he said. "Why were you wearing your Kevlar vest?"

"It saved my life in Amsterdam a couple weeks ago. Figured I'd keep it on," Zack said.

Private detective Zack Stack returned from the Barnes-imposed hiatus in Amsterdam earlier that day with his business partner, Andre Kitchell. After a long four months away from home, Zack and Andre were excited to return home. Today's post-arrival events ruined the homecoming.

"Did you suspect someone was going to shoot you?"

Zack shrugged. He noticed Stefani moving items from a cart into a storage unit in the room. She pretended not to pay attention. "No. I put it on in the airport because I was tired of carrying it and because Dre and I suspected we were being followed."

"Did you tell anyone you were coming home today?"

"Just Jules. Did you?" Zack returned.

Barnes shook his head. "So how did anyone know exactly when you deboarded a plane today after being in Europe for four months?"

"That, Lieutenant, is now a question for you to find the answer. You were a detective once, weren't you?"

Barnes smiled. "Screw you, Stack."

"Why don't you ask the three guys that jacked Dre and I at the airport?"

"Well, one is missing his head," Barnes began.

"That was all Dre, not me."

"The second guy was thrown from the vehicle in the roll on the Interstate, and we found him planted in a parked cars' windshield below the overpass."

"Sucks to be the owner of that car," Zack said. He heard Stefani stifle a gasp.

"And the third guy was thrown and embedded on the grill of a fast-moving Mack truck heading the opposite direction."

"That's why Dre and I always fasten our seatbelts."

Barnes rolled his eyes. "There's no seatbelt on that motorcycle of yours."

Stefani interrupted. "You ride a motorcycle?"

Zack and Barnes both looked at her.

"I'm going to take pictures of all the riders we get after accidents and send them to you. Those things are dangerous."

Zack shook his head. "You could be my fiancé," he said. He looked at Barnes. "Anything else you want to get her to nag at me about?"

"Let me get my list," Barnes said.

"Seriously, Zack, if you saw the things I saw, you'd never ride again."

Zack opened his mouth but stopped short of saying anything. "So why are you here, Lieutenant? This visit is unusual."

Ted nodded and held the bag he got from Julie out. "Here," he said. "This is your fiancé's bag. It's a long story that I don't feel like retelling right now. Just keep it safe until you get home and then I don't care."

"You have a fiancé?" Stefani asked.

Zack took the bag. "How did you get this?" He put the bag beside him on the bed.

"Long story short then. Someone attempted to kill Senator Rosler today. Julie was there covering the rally and was caught in the middle of it. She's fine, but Rosler's security was searching everyone's phones and purses and belongings, and Jules didn't want them to see, so she gave it to me. Now I'm giving it to you."

"Julie is here?" Zack sat up in bed, immediately regretted the sudden movement but his excitement to see her was not quelled. "Where? Did you tell her I'm here?"

"Easy, big shooter," Ted said. "She's not allowed to leave so no; she can't visit you."

"What? Are you kidding me? Why not?"

Ted shook his head. "Rosler's camp is being overprotective right now. She's fine. I'll find her on my way out and tell her you're fine."

Zack slumped back on the bed, irritated and disappointed.

"Rosler was shot?" Stefani asked.

"The Prince of Darkness is probably bullet-proof," Zack said. Barnes chuckled.

"What?" Stefani said. "I like Rosler!"

"Of course you do. For some odd reason, all women do," Zack said.

"Good looking, rich, powerful," Barnes said. "What's not to like?"

"Shut it, Ted. I don't need to hear that right now."

"Why not?" Stefani asked.

"His fiancé, Julie, is working for the dashing and debonair senator," Ted said with a wink.

"Dashing and full of crap," Zack said. "He's a lying sleazeball."

"Oh stop, sounds like you're just jealous," Stefani said.

"Call it what you want. Right now I don't want to hear about Rosler."

Ted smiled. "Right. I'll try to remember. So why did you and Dre get into the Escalade with the three gentlemen who are too dead to tell their story?"

"One had a Glock pointed at my chest; another had one pointed at my back. We didn't have much choice," Zack said. Barnes looked at Stefani.

"Stefani, would you mind?"

"She's fine, Ted," Zack said. He looked at Stefani. "Stef promise you won't repeat anything you hear in this room and will deny hearing anything. Ok?"

She nodded. "I promise."

"What did they say?"

Zack shook his head. "They simply said, 'Get in, we're your ride.' Once we got in, I tried to talk; they weren't in a conversing mood, they threatened us and told us, me specifically, to not take on any new cases and don't investigate anything for a while." Zack remembered the voices, the faces, the tones. The men were serious and the gun pointed at his head was serious. "I asked them nicely to drop us off at a bar since we heard their message loud and clear. Then, some teenage boy texting while driving caused an accident, the driver jerked the steering wheel one direction, Dre and I went for their guns, I got shot in the ribs, thankfully a glancing hit, you know the rest. I must have blacked out because the next thing I remember is someone yanking me out of the overturned vehicle. Then, the ambulance arrived."

Barnes stared at Zack. "We'll do a background on the men — prints, all that," he said.

"You won't find anything," Zack said.

"Why do you say that?"

Zack shook his head. "Because the kinds of guys that force guys like Dre and me into a vehicle at the BWI Airport in midday with security everywhere are the types of guys who don't have backgrounds."

"Which means what, Zack?"

Zack leaned back and closed his eyes. "I have no clue. But I intend to find out."

CHAPTER 4

Mid-morning the following day; Zack Stack limped up the stairs of the Dre-Zack Detective Agency carrying Julie's bag with the hospital admission bands still on his wrist. He pushed open the double glass doors. Andre sat on the corner of Michelle Bormann's desk, the office manager, a cup of steaming coffee in his hands.

"Where the hell have you been?"

"Me?" Zack shook his head. "Didn't anyone know I was stuck at the hospital? They wouldn't let me out until this morning, and I ended up getting a ride home from the nurse that took care of me," Zack said disgusted at the events. He put Julie's bag inside his office and grabbed a Pepsi out of the small fridge behind Michelle's desk.

"Why didn't you call me?"

"My phone didn't survive our run-in with yesterday's goon squad," Zack said. "Anyway, at least Stefani the nurse was super cool about it."

"Yeah? She hot?"

"I'm engaged, Dre." Zack sat on the couch along the wall. "She is hot though. Pretty sure she's into me." He drank from the soda. "Jesus Christ I hurt all over."

Andre moved slowly as well, sore but relatively unscathed compared to Zack. He sat on the other end of the couch. "How's Jules? She must be shaken up after the assassination attempt yesterday."

16

"I don't know. I haven't heard from her and can't find her." Zack shook her head. "It's pissing me off. I couldn't see her at the hospital, and when I was released, she was gone. I don't even know if she tried to call me."

Andre was silent.

"How long you been here?"

"Ten minutes or so," Andre said. "Michelle called all panicky and shit. Upset that she hadn't heard from you yet. There's a crisis, according to her."

Zack leaned back and closed his eyes. "Does she know about yesterday?"

"Not everything. Michelle's in the bathroom. She's in one of her moods. Be prepared."

Zack smiled. "When is she NOT in one of her moods?"

Andre chuckled. The door opened from the bathroom. Michelle walked out and saw Zack sitting next to Andre.

"There they are, my favorite inter-racial couple." She laughed, let out a gleeful yell, ran to Zack and jumped onto his lap. The surge of pain caused him to buckle and grimace.

Andre shook his head and smiled.

"Believe it or not, I missed you! It's about time you're back," Michelle said into Zack's ear and kissed the side of his face.

"I missed you, too, Michelle," Zack said. "Wow, that's the best greeting I got from you since the last time I returned from deployment."

"I was younger and dumber then." She pulled away from him, looked into his eyes and lost her smile. "Now where the hell have you been all day? Do you know what I've been dealing with? Jesus, Zack, you are lucky I didn't pack up and leave you!"

"Now that's the greeting I'm used to."

"Where have you been and why weren't you answering your phone? I've been trying to reach you since you landed at the airport yesterday. You were supposed to call. What happened? Why are you acting like you're in pain?"

"Because I am," he said and gently moved her off of him. "And I need a new phone. Can you do that for me?"

Just then, the doors opened to the office, and a middle-aged woman entered, dressed well, with a purse strap over her forearm. She stopped and saw the three people on the couch to her left. Michelle got off Zack's lap and straightened her clothes.

"Ahh, Mrs. Blumenthal," Michelle said. "Here is who you want to see." She looked at Zack. "Zack, Mrs. Blumenthal is here to talk to you. I'll take her into your office while you get organized."

Michelle led the woman into Zack's office, then reappeared and shut the office door behind her.

"Who the hell is that?" Zack asked as he stood.

"A paying customer," Michelle said.

"Michelle, this is not a good time. Seriously, you need to send her away."

Michelle grabbed his arm, forcibly walked him to his office door, and eyed him. "The world doesn't stop just because you sleep in. Now do your damn job." She smacked his rear end. "Get in there and make that woman happy."

"If I only had a nickel for every time I've heard that," Zack said.

"You'd have what? Ten cents?"

Zack entered his office and saw the lady, her hands in her lap and a slight smile on her face. Well dressed with an aura of well-to-do about her, she was attractive and had jewelry on her wrists, her neck, big earrings, and rings on both hands and held a thick file folder. A massive diamond on her wedding ring caught Zack's eye. The lady smelled of expensive perfume, flowery and sweet but not overpowering. She hid her graying hair with highlights and dye. Zack walked behind his desk.

"Mr. Stack, my name is Cheryl Blumenthal. I'm relieved you're finally here. I waited for two hours yesterday, and this is my second stop this morning. I would think your secretary would have a better idea of your whereabouts."

Zack hid a smile. *Michelle would throw you out if she heard you call her my secretary.* "I'm sorry. I just got back into the country yesterday, and it's been hectic ever since."

"Well, she kept telling me you would arrive any minute."

"Again, Mrs. Blumenthal, I'm sorry. How can I help you?"

"Mr. Stack, I need you to investigate the death of my daughter Ashley."

Zack frowned. "I'm sorry for your loss."

"Three other private investigators gave up, and the police dismissed me. You come highly recommended."

Zack raised his eyebrows. *Fourth? Highly recommended but I'm fourth?*

"Mr. Stack, the police don't believe my Ashley was murdered. I kept pushing but all Lieutenant Barnes could say was that perhaps you could help me."

Zack noted to tell Barnes what he thought of the unsolicited referral.

She put the file folder on his desk and slid it forward. "They said Ashley drowned while at college in a shallow pond on campus. It's behind her chateau quarters on campus. There was a party one night, and she supposedly drowned."

Zack shook his head. *That's why I never water down my drinks.* "Why do you say supposedly?"

"She won the state championship in freestyle swimming in high school. She was a swimmer for the college swim team, lettered all four years on varsity. She knew how to handle herself in water, Mr. Stack. Believing she drowned is simply inconceivable."

Zack opened the file folder. The listed COD was drowning. There was no autopsy per demands by the father. Zack saw the medical examiner's signature. He recognized the name.

Cheryl Blumenthal showed a tear in her eye. "Mr. Stack, please, my husband can never find out I'm pursuing this. This has to be our secret."

Zack looked up from the file. "Mrs. Blumenthal," he began. There was a knock on his door. Michelle entered carrying a plastic bottle of Pepsi for Zack and a cup of coffee for Mrs. Blumenthal.

"Mrs. Blumenthal, again I apologize for Mr. Stack's lack of promptness. Here's some fresh coffee if you'd like."

Mrs. Blumenthal accepted the coffee. Michelle gave Zack a dirty look out of Mrs. Blumenthal's sight and exited.

"Mrs. Blumenthal," Zack began again.

"Call me Cheryl."

"Cheryl, I just," he paused, "look, I don't want to be rude." He sighed. "I know Lieutenant Barnes. If he said this was an accident, chances are it was."

"Mr. Stack, I know my daughter. This was not an accident."

He nodded with a frown. *This is not a good time.* "What does your husband do?"

"He's a circuit court judge."

Zack nodded. "How long ago did she die?"

"Five months ago, near the end of the school year. I want answers, and you are my last hope."

That's a tad over-dramatic. Who am I, Obi-Wan Kenobi? Zack looked at the file. "The file here is everything?"

"Yes."

Zack remembered yesterday's 'courtesy' ride. He knew Cheryl was talking, but only could hear the man in the front seat of the SUV with the Glock pointed at his chest telling Zack and Andre 'you are not investigating anything. Take a vacation.'

"So, you'll take the case?" She asked.

"Mrs. Blumenthal. I have no idea of what you must be going through, and I'm sorry for your loss." He looked at a page in the file. "I know the lead investigators from the police," he said. "Schmidt and O'Malley do good work." *For fat-ass donut-eating morons.* "I'm not sure I'll be able to give you an answer any different than you already have." *How do I get out of this?*

"I believe you can. I know you've put murderers in jail before. I researched you. I know in my heart that something happened. I know my daughter," Mrs. Blumenthal argued. "And I know she didn't drown."

Zack nodded and returned his gaze to the paper in front of him. *No evidence of foul play. The cops concluded that without an autopsy? A medical examiner signed off on that?*

"Please, Mr. Stack. Just read the file. Here's a retainer fee. Document your time, and I'll double your normal fees. But please only contact me at this number." She handed him a business card and a signed check. "And please only contact me between nine to four. I can't have Albert finding out."

Zack saw red flags rise all over the case. *$5000 bucks just to determine a college girl drowned while drunk? Shit, I can't say no now.* "Ok," he agreed. "I'll look into it."

"Thank you, Mr. Stack. Thank you so much." Her face lightened, and she smiled. She stood. "I'll be waiting for your findings." She left the office.

Zack stared at the file and his littered desk. The desk stared back covered with mail, notes with numbers and names and a prominent note on his office phone saying, "Check your messages now, Zack!" Michelle's handiwork. Everywhere he looked he saw piles of clutter that needed his attention. He remembered his ride home yesterday. *No way this is related. Why would they not want me to investigate this?*

He opened the Pepsi, swigged from it and screwed the cap tight. *Second day back and I already need a vacation.* Within thirty seconds of Mrs. Blumenthal's exit, Zack couldn't sit any longer and entered the front office.

"I knew you'd take the case," Michelle said from her familiar perch behind her desk in front of three computer screens.

Andre exited his office. "What was that about?"

"Dead girl. Mom disagrees with the answers."

Andre nodded. "What do you think?"

"Red flags all over this one. My gut says flush it, but she gave us a large check, and this seems like an easy one." Zack gulped more of the Pepsi.

"You think it's connected?"

The vague question went right over Michelle's head. Zack was glad. *Smart phrasing, but she will be pissed when she finds out.* "No, I don't. Why would it?" Zack walked to the window in the office. "You hear from Barnes yet?"

"He called me this morning. So far, there is nothing."

Zack nodded, frowned and turned to Andre. "So, Vigo, Vlad, and Chuck don't exist?" Zack chuckled. "Who would have guessed that?"

"Who are Vigo, Vlad, and Chuck?" Michelle asked.

"Met them at the airport yesterday," Zack said.

Andre smiled. "What now?"

"Wait, what?" Michelle interrupted. "What aren't you telling me?"

Zack sat on the arm of the sleeper couch along the wall that faced Michelle's desk. "You know what I can't figure?"

"Why are you ignoring me, Zack?"

"Talk to Dre," he said. "It makes no sense."

"What?"

"Why would anyone want to kill Rosler?"

CHAPTER 5

Zack leaned against his kitchen counter and watched the national news gush over a man they had rarely mentioned: Michael Rosler. Heroic and brave were two adjectives they often used in their description. But the attention was a double-edged sword, Zack knew. It was the attention Baltimore didn't want. It was the attention Ted Barnes didn't want. However, Senator Rosler was the Golden Boy of Maryland; the whole state was proud of him. And this was news.

Thanks to Julie's job, Zack already knew the score on Rosler. His resume included a successful CEO, a brief stint in the National Guard, amassing legislative victories in Congress also while considered a budgetary hawk. His supporters believed Rosler would win the nomination and become the next President, but the polls weren't favorable.

The reporter stood outside the hospital door and said what everyone else said: no news on Rosler's condition, but he was believed to be in stable or fair condition. Zack scoffed. *I hope he paid Jules in advance. Of course, if the sonofabitch had died, they would have already erected a statue of him.*

Rosler married his college girlfriend who took over as CEO of the family company when Rosler entered the political world. Rosler was handsome which all the women loved, and he talked about his mother and two sisters often in his speeches to show he was in touch with families despite not having children himself. Rosler came from money, and the money only grew when Rosler stepped into power. Rosler was an insider as much as he portrayed himself an outsider. The regional press loved Rosler, but lack of name recognition suppressed his run.

Zack flipped channels. A pundit on one of the political channels said again that name recognition was Rosler's biggest challenge. *I think his problem of name recognition is solved.*

He looked at his new cell phone. Julie was supposed to arrive at any minute. Zack couldn't wait. He was anxious and nervous to see her; it had been over six weeks since he saw her last. The last words she said were "I love you," and then she planted a long, wet, deep kiss on him and walked away. Now, she was about to step into his apartment again.

A different newscast moved on from Rosler and talked about the other victims.

"The two victims have been identified as Maryland State Senator Sam Polzinski, a long-time friend of Senator Rosler and a staffer on his campaign, Hannah Davison." The news anchor took a breath as the picture changed back to Polzinski. "Polzinski was widely speculated to run for Senator Rosler's seat after the Presidential election."

Zack flipped through an enormous pile of mail as the broadcast covered Polzinski and Rosler's relationship. *Thank God for Michelle paying my bills for the last four months. Ahh, Publisher's Clearing House. Ahh, nope, I lost.*

The news talked about the deceased Hannah Davison. The camera switched to a spokesman for the Rosler campaign. A sleazy looking guy named Jerry Pantalini, Rosler's Chief of Staff and top advisor, said how vivacious Hannah was and what a bright future she had and how sorry they were that "this misguided, unfortunate tragedy claimed two innocent lives."

Zack looked at the television as they showed her picture and talked briefly about her. Nothing stood out until they said where she had been attending college: the same as Ashley Blumenthal.

"What a coincidence," he said. *We don't believe in coincidences, Zack.*

His new cell phone rang. Zack stared at the number, didn't recognize it and answered.

"Stack here."

"Zack Stack, private detective extraordinaire?" The voice was deep, male, and pointed.

"Speaking." *Didn't know I was extraordinaire.*

"I'm glad you're back. I think you owe me something."

"Oh yeah? What is that?"

"My freedom, namely. You messed up. Now I'm giving you a chance to fix it."

"Who is this?"

"Look at your past, Mr. Stack. I have, and I know all about you. Do your job, and no one else will learn what I already know."

Zack stopped cold. *Maybe it's just a prank.* "Yeah? What do you think you know?"

The voice laughed. "David Staechel don't mess with me. I know what you're hiding, and I know full well what would happen if that information became public. You have two weeks."

Chills shot through Zack's body. He had hoped his secret remained a secret back in Indiana and to the few people who knew him in Baltimore. He felt his hands shake. "Two weeks? I don't even know what I did."

"Pay attention. You know." The line went dead.

Zack put down his phone and let out a deep, frustrated breath. *Sonofabitch! I need a reset button or should go back to Europe. What the hell is going on?*

Zack didn't have time to think anymore. The door unlocked and the familiar sound of her light footsteps up the wooden stairs to his second-floor apartment filled the air. Zack smelled her scent first, then saw her face and her gorgeous enthralling cerulean eyes. Then she reached the top of the stairs, saw him and stopped.

"Oh my God, Zack. What's wrong?"

"What?"

"You're white. It's plain as day. Honey, you look awful. What happened?"

Where do I begin? "Can I get a hug first?" Zack exhaled. "I've missed you so much."

* * * * * *

ANDREW GRUSE

"You look like shit, Zack," Dre said as they rode in Andre's car. "Did you even sleep last night?"

"No. It was not the reunion I hoped for with Jules," Zack said. He chugged Pepsi for any caffeine kick it would provide.

"No? What happened?"

"Meh, I don't want to talk about it. I don't understand why they needed her this morning so early," Zack said.

"I heard they are releasing the dude from the hospital this morning," Dre said.

"What? The dude took one to the chest," Zack said. "How the hell could," but he stopped in mid-sentence and looked at his partner. "He was wearing a vest."

"Maybe."

"Why though? I mean, is he that paranoid and narcissistic to think he's a target of anyone? Hell, no one even heard of him before two days ago."

"Well, we're here. We can talk about it later. Now, why are we here?"

"Because we don't believe in coincidences and Jules freaked all night about me being alone after she learned of our ride home from the airport." Zack shook his head. *She doesn't even know about the phone call!* "I took my shirt off and ballistic would be the proper term for her reaction." He looked out the window. "I mean, it is pretty black and blue and looks terrible and hurts like hell but could be worse."

Andre laughed. "Buy her some flowers, take her to a nice dinner and have an expensive bottle of wine waiting at home afterward. That should help."

"If I see her. Anyway, I want to get inside the room of Ashley Blumenthal and see if she knew Hannah Davison," Zack explained. "Would you mind doing recon? Check out the pond Ashley drowned in, see if we're being followed, all that stuff."

Andre nodded. "You got it, man. I'll be here."

Zack exited the car and walked down a sidewalk which led him to the chateau-style housing Ashley Blumenthal had stayed the previous spring. He knew it was a longshot at best; a new school year and likely new students were there. Zack doubted any connections existed anymore.

26

Zack surveyed the area as he walked towards the chateau Ashley had lived. Several buildings lined small man-made ponds, surrounded by mature deciduous maples, lindens, and oak trees. The red-brick buildings with white trim around the windows and doors, black shudders and gutters were stately and elegant. Shrubs and flowers in finely manicured beds dotted the thick green grass around the buildings. An occasional school flag hung from a window and flapped gently in the light breeze. Zack suspected rooming in these was not cheap.

He stared at the pond which claimed Ashley's life. About the length of a football field but not as wide, the water was blue with below-surface aerators in each corner, and a decorative fountain at each end kept the water moving and algae free. Picturesque for a recruiting postcard.

With the picture he had of Ashley from the file, he randomly stopped students and asked if they knew her. All said the same thing: sweet girl, a smart student, terrific swimmer and couldn't believe it happened. Every single person that knew Ashley wondered how she drowned but not one person suspected foul play. *I should be able to get this off my radar quickly.* Zack scratched his head and frowned. *Dig deeper, Zack. Cheryl deserves at least some effort.*

Zack knocked on the door of the chateau and waited. A college girl answered the door. She looked at Zack and asked in a short tone, "who are you and what do you want?"

Zack took a deep breath and decided not to waste any more time. He lifted the picture so the girl could see it and asked, "do you know this girl?"

The girl paused, and her face paled. "Why?"

Zack lowered the picture. "Do you know her? Her mother hired me to investigate her death. I was told she lived her last year."

"That's Ash," the girl said. "She roomed across the hall from me."

"So you knew her well?"

"Very," she said.

"Look, would you mind if I came in and asked you some questions?"

"Sure. About what?"

"Her death. Do you think it was an accident?"

"No. Come on in."

CHAPTER 6

She led him to Ashley's former room; the roommate was absent. The girl sat on the bed as Zack sat at Ashley's old desk. Pictures and other items covered it. The girl said Ashley's roommate asked Ashley's parents to leave them.

"Why don't you think her death was an accident?" Zack asked.

The girl shook her head and was hesitant to talk. "Who are you?"

"My name is Zack. I'm a private detective. Her mother hired me, and I want to find the truth."

"Really? The last guys she hired didn't care too much about that," the girl said.

Zack sat back and looked at her. *She knows something.* "Well, I'm not them." He leaned forward. "Do you know something about what happened that night?"

"I wasn't here," she said quickly. "You want to look through her desk?"

Subtle. What is in here? Zack nodded and turned to the desk.

Zack sifted through the items not knowing what he was looking for or if he'd find anything, but he continued. Ashley was a beautiful girl; she was tall at five feet ten, with a dominant athlete's physique. Dull blonde hair she usually wore in a pony-tail with pretty blue eyes, she was the All-American Girl. Many of her pictures were with two other girls who were equally as beautiful.

"Do you know who these other two girls are?" Zack asked the girl.

"The tall one on the right was Ashley's roommate, Meg and the one in the middle is Hannah Davison."

Zack's heart stopped. "Hannah roomed here?"

"Yeah, she was my roommate."

He looked at the girl and saw tears in her eyes. Suddenly, Zack felt like a jerk for being there.

"I know she's dead. Two men came here and told us."

"I'm sorry," he said. "Would you prefer me to leave?"

"No. I'd prefer you to stay. It would be nice to talk to someone." The girl looked at the floor. "It's so sad. Hannah was a good friend," she said and broke into tears. Zack quickly moved to hug her. After a few minutes, she pulled away, apologized and stepped away from Zack.

"It's OK. I happen to be an expert on making girls cry so giving them a shoulder to cry on is natural," he joked. She smiled. "Is Meg here?"

"No," the girl answered. "No one has seen her since Hannah died. It looked like she packed some things and left, but no one knows where." She took a breath. "She lost her two best friends in the last five or six months; she probably went home."

"What two men came here?"

"I don't know. I think they were cops. They wore suits and had badges and wanted to look through Hannah's stuff they said for security reasons."

Zack looked back at Ashley Blumenthal's desk, the one that Meg didn't want to be touched. *Why? That is so odd. Why look at reminders of a dead girl every single day?* "Did they take anything?"

"Just her phone. They wanted her computer, but that disappeared," the girl said. "They searched everywhere and asked a lot of questions. It was almost like they were interrogating all of us here."

He opened the center drawer of Ashley's desk. Nothing unusual. Just the typical laundry list of items a college kid would have in a desk drawer. He opened and closed the top two drawers on the right side of the desk, nothing but in the bottom-drawer was a stack of glossy photos held by several rubber bands.

He leafed through the photos until something caught his eye. He flipped back and slid three pictures out of the stack. He put them on the desk and flipped through several slowly and removed seven more.

"Do you know who these two guys are?" Zack pointed at three pictures. In each image, Ashley was arm-in-arm with a different man.

"That one is her boyfriend, Steve," she pointed. "The other is the swim coach."

Zack looked at the pair in the picture. "You said this one, Steve, is her boyfriend?" The girl nodded yes. "And this is her swim coach?" The girl nodded yes again. "Tell me something, does this look like a coach and one of his swimmers?"

The girl's eyes looked down and to the right. Zack smiled.

"What is your name?"

"Claire," she said.

"Claire, there are several pictures of the coach and Ashley. In these, the two are at a beach somewhere together taking a selfie."

Claire remained silent, and her eyes dodged Zack's.

"You can tell me. Ashley and her coach were lovers, weren't they?"

Zack saw the hesitance on Claire's face. The tightening of her skin as it flushed. Claire knew. Her loyalty was to Ashley.

"It's ok, Claire. I won't tell anyone you told me. I was a Marine. We don't take honor lightly."

Claire exhaled. "I think there was more there than met the eye."

And the dog's name was BINGO! Now we're getting somewhere. The fat flat-foots didn't have that in the report. "Did her boyfriend Steve know?"

"I'm not sure."

Zack convinced Claire to let him search the desks of Hannah and Meg. Meg's had little; as if Meg weren't there. In the bottom right drawer, after nothing in the other drawers, he found a few papers and pictures.

"You don't know where Meg is?"

Claire shook her head no.

Zack put the pictures down except for one nice shot of Meg's face. Then he saw a check stub. He looked at it. "St. Michael's Winery? She works there?" Zack looked at Claire.

She paused, "Uh, she worked there over the summer. Obviously not now." Claire smiled and shrugged.

"You have no idea where she went?"

Claire shook her head no again. "No one knows where she went."

Zack turned to Hannah's desk. It was, in every aspect, the desk of a college girl with a full load of classes. Nothing was of special interest except for one picture in the bottom left drawer. It was her with another man. The same man Zack saw in a picture with Ashley Blumenthal. Both girls now dead and in separate pictures, both arm-in-arm with a smiling man at a remote location: Senator Michael Rosler.

* * * * * *

An hour later Zack and Andre knocked on the door of a frat house. Claire told him Ashley's boyfriend lived there.

"You got the lead on this one?" Andre asked.

"Yeah. Just look mean and ready to rip a head off," Zack said. Zack saw the three different Greek letters. The Greek alphabet was not a subject Zack knew. "What do you think those letters stand for?"

Dre chuckled. "White privilege?"

"Could be," Zack said. "I think maybe they mean 'Ima Giant Douche.'"

"I'll give you a twenty if you're right," Dre said.

The door opened, and both Andre and Zack smiled.

The male at the door said, "Hey, what's up?" He wore worn-out sandals, white socks, sweatpants with the school's name on the side of one leg, a t-shirt one size too small, so it clung to his shaped upper body and had long greasy hair coming out from under the baseball cap that he wore backward.

"We're looking for Steve Moreland. Is he here?"

"Yeah, sure. What about? I mean, who are you?"

Whoever said 'manners maketh the man' clearly studied frat houses. Zack guessed the guy had at best a 1.6 GPA and his major was some non-specific business degree that had the sole purpose of educating this punk on how to spend daddy's trust fund.

"My name is Captain Jack Sparrow," Zack said. "This is my partner, Will Turner. We're here about a piracy issue."

The guy looked confused. "What?"

"Is he here or not?"

"Yeah, ok. Steve is in here."

Zack and Andre followed the guy into the frat house. Their first impression was simple: guys in frats were slobs. Soiled dishes and empty pizza boxes littered the tables, and the corner recycling bins overflowed with liquor bottles and beer cans. Dust, shoes, and dirty socks littered the floor and food crumbs lined the edges of the floors.

Two guys sat on a worn-out soiled couch, each with a game console controller playing a game that Zack didn't recognize. He wondered if that was because he grew up or didn't have time.

"Yo, Steve, these dudes here wants to see you about some piracy thing."

Steve looked at Zack. "What? Who are you?"

"Are you Steve Moreland?" Zack asked.

"Yeah. Who are you? I'm kind of busy."

Zack looked at the television and saw guys in heavy militarized uniforms using guns that only existed in computer games running back and forth shooting monsters that likewise only lived in games.

"What pirate thing? Who are you, man?"

Zack sighed. "Whatever happened to politely introducing yourself? Is that what this overpriced college is teaching you guys? How to be rude?"

Steve and his playing partner stopped, and both looked at Zack.

"Lighten up, man," the other said. "We are in the middle of an epic battle."

"Epic battle? These punks should join the Marines," Andre said.

"Youth is wasted on the young," Zack said. "Were you dating Ashley Blumenthal?"

Steve stopped and looked at Zack. Zack watched as Steve's character got vaporized on the television. Steve swore and put down the controller. He stood from the couch as if to be tough, but Zack had three inches, and thirty pounds of muscle on the kid and Andre was just as imposing. Steve frowned.

"Come on; we can talk outside."

Zack looked at the other guy on the couch as Steve went to the front door. "Good luck in your epic battle, man." Once outside Steve stopped and turned to Zack and Andre.

"Who are you?"

"We're private detective's investigating Ashley's death. I heard you were dating her."

"Yeah, I was. So, what?"

"We have a few questions so relax. If you're telling me the truth, you can go back to your children's game in a couple of minutes." Zack watched Steve's face turn red.

"Shoot."

"How long did you two date?"

Steve looked frustrated. "Two years give or take."

"Did you have any reason to think someone wanted to hurt her? Did she have any enemies or anything?"

Steve paused. "No."

Andre picked up on the pause. "Was everything good between you two?"

Steve paused. "Yes."

Zack nodded. *He's hiding something.* "We've talked to a bunch of students, and they all say the same thing. But if there is any chance that there was foul play involved, we have to follow that lead, you understand?"

"I get it."

"Did you suspect that she was having an affair with her swim coach?" *He knew. Let's see if he admits it.*

Steve paused. "Who told you?"

"Ashley was sleeping with her coach, wasn't she?"

Steve wouldn't make eye contact. Steve put his hands on his hips, and his face went to stone. Zack suspected that Steve wanted more with Ashley, but she wouldn't capitulate.

"She was graduating, and it was over between you two, wasn't it? She wanted to be with her coach?"

"I didn't kill her."

Maybe not, but that's motive. "So, am I right?"

"Yes, she was screwing her coach. That prick has a reputation of sleeping with as many of the girls as he can only the administration won't do anything because the jerk won a bunch of Olympic medals and now the swim program is outstanding and makes money for this place."

"Is this fact or speculation?" Andre asked.

"I caught them doing it! They were at her place, and she broke off our date. Told me it was over but never said why. I wanted an explanation, so I went to her place and walked in and boom. There they were butt naked on the couch."

Zack stared at him.

"But I didn't kill her!"

Zack knew the alibi. Steve was at his parent's house when Ashley died, and Steve gladly repeated it to Zack. The police did at least get that much out of Steve. But they didn't discover the swim coach.

"Just one more question, Steve. Where can we find that coach?"

Moments later, they got back to Andre's car. Andre looked at Zack. "Call the bet even?"

"Yeah, definite tie."

CHAPTER 7

Zack and Andre drove to the other side of campus to the swim coach's office. The two exited the car and walked across the parking lot.

"You sure this is a good idea?"

"I never said it was a good idea," Zack said. "We have a tail or not?"

"I couldn't tell. I saw a car with a couple of dudes that looked oddly out of place, but they drove off, and I haven't seen them since. I'm more worried about Dean Smith, or whatever his name is, calling security and having us arrested," Andre said.

"The Dean is really named Dean Smith?"

Andre shrugged, and the two laughed. Zack opened the door to the natatorium. "Good old fashioned detective work," Andre said. "I miss this stuff."

"You aren't the one getting shot lately," Zack said. "I don't miss that."

Zack knocked on the door of the office of swim coach Gary Tanner. On the wall outside his office, replicas of all nine medals he had won in two different Olympics hung with events like medley, butterfly, freestyle, and backstroke. *Impressive. I bet those medals draw in a lot of talent.* "Does he get cash with those medals?"

Andre shrugged. "I don't know. I don't follow swimming."

"Why not? You afraid of the water?"

Andre smiled. "Dries out my scalp." He ran his hand over his smooth-shaven head.

Zack knocked on the office door again. Two shadows scurried behind the glazed window of the door. The door opened, and Zack stood face to face with Gary Tanner, Olympic Medal Winner. He was six feet tall, white, shaved his head and was well cut. *Staying fit to impress the girls or make a comeback?*

"Can I help you?"

"Yes, you can," Zack replied. "We need to ask you some questions about Ashley Blumenthal."

Gary looked perplexed. "What? Who are you? Are you with the police?"

"No, we're not. I'm Zachary Stack. He's Andre Kitchell. Private investigators."

Gary shook his head. "And you're asking me about her because I coached her?"

Attitude? Really, Gary? "No, we're asking you because you were sleeping with her."

His face paled. "You have no proof, that's a lie."

"We have an eyewitness, Gary." Zack leaned forward to look inside the door. "I see you have company. Did we interrupt something?"

"Yes, as a matter of fact, you did. I'm having a training session with one of my swimmers so if you could come back later."

The disheveled appearance didn't slip by Zack's attention. The easy access shorts Gary wore didn't escape Zack either. Nor did the sweat beads on Gary's forehead. "I'm sure you can make the girl in there come later."

Andre smiled. "Probably make them come often, huh, Gary?"

Gary's face tightened, and he stepped forward. He closed the door behind him halfway as he looked back at the college girl that hid in the corner of his office. "I don't know who you two think you are, but you're out of line, and I have nothing to say about Ashley."

Zack shook his head. "Don't make this hard on yourself. A credible source saw you screwing Ashley. Two nights later she was found dead. You can talk to us or the police."

"Who the hell? What, you two think you can come here and intimidate me?"

"Yes," Andre said calmly.

"Quit playing tough guy, Gary. You either talk to us, or we talk to the police. Or the Dean. I'm sure he'd love to hear about how you're diddling all your swimmers."

Gary's face tightened with anger, and his eyes shot through Zack.

Zack smiled. "Don't even think about it, Gary. You'll be on the floor before you're done missing me with a wild punch. And the girl in there won't think as highly of you after she sees you get your ass kicked. Now save yourself the embarrassment and tell us about your relationship with Ashley Blumenthal."

Andre crossed his arms and flexed. Zack opened his coat to show his gun.

Gary looked at the gun, at the two men, the floor and exhaled. "All right. Come inside."

They followed Gary into his office and saw the girl in the corner on the couch. Seeing Zack and Andre, she quickly threw her shirt over her sports bra. She had a swimmer's build; dark blonde hair pulled back into a ponytail.

"It's ok, Melissa," Gary said to her. "Can you come back later? We can finish our session then."

Zack smiled. *As if I don't know what was going on in here.* The girl left, Zack shut the door and turned to Gary. "Ok, start talking."

"Ok, ok," he said. "Yes, I was seeing her. But Ashley was special. It didn't start until her senior year."

Of course, he's going to say that. Having an affair with a twenty-one-year-old is a lot different than an eighteen-year-old. Or even younger as some of the freshman girls were still seventeen and statutory rape would not look good on his record.

"Her boyfriend caught you two having sex two nights before she died. Is that accurate?"

"Yes, she dumped him, but he wouldn't let her go. He barged in on us."

"And then what?"

Andre looked at the pictures, posters, framed newspaper clippings and awards that filled the walls of the office while Zack did the interrogation.

"Then nothing. Steve left. Ash and I spent the night together." Gary moved a little. "Look, she was a terrific person. Everyone loved her. I loved her," he said. "She was a great swimmer. She had a chance to qualify for the Olympics. She was that good."

"If she was that good, how did she end up drowning in a shallow pond in the middle of the night?"

"I don't know."

"Who else knows that you are screwing your swimmers?" Andre asked.

"I'm not," Gary tried.

"Don't lie to us, Gary," Andre said. "We don't have time for that."

"Look, no one knows. It would ruin my career. I'm a good coach. The school wants me, and sometimes I have a relationship beyond the pool," Gary explained.

Zack shifted his weight. "Where were you the night Ashley died?"

"I didn't kill her."

"I didn't ask that." *Steve said the same thing. Is it that hard to believe she drowned? Why did Barnes' men conclude so quickly it was drowning? They didn't even know about Gary the pervert.* "I asked you where you were the night Ashley died."

"I was in Towson scouting a swim match."

Scouting for fresh meat, no doubt. "You can prove it?"

"I have witnesses."

Zack stared at Gary. "Ok, Gary. That's all we have. But do yourself a favor: first, you won't mention to anyone we were here. You will convince the girl we caught you banging not to mention it either, and in return, as long as we can't prove you had anything to do with Ashley's death, we won't ruin your career. Do you understand?"

Gary stared at Zack with hate in his eyes, glanced at Andre but merely nodded.

"We didn't hear you, Gary. Do you understand us?"

"Yes."

The two men left the office and got back to Andre's car. Zack clicked his seatbelt and sat back. "What do you think?"

"I think he's a sleazeball taking advantage of vulnerable college girls," Andre said.

38

Zack nodded. "That's not what I meant."

"I know. What do you think?"

"I think he's telling the truth."

"So do I."

"Curious though. Why didn't the cops get this far?"

Zack checked his phone as Andre drove. A couple of hours earlier, he thought this case would wrap up quickly. Now, Zack kept finding questions that no one asked. "Dre, Barnes wouldn't sign off on this if he knew what we know. So, did he know? What about the medical examiner? He wouldn't give a COD without a proper exam. What about Hannah? Is this connected to Ashley?" Zack shook his head. "I figured you were going to ask what I'm thinking."

Andre chuckled. "Good old fashioned detective work."

The phone conversation played in his head. *David Staechel. How did whoever that was find out? Is it connected to Michigan City? Why was Senator Rosler with these college girls? Why hasn't Jules called or texted me today? Sonofabitch. This thing is spiraling out of control, and I don't even know what the hell is going on.*

"So what now?" Andre asked.

"Keep digging, I guess."

CHAPTER 8

Zack got home late that night, hungry and thirsty. Since he had only been back from Europe two days, he had no food in his apartment. He called Julie hoping she could meet for dinner.

After another no answer from Julie, he decided to take matters into his hands and walk to a nearby Bar & Grill. He didn't frequent it often, but he was there often enough to know he could get a cold beer and a good hot plate of food with a seafood flare to it which appealed to him. He left a message on her phone saying he was going to the Red Star and footed it there.

Zack sat at the bar and expected no one to meet him there. *Where is she? Even when she is mad, she still texts. Does that lying scumbag Rosler still have her working on his stupid book?* Zack, as he enjoyed a Long Island Iced Tea, let seeds of doubt creep into his mind. He hated it. Zack fought them out, but still, they edged. *What if she can't deal with my past?*

He switched to the Sam Adams Seasonal while he enjoyed his dinner. Zack didn't remember what he ordered, but he knew there was crab meat, shrimp, scallops, and lobster meat in the dish, and it was succulently cholesterol heaven, and he'd pay for it later, but it was good, as were the three pints of Sam Adams. He didn't hear from Julie. *Where is she?*

Then, one of the televisions above the bar showed Senator Rosler walk out of the hospital, with the help of his Chief of Staff and security, smiling and waving at the crowd. The scroll across the bottom of the TV talked about how brave and courageous he was. A hero, they said, for not cowering to the assassin that tried to take his life. He was healing remarkably fast and was continuing not only his campaign, Rosler announced, but his fight in Congress for the great people of Maryland and the United States.

Zack wanted to vomit. No matter what spiel came out of Rosler's mouth, all Zack saw was something off. Something wrong. Zack suspected lies and secrets. Zack finished his pint and knew he hated this guy because of Julie. He tried to shake it off but his blood boiled, and he knew he turned twenty different shades of fire red because there was Julie on the television screen getting into the Senator's limousine. Zack was too mad to vomit now. He wanted to hurt something. Or more specifically, someone that held a public office.

* * * * * *

Zack walked along the sidewalk and enjoyed the brisk evening and light breeze coming from the southeast despite having a foul mood because he didn't know where his fiancé was. It was dark and past ten o'clock. The sidewalk was empty, the streets quiet and the sky clear. He thought what a beautiful night it would be to spend with Jules if he knew where she was.

He listened to her cell ring and then her message. Zack frowned. "Jules, it's me. Missed you tonight. I figured you're busy. Sorry for calling so late," he paused. "I'll call you in the morn…"

He hit the wall hard. His phone broke on the concrete and an arm pressed against his neck while a hand grabbed his right arm, twisted it behind his back and wrenched it up towards his shoulder blade. For good measure, the assailant yanked him back and slammed him into the brick wall again.

"Do I have your attention?" The man said with his mouth close to Zack's ear.

Zack struggled and made a grunting noise. The assailant slammed him against the brick wall then flipped him around and slammed him once more. Zack cleared his fuzzy vision and saw three men wearing black masks in front of him. One expertly pinned his legs and arms so Zack couldn't move.

"Do I?"

"Yes," Zack forced out.

41

"Good. Listen carefully," the main man said. "We know what you're doing and what you're investigating. We know everything."

"Great," Zack mumbled. "Can you tell me who shot Kennedy? Been bothering me for years."

"We warned you. Stop, or you will feel pain, and you will get hurt."

"Not sure that I like where this is going."

"And you won't. Just walk away now before it gets ugly."

"You mean this isn't?"

The man leaned forward, his head inches from Zack's. "It's going to get a lot uglier," he said.

"Yes, it is," Zack said and headbutted the bridge of the man's nose once, then again. The man fell backward and let go.

The other two moved quick. Zack landed a right cross on the man to his left and a kick to the crotch of the headbutted man before the third man stopped Zack cold with a punch to Zack's lower right ribcage and a second punch to the side of his head. It buckled Zack, and he fell to the ground.

The men kicked him several times. The main man leaned over close to Zack. "Don't make us warn you again, Stack." The men disappeared in the darkness.

Zack laid on the ground; sweat dripped from his brow. Slowly, he sat up and rested his back against the building and caught his breath. The pain subsided but he knew his body would remind him of this encounter. He looked around and realized one thing: *clearly, I am looking at something that someone doesn't want looked at.*

CHAPTER 9

Two mornings later, Zack walked a trail around Lake Roland, north of the city.

His eyes scanned the lower levels of the trees and the treetops. The wind was calm, which he liked so most movement would be what he was searching for: birds. Migration was always a fun time for Zack. Fall migration was especially challenging, but Zack loved a challenge.

The area was quiet to his delight. No other birders or joggers or even people walking their dogs were around which Zack despised because their rapid movements and noise scared the birds away from the trails. So, as he stood still watching what looked like a Vireo flitting about a tree, hearing two sets of footprints approach from behind him both irritated and alarmed him.

Zack knew no one followed him. After the incident the other night, he vowed that wouldn't happen again. And he was armed. He lowered his binoculars; his right hand slid inside his jacket under his shoulder.

"Easy there, big shooter, it's just us," Andre said. "You can relax."

Zack turned and saw Andre standing beside Lieutenant Ted Barnes.

"Good morning, Zack," Barnes greeted. "Early riser today?"

"Best time to see birds," Zack said. "How did you find me? And what are the two of you doing together? Is this an intervention? To keep me from enjoying my getaway hobby or something?"

"He found me, too," Andre said. "Told me he needed to speak to both of us."

"So how did you find me? I've never told anyone about this place. You tracking me?"

"Tracking you isn't a bad idea," Barnes laughed. "You told one person," he added. "It's Sunday. Shouldn't you be headed to Church or something?"

Zack chuckled. "Probably something." The phone call re-entered his mind.

"With the luck you've had, maybe going to Church would be a good thing for you."

"Oh, Jesus Christ. Please don't tell me that you're one of those too, Ted? Don't ruin my picture of you."

Barnes smiled. "Just saying. You've been lucky lately."

"Yeah, well. Maybe. So why are you here?"

Barnes handed Zack and Andre a manila envelope each. He said nothing. They opened the envelopes. They were duplicates.

Zack let his binoculars hang from his neck and pulled out a stack of pictures.

"Hannah Davison. The girl shot and killed on stage." Andre said.

Barnes nodded. "Zack, you ok?"

"I was in her college dorm room a few days ago. Pure coincidence," Zack answered.

"I thought you don't believe in coincidences?" Barnes asked.

"We don't. But this is too bizarre. I saw pictures of Hannah in the desk of Ashley Blumenthal."

"That name sounds familiar," Barnes said. "Why do I know that name?"

"The mother just hired Zack to prove her daughter's death was murder," Andre said.

"She was found dead in a pond behind her chateau. You investigated it," Zack said.

"Oh yeah, her mother talked to me about it again when you two were in Europe, so I sent her your way," Barnes scratched his chin. "But, Schmidt and O'Malley couldn't find anything that would help me think foul play since her father didn't allow an autopsy."

"Yeah, that was the first thing I asked. Wonder why old man Blumenthal wouldn't?"

Barnes shrugged. "So, Mrs. Blumenthal hired you?"

"You did recommend me."

Barnes smiled. He met Zack over three and a half years earlier while working a murder case. Zack turned out to be working a cheating spouse case. The two solved the case with a lot of Zack's help, and the two had been friends ever since. "Yeah, I did. Ashley and Hannah were friends?"

"Yeah," Zack said.

"Find anything yet?"

"Not a thing. There was nothing until now."

"Because she knew Hannah?"

"Yup."

Andre pulled a picture out and showed it to Barnes: the bullet wound on Hannah's chest. "How are the Feds explaining this one?"

"Collateral damage."

Andre shook his head. "This is precisely placed on her heart."

"No shit," Zack added. "This wasn't collateral damage. This was an execution."

"Not how they see it."

Zack finished and slid the pictures back into the envelope and gave it back to Barnes. "They are wrong." He picked up his binoculars and focused on a little bird flitting about in a tree. "I suck at fall warblers," he said, but Barnes paid no attention.

"What happened to your head? You get into a bar fight or something?"

"Not exactly," Zack said. "I think that's a Cape May Warbler." He shook his head. "So much easier in spring when they have their breeding plumage." Zack rested the optics on his chest. "Why are you telling us?"

"Officially, I'm not," Ted said. They stared at him. "But unofficially, I want you two to do your thing and snoop around as discreetly as you can."

Zack and Andre looked at each other and laughed. "Yeah, that isn't going to happen," Andre said.

Barnes was silent and stared at the two with a look knowing he was going to get his way. Barnes knew the game, too. The first one to speak loses.

Zack shook his head. Andre grabbed his arm. "Zack, no."

"Are the Feds involved?" Zack asked.

Barnes smiled. "Not yet but they are pressing, and if I don't get something quick they'll take it over."

Zack shook his head again. He knew the game. Played for a sucker. He knew he lost. But he needed to know if Ashley and Hannah were a coincidence. "Who do you have working the assassination?"

"Assassination attempt," Barnes corrected.

"Keep telling yourself that," Zack said.

Barnes smiled. "Schmidt and O'Malley have the lead. They have Jenkins, Kendricks, Tanner, and Bloom working with them. Everything goes through me, and I share if I think it's necessary with the Feds."

"What do they have?" Andre asked.

Barnes shook his head. "A couple of possible locations of the shooter,"

"Or shooters," Zack said.

"ID's on the bullets that killed the girl and Polzinski."

"What kind of rifle? M24?" Andre asked.

Barnes looked surprised. "Yeah, exactly. How did you know?"

"Easy gun to get and a sharpshooter's gun of choice in the states," Andre said.

Barnes shook his head. "Well, anyway, that's about it right now."

Zack laughed. "Are you freaking kidding me?"

"What? You think you can do better?"

"How could we do any worse?" Zack laughed. "I think Schmidt and O'Malley may not be your best detectives."

"Yeah, well, I need a win, Zack," Barnes said. "My department needs a win. And the press wants to crucify the department because there is still a shooter on the loose. So, here I am telling you two that you are going to help me with this."

Zack and Andre looked at each other.

"Unofficially of course. Officially, you know the drill."

"Of course," Andre said. "You never spoke to us about any of this, and we were freelancing, possibly obstructing an official investigation and you'll be throwing us in jail once the shit hits the fan."

Barnes nodded. "Somehow I trust you two won't let the shit hit the fan."

Zack lifted his binoculars again and let out a deep sigh. *It feels like it already has.*

"You aren't going to tell me what happened to you?"

"I was dropped at birth," Zack said.

Andre laughed. "Ted, come on, now. You don't think having us get involved is a good idea, do you?" He pointed at Zack. "Especially with the trouble always finding this one?"

"Let me put it this way," Ted began. "You two owe me." He stared at each one. "You owe me big. And I'm cashing in one small payback chip. Just stay out of the news." He stared at the two again for an extended moment of silence. "Have we reached an accord?"

Zack didn't change his expression. Andre looked at the ground.

Barnes smiled. "If I ever retire, the three of us should open a detective agency. I think you two would flourish with me as the boss." He winked at them. "So, this is what you do when you disappear? Watch birds?"

Zack nodded. "Yup."

"I can't believe you're a birdwatcher."

"Birder," Zack corrected.

"Sorry, didn't mean to offend you," Barnes laughed. "Nothing through unwise channels, got it?" The two nodded and said nothing.

Barnes looked at the tree as Zack stared through the binoculars again. "Keep me informed." Barnes turned to walk away.

"Hey, did you send two guys to Hannah's college?"

"No."

"Did Schmidt or O'Malley?"

"Not that I know of. Don't know why they would since your buddy Rosler was the main event," Barnes said. "Why?"

"Because someone did, and they took her phone," Zack said.

"Who were they?"

Zack shook his head. "If I knew I wouldn't have asked you."

Barnes smiled. "I'll ask around. Good luck with your Cape Fear Bubbler or whatever made up name you called it."

Zack smiled, Barnes left, and Zack returned his focus to the tree and identified a Black and White Warbler. He looked at Andre. "You drove separate; I take it?"

"Yeah." Andre looked at his watch. "I have to meet my girl for church with her family in a few hours. Want to catch breakfast?"

"I have a wave of warblers passing through. We can talk while I bird." Zack raised his binoculars to his eyes. "Did you tell Barnes about my encounter the other night?"

"No. Didn't have to."

Zack looked at Andre.

"Your fiancé did. She thinks you need to be watched when she's in Iowa with the Senator following his campaign for the book. Why didn't you tell me that?"

Zack lowered the binoculars. "After she told me, we fought all night." He looked at Andre. "She went back to her place, and I haven't talked to her since. That's all we've done since I got back: fight. I tried texting her, told her I was here, which is how you found me, but nothing from her."

Andre shook his head. "Your jealousy is going to be the death of you."

"I should be so lucky." Zack looked at another warbler species. It looked like a Chestnut-sided Warbler. "Good birds today."

Andre looked into the trees. "Someday I'll have to see what this is all about."

"Couldn't hurt," Zack said.

"Black guy walking around a park looking through binoculars?" Andre laughed. "You white folk would freak and call the cops on me."

Zack smiled. "You know, we all aren't racists." He took his gaze away from the warbler and looked at Andre. "Hell, I'm still waiting for that invitation to your mother's to taste her famous fried chicken. A Sunday afternoon with your family would be a treat."

Andre shook his head. "Maybe we're racists."

Zack's smile left his face. "Dre, what am I going to do with Jules?"

"You have to communicate, both of you," Dre said. "Swallow your damn pride, stop being so damn stubborn, and quit freaking about her with Rosler. It's just a job."

Zack stared at Dre and nodded. "I know," he said defeated. "There's just a lot of shit going on, and I'm not sure she and I will survive it."

Andre grabbed Zack's shoulder. "You're overthinking this. Come on, let's eat. You can come back another day for the birds."

"Umm, Dre, it's migration. These birds won't be here another day."

Andre rolled his eyes. "Fair enough. But we just got enlisted to do a backdoor investigation on the assassination attempt of a Presidential candidate, who happens to be employing your fiancé. I think this takes precedence."

CHAPTER 10

His phone had no new notifications. No Julie for day three. Zack knew why. *Ok, so I may have been an ass, but I bet she wouldn't like it if I disappeared for two weeks with another woman!*

Jealousy got the best of him. Zack knew Julie wouldn't do anything with another man, especially one like Senator Michael Rosler. She despised men like him. This was just a job.

She said she was leaving to follow Rosler's campaign through Iowa for two weeks. "I'm leaving with Michael for two weeks to cover his campaign. It should make for a nice wrap-up for the book," she had said. *Michael. Whatever happened to Senator Rosler?* First name basis and no discussion. That started the argument.

Julie was right. Zack had been an ass. She called him worse, but he settled on ass in his mental recap of the fight. The worst they have ever had. She hadn't even been that upset when she learned he had been lying about his real identity ever since he left Indiana at age 17. At least that was warranted. David Staechel had to stay dead. Too much would be destroyed if the truth came out. Even

Lieutenant Barnes fully understood. *And now someone else is extorting me because of my past.*

The only positive thing that happened in the last three days was his finding the recording of the assassination attempt Julie snuck at the rally. He watched it over a dozen times. *Deal with that as soon as I reach Dre.*

Zack opened his computer to check the morning headlines. *Try to focus, Zack.*

Zack scanned the headlines on his computer's homepage, saw that most were about the windbag his fiancé was about to embark with on a trip. *This jagoff is getting more free press than anyone right now.* The authorities at the Baltimore County Correctional Center still did not know why the near-riot took place that left two inmates dead and several other inmates and guards injured. *Wonder if it's anyone I helped put in there? Like the dude who called me.* He made a note. *Who did I put in there three years ago?*

He sifted through the pictures he obtained at the desks of Ashley, Hannah, and Meg. The three were close. Why was Rosler in pictures with Ashley and Hannah but not Meg? *Two are dead, and Meg is missing. Where is she? Claire wanted me to see these. Why?* He put the pictures down and walked to the window. *How were Hannah and Ashley involved with Rosler but not Meg? Maybe Meg tried to kill Rosler. I don't blame her. But why kill Hannah and a no-name state representative? Ok, it wasn't Meg. Where is Jules? I should call her again. Damnit, Zack. You screwed the pooch on this one.*

* * *   * * *

The morning sun barely peaked over the rooftops; occasional rays shone between the buildings and warmed her. Julie walked quickly towards Zack's apartment. Three days was too long. He did deserve it, but it was time to talk with him.

She used her keys to unlock his door, she locked it behind her, reset the security alarm and climbed the stairs. No need to *act* mad, he already knows it. But enough is enough.

She reached the top and saw Zack in the kitchen washing dishes. A quick scan of his apartment revealed a surprisingly clean place. *So he's been here the last three days. Good.*

He looked at her. She looked at him; arms folded across her chest.

"Were you planning on calling me today?"

He nodded.

"Good." They were silent, and she walked to him. "When was the last time you showered?"

"Yesterday morning."

She took in a deep breath through her nose and let it out slowly. "You're a mess. Go shower. We need to talk because frankly, I'm tired of this."

"Good. So am I. Shower with me. We can talk in there."

* * *   * * *

Three hours later, Zack walked out of his bedroom, freshly showered wearing a pair of navy gym trunks. He looked at his phone, saw missed calls from Andre and Michelle, put the phone down and walked to the kitchen.

Moments behind him was Julie, hair wet, one of Zack's tee-shirts clung to her damp upper body and just past her bottom. She followed him to the kitchen, took the bottle of water out of his hand, ran her hands across his chest, over his broad shoulders and planted her lips on his.

"I hate it when we fight," Zack said after the kiss ended.

"Then don't fight anymore," she said with a wink. "Make me breakfast; I'm famished."

Zack smiled. He watched her long bare legs walk to his couch. She turned and plopped on it, flung her hair over her shoulders and stared at him. "You know, you should have been a model," he said.

"Oh, shut up."

"I'm serious; you're gorgeous. Just watching you wearing nothing but my shirt is a turn on."

"You aren't so bad yourself," she said. "But after that performance, I doubt even you can rebound, and without any nourishment, I'm completely wiped."

"Drink some water. Rehydration is key," Zack said.

They were silent as Zack opened his refrigerator and cupboards to make a list of all he didn't have in his kitchen. The last three days he ate out every meal.

Shopping for groceries never crossed his mind. *Slight oversight I am now regretting.*

"What are you working on anyway? You never told me why you were jumped the other night."

Zack finished his list and exited the kitchen. "I stirred the pot where I shouldn't have."

"You do that a lot lately," Julie said.

"Yeah, well." He sat beside her and put his arm around her shoulders. "Did you know Hannah Davison?" Julie shook her head no. "She worked for Rosler in some capacity. As far as I can tell she was an intern on his campaign force."

Julie shook her heard more. "I remember seeing her on stage that day, but there are so many women around Rosler it's hard to tell one from another."

"Do you know she went to the same university as Ashley Blumenthal?"

"The girl that drowned last spring?"

"Yup."

"Oh my God! Seriously?"

Zack nodded. He suddenly realized how little he and Jules had talked since he got back to the states a week ago. It made him feel like a heel. "Caught me by surprise, too."

"Zack, that is so weird. Remember the story I did last May right before you left to save Darnell in Indiana?"

"Not really."

She turned on the couch, her leg suddenly folded under her, and she faced him. "Ashley Blumenthal had just drowned, and I heard a passing comment on a news story about how six other girls had died in the last six years. Ashley was number seven. Remember?"

"Sweetie, I'm sorry but that was a while ago, and you do a lot of stories."

Julie's excitement wasn't squashed. "I decided to do a follow-up story on those deaths — kind of a how-do-the-parents-move-on piece. I mean, is anything in life more tragic than losing a child? It took about a month, and I got it finished right before you left for Michigan City. Anyway, got paid pretty well for it but Hannah would be the eighth. I remember asking if it was a curse. Eight girls in six years? What do you think?"

Zack perked up. "Only females?"

"Yep. Not a single guy died at that university in the last six years. With all the stupid frat house shit going on, I was surprised."

"Did you find any links between the girls besides they died?"

She shook her head. "No, I wasn't going for that angle. Each case was an accident, or something stupid. Like drowning, overdose, car accident, fell down steps while drunk, another car accident, one drank too much and died of alcohol poisoning, another suffered a heart attack. I know the M.E. that worked each case, and he didn't think anything was suspicious for the first six."

Zack nodded. He looked her up and down, liked where his tee shirt rode up on her thighs and how her hair frizzed as it dried. "God Damn! You are so freaking hot right now. However, my mind is racing so I'll make you a deal: I'll make you whatever you want, but we have to get it. Then I'll make you breakfast. Then, believe it or not, I'm going to research that."

She chuckled. "I know how you hate research. Come here," she said and pulled him forward to kiss him again. Their tongues met, their hands explored each other, and right before he moved to get closer, she pulled away. "Don't ever be a jerk to me again, you understand? I love you; you got it? Don't worry about me and any other man because no other man will ever, ever, ever have me. Understand?"

He nodded yes.

"And if you ever begin to doubt, remember me sitting on this couch, your hands all over me and mine on you and realize you do not want to lose this. Got it?"

"Loud and clear. I'm sorry."

"I know." She kissed him, bit his lower lip and held it in her teeth gently for a moment. "I'm spending all day here. Naked." She kissed him again. "I suggest you plan our meals appropriately."

Oh my!

CHAPTER 11

It was only eleven in the morning, but it seemed like a full day already for Zack.

The argument with Jules, the love-making with Jules, the shower, more love-making, talking, an expensive trip to the grocery store, breakfast, research, he needed a nap.

But work had to be done. He called Michelle. She answered politely. "Hey, Michelle, it's me."

"I know. I was being polite."

He shook his head. "I'm going to miss you when you're gone. Where is Dre?"

"Not my day to watch him," she answered.

"But then again, maybe I won't."

"Ha-ha. What do you want? You only call when you need something."

"Michelle, darling, how can you be so cold?"

"Because of who I'm talking to. What do you want? I do have a job to do, remember?"

"I do, it's working for me, remember?"

"Touché."

"Sweetheart, I need you to work your magic."

"Of course, you do. I don't know where you'd be without me."

"You know damn well I'd probably be dead in a ditch somewhere. You finished giving me grief yet?"

"Maybe. Are you coming in today? You haven't been here in three days."

"No. I'm busy here. But I'm on kind of a time crunch, so I need this to be a top priority." *My anonymous extortionist probably won't accept I'm slow as a researcher as an excuse to delay his deadline.*

"Of course, you do. Andre will be happy."

"If he calls, have him call me. First, I want you to access Ashley Blumenthal's medical records. The file had her family doctor, and ob-gyn listed so start with that."

"Why?"

"Well, you won't appreciate my line of thinking but if you want to hear it,"

"I do."

"Well, Ashley was sexually active. Her coach was sexually active; I'm guessing the other partners in that circle were active as well."

"Yeah, and?"

"Maybe one of her doctors had issued an STD medication or something."

"And what will that tell you, Zack? That she drowned of chlamydia?"

Zack chuckled. "I'm not sure what I'm looking for. Probably a dead end but no one has dug this far. So, can you do that for me?"

"On it. Anything else?"

"Have Andre call me if you hear from him." Zack hung up and looked out the window. Rain beat against the pane. He opened his computer and logged on. Minutes later he read Julie's article about the dead girls from the college.

His phone rang. "Dre, where are you?"

"Hey, Zack. I'm at the park where Rosler got shot."

"Why?"

"Because. How soon can you get here?"

Zack sighed. "It's raining, and I have Jules' video of the shooting. You need to see it."

"I will. But get down here first."

Zack frowned. "Dre, I don't have wheels and Jules is at my apartment today. I want to spend the day with her."

"This will only take ten minutes. Bring her down. Hurry up. I'll buy lunch."

56

* * * * * *

Zack adjusted his green rain jacket while Julie tightened the hood around her face as they walked across the sidewalk and into the park. Any evidence that there had been an assassination attempt days before was long gone. The park was empty thanks to the rain, except for Andre who stood where the stage had sat.

Zack and Andre shook hands. "Ok, you got us down here. What do you have?"

"You ok with this, Jules?" Andre asked.

"Other than I have to redo my hair, yeah, I'm fine."

Zack smiled.

"This is about where the stage was, right?"

Julie looked around. "Yeah, I was sitting about here." She moved to where her seat was.

"Ok, Zack. Look out there. What do you see?"

"Rain," Zack said as Jules moved beside Zack and wrapped her arm around his.

"Come over here," Andre said as he moved several paces to the left. "Now look out here and tell me what you see?"

"More rain," Zack said. He looked at his watch: noon. His stomach grumbled. "What do you see?"

Andre pointed out. "Somewhere along this line two shots were made that killed Sam Polzinski and wounded Rosler," he said. He grabbed Zack's arm and pulled him back to the first spot. "Somewhere out there the same shooter made another shot that killed the girl."

Zack stared out over the park into the city behind it and remembered what he saw at the other spot. "Jules, do you remember anything odd about that day?"

She walked to where she had been seated and closed her eyes. "Rosler was talking, he paused, and I saw Hannah slump." She opened her eyes and walked forward. "I thought I heard something," she pointed at the podium. "I looked and saw Polzinski get shot, Rosler fell the same time." She looked at Zack. "After that, it was chaos."

Zack put his arm around her. "That makes it sound like the prize of the day was shot last."

Andre nodded. "Which makes sense in a way." He looked back over the park. "Barnes said they hadn't found the location of where the shooter was, only a couple suspected areas. No one saw anything. The rooftops were clear. Right now, almost a week later, what is the chance they find anything?"

Zack stared into the distant city. "I'm beginning to think zero is a safe bet."

Andre's voice quickened with excitement. "Of the two different angles we looked at, there is only one spot that works." He pointed to a building that was to the right of center. "The police figured the shots had to be head-on, so to speak, straight out from the stage due west where the sun would have been behind the shooter. The only way you can make those shots is from over there. Every other place is too difficult. Too many variables," Andre said. "Too many trees, power lines, light poles and the day of the shooting, speakers and more lights on stage. It had to be from over there." He pointed to an old brown building in the distance to the right of center.

Zack looked again. He went to both spots, looked and knew Andre was right.

"What if there were two shooters?" Julie asked. "From two different locations?"

"Ballistics," Zack said.

"What?"

"Barnes told us the bullets from the girl, and Polzinski were from the same gun," Andre said.

"What about the one that hit Rosler?"

"They got rid of it. Police can't find it," Zack said.

"Well that's odd," Julie said. "Isn't it?"

"Extremely."

"So, one shooter took all three shots?" Julie asked.

"That's the official story," Zack said. His hands made air quotes.

"What? What is that?"

"Yeah, why did you do that, Zack?"

Zack looked away and stared out through the heavy rain and towards the building Andre identified. "You need to see Jules' video of the shooting."

"What's on it?"

Zack frowned. "Answers," Zack said, and Andre stared at him with the 'just tell me' expression on his face. "Trust me, partner, you need to see it first." He looked right at Andre. "I need you to look at it without any bias. Tell me if you see what I saw."

Andre nodded. "What I can't figure out is why aren't they asking why."

Zack nodded. "Schmidt and O'Malley will never figure it out." Ever since he saw the assassination attempt, Zack was asking why. He knew something was off. He and Andre were expert sharpshooters in the Corps. They participated in competitions and did well. In one contest, Zack won, and Andre finished second. Andre disputed the results ever since but they 'retired' from those competitions following that year. Both were deployed to the Middle-East afterward. Shooting meant something different over there.

"I'm going to follow up on this. What are you going to do?"

"I'm going to enjoy the lunch you promised to buy Jules and me," Zack said. "Then I'm going back to my apartment and doing some research."

"On what?" Andre asked. They headed towards their cars.

"Ahh, I'll tell you if I find anything," he exhaled, "probably grasping at straws."

"Ok," Andre said. "Look, instead of lunch, what about dinner? You and Jules want to go out with Alysha and me tonight? The lunch places nearby aren't that good anyway."

Zack shook his head. "I knew you'd cheap your way out of lunch." The two laughed. "Is that ok with you, honey?"

Julie smiled; her arm still clutched to Zack. "Call us with a time and place."

Andre unlocked his car door and opened it. "You got it. Thanks for coming down."

"Trust me, Dre," Zack yelled as he opened Julie's car door, "you need to see that video."

CHAPTER 12

Andre descended the steps of the building slowly. He found the landlord and paid the guy a couple of Franklins to get access to the upper floors. The old brick building was formerly a furniture company long since out of business. Investors bought it and saw it as an essential redevelopment project near downtown to keep Baltimore vibrant. They renovated the lower floor so that offices could occupy it and had the next two stories developed into studio apartments designed for the younger, hipper crowd. The flats hadn't filled yet, which cramped the finances, so the upper four levels were mostly untouched.

The rooms on the upper floors varied and mainly were small offices on the outside walls with much of the interior of the level open with occasional load-bearing posts spaced evenly across the area. But one thing Andre noticed immediately was dust, dirt, and debris on the floor, and no one lived or frequented the top stories.

Andre checked the east side of the building only. He studied each window on the top level. Andre was sure there would be a sign that someone, namely the shooter, had been there. Instead, he saw nothing.

Andre went to the sixth story and examined every window facing east. Nothing. Not even pigeons or rats had been on the sixth floor and the same with the fifth. He did like the layout though and decided he and Zack should invest. But that thought disappeared quickly as his confidence sagged after another nothing floor.

Andre descended to the fourth floor. He walked to the center and listened as he scanned the floor in every direction. He heard raindrops. A window was open. To the east. Then he saw footprints. Two sets. *Two sets? What?* The dust had scattered and settled, there were no tread patterns, but there were two sets of prints. That was clear. He followed them right into the fifth room from the southeast corner, saw the partially opened window, walked to the window without disturbing the footprints and knew instantly that's where the shots fired. He smiled. *It took me one day. ONE!* Andre shook his head. "Something is not right."

* * *   * * *

Zack clicked through the windows on his computer, each with a different story but none with enough detail. He found articles on the dead girls and what happened and a brief background for each girl. But no connections. The rain fell against the window, a soft, comforting rhythm. Perfect for sleeping, or for making love but when he looked at Jules, her face was buried in her computer, reading glasses on and her hair in a ponytail. A pencil rested behind her ear even though she only tapped the table with it when thinking. She never wrote with it. Zack knew she was not in love-making mode. So, he continued.

Julie looked at her watch and stretched her back and arms. She looked at Zack at his computer at the kitchen table. He stared into the screen intent. She smiled and was glad she convinced him to spend the next three days with her before she was leaving with Rosler on his first campaign trip to Iowa.

She heard the rain pitter-patter on the windowsill. *I bet Zack wanted to ask me to make love. He always does when it rains. Zack can pretend he is concentrating on his computer, but I bet all I have to do is ask if he wants to take a nap and he'll be in that bed faster than I can close my computer screen. I love that man!* She typed in another query about Polzinski and Rosler.

The page filled quickly with articles and reports, and all seemed familiar until she hit the bottom of the page. The headline caught her eye: "Pals Polzinski and Rosler Clash on Key Issues." That was enough to capture her interest.

She opened the article, and after only reading two lines she copied and saved it on her computer and found another link. It was what she was hoping for:

finally, something that proved that not all was as seamless as the press wanted the people to believe between Sam Polzinski and Michael Rosler.

"Zack, come see this."

"What is it?"

"Just come here. It's too hard to explain."

He walked to the couch, sat beside her and read the article on her screen. "Donald freaking Fairfax! I'll be damned." Zack sat back. "He was friends with Rosler and Polzinski in college? How the hell did I miss that when we investigated him?"

Donald Fairfax over three years earlier was the CFO of Valentino Industries; Michael Rosler's family started the company about the time of the industrial revolution Zack figured. Fairfax got a job there out of college and worked his way into the CFO's position. Rosler left as CEO to become the US Senator, but Fairfax remained the CFO while Rosler's wife took over as CEO.

Fairfax's wife hired Zack to determine if Fairfax was having an affair. She had no idea who, just that he was. It was one of Zack's first jobs and his most important case at the time and the one that tied Zack to Lieutenant Ted Barnes. While investigating, Michelle discovered some financial irregularities that eventually led them to evidence that Fairfax wired large sums of money into offshore hidden accounts. Michelle determined over three million dollars vanished. The embezzling charge never stuck, nor did Valentino Industries lawyers go after it.

Zack knew Fairfax was having some side fun and went to Fairfax's wife to show her pictures he had of her husband getting intimate with another woman: a tall, sleek brunette that was very careful. Zack arrived at the house, knocked on the door, it was cracked open, and he walked inside to find Fairfax's wife on the living room floor in a large pool of her blood, slit open with a knife from her throat to below her abdomen.

It was the most gruesome murder he had ever seen. A knife was nearby as were footprints in the blood that left out the back door. All the evidence circled right back to Donald Fairfax: fingerprints, shoe prints matched his size though the shoes were never found, and Donald's blood on the handle of the knife. The security alarm had not been breached nor was there any forced entry, so it was determined that Fairfax's wife Jane knew her attacker. Later after his arrest, the police asked about a small cut across his fingers. The prosecutors speculated it happened during the stabbing. He offered no alibi. Fairfax provided nothing for his defense team, and that helped seal his fate.

He was found guilty and sentenced to life at the BCCC, the Baltimore City Correctional Center. The case put Zack on the map though he still burned about not finding out who Fairfax was diddling on the side. *He's in prison, and he knows Rosler. It's him. It has to be. But how could he find out about my past?*

"We didn't look back at his college years. No reason to," Julie said. "Look at this one."

She clicked, another picture popped up, this one with the three men and a woman. A young attractive tall brunette with a broad smile, round eyes, and a soft nose stood between Rosler and Fairfax.

"Is that...?"

"Yep," she answered. "That's Rosler's wife."

"Wow. Quite fetching."

Julie snorted. "Shut up, jerk. Look at this one."

Another picture showed just the three men, but the woman's head was on Fairfax's shoulder while Fairfax held her around the waist and Rosler was off to the side looking a different direction.

"Rosler married his college girlfriend. You tell me, Zack, does that look like his girlfriend in that picture?"

"Nope," he said. "But they were best friends. Looks like the whole group spent a lot of time together and got friendly at times. Especially in college when they're passing around blow, weed, booze, and God only knows what else. Who's the weasel with the three amigos in that picture?"

Julie smiled. "Zack, that's Jerry Pantalini. He's Rosler's Chief of Staff."

"Are you serious? These nitwits have been together since college?"

"Yup. I found this picture of his grades at the end of his junior year. Rosler was an average student at best. Both Fairfax and Polzinski were heads and shoulders above Rosler grade-wise," she said.

"So? When you're rich, brains don't matter."

"Well, it just little bits and pieces of stuff like that I keep unearthing. Rosler's transcripts are sealed. The university won't give them out but what he says his grades were in college didn't match what they actually were by a long shot."

"He's a liar. We already know that, Jules."

"Nothing adds up. The image and what people think is the truth about Rosler isn't. And this Fairfax thing and Rosler's wife confuses me. Throw in Polzinski's background with Rosler, and it gets worse. I mean, Polzinski wasn't in the millionaires by birth club like the other three. Everything I could find says he had to scratch and claw for everything he had."

"Ok, so what prompted this search?"

Julie leaned back and twirled her pony-tail with her right forefinger. "I have to do some research about Rosler for the book. You know, his past and stuff like that."

"Doesn't the Rosler propaganda machine already have a pre-printed file of lies for the book?"

Julie rolled her eyes and smiled. "Of course, they do, but I like doing my own research. After all, my name is going on the book. I want it to be accurate."

Zack laughed. "I don't think accuracy is anywhere near the top of Rosler's priorities."

"Oh stop, he isn't that bad."

"Don't defend him. That doesn't make me feel any better about you leaving in three days to spend two weeks with the God of the Underworld."

Julie chuckled. "What did I already tell you about that?"

"Maybe you should remind me. You know how I love spending rainy days with you."

She leaned forward and kissed him. "You better get started then. We have to meet Andre and Alysha in a couple of hours."

He stared into Julie's cerulean eyes. He kissed her, but in the back of his head, a voice spoke. It was soft but steady.

They embraced in a deep kiss. But the voice grew louder in Zack's head. *Do NOT let her go to Iowa!!*

CHAPTER 13

Andre stopped his car in the gravel parking lot of a shooting range, his third that day, and stared at what was around him. It was early afternoon, and he was running out of options.

The parking lot wasn't as much a parking lot as it was a worn-out grassy area where the patrons parked their automobiles. The owner over the years added gravel where holes formed so the vehicles wouldn't get stuck. Over the years he spread enough gravel so there was no grass left except on the edges where the cars and trucks stopped. Today only one pickup truck parked in the lot.

It faced an extended mobile home trailer which acted as the office and offered a resting place for the owner when he felt like it. Gray vinyl siding covered the building. The few windows were dusty and blocked on the inside with blinds, and the roof shingles looked old and tired and probably leaked.

This shooting range was the closest one to Baltimore that shot out to one thousand yards. No other range went past five hundred. Simple math and logic. It was only a little over an hour and a half drive to just north of Fredricksburg, Virginia up in the hills. *Logic and logistics. It should be that simple. Two days and I need a break.*

He walked to the single door with a hand-scribed wooden "ENTER" sign above it and an open sign swinging from a hook in the center of the steel door. The sturdy door swung open silently and effortlessly. Andre walked inside, and behind the counter stood an older man, white, wearing a USMC cap, blue jeans, and a denim shirt.

"May I help you?" The man said in a gruff but friendly voice.

"Hoorah," Andre smiled.

"Hoorah," the man answered. "Jarhead?"

"Semper fi. Where'd you serve?"

"Nam, two tours 1972 and 73. You?"

"Iraq and Afghanistan among other places."

The man offered his hand and shook Andre's. "I don't often see Marines come through here. Usually Army and wannabe's."

"They need more practice than us," Andre joked.

"What can I do you for?"

Andre smiled. "I'm looking for a shooter. My guess is ex-military, probably Army. Shooting an M24 and probably one of the best shooters here."

The man's smile left his face. "Why?"

Andre shrugged. "I'm just doing research."

"What kind of research? And don't try to bullshit a fellow Marine. I don't want to believe any of my brothers would stoop so low."

Andre nodded. "I'm researching the kind of shooter that would have tried to assassinate Senator Rosler and killed two other people."

The man stared at him. "I suppose you're going to issue some threat or promise about sending in the cavalry to interrupt my business if I don't cooperate?"

Andre stared at him. "I don't think we have to go that route."

"And you're sure the shooter uses my place?"

"He needs to practice. He needs a long range, and he's a good shot. The odds are ex-military."

"All valid points. Any of this going to come back on me?"

"Not a chance."

"How can I be sure?"

Andre smiled. "Semper fi, brother. That's enough where I come from."

The owner smiled. "Ok, there are quite a few ex-military shooting here."

"Who's your best?"

"Well, that's simple. Jeremy Axford. Ex-Army."

Andre smiled. He recognized the name. Axford was in every competition that Zack and Andre entered and never finished better than fifth. He was a weasel-like little man with a big chip on his shoulder. And he was a racist and hated Andre which meant he hated Zack because Axford believed that no white man should hang around any black man.

"Thanks, that's all I need." Andre pulled out his wallet, removed five twenty-dollar bills and placed them on the counter. "I don't suppose you could give me an idea of when he's here?"

The man smiled. "You never heard this from me."

"We never spoke as far as I'm concerned."

"Good. Here's what I know."

* ** ***

Andre entered the office late in the day, right as Michelle readied to leave. He had an extra pep in his step and stopped at her desk. "Going home?"

"It is five o'clock. Unless you and our fearless leader changed hours around here, that's my quitting time." She stood from her chair and clicked off a computer screen.

"I need you to do your magic," he said.

"Leave me a note. I'll get to it in the morning."

Andre chuckled. "Sorry, honey, I need it now."

She stopped and looked at him. As if the constant messages from Zack all day asking how to do this and that and how to find this and that didn't irritate her enough, he should have just asked her to do it and saved everyone a bunch of time, now overtime?

"Please tell me you are joking. Do you know what a pain in the ass Zack has been today? It's like he's on a mission or something. Why does Zack want me to find a phone number for Mrs. Linda Polzinski? Why does he want to talk to her? Her husband just died." She let out an annoyed Ugh and shook her head. "I swear, I know he's hiding something from me and when I find out, you both are going to suffer."

Andre stared at her with a half-smile. He knew full-well the torment he and Zack put her through with their requests. That was part of her gift and curse.

"Michelle, you are the best, you know that. I don't know what Zack is up to, but I need you right now. Put it down; you'll get time and a half for OT."

"I want double time and dinner. Delivery is fine, and you're leaving a tip," Michelle demanded.

Andre smiled. "That's why we love you, 'Chelle."

"Can the smooth talk, jerk. What do you need and why do you need it now?"

"Find out everything you can about an ex-Army guy named Jeremy Axford. I think he was discharged within the last five years."

"Why?"

"Because I need to know all about him," Andre said. "And I need it yesterday."

"You two always do."

She sat behind her desk and clicked her computers on. "Ok. Do we have a starting point for me?"

"Yeah, I think he's a mercenary." He grabbed a mug of coffee as her computers rebooted. "Do you know what Darnell is up to? I haven't talked to him in a couple of days."

"He's working that insurance fraud case and about to give the evidence to the insurance company. Some dude is scamming them out of hundreds of thousands of dollars. He's claiming he got injured in some accident, blamed it on faulty equipment, and he's now acting crippled and can't work. Somehow, he's gotten away with it so far, but Darnell says, and I quote 'the hammer is about to get dropped on his idiot ass.'" She smiled. "You guys can be so poetic at times."

Andre laughed. "I'm glad Zack brought him on."

"Me, too," Michelle said. "Since he's the only one around here working on paying cases."

"Ha, funny. Don't worry about the money. We always find it. Jobs keep finding us."

"Yeah well, you and Zack better hope so."

Andre shook his head. "By the way, did you tell anyone when Zack and I were coming home? Somehow someone knew exactly when we got back from

Europe." He looked at Michelle. "I didn't tell anyone other than Alysha. She told no one."

"I didn't tell anyone," Michelle said. "I didn't email it or anything, and I do a daily sweep on my computer and know no one has hacked in and no one even told Darnell."

Andre nodded. "Well, Zack doesn't have that big of a circle, so we should be able to figure it out." Julie popped into his mind. *But who did she tell?*

Michelle scooted closer to her keyboard. "Ok, so why do you need info of this guy?"

"I think I found Rosler's almost assassin."

CHAPTER 14

Zack sat on the edge of the bed; the morning sun peeked through the cracks of the gray curtains in the bedroom and Julie laid curled next to him. He stretched his legs and back and arms. He tried to stretch his aching ribcage. Better but still sore.

Zack turned to see Julie's eyes open with a smile on her face. "Good morning," he said. He leaned over and kissed her.

She put her arms over his bare shoulders. "I wish I didn't have to leave."

"Don't go then," he said and kissed her again. The voice in the back of his head hadn't silenced.

"I have to, baby, you know that."

They stared into each other's eyes. "Ok. Then get up and get ready. We have some work to do today."

"You want to go through with it?" She sat up and slid a tee shirt over her head. She flung her hair from under the collar.

No, I want to stay in bed with you all day. "You want to get to the bottom of this as much as I do. So yes. I'll start breakfast. Get in the bathroom. You have fifteen minutes."

He kissed her again and disappeared into the kitchen.

She smiled as she got out of bed and walked into the bathroom. "Fifteen minutes isn't enough, and we need two bathrooms!"

* * *   * * *

Andre entered Lieutenant Ted Barnes' office early that morning. Andre hadn't lost that extra bounce in his step: he was about to solve a big question for Barnes.

Barnes looked over his reading glasses and motioned for Andre to shut the door. Andre sat down as Barnes closed a file and hung up the phone.

"Jesus, what a nightmare," Barnes said. "That was just the Feds. They aren't happy that Senator Rosler's would-be assassin is still at large."

"Sending in their experts?"

"Yep."

Andre slid an envelope onto the desk. "Well, I may have just saved your job."

"What are these?"

"Fingerprints. Can we run them?"

"Should I ask where you got them?"

"Yeah, from the windowsill of where the gunman killed two people and inexplicably missed Rosler," Andre replied.

"You and Zack keep pushing that narrative. Why?"

Andre shook his head. "Because it makes no sense."

Barnes looked down. "Well, we'll see. So, you found the shooter's spot? We've been searching that area for days."

"You asked us for help, remember?"

"Unofficially."

"Of course. I found it one day."

Barnes was silent for a moment. "You found it in one day?"

Andre nodded. "Yup. And the next day, I may have identified the shooter."

Barnes was silent. His puzzled look hid his anger.

"Zack and I are thinking that Schmidt and O'Malley should stick to writing traffic tickets. They couldn't find their ass in their pants," Andre said. "After Zack and I looked at the area again, we knew it could only be from one angle."

"And you're sure you found it? I had my men looking all over. We found likely places, but no evidence and you're telling me right now that you found it in one day on your own after you and Stack looked at the site?"

"That's what I'm telling you. I found powder residue and pulled these prints. Here's the address," Andre slid a sticky note across the desk. "What was odd was that there are two sets of footprints on the floor in the room."

"What?"

"Yeah, that's what I said. I think maybe the shooter had a spotter."

Barnes stared at the note. He picked up the phone. "Schmidt, this is Barnes. Take a team to this address," he recited the address. "Fourth floor, southeast corner. Get forensics. We may have our location, and I don't want it messed up. Keep it quiet too." He hung up and looked at Andre. "Good work." Barnes rose from his desk. "Let's go check these prints."

Andre followed him to a processing room for prints in the back of the precinct. Barnes talked to the tech and told him those prints were a top priority. The techie dropped what he was doing and went to work on Andre's prints.

"These aren't the best quality. Did one of our guys pull these?" The techie asked. "If so, we need another training class."

Barnes looked at Andre and smiled. "I'll see to it."

They watched the techie do his job and continued to small talk.

"At least they're good enough to make a composite so I can run it through the system."

Barnes nodded. "Run it through them all." He looked at Andre. "This could take a while. Did you do this alone or was Zack with you?"

"Alone."

Barnes nodded. "Let's get some coffee. Do you know what he's pursuing?"

"The Ashley Blumenthal case for one."

"Why is he doing that?"

"My guess is he wants to find some answers for her mother. And to see if there are any connections there."

"With what?"

"Hannah Davison." Andre poured himself a cup of coffee. "Jules is leaving in a couple of days. Traveling with the Senator's campaign for a couple of weeks. He's worried about that. You know him. I think he'd be lost without her."

Barnes laughed. "Seriously? Is he worried about her leaving him? Why? She loves him, and if she kept finding reasons to stay with him up to this point, he never has to worry again." The two men laughed. "Well, like Zack suspected we found nothing on the three DB's from the SUV. It's like they never existed. There is no match for their prints, nothing. Who were they?"

Andre shook his head. "More importantly, why would anyone be following and threatening us and how did they, whoever they are, know exactly when we arrived at the airport? Did you tell anyone?"

"Me?" Barnes laughed. "No, no one at all. I didn't want anyone to know that you two were back and now seeing the trouble I have since you returned I think I should have kept you in Europe." He shook his head. "Who else knew?"

Andre thought of Julie again. *It had to be her.* "I'm not sure, but I'll stay on it." They talked for another thirty minutes before they headed back to the lab.

"No hits sir," the technician said.

"Run it through the military database," Andre said.

The techie looked at Barnes. Barnes nodded, and he did.

"When we were in Europe did you detect anything that gave you a reason to think Zack's out of state trouble followed him here?"

Barnes shook his head. "None whatsoever. We were pretty vigilant about that but saw nothing."

"If not that, then what?"

The two talked another twenty minutes.

"Sir," the techie interrupted, "we have a possible match."

The two looked at the computer screen.

Barnes leaned forward. "Ok. Here's the million-dollar question: who the hell is this guy?"

Andre stared at the picture. "A mercenary. You have plans today?"

"What for and how long?"

"Let's go talk to him. We'll be gone most of the day."

Barnes nodded. "We need backup?"

"Not your jurisdiction, I'm afraid. Before we go all balls to the wall and fry his ass, I'd like to try to get him to talk. I would appreciate it if you kept this our secret until we get some answers."

Barnes nodded again. "Meaning don't tell the Feds."

"Or anyone."

"Ok. Fill me in on the rest on the way, but we're going in tactical. Now tell me exactly how you found this guy. After we arrest him, I need to make sure some hot shot lawyer doesn't get him off on some stupid technicality."

"We have to arrest him first."

CHAPTER 15

Zack dialed the number provided by Michelle and waited. On the fourth ring, he heard a tentative hello.

"Hello, Mrs. Linda Polzinski?"

"Yes."

"Mrs. Polzinski, my name is Zack Stack. I was wondering if I could talk to you about your husband."

Click. Linda hung up.

Zack took a deep breath. He heard the shower run and dialed again.

"Hello?"

"Mrs. Polzinski, it's Zack Stack. Please, don't hang up," Zack rushed.

"How did you get this number? It's unlisted."

Not to Michelle. "I can explain that later. Mrs. Polzinski, can I meet with you to talk about the Senator?"

Click. Zack stared at his phone. The line disconnected. *Ok, so do I push this or not?* He dialed again. He knew she answered, but she said nothing. "Mrs. Polzinski, please listen to me, I only need a few minutes of your time."

"I am not interested in talking to any reporters and answering questions about the precious Michael Rosler! Now if you don't stop calling me, I'm calling the police."

Click. She hung up again. *Fourth time is a charm, right?* He dialed. It rang and rang. After the tenth ring, an answering machine picked up. It said only to leave a message.

"Mrs. Polzinski, Zack Stack again. I'm sorry to bother you, but I need to talk to you. I know you're listening to this and ready to call the police but hear me out first." Zack took a deep breath, unsure of what to say. "I am not calling about Rosler. I'm calling about your husband. I think he was the target, not Rosler," he said. *With nothing to prove it either.* "I'm not a reporter. I'm a private investigator. I can explain if you can give me ten minutes of your time. Please. My number is..."

"I'm here," Mrs. Polzinski said after she picked up the phone. "Why is a private investigator investigating the death of my husband? It's a police matter, and I was told he was collateral damage."

"I disagree," Zack said. "Look, I can explain, but I would prefer to meet with you. Are you free any time today?"

There was silence.

"Please Mrs. Polzinski, I'm asking you to trust me. Just a few minutes of your time and if you don't like what I have to say, just say the word and I'll leave you alone."

Zack could hear her breathing.

"Look, you can look me up online. My office number is right there. If you research me and find anything you don't like or trust, just call the office and let my office manager know you can't meet. I won't bother you again then," Zack said. "But know this: I do believe your husband was a target, and so was the girl. But I need information to help me prove that."

Mrs. Polzinski let out a deep breath.

Zack waited. *If she says no, where do I go from here?*

"Very well. I can meet you today at three o'clock. Do you know where I live?"

"Yes, ma'am, I do. Thank you, Mrs. Polzinski. I will see you then."

Zack hung up, and he looked at the time. He walked into the bathroom and pulled back the shower curtain. "We have time to spare. Can I join you?"

Julie smiled. "Can you wash my back for me?"

He closed the curtain behind him and stepped into the hot stream of water. Zack put his arms around Julie and held her naked body tight to his as the water splashed on his shoulders. "I can wash your back, your front, your sides, your top, and your bottom," he said. "I'm talented like that."

Julie smiled. "Well, let's start with my back and see what happens." They kissed. "Did you make your phone call?"

"I did," he said. "Took some persuasiveness, but Mrs. Polzinski agreed to meet us," he said and then realized he never mentioned Julie would be with him.

"What time?"

"Three o'clock," he said.

"So what do we do until then?"

Zack grinned and nibbled on her exposed neck. "After we shower, and whatever else, and breakfast of course," he said between more kisses, "we need to find a link between all those girls and Rosler."

"How about if we talk about that later?" She said. She moved her hands to below his waist. "I think I should clean this for you."

"Hey, remember, blood pressure in the shower?"

She stopped and laughed at him. "I am sure you're not going to have a stroke because you're making love to me in the shower!"

"Is it worth risking?"

She dropped to her knees. "You tell me."

"I'll risk it."

* * *　* * *

Two men talked in an office three stories above street level in a plush office. Both wore suits, one the power blue suit with a white shirt and red tie while the other wore a black suit and tie. The blue-suited man sat behind a desk when the black-suited man's cell phone rang.

"Yeah?"

"Stack set up a meeting with the widow," said the voice on the phone. "Three o'clock this afternoon."

"Well that's unfortunate," the black-suited man replied. He stared ahead. "I'll get back to you." He hung up his phone and looked at the other man.

"Problem?" The blue-suited man asked behind his desk.

"Stack is meeting with the widow today."

"Why?"

The black-suited man smiled. "Well since he investigates for a living, I'd venture to guess that he is investigating."

"Investigating what?"

"What the hell do you think, Jerry? Jesus Christ. Isn't it obvious?"

"What?"

The black-suited man stood. "Why else would he be talking to the widow of Sam Polzinski?" He waited as Jerry stared at him. "Christ, it wasn't rhetorical. He's investigating Sam's ties with Rosler."

"Oh," Jerry said as if a lightbulb finally clicked. "What do we do?"

The black-suited man walked to the window. "I'm thinking."

"What about a payout? Just throw some money at him. It worked before."

"It won't work with this guy. He's too principled."

"Bullshit. Every person has their price."

The black-suited man retreated to a wet bar and poured himself a glass of bourbon. "I'm sure they do, but you don't have enough to buy this guy. Trust me."

"Come on, a quarter of a million should do it."

"Jerry, listen to me: it won't work. We already tried talking to him, and he and his partner killed three of my guys. What does that tell you? Listen to me: I've seen this guy's military file and his partner's too. They are decorated combat soldiers. United States Marines. Do you get it? They don't like to lose. They don't quit either. Stack went to Europe just to catch a guy who skipped bail. Spent four months there until he caught him and came back. Get it now?"

Jerry shook his head. "Well, we have to do something. Does she know anything?"

"She probably knows what Sam knew." The black-suited man sipped his bourbon. "Which means she knows enough to point Stack in the right direction."

"Listen, bud, you know I don't like interfering with what you do, but that could be bad. Real bad."

He stared at Jerry and nodded. "I know." He finished his bourbon. "We should have just castrated our boy six years ago." He stood. "I'll take care of it."

CHAPTER 16

The trip to the shooting range in rural Virginia took an hour and a half. Lieutenant Barnes steered his car into the gravel parking area and saw six vehicles in the parking lot. Four of the trucks had Virginia plates; two had Maryland. Three Chevy trucks, three Ford trucks sat silent.

Frequents 'pops' echoed from behind the building. Lieutenant Barnes shook his head and pulled his Glock out of his holster. He checked it, loaded the barrel, clicked on the safety and re-holstered it. Andre did the same with his .45 revolver.

"Is that your only piece?"

"No." Andre lifted his pants leg and showed a Colt .45 automatic. "Where's your .357?"

"Home. Don't you think the .45 is more practical than a six-shooter?"

"Not if I don't miss," Andre smiled.

Barnes snorted and laughed. "Are you and Stack brothers?" He shook his head. "Let's hope we don't need them. You recognize his truck?"

"Yep, the black F250 is his. If Michelle's research is accurate," Andre answered.

"It always is. Let's go."

The two walked into the office. Andre opened the door of the office, and he followed Barnes inside. Behind a long narrow table was shelves filled with bullets and boxes of casings and caps and ammunition. The man behind the counter carried a .357 Magnum on his belt, and a semi-automatic rifle leaned against the wall beside him. On a table behind him was an M1 rifle, the man's gun of choice on the range. He saw Andre and smiled.

"Can I help you, gentlemen?"

Lieutenant Barnes removed the sheet of paper Andre handed him earlier from his coat pocket and looked at the name. "Yes, we're looking for Jeremy Axford."

"If you say he's here, he's gotta be out back shooting," the man said.

"Thank you," Barnes said.

"Hoo-rah," the man said as Andre walked towards the front door.

"Hoo-rah," Andre returned, and they stepped outside.

"Marines, I should have guessed," Barnes said.

They stepped out the back of the trailer and looked over the range. Tall deciduous trees surrounded the property atop mounds that completely surrounded the shooting lanes. Behind the range were the low, rolling hills of eastern Virginia and miles and miles of forest.

Andre and Barnes saw five men in various positions, one standing, one kneeling, two lying down and all shooting long range rifles at targets spotted at different distances. The man lying at the far end was shooting at the most distant target away, 600 yards.

Barnes looked from end to end. "Shall we approach Mr. Axford?"

"With pleasure."

They walked across the wooden patio past the other shooters and towards the man at the end. The man at the end, Jeremy Axford, emptied his five-shot clip and eyed the target through a spotting scope. He heard footsteps, looked up and saw Andre and Barnes beside him.

"Jeremy Axford?" Lieutenant Barnes asked. "I'm Ted Barnes; this is Andre Kitchell. We'd like to have a word with you."

Axford looked Barnes up and down and then looked at Andre. He couldn't hide his recognition of Andre. "What do you want? I'm busy." He pretended to pay no attention and reloaded his rifle.

"Mr. Axford, I'm with the Baltimore Police Department, and we're investigating the murder of two people in conjunction with the assassination attempt of Senator Michael Rosler. Are you familiar with it?" Barnes sounded non-confrontational but kept his right hand perched atop his hip holster.

Axford rolled to his side, his rifle shifted ever so slightly towards the two men but still safely away from them. "And why would you be asking me? Because I can shoot? A lot of guys can shoot. You ask all of them yet?"

"Well, Jeremy, you may want to explain what you were doing in a room of the Armiture building on the fourth floor at the window that day," Andre cut to the chase quickly.

"I wasn't there, nice try Kitchell. Say, whatever happened to that friend of yours, the white kid? As I recall, you two could shoot pretty well too," Axford answered with bitterness and resentment in his voice. "Did you question him?"

Barnes looked at Andre.

"You see, Lieutenant, Jeremy here is a good sharpshooter. For three years in a row, he'd enter the military sharpshooter contest as did me and the white kid," Andre didn't hide his distaste for the term Axford used for Zack. "One year, Jeremy shot better than he ever did, but after all was said and done, that white kid won, and I finished second. Jeremy here finished fifth. He never finished in the top ten any other year. Sounds like he's still a little bitter, doesn't it, Lieutenant?"

Barnes nodded. "Sounds like he doesn't like either of you." He turned back to Axford. "See, here's the thing, Axford," Barnes let out a sigh. "We know you were in that room and that room is the perfect angle, distance, and sightlines to be involved in that shooting. So, we want to know what you were doing there."

"Bullshit, you're fishing. I wasn't there. You can't prove shit," Axford said. The gun moved slightly again.

"What I collected says differently," Andre said. "See, dumbass, you used the bathroom when you were there. You left your fingerprints on the windowsill and the toilet. That's what we call being stupid." Andre moved his hand to his hip holster. "And I'd appreciate it if you would quit moving the aim of that rifle towards us."

Axford glared at Andre, the hate evident. The fire in his eyes burned hot. His eyes shifted back and forth, computing what he heard. "That's a lie!" He wanted to say he was wearing gloves. "You didn't find my fingerprints in that room!"

"Yes, I did, Jeremy. Baltimore Police Crime Scene Investigators were there yesterday too. You were there. Now tell us why."

Axford's face turned colors again. "Ok, I was there. A few days ago, I was there. I looked at a lot of rooms. I was checking the place out to see if I wanted to move in once it gets renovated. Was even considering being an investor to help get it done. Ain't no law against that."

"There's evidence that you were in just one room. The one where the gun fired that killed two people and wounded a third," Andre said.

"Maybe you weren't looking hard enough," Axford tried.

"That's an M24," Barnes noticed. "Nice gun."

Axford said nothing.

"Where were you the day of the shooting?"

"I was here, there. You know, running errands and stuff. Hell, I don't know. That was what, like a week or so ago? A lot has happened since then. I can't remember what I was doing."

"Would you mind if we recovered a bullet or two of what you just fired? Compared it to what we recovered from the shooting?" Barnes looked at the other shooters on the range. None seemed to care about Barnes, Andre, and Axford.

"Goddamn right I mind! I don't know who the hell you think you are coming in here and accusing me of murder, but you are way out of line, and way out of your jurisdiction, so I suggest you get back into your car and get the hell out of here," Axford snapped.

"Or what?" Andre said. "Are you threatening us?"

"Nope," Axford said as he got to his feet. "I'm just answering your questions."

Andre continued. "Look, Jeremy, it isn't looking good for you right now. We haven't told anyone else about what we found but if we give what we know to the Feds your life will get a whole lot messier," Andre warned him.

Barnes took over. "So, in the spirit of cooperation and saving your ass, we'd like to do a ballistics check with this gun and ask you a few questions where

83

it's a little more," he looked around, "warm. Like inside somewhere. What do you say? Is that your only rifle?"

Axford stared at the two, nodded and then shook his head with pierced lips. "I have to give it to you fellas; you sure seem to think you have it all figured out, don't you?"

"We're trying, Mr. Axford," Barnes answered. "How about we leave this place and go check that gun to clear your name?"

"Well," Jeremy sighed, "I suppose we oughta get this over with. I have my other rifle in the truck. How about I get that and meet you boys out front, so you can get on with something else after I prove you wrong?"

"Splendid. Lead the way."

* * *   * * *

Linda Polzinski wasn't skilled on the use of a computer but searching was easy. She typed words into the search engine and read the pages one at a time. The search results for Zack Stack, Private Investigator, proved fruitful.

She read them thoroughly until she saw a newspaper article, written by a reporter named Julie Fletcher, that highlighted Zack's involvement in the arrest and conviction of Donald Fairfax. That cemented her decision. Linda's hands slightly trembled as she read the article. It was gruesome but thorough and brought back horrid memories.

She turned off the computer. Linda knew she made the right choice. Zack Stack is the right man. Linda Polzinski, the widow of state senator Sam Polzinski, married for twenty-two years, vowed this would be the end of her fear, and she knew exactly what to do. *Zack Stack is going to learn about everything.*

CHAPTER 17

Barnes and Andre followed Axford to his truck. They stopped twenty feet away from the Ford truck as Axford opened the passenger door and leaned inside. Barnes kept his eye on Axford and Andre surveyed the area.

The trees on the hills showed hues of red, orange and yellow amongst the coniferous green. Leaves floated to the ground begrudgingly. Andre watched as fluffy white clouds kept the sun in a game of hide-and-seek. A light breeze rustled the leaves. A beautiful setting to Andre, he thought of bringing his girlfriend out to something like this the upcoming weekend for a romantic interlude.

"What is taking him so long?" Barnes asked.

Andre scanned the top of the hills and saw a flash as the sun popped out. He focused on it. It looked familiar; the sun disappeared and then reappeared; Andre saw it again and recognized it.

He grabbed Barnes and jumped to the ground just as the gun fired. It missed. The two rolled and scrambled to the side of the office as three more gunshots rang out and ricocheted off the ground near them.

Andre leaned tight against the building and checked his .45. "I think we just found his accomplice."

"I'd say so." Barnes glanced around the corner and saw Axford with two rifles run into the hills.

"They'll disappear into those hills, and we'll never find them if we call for backup and wait. Too many escape routes around here. We have to go in."

A bullet exploded through the wall between their heads. They hit the ground and scrambled away. They reached the far corner and peered around it.

"It's now or never," Andre said.

Barnes nodded. "Let's do this then. On three."

Barnes said one, two, and ran for it. Two shots fired, both missed at his feet before Andre raised and fired his handgun towards the trees. He fired four shots and saw Barnes dive into the tree line.

Andre re-loaded his gun, took a deep breath and sprinted to the tree line. There was no return fire.

"They're running."

"They'll stick to the ridge tops," Andre said as he eyed the surroundings.

"Plan?"

"Yeah, stick close to the trees, don't make a move unless it's solid and covered; we'll work our way east towards them." Andre took a deep breath. "Don't get too close. We don't want one shot taking us both out."

Barnes nodded as he surveyed the area. The hills rose and fell sharply, years of time and water dug canyons and streams between the peaks. The ridges rose as they went east and south. Barnes looked at his watch. "Move out; I don't want to be anywhere around here by dark."

"If we aren't out of here by dark, we're dead."

The two dodged from tree to tree and soon were away from the parking area and out of sight of the shooting range. Ten minutes turned into twenty. The pecking of woodpeckers and calling of Blue Jay's warning of intruders silenced. Andre could barely see the movements of Barnes through the thickness of the trees. It was too quiet. Andre leaned out from behind a thick oak tree and heard three shots. Two of the bullets ripped into the bark of the oak near his head. He felt something burn on his face and dove to the ground.

Barnes fired his weapon three times towards the shooters. The return fire shredded tree branches. Barnes scrambled away from that tree, leaned against another. Barnes thought he saw movement and fired twice, dove to the ground, rolled away from that tree and popped to his knees when he saw the flash of the automatic rifle rip off a dozen shots.

Barnes fired and saw from the corner of his eye Andre shoot his handgun towards the gunman. It was silent again. The two maneuvered their way another two hundred yards away from the parking lot. Andre looked at the ground while Barnes watched ahead, behind and around them.

"I don't like this, they are drawing us further away," Barnes said.

"I'd guess a mile by now, but looks like we got lucky," Andre answered. He pointed to a blood-soaked leaf. "One of them is bleeding."

"Well partner, so are you," Barnes said and pointed to Andre's face. "You get hit?"

"Tree did. Must have caught a splinter or something. How bad is it?"

Barnes examined it. "Looks like hell. But you probably won't even scar."

"Come on, stay behind me about ten feet. Keep low."

* * *   * * *

Andre crouched and crept from tree to tree, through brambles and brush, with Barnes ten feet behind him. The trail alternated from sunlight to shade as the foliage thinned and thickened and the sun continued its game of hide-and-seek.

Andre motioned for Barnes to take a position to his left where the ridge top widened. Automatic gunfire filled the air. Bullets peeled the bark of the trees and shredded leaves. Barnes shot his Glock. The shooting stopped almost immediately as it began. Both Barnes and Andre re-loaded when Barnes spoke.

"Axford, we know you can hear us," Barnes yelled. "We know you have a partner and he's with you. We can put you at the shooting; we can tie you to the bullets that killed Polzinski and the girl."

Two guns opened fire for a few seconds then stopped. Barnes and Andre shot their weapons towards the shooters then ducked.

Barnes yelled again. "Look, if there is more to this than you just going psychotic and blasting away another worthless liar of a politician, then talk to me. We can work this out."

Silence.

Barnes wouldn't give up. "Come on, Jeremy! No need to die or rot in prison for this. Just tell us who hired you, and we'll walk away!"

Andre pointed to another spot of blood on the ground. Barnes nodded.

"Axford!" Barnes yelled, anger in his voice. "Listen to me. It doesn't have to end this way. It's just a matter of time before these hills are swarming with cops. You have no chance of getting out alive. I'm offering you one. Tell me what I need to know."

Andre pointed with two fingers to his eyes and then ahead, then made a walking motion with his fingers and looked to the next ridge south. Barnes nodded, and Andre started down the hill as quiet as he could.

Silence.

"Axford," Barnes yelled again as he crept forward, "we know one of you is wounded. You won't get far trailing blood. Let me help you. I can get that wound taken care of with no questions. You can go free. Just tell me what you know. That's the deal."

Silence. Andre disappeared. Barnes didn't like that and moved forward. More silence. Things changed fast; eerie turned to creepy and then scary in moments. Barnes stood next to a thick maple and looked around. Andre appeared and motioned to something up ahead.

Suddenly they heard a single shot, a man yell and then silence. Both men paused. Andre ran ahead to the next ridge. Barnes met him there and saw it.

A body lay at the bottom of a gulley between two ridges: a bowl-shaped gulley filled with tangled brambles and short-stalked trees. They knelt and looked all around; guns pointed. The wait, only moments, seemed like minutes. The silence returned. Barnes lost patience and motioned; he went down to look. Andre looked up and down every tree, behind every rock and crevice, but there was nothing.

Barnes reached the body. Dead. It wasn't Axford. Barnes shrugged as Andre came down the side of the ridge. "Axford sacrificed his partner so he could escape. You recognize him?" Barnes asked.

Andre shook his head while he continued his surveillance of the surrounds.

"He's gone. We were right; he knew he couldn't escape with a wounded partner, so the sonofabitch shot him and tossed him into the ravine. What a prick move," Barnes said. "One in the heart and one in the stomach which I'm guessing was from me," he looked up at Andre and smiled. "Just a guess."

"Keep telling yourself that," Andre remarked. "Well, we have a runner. You better call it in."

Barnes looked at his cell phone. "I have no coverage. Maybe up top, I'll get a bar." He shook his head. "Can you hear me now?" He mocked. "My ass."

The two reached the top and walked around until the cell phone picked up a signal. Barnes dialed a number. "It's Lieutenant Barnes; I need you to locate me on my cell and send a team. I have a dead body and an ID on the shooter." Moments later he hung up and stared at Andre. "Well, partner, this has been a fun day."

Andre stared at Barnes.

"Now we park our butts at the top of that ravine to make sure a bear doesn't eat our DB and wait for the cavalry."

"You want me to stay here while our shooter flees?"

Barnes nodded. "Better to stay together. We just possibly upset a bunch of gun-nutter ammosexuals who think we are," he changed his dialect to mock the southern drawls they heard at the range, "interferin' with their rights as guaranteed by the Second 'Mendment of the Constitution," he smiled and switched to his normal voice. "I don't want to walk into an ambush alone. Do you?"

Andre frowned. "Hell no. But we can't sit here. We have to go after Axford."

"No, Dre," Barnes began, but Andre already turned and ran after Axford. He shook his head. "I should have never gotten involved with those two idiots." He took a deep breath and ran after Andre.

CHAPTER 18

Andre ran along the ridge top for a half hour. He knew he was on the right track, but there was no sign of Axford. There was no sign of Barnes either. He was on his own.

The ridge descended into a valley, and a stream raced at the bottom. Andre stopped and looked in every direction. The thick trees and dense shade restricted the view. *What is he thinking?* Andre pictured himself as the runner. *Stay high. He's running in the valley for cover.* Instead of descending into the valley and following the stream Andre followed the elevated ridge south. He picked up his pace and ran as fast as he could. He knew night would fall soon and then Axford would disappear. Andre ran faster. *Axford is not getting away today!*

* * * * * *

Jeremy Axford didn't want to kill his buddy, but he had to. The cop was right: with his buddy bleeding, they wouldn't be able to get away. He did come to Axford's aide, and Jeremy would always be grateful.

Axford didn't know how he was going to get away from the pig and the arrogant coon from the Corps. What was he doing working with the cops anyway? And how the hell did his fingerprints end up in the room? *Those bastards set me up! After I get out of this, I'm going to find them and teach them a lesson.*

Axford ran along the stream bed quickly, but it was slow. The water was cold, rapid and the footing was slippery and treacherous. He had fallen twice, but after the second time, he realized he let his emotions take over. So Axford settled down and watched his footing. The progress was still slow, but he was far away from where he had to shoot his buddy. He knew the pig would stay there. That body was evidence to them, Axford knew. *Only it was a dead-end.*

Axford smiled at the pun. If he was correct, the stream fed a small town's reservoir a few miles away. Once there, he could get a vehicle and disappear on the backroads of the mountains all the while heading south. Then Axford would access his account and buy a one-way plane ticket to Belize or someplace in the Caribbean and never be seen again. Two-hundred and fifty thousand would last a long time there in addition to the money he saved doing other mercenary jobs.

A fallen tree across the stream blocked his path; he jumped over it, but his foot landed on a wet slippery rock. He crashed into the stream face first. Axford grimaced, adrenaline surged through his body, perspiration dripped, and he grasped his throbbing ankle. Sprained. That would slow him down. Made him wish someone had hired him to kill Kitchell and his white trash friend. *No one would miss them two losers. They rigged that last competition to finish first and second. They had to! Everyone in the Army knew Jarheads couldn't shoot. They were the first ones sent in because they were the stupid ones.* He looked around and headed south again but now even slower.

Ten minutes later he reached a crisis. The stream plunged seventy feet into a pool before continuing its path south. The only way down was to scale down the cliff. Following the ridge could take hours; hours that he didn't have.

Axford shook his head and slung his one remaining rifle over his shoulder and climbed down. The sun hadn't set, but it was below the tree line, and the shadows overtook the forest. He continued downwards.

The cold water made it hard to grip the wet rocks. Footing was even worse, but Axford continued. Not much further. He looked below, and the best way was to cross the waterfall and get a foothold on the other side. He reached out his foot and stretched further and further…

Axford plunged the last thirty feet and splashed into the pool. He disappeared underwater and lost his rifle. He scrambled to the surface, paddled to the shore, pulled himself out and stood on the edge looking for his gun. Axford panted and saw his rifle on the far shore of the pond. He jumped into the cold water; anxiety welled inside him.

He reached the shore, cold, his body shivered, and the daylight waned. The temperature dropped. He grabbed his gun but then heard the unmistakable sound of a .45 caliber revolver cocking.

"Don't...make...a...move."

Axford looked at the barrel of the handgun; a six-shooter with all barrels loaded and saw a big black man on the other end with a smug smile on his face.

"Drop that rifle, Jeremy. I don't want to kill you."

Axford calculated his odds. They weren't in his favor. He dropped the rifle.

"You want to talk to me, or you want to wait until the Feds get here?"

Axford glared at Andre Kitchell. He hated the man in front of him. Axford hated how Kitchell held that second place trophy and how Kitchell hung out with that white kid. Mostly, Axford hated that a black man had just gotten the best of him.

"I know you weren't alone. Tell me who was with you and who hired you?"

"Go to hell."

Andre smiled. "I should just put a slug in your leg and cold-cock you then drag your ass back, so I don't have to deal with your crap. But, I'm going to give you a chance. You can't win this one, Axford. Talk to me. Tell me what happened, and we can work a deal."

"I ain't trusting no coon."

Andre shook his head. "What is with you stupid, uneducated rednecks? You keep that dumbass racist flag on your truck because you think it's cool, but it makes you nothing more than a bigoted, small-minded idiot. Listen close: The South will not rise again. The war is over, and slavery is not coming back. Get over it! Look, Axford, you have a choice here. Tell me what happened, and I'll let you run. You can take your chances of getting out of the country. Or you can be the moronic, ignorant racist jackass you are and end up someone's bitch in prison the rest of your life. What will it be, Johnny Reb?"

Axford figured he had one chance. "It wasn't my idea. I was doing a job. I just had to take out the girl. Two shots. That was it. And my fingerprints were planted. I wore gloves, man."

"You shot twice, both at the girl?"

"That was my job."

"Who hired you? Who was with you?"

"That's all I'm saying. If they find out I talked, I'm dead."

"Jeremy, no one will ever know you talked. I promise. You may hate me, man, but we're both ex-military. We have a code. You can trust me. Tell me what happened that day. Who hired you? Talk to me, man."

Axford stared right into the big black man's brown eyes and slowly moved his right hand closer to his pistol. "They'll kill me, man. You have no idea! You figure it out."

"We will figure it out and quit moving your hand towards that gun behind your back," Andre said, his Colt pointed square at Axford's face. "Do you want your brains splattered all over?"

Axford's eyes burned holes through Andre. If looks could kill, Andre would be dead. "No nigger is taking me in."

* * * * * *

Andre stared at Axford. The N-word used to infuriate him. Now, it just proved a point: *Just another low-life ignorant redneck. Dumb as a stump and no one ever taught him along the line that he was wrong about his views.* Then Andre realized that Axford wasn't ignorant. He was just plain stupid. *You can teach an ignorant person, but you can't fix stupid. And he's hatching a plan to get out of here.*

"Well, then we're at what they call an impasse. So, tell me, what's eating you more, Jer? The fact that a good ole' nigga like me caught your dumb pasty racist ass?" Andre smiled. "Or that you're never going to get credit for making those shots? Even I admit they were good," he paused and smiled wide, "for a fifth-place finisher."

Axford's lips disappeared, and his face reddened.

"So, what's your move?" Andre smiled. "Cracker."

Axford screamed and lunged at Andre. The next and last sound Axford heard was the sound of a .45 shell firing out of a six-shooter.

Andre heard a twig snap and spun, ready to fire.

"It's me, Dre," Barnes said. "Did you have to shoot him?"

93

"No one will miss one less a-hole. I did us all a favor and saved the taxpayers a lot of money," Andre said.

"Jesus, you sound like Zack." He shook his head. "What did he say?"

"How much did you hear?"

Barnes holstered his weapon and grabbed his cell phone. "I heard enough."

"He only took two shots."

Barnes hesitated. "When the cavalry gets here don't mention that part." Barnes looked at his phone. "If there's another shooter out there, let's make him believe we don't know it," Ted said.

Andre hesitated as he processed the information. "Whoever hired him, he's afraid of them. He said they."

"They," Barnes repeated with a deep sigh.

"Yeah," Andre replied and holstered his gun.

Barnes nodded. "Well, for now, we sell the Feds that this was the only shooter, got it? With luck, the gun we recover will make a ballistics match. Then we make up some bullshit about Rosler's stance on whatever pissed off Axford."

Andre looked from the dead Axford to Barnes. "So, we do a misdirect strike."

Barnes looked at Andre.

"That's what Zack and I would call it."

Barnes shook his head. "I don't even want to know. Wait, I think maybe I should know. You two keeping secrets from me isn't good."

"Maybe later. Here comes the cavalry."

CHAPTER 19

Zack sat in the car and watched the side view mirror. He saw no signs of a tail.

The house appeared on the right, and Julie stopped the vehicle on the street in front of the house. Zack looked at the Tudor style house with brown brick and white trim.

"Forget about it," he said to a smiling Julie who stared at him.

"What?"

"Too many gutters. I'm not spending my weekends all fall cleaning them," Zack said.

"You hire someone to do that," Julie said.

"Too far away from Fells Point, too," he said.

Julie smiled and shut her door. "We'll see."

He knew what that meant; *she likes this house and wants suburban life. Maybe that's better for children. I don't know. Who wants to waste every weekend taking care of a yard?*

"Besides, honey," Julie said, "think of all the birds you could attract in a yard like this?"

He smiled. *Now she's trying to bribe me.* "We'll see." Zack knew his attempt to turn things around didn't work. But, at least she understood his position. They walked on a long sidewalk to the house, leaves crumbled under their footsteps.

Zack looked at Julie as they reached the door. "Well, let's see how this goes." He pressed the doorbell, and they waited.

He pressed it again and looked around. The quiet neighborhood showed no signs of life.

"What time did she say to meet?"

"Three," Zack answered and looked at his watch. "It's 2:58," he said.

"Hmm," Julie pierced her lips and tried to peak through the small half-moon window in the top of the door.

Zack knocked on the door, and it creaked open.

They looked at each other. The door wasn't latched. Zack motioned for her to get behind him and he pulled his Sig from under his arm. "If anything happens, you call 911 immediately and get back to the car. Don't wait for me, just get out of here," he told her.

He put his hand on the door, nodded to Julie and gently pushed it open. "Hello? Mrs. Polzinski?"

Silence ensued. Zack entered with Julie close behind, his gun clutched in his hand and pointed where he looked. He looked straight, to the right and to the left. The living room to the left was filled with bouquets of flowers and blocked the vision across the room.

"Mrs. Polzinski, are you here?" Zack called out.

Silence.

He looked at Julie, and the two entered the living room to the left. On the far side of the room was another room also filled with flowers. Zack took a step towards a love seat and then saw Mrs. Polzinski in a chair, her arms splayed to her sides, her legs limp. Her head laid back, her eyes and mouth wide open.

Julie gasped and covered her mouth.

Zack lowered his gun, still alert for noise but heard nothing. He walked to her and put two fingers on her neck pulse.

Linda Polzinski was dead.

Zack looked at a round table beside her chair. An empty bottle of vodka and an open container of prescription pills sat on it. He leaned over to see the pill bottle closer: imipramine. "Antidepressant," he said softly to Jules who slowly moved closer to the body. "Overdose most likely."

"Oh my God, Zack," Julie said. "What do we do?"

"First, you call the police. Second, don't touch anything. Third, I'm going to clear the house."

"She was to going to talk to us, Zack. Why would she kill herself?"

"Is your medical examiner friend on duty? I want him on this case."

Julie held her cell phone to her ear as Zack left the room.

* * *   * * *

Zack and Julie leaned on the bumper of her car in the street in front of the Polzinski house two hours later. The police arrived, an ambulance arrived, detectives arrived, and the questions began.

The medical examiner arrived. As he left after examining the body, he spotted Julie and winked at her.

"You have a bad habit of being in the wrong place at the wrong time, Stack," the lead detective said to him.

"I guess that's a matter of perspective, O'Malley," Zack replied.

"Her husband gets killed in an assassination attempt a week ago, and you show up here the day his wife commits suicide?" O'Malley shook his head. "What were you doing here?"

"First of all, O'Malley, we don't know she committed suicide. It looks like an apparent overdose. Second, I told you already, and no matter how many times you ask me or how many different ways you try to spin it, you're going to get the same answer: I had a meeting with her at three o'clock. I called her this morning. We arrived here at 2:58, I knocked on the door, and it creaked open. We entered, announced our presence, found her in her living room and called 911. I cannot spell that out any more factually or with brighter color crayons for you to understand. We have not committed any crime so are we free to go?"

O'Malley stood straight and took in a deep breath. "But what were you doing here? Why were you meeting her? What was your meeting about?"

Julie spoke. "I'm doing a story on her husband and his legacy. She agreed to talk to us about that. That is my job."

"But what is he doing here?" O'Malley pointed at Zack. "He said he had a meeting with her."

"I am helping Jules with her story," Zack said. "Are we done here? Seems to me, you have no cause to keep us here any longer."

O'Malley stared at Zack and shook his head. "Yeah, you're free to go."

The two stood and walked to their own car doors.

"And Stack, don't let me catch you interferin' with this investigation," O'Malley barked.

"What investigation? I thought you already declared it was a suicide?" Zack got in the car and shut the door. Julie started the car. "I assume you're thinking what I'm thinking?"

"Yep. Let's go visit the medical examiner."

* * * * * *

Doctor Steve Patterson, M.E., processed the body of Linda Polzinski like he did to hundreds of bodies before. It wasn't personal, and this body was no more important than the last, or the next. His job was about science and death, and science is fact and death has no bigotries. No preconceptions, no lies, no rants or diatribes, and no fallacies impacted what he learned from the bodies on his table. He liked it that way.

Except this body was more important than the last and the next. The entrance into the lab by a sandy-blonde-haired blue-eyed investigative reporter told him that. The man behind her, tall, muscular, short dark-blonde hair and who looked like he had been in several cage fights lately reinforced his assessment that this body was different.

He looked over the top of his glasses and smiled at the woman. "Miss Fletcher, I suspected I'd be seeing you soon. Not sure why."

Julie smiled. "Hey, doc. I'll tell you why," she said.

Patterson looked at Zack and back to Julie. He knew Zack well enough; Zack had been in the lab before as well, and Julie talked about Zack to Patterson in the past, but this seemed unusual, and Patterson acted like he expected an explanation.

"Doc, this is Zack, remember him?"

"We've met before," Zack said.

"We're curious. What have you found so far?"

98

"It's only been an hour," Patterson said. "Other than apparent overdose, I don't have anything to give you yet."

"Vodka and imipramine," Zack said. "Lethal concoction?"

Patterson smiled. "Come on, Zack, you know better than that. Everything is toxic. Even water. So yes, to answer your question. And a woman of her weight, which was normal, wouldn't need much to be lethal. Like I said, I'll know more in a little bit."

Julie nodded. "Do me a favor and call me as soon as you have some results."

Patterson looked back to the body. This was the typical arrangement between the two.

"Hey doc," Zack asked before he and Julie left, "would you be able to tell if someone forced her to ingest the booze and pills?"

"Maybe. You think there was foul play involved?"

Zack shrugged. "I don't know. But, it would be nice to know."

"I'll pay attention. Now let me get back to work."

Julie left with Zack behind her. They got to her car and sat inside.

"So what now?"

Zack shook his head. "I don't know."

Julie started the car. "My place or yours?"

"Let's go to your place. That way you won't have to leave before dawn tomorrow."

"Plotting I see," she said softly. "Good. Let's go."

CHAPTER 20

The morning came early for Zack. The sun shone through the window right onto his face. He overslept; Julie's rule was he would leave before sunrise. Retribution from her religious mother scared her still. He looked at Julie, asleep peacefully with her hands under her pillow as she laid on her right shoulder facing him. *I better get up and dress in case Mother Religion shows up and tries to burn me on a cross.*

He was in and out of the shower and had her coffee started when she finally stirred. He heard Julie rumble in the bedroom, then the bathroom. He'd see her in thirty minutes.

Zack stared out the window at the street with his mind full of questions and thoughts and doubts and worries. *She is leaving tomorrow. How can I get her to stay?* Zack had no answer. Time didn't stop, much to his dismay, so he started breakfast. *Make the best of it, and maybe she'll change her mind and stay home.*

Julie came out of the bedroom, dressed with her hair still wet. Zack handed her a cup of coffee, but she kissed him before she drank. "I thought we could stay here today. I have to do some work, but I want you around. Then maybe we could go to your place for dinner since I know you have food now."

"I wasn't planning on leaving you at all," he said. He kissed Jules.

She leaned close to him. "Get dressed. You just in boxers is enough to make me want to jump you right now."

"That was the whole plan." Zack winked at her and lightly smacked her butt.

"It's working. Just not until after breakfast. I'm starving."

Zack disappeared into her bedroom and found his spare pair of clothes. He was allowed one set in case of an emergency. Zack learned early in their relationship that her mother checked those things. *Her daughter has been long past pure, Mrs. Fletcher.* Zack smiled as he zipped his pants.

A knock on her front door surprised both of them. Zack stayed in the bedroom silent. *Who the hell is here this early?*

"Senator Rosler! What are you doing here?"

Senator Michael Rosler, dressed in his dark power suit, smiled at Julie and hugged her. "Hey, we're past the Senator stuff. Call me Mike or Michael, remember?" He stepped inside the doorway; his two security men waited outside the door. "I was on my way across town, thought I'd stop in and see how my favorite writer is doing? Excited about the trip?"

"I'm excited to wrap this up so I can finish the book," she said.

He grabbed her shoulders. "I can't wait to read it. I bet it will be perfect."

Zack remained silent. *If that slime ball makes a move on Jules, he's a dead man.*

Julie smiled but added nothing.

"Listen, we have some early Sunday meetings, so we'll be leaving earlier than originally planned," Rosler said. "I'll have Jerry let you know the specifics. We'll pick you up here."

"Ok," she said.

"I know it will be a long two weeks, but it will be worth it, you'll see," Rosler said.

Julie remained silent but smiled.

"I forget the name of the town, but they have one of the best restaurants in the Midwest. It's an Italian joint. Very romantic. Plan on dining with me. If you don't want to pack anything nice, don't worry. We'll get something for you on the trail."

"Senator, I'm going to Iowa to write, not dine with you," Julie said, but he cut her off.

"Hey! I said call me Michael. After all, we are going to spend a lot of time together. Might as well enjoy it."

"I'm there for work."

Rosler laughed. "You know what they say about all work and no play?"

Julie smiled.

"Don't worry about it. Your boyfriend doesn't need to know. What happens in Iowa stays in Iowa."

Zack clutched the door handle. *He's hitting on my fiancé!*

"That's because nothing is going to happen in Iowa," Julie said.

"Oh, something is," Rosler said. "I mean, the Rosler campaign is happening there, and Iowa will never be the same." He laughed. "Is the guy you're seeing ok with you leaving with me for two weeks?"

The smile left her face. "I'm following your campaign through Iowa to finish the book. That's a bit different than leaving with you for two weeks and no, he's not ok with it."

Rosler laughed. "Well, I'm hoping you can sway his vote for me." Julie didn't laugh. "But hey, he should be supporting you which means he would be supporting me. And if he isn't, then maybe he isn't the guy for you."

She ignored his statement.

The Senator stared into her eyes. "You have the most beautiful eyes."

"Senator, thank you. I am sure you have better things to do than stand in my apartment and flatter me. I have work to do."

Rosler put his hands on her arms. "You're right. I do have meetings. Listen, Julie, honey," he hesitated, "if you need anything at all and I do mean anything, you call me direct. You understand?"

She smiled and nodded. "I'll be ready to go on Sunday."

Rosler leaned forward and kissed her forehead. He held her for a second longer, smiled and turned and left. She walked to the door, locked it and leaned against it before she turned to see Zack stare at her. The expression on his face told her everything.

"Zack, wait, don't go ballistic, ok?"

"After what I just saw?" He nodded. "Ok. I'm listening."

"Zack, we talked about this," she said. "You have to trust me."

"Trust you? It's him that clearly has an objective."

"But that isn't mine," she said.

He stared at her. "I think," he said slowly, "that the best thing for us right now is for you to find a reason not to go on that trip."

"Baby, I have to go. I committed, and we need the money. I don't care what he thinks or what you think. I'm not sleeping with him."

"That guy has one idea and one idea only about what is going to happen," Zack said. His cell phone rang.

"Nothing is going to happen."

Zack looked at his phone.

"Are you going to answer it?"

Zack frowned. *I can't push this, or she'll shut down and close me out for two weeks.* "It's just Michelle. Probably going to complain about me not stopping at the office."

Julie crossed her arms. "You had a relationship with her. I still trust you."

Zack nodded. He walked to her and exhaled. "I'm sorry. I do trust you, but I know how men think, and I don't trust that snake at all," he said. He kissed her lips softly. "Look, I need to stop at the office." He shook his head. "You want to come with me? Maybe Michelle found something out about Ashley Blumenthal."

"Give me a few minutes. And listen to me one last time: I love you! And only you. So, please not another word about that damn trip, ok?"

* * *   * * *

Zack opened the door for Julie. They walked in to see Michelle and Andre huddled over a file on Michelle's desk. Michelle looked up.

"It's about time you got here," Michelle said.

Zack slouched. The constant bombardment from Michelle wore him down. "Don't start. Please, not today. Do you have anything for me?"

Julie hid her smile. Michelle took a deep breath and pointed a file on the opposite corner of her desk.

Zack picked up the file and read it.

The others talked while Zack read. And then he turned the page and found a smoking gun.

"Holy mother of pearl!" He spun around to the three. "Ashley Blumenthal found out she was pregnant ten days before she died."

"What?"

"She was pregnant, Jules." Zack was expecting to see prescriptions for antibiotics. Not this.

"How?" Julie asked.

"Birds and bees, dear," Andre said.

"I mean, how is that possible?" Julie smacked Andre's arm. "I mean, how is that not in the police file? How did no one know?"

Zack smiled and closed the file. "How do we know no one knew? It smells like motive to me. I say we ask her boyfriend and the swim coach. See which one rolls over on the other first."

"And then what? Both had alibis," Andre said. "Couldn't have been either of them."

Zack frowned. "Well, we've gone this far. Might as well keep going and see where it leads."

* * * * * *

Julie drove past the office buildings, down the windy road through the campus past the historic buildings, the striking architecture of the stone buildings and well-maintained landscaping of the campus. The road made a wider loop around a large parking lot near the natatorium and gymnasium, and she followed it to the far end of the parking lot per Zack's directions on their way to interrogate the swimming coach.

Coach Gary Tanner was alone in his office. Considering the time of day Zack was surprised he was alone. It was late morning, and Zack thought for sure Tanner would have one of his swim girls doing laps on him. Zack pushed open the door and smiled at Tanner.

"Knock, knock," said Zack.

"What do you want?"

Zack stepped inside. "Hey, buddy. Have a minute?"

Julie stepped past Zack. "You must be Gary Tanner?"

Tanner ignored Julie and watched Zack. "I have nothing else to say."

Julie spoke. "We have a couple of more questions."

"I told you I had nothing to do with her death. There's nothing else to discuss."

"She was pregnant," Zack said. "Did you know that?"

"What?"

"Ashley was pregnant," Zack said. "She found out, then ten days later, she's dead. I smell motive, don't you?"

Tanner's face went white. "No! I,"

"You knew she was pregnant, didn't you? And that was going to ruin your career, so you killed her, is that it?"

Gary shook, and his breathing quickened. His eyes were huge. "What? What are you talking about? I swear I didn't know she was pregnant!"

"Her boyfriend said you knew and it scared you. He said you knew the administration would fire you. You'd never get a job again," Zack said.

"That's a lie!" Gary jumped to his feet. "He's lying to hurt me because Ashley wanted to be with me, not him!"

Zack stared at him.

"Gary," Julie said, "we can help you. But you have to tell us the truth. Is any of what her ex-boyfriend said true?"

Tanner stood motionless, his face white, mouth open and his eyes reddened.

Zack sat on the edge of the desk. "We have motive now, Gary. She found out she was pregnant ten days before she died," Zack repeated. He watched Gary's reaction. "The police didn't know about this then, but I have to tell them. Then, they'll get a warrant and tear your life apart."

Gary slid to the floor, sat on his rear and looked devastated. "I didn't know she was pregnant," he uttered. "I didn't know she was pregnant."

Julie walked around the desk and knelt beside him. "Coach Tanner, are you telling us the truth? Everything? We can help you, but you have to tell us everything."

Tanner shook his head slowly. "I swear on my life; I didn't know she was pregnant." Tears ran down his face.

Zack wondered if they were for Ashley or his soon-to-be-dead career.

"I was out of town. I texted Ash that evening," Gary said. "Said I'd be home about eleven and asked to see her."

Julie looked at Zack.

"She texted back that she was at a party but had to meet someone later and that she'd see me the next day." Gary struggled to catch his breath and stop from crying.

"Did she say who? Her ex-boyfriend was out of town. Was she seeing anyone else?"

Tanner looked at Zack. He opened his mouth but could only shake his head.

"Come on, Gary, what do you know?" Zack said with a lack of compassion that made Julie look at him again. "You must suspect something."

"She may have been, but I'm not sure, all right?" Gary snapped. "Ash was getting texts all the time when we were together, but she'd never tell me from who. Ash said not to worry and that it was just one of her friends. All I know is that she said she was supposed to meet someone later that night and when I tried to call her the next day, she was dead. But I swear to God, I didn't know she was pregnant. I swear."

"You have to suspect something, Gary," Zack snapped. "Did she have a job? Was she working for anyone? You had to see something on her phone at least once. Come on, Gary. Think."

Julie looked at Zack surprised at his lack of compassion.

"Job? No," Gary said, near tears. "Wait, she did. She was a staffer on Senator Rosler's campaign." Gary looked at Zack, then to Julie. He kept his eyes on Julie as she was comforting. "I saw a text a couple of times, odd hours of the night, all it said was 'I want you.' I asked her about it, and she told me it was just a short message letting her know she was needed by the campaign. I swear, I'm telling you the truth. I didn't know she was pregnant and if I did and it was mine, I would have done the right thing!"

"Why didn't you tell the police she had a meeting that night and that you suspected her seeing someone else?" Julie asked, the compassion evident in her tone.

Tanner covered his face in his hands. "They never asked. And I was afraid I would," he stopped and broke down. Zack knew the interview ended.

Julie stood, and Zack nodded. "We don't know whose it is, Gary."

He looked at them and caught his breath. Gary wiped his face dry. "How will I know if it was mine?"

"We want you to give us a sample for a paternity test," Julie said.

"Ok, anything," he said. Julie had a vial and Q-tip handy and swabbed his mouth.

"How long will it take? How will I know if it's mine?"

Zack opened the door. "Watch the news. If it's yours, you'll know." The two left the office and shut the door behind them.

"That was pretty harsh," Julie said softly in the hallway.

"Tell that to Ashley's mother," he replied. They reached the exit door, and Zack opened it for Julie. She eyed him. "I'm sorry."

He followed her out the door and through the parking lot to her car. "You believe Tanner?"

"Yeah, I do," Zack said. "Do you?"

She nodded. "What are you going to do now? Tell Barnes?"

Zack exhaled. "No."

"Why not?"

Zack looked at her. "The police never checked her text and call record for that night thus never found out about Gary or her meeting, or they did and chose to bury it. Either way, me telling Barnes his men did a shitty job isn't going to accomplish anything. Gary isn't our man. I don't think Gary deserves his life ruined over this."

Julie, surprised by Zack's about-face with his attitude towards Gary, drove the car off the campus. They were silent for a long while.

"Nice thinking with the mouth swab." Zack ended the silence. "Of course we don't have a sample to compare it to. So what good is it?"

She bit the corner of her lip and thought. "We just saw the medical examiner who probably examined Ashley's body. Let's go see."

* * * * * *

107

They arrived at the Chief Medical Examiner's office at two that afternoon. She parked the car and smiled at Zack. "Are you ok?"

Zack nodded. "Yeah, just thinking."

"About what?"

"I'm sorry for snapping at Gary. I know it isn't his fault Ashley is dead."

Julie smiled. "Well, if you wanted him to feel bad about his actions, you did."

"This case makes no sense, Jules."

She squeezed his hand. "Let's make sense of it."

They entered the building and Julie in typical Julie fashion winked at the receptionist and walked beyond the desk into the back room. There was Doctor Patterson. He looked over the glasses at the end of his nose and smiled at Julie.

"Hey, Doc, we're back."

"Two visits in two days," he said. "This must be important stuff."

"It always is when I come here," Julie said.

"Yesterday's DB, right?"

"For starters. What can you tell me?"

"Well, not a lot, really. She overdosed. The technical terms are in the report on my desk."

"Anything odd about it?"

"Well, she got the prescription yesterday morning. Doctor Frank Hewson wrote it," Patterson said. "My guess is she was depressed about losing her husband."

"And the first thing a doctor did was give her a prescription?" Zack shook his head. "Is that normally how things work?"

Patterson shrugged. "I don't deal with the live ones, that's your jobs."

"Ok, any marks or anything on the body? Any signs it was forced?"

"There are, but nothing that can't be passed off as self-inflicted."

Zack looked at Julie. Julie crossed her arms. "Let's shift gears then. Doc, we have a dilemma." She leaned against the metal table. "And I'm hoping you can help."

"You always do. What?"

"We need to prove or disprove that a person is the father of a child."

"Get a paternity test. Pretty easy these days."

"Well," Julie shifted her body to protrude her chest a little more. "It isn't that simple."

"Why not?"

Zack shook his head. He hated watching her flirt though he loved the sight of her breasts. "Because the child was never born and the pregnant girl is in a cemetery six feet underground."

Both looked at Zack like he had broken some unspoken protocol and violated every law inside the building.

"What?" Zack held out his hands.

Julie smiled and shook her head at him. "He's right, Doc. The girl supposedly drowned ten days after she had discovered she was pregnant."

"What about the autopsy?"

"The father forbade it."

The doctor checked his memory. "Wait. Did this happen back in May?"

"Yep."

"I vaguely remember. What was the girl's name?"

"Ashley Blumenthal," Zack said. "We just learned that she was pregnant and have an idea of who the father is. We're trying to determine if it was murder."

"Would have been done already had the father allowed me to do an autopsy. He fought me every step of the way. Insisted there could be no autopsy, or he'd have my job."

"But you signed off on a COD anyway?"

Again, Julie and the doctor looked at Zack.

"What? I saw his name on the report."

Julie shook her head again. "What happened, doc?"

"The mother arrived first to identify the body. She asked about the autopsy then the father showed up. She cried, they hugged, and then he immediately said no autopsy. Said it was for religious reasons."

Zack looked confused. "They're Lutherans." He shook his head. *People kill each other in the name of religion every day but no autopsy?* "Ok, so then what?"

"Well," the doctor shifted and smiled a wry smile. "I agreed, they left, and I prepped the body."

ANDREW GRUSE

Julie suddenly stood straight. "Do you mean?"

The doctor nodded. "Something didn't seem right. So, I took some samples after they left."

Julie jumped onto the doctor, hugged him and kissed his cheek. "Doc, you are a genius! Now, where are they?"

"I have an oath," he tried.

"Oh, cut the crap. This is me you're dealing with," Julie said more excited with each sentence. "You know something so spill it."

"Ok, right this way."

He took them into a separate room filled with metal doors with numbers and letters on them. The doctor opened the door and LED lighting lit the room. He scratched his chin, snapped his finger and opened a door of a giant stainless-steel freezer.

"Right here." He bent over and grabbed a box from the bottom shelf tucked behind vials, tubes and jars all labeled in script Zack didn't understand. "Now this wasn't allowed to be done so you can't use this evidence at all, you understand that, right?"

"Yes," Zack said quickly.

"What do you got?" Julie leaned in close to look inside of the box.

"Well, she didn't drown, and she was pregnant. I can tell you that much."

"But you signed off as drowning being the cause of death," Zack said. "Why did you do that?"

The doctor leaned against the table and crossed his arms. "I didn't. But you know you can't mention any of this to anyone. I'll lose my job and my license. And none of this can be used in a criminal case, you know that, right?"

Zack looked at Julie. "So we have nothing is what you're saying."

"No. We have a start," Julie smiled. "We can run a paternity test to see if Gary is the father."

CHAPTER 21

Julie sat on the tour bus that Sunday afternoon and wished she had stayed in Baltimore. She knew she saw tears in Zack's eyes when she walked out the door of her apartment. He promised he'd stay out of trouble and stick to the office and not worry about her. She doubted Zack would accomplish any of those. She hoped he would spend the day birding. At least that cleared his mind.

Julie, on the other hand, went from a plane to a bus and was somewhere in Iowa and her mind was anything but clear. She didn't want to leave Zack, but she had to go to finish her association with Rosler. She would finish the book the second the trip was over. They only wanted one more chapter and the beginning of the campaign, the Rebuilding of America as Rosler called it, would make a perfect end of the book. It was just two weeks she told herself and then she wasn't leaving Zack again.

"Senator, we will be at the next event in an hour."

Julie looked up and saw the Senator approach her on the bus, with his campaign manager behind him. Until then, she was alone and worked in peace. The Senator smiled at her.

He looked at his campaign manager. "Good. Q and A, or just a speech?"

Jerry Pantalini ignored Julie. "Speech, no Q and A at all. I'll get you the transcript."

Rosler sat next to Julie. "Ok. I'm going to catch up with our writer on the book."

Jerry nodded. "Very well." Jerry returned to the front of the bus.

"I think I'll need to get back to work just to relax after this trip," Rosler said with a laugh. "By the way, have you seen the latest polls?"

Julie nodded. Rosler led his party rivals by over fifteen points. The assassination attempt and his statements and appearances since changed the polls. Rosler was a household name. Julie wondered if it was sympathy but knew the free press coverage that made him the hero for surviving the attempt, dealing with losing a campaign staffer and a close friend played the role his campaign staff silently hoped.

"Yes, I have. You're doing very well."

Rosler shook his head, clenched his fist and lightly tapped it on the chair armrest. "I want my popularity to be because of the issues. That's why we have to hit the road and get in front of the crowds, to put this behind all of us and move forward with winning this election for the right reasons. And that's to move this country forward, to make it strong again." He looked at his watch. "This trip will be good for us, Julie. You'll see."

Julie said nothing and returned to her computer.

"Julie, you seem upset. Is something bothering you?"

She took a deep breath. "Senator, haven't you heard? Linda Polzinski was found dead yesterday."

Rosler paused, his eyes shifted. "Yes, I did hear. She committed suicide by overdose," he said. He shook his head and frowned. "It must have been terrible losing her husband of all those years like that."

Julie looked at him. "Is that how she died? I didn't hear that," she said.

Rosler nodded. "Yes, that's what I heard." Jerry returned with a tablet. "Ahh, back to work. I wish we could talk more, Julie. You are a breath of fresh air." He winked and went back to the front of the bus.

Julie shut her eyes. *I should have stayed home.*

* * * * * *

Zack had enough of being inside. Julie's apartment was a reminder she was gone. His apartment was a reminder he was alone. Too many things swirled in his head, and there were no answers in his apartment.

He locked up and walked to the office. There were no answers there on a Sunday either. But he could try to keep busy there. He entered his office, sat down behind his desk and watched the video of the assassination attempt on Julie's recorder again. He watched it on the big screen TV, and it told him the same thing. Zack knew he had to have more eyes on it.

On the fourth ring, Zack heard a familiar voice on his cell phone. "Dre, hey man, what are you doing?"

"It's Sunday afternoon. I'm with Alysha and her family. What's up?"

Zack sighed. "Nothing," he said. "I'm at the office and just watched Jules' video of the Rosler shooting again. You need to see it."

"Can it wait until morning?"

"Yeah," he said. "Sorry. It will be on your desk. Look at it first thing, ok?"

"Yeah you bet," Andre said. Zack was silent. "Hey, man, are you ok?"

Zack snapped back to attention. "Yeah. Hey, have a great day and tell Alysha I said hi. We'll catch up tomorrow." Zack hung up, put his phone down and looked out the window. *Take the rest of the day off, Zack. Nothing you can do today.*

Zack knew that was the best thing to do. Only he didn't take his own advice.

Twenty minutes later, he drove Julie's car out of town towards the campus. Zack didn't want to be anywhere near the Rosler case, but everything he did drew him closer to it. Rain fell over the area; a steady soaking rain. It felt apropos.

The rain made driving treacherous. Zack felt like everyone became a worse driver when it rained. Some drove slower and refused to change lanes. Must have been afraid they'd lose control of their vehicle at twenty miles an hour. Those in big trucks and SUV's usually drove wild, apparently convinced there was no way a little weather would make them lose control of their vehicle. Zack hated it. *I should have stayed home today.*

Traffic stopped at a light, and Zack remembered when he was young. The rain where he grew up seemed different. He remembered fast moving fronts and storms that sped across the lakes to get to the east coast and then stall. With snow it was different. Zack remembered all day snows and blizzards. He loved lake effect snows. It was fun to miss school and play in the snow drifts higher than he stood. *Of course, the shoveling sucked.* But today, where he was, there was just rain. *I should definitely have been a weatherman.*

It fell steady and hard, an occasional gust of wind made it more miserable. And Julie's windshield wipers needed replacement. *These cars are maintenance whores, and Jules wants me to buy one of these things?*

*** ***

A black-suited man stood just off stage and listened to the man speaking behind the podium. His cell phone buzzed. "Yeah, what is it?"

"He's at the campus again sniffing around the girl's dorm."

"I guess he didn't get the memo," the man answered.

Another man walked beside him. "What is it?"

"The detective is doing his thing again," he answered and talked into the phone. "Has he talked to anyone?"

"He talked to some girl, might be looking for the girl that let him in the last time. Now he's standing in the rain staring at the pond."

The black-suited man nodded. "Take care of it." He slid his cell phone inside his coat and looked at the man next to him.

"How bad is it?"

"Oh, I don't know. Ever hear of the Lusitania?"

"What? The ocean liner?"

"Yeah. Torpedoed. Imagine that same thing only with all of us going to jail, too."

"You're here to fix things." He looked at the man. "So, fix it."

"Jerry, this is going to cost money."

Jerry looked at the vibrant man on stage and heard the crowd roar in approval. "Ok. Do it whatever it takes. I need all of this gone now. Make sure none of it comes back to us. Especially him," Jerry pointed to the man on stage.

"I have a team in place already. Wire the money. These guys eat nails for brunch. You don't want them waiting for their money."

"Consider it done."

The crowd erupted as the man on stage finished and waved.

"Better go collect your meal ticket, Jerry, before he finds a teenager in the crowd to screw."

CHAPTER 22

Zack stared at the pond. It was about a football field long, but only about 70 feet wide. The aerators and fountain still operated. Signs around the area read NO Swimming, complete with the red circle and line through it. A steady rainfall soaked Zack, but he stood still and stared at it.

A covered John Deere Gator maintenance vehicle stopped behind him. A middle-aged man wearing a uniform stepped out. "Can I help you?"

Zack saw the name on the shirt. George. "You work on the grounds here?"

"Twenty years," George said. Zack shook his hand and introduced himself. "What's your interest in this pond?"

"A girl drowned in this pond last spring, and I'm wondering how the hell did that happen?"

George shook his head. "Beats me. It's only about six foot deep. Even at night with all the lights around here, it isn't like you couldn't find the shore. Maybe she was just too drunk."

"Yeah, maybe. What's the base?"

"Sand."

"You say it's only six feet deep?"

"Yep."

"And you're sure of this?"

George looked at him and laughed. "Every year I have to wade into that thing and clean the filters on the fountains. I know."

Zack nodded. "I'll trust your word."

George laughed. "You don't want to go swimming to check?"

"Not particularly."

"We clean it annually, too. The base is firm and the cables are buried." George shrugged. "Believe me, it's been bothering me since it happened and I can't figure out how the girl drowned in that pond."

Zack and George stared at the pond.

"I gotta run, but if you have any more questions, come find me." George climbed back into his maintenance vehicle and drove away.

Despite the rain and the wind, Zack stared at the pond for several minutes before he walked back to the car still confused about how it happened.

Zack found a blanket in the trunk and dried off inside the car. He sent Julie a text: *Call me later if you can, I'll be home early.* Sufficiently warm, he turned on the sub-par wipers, slid the phone into his front pocket and drove away.

He kept his eye on the rearview mirror as he turned onto a county highway. A charcoal Ford Taurus turned behind him. *I've seen that car before.* The hairs on the back of Zack's neck stood straight: he was being followed. At an intersection, instead of turning right for home, he turned left and drove west on the four-lane highway.

Zack switched lanes, sped up, slowed down, switched lanes again. The Taurus stayed the same distance behind Zack. The rain and the water kicked up by the tires made it impossible to see who or how many were in the car behind him. *Friends of my extortionist or the goons from the airport?*

The Taurus closed the gap. Zack couldn't accelerate because of traffic in front of him and couldn't change lanes. A white cargo van boxed him into the passing lane. It felt too close. He couldn't see the driver, but it edged closer. Zack swerved away from the van, and the van veered with him. Zack slowed but so did the van; he accelerated, and so did the van. The Taurus behind him did the same thing.

It looks like I picked the wrong day to quit swearing. And drinking. And shooting people.

117

The van slammed into his car and forced Zack into oncoming traffic. Zack turned back into the vehicle and pushed it away. Zack slowed to try to get behind the van, but the Taurus slammed into his rear end. The van slammed into him again. This time it had the momentum and the angle. It drove Zack into the left lane of oncoming traffic.

Zack fought to steer right, but it wasn't happening. A break in the oncoming traffic saved him, but then a semi-truck drove around the corner. Beside it was a large pickup, going side by side. The van sped up and pushed Zack further into the path of the oncoming truck. The semi's horn roared.

Zack floored the accelerator, turned the steering wheel to the left, dislodged from the van and shot across traffic.

But not fast enough.

Zack missed the semi. Car tires screeched, and more horns blared. The car traveled too fast into the corner. The pickup truck swerved but couldn't avoid Zack's car. It side-swiped Zack and launched Zack over the curb, into the guardrail around the curb. The vehicle drove off the guardrail like it hit a ramp and was airborne.

The car flipped upside down as it crashed into small suckling trees. It snapped the trees in half and hit a stream with a splash. More car tires screeched to a halt; horns continued to honk; three autos slammed into each other. The white van sped off as did the Taurus.

Zack opened his eyes and felt water drip on him. He realized he was upside down in a stream. Zack heard people yell.

Get out! He heard the screams in his head. *Move! Move! Unlatch the seatbelt!* He lifted his head to get a breath as the water filled the inside of the car.

Someone fought with the door, but it wouldn't open. The car sank, and water rushed inside the vehicle. Zack raised his head, but the water level was too deep. He fought with the seatbelt.

In every stinking movie, the seatbelt gets jammed. Goddamnit! Zack twisted and turned and expelled the last of the air in his lungs. Finally, Zack ripped the seatbelt holder off the side of the car. Still latched but now loose, he contorted his body to release himself as the vehicle settled in the mucky river bottom. Only the tires remained above the water level.

The door wouldn't open. Zack knew his gun wouldn't fire underwater. He kicked and pounded on the windows but couldn't get enough pressure due to the water resistance. The door wedged into the creek bed and wouldn't budge. The inside filled with water. There was no way to get out. He knew someone was outside the car fighting with the door, but it was too late. Zack blacked out.

Two men standing in the chest deep water felt otherwise. One of the men used the blade of a knife he carried and pounded the center of the side window. It shattered. He went under and saw the man in the car floating, unconscious. He grabbed his shoulder and yanked him towards the window. Moments later, they were on the shore.

CHAPTER 23

Zack opened his eyes; fog enveloped his field of vision. He heard a rhythmic beeping and felt a clip on the end of his finger, bands around his wrist and tubes stuck in his hand and forearm and small tubes in his nose. Zack didn't feel much of anything other than woozy. He blinked over and over; the fog lifted a little. He saw the figure of a person wearing blue. His mind clicked on: nurse scrubs. The nurse turned around and held his wrist, saw his eyes open and asked how he was feeling.

Zack tried to smile and tried to talk. He heard nothing come out of his mouth.

"Shhhh," she said to him. "You need some sleep. You'll feel better in a few hours."

He saw her fiddle with a bag that dripped into a tube hooked to his arm, and he decided it wasn't worth fighting. He shut his eyes. *I'm alive and in a hospital.*

He fell asleep.

* * * * * *

After a soft touch on his wrist, he opened his eyes. A nurse placed her fingers on his wrist and watched the clock. He blinked several times. His mouth was dry, his head hurt, and his body ached. She finished with his wrist and typed into a computer in the corner. She looked at him, saw his eyes open and smiled.

"Hi," she said. She watched Zack's eyes. "Are you thirsty?"

He nodded, and she held a cup of water with a straw near his mouth. She guided the straw into his mouth.

He felt the rush of cold water right into his stomach, and it felt great. He forced out a dry, raspy and weak inaudible sound. She smiled.

"It must be fate, Zack. This is the second time I've been your nurse. I think you may want to think about your life choices." She smiled and checked a drip of a tube hooked to his arm. Stefani, the nurse, stood over him. She touched his arm gently.

"How long have I been here?" His voice came back stronger with each syllable and each sip of water.

"I think you got here yesterday around five."

Zack thought about it. "What time is it?"

"Eight in the morning. Monday. Don't worry about the time. Just rest."

"How am I?"

She smiled again. "Well, you're going to be sore for a while, but nothing is broke."

"Doesn't feel like it."

"Just lie still," she said. "I'll take good care of you."

He felt weary and knew he'd be sleeping soon. "My phone," he whispered. "I need my phone."

"Sorry, hon. Your dip in the river killed your phone."

Zack mouthed a word, but his eyelids closed before he could say anything.

* * * * * *

Fall in Iowa can be as beautiful as any other part of the country. The leaves on the trees on the hills just past the hotel parking lot highlighted shades of red, orange, yellow and shades of pale green. A light wind made the leaves dance back and forth in unison. Purple and gray clouds edged nearer from the west and promised rain and cooler temperatures.

Pete Kilgas stood at the window of his suite, he held a cup of coffee in his hand and watched the trees and clouds and decided he hated fall. He hated everything about it: the leaves, the colder weather, the incessant pumpkin-flavored everything, and the advent of winter. A beach in the tropics was his preference. *Once I get this sonofabitch elected, I'm out of here.*

The cell phone call snapped his focus off the weather. "Yeah?"

"It's done."

"Are you sure?"

"Yeah. Stack flipped the car into a river. We had to get out of there, but I doubt he survived. The way the car smashed through the trees he may have been dead on impact."

"But you don't know for sure?"

There was silence.

Kilgas exhaled. "I am certain he is at a hospital. Find out which one, go there, find out if he is still alive, and if he is," he hesitated. "If he is, make sure he doesn't get out alive."

"Got it. Standard operating procedure or making a statement?"

"S.O.P. this time. Needs to look like an accident. We don't need any more attention on him."

He hung up, and his door opened.

"Pete, how is it going today?"

Pete shook his head. "Not getting the results I want as quickly as I want, but the main target is currently incapacitated."

"Good. I'll let the boss know."

"Jerry," Pete said at length, "there is no turning back now. If he survives, he'll want retribution."

Jerry smiled. "You said you're the best. Make sure he doesn't survive."

* * *   * * *

Andre Kitchell arrived at the office before eight Monday morning, even before Michelle. The video was cued on his desk like Zack said. He started a pot of coffee, turned on Michelle's computers and his, checked Zack's office to see if he was there then returned to his desk with a steaming fresh mug of coffee. The smell invigorated him, and he wondered why Zack hated it so much.

He saw the note Zack left on his desk and pressed play. Andre stopped the video, replayed it, rewound it, replayed it again. Then moved it to the big screen TV on his office wall and watched again with the sound.

"Holy shit snacks," Andre mumbled after he watched it at a slower speed. "Zack is right."

He watched it again and heard the familiar footsteps of Michelle. "Barnes lied to us. Sonofabitch." Michelle stuck her head in Dre's office.

"Hey, good morning. Did you say something?"

"Hey, 'Chelle," Andre said as he dialed his phone. "No, just talking to myself." Zack's phone went straight to voice mail. "Shit." He walked into the main office near Michelle who filled her giant mug with coffee. "Have you heard from Zack yet today?"

Michelle laughed. "It's Monday and before ten. What do you think?" She walked to her desk.

"If you hear from him, have him call me immediately, ok?"

She stared at her desk.

"What is it?"

"Zack was here. Don't know when but he left a list of things to find out."

"Like what?"

"Like what is the name of the guy in this picture?" She held up a picture Zack captured off the video of a man in a black suit and tie next to Rosler before the shooting.

Andre knew why: that man was not present when they pulled the wounded Rosler off the stage.

"And he wants to know who Dr. Frank Hewson is and if he prescribed Linda Polzinski any medications recently." Michelle looked at Andre. "Is there any reason for this?"

Andre smiled. "That's our boy. He's onto something. Have him call me as soon as you hear from him." Andre returned to his office to examine the video more. He shut the door behind him. *Zack is right. Two shooters and Rosler was not the main target. But why?*

* * *　* * *

Zack felt the same soft, delicate touch of Stefani the nurse on his wrist again and opened his eyes. He had no idea how much time had passed or what day it was or how long he had been there.

"You're awake," she smiled at him.

"How long have I been out?"

"A long time."

"You've been here the whole time?"

She nodded. "No. My shift ended, I went home, and now I'm back."

"Why?"

She smiled at him. "That's my job."

Zack sounded better and felt stronger. Images of the crash went through his head. The bits and pieces formed together, and he remembered more and more. "I need my phone," he said. "I need to make some phone calls. Does anyone know I'm here?"

"No one does. We didn't know who to call. And I told you already; your phone died when you went into the river. The police want to talk to you though," Stefani said. "As soon as you are with it."

"How did I get out of the car?"

"Two men saw the crash and rushed into the river to get you out. You should thank them. You should be dead."

Zack closed his eyes. "Believe me, I will. Can I borrow your phone?"

Stefani looked around as if she wanted no one to see. "I'm not supposed to let you make any phone calls," she said. She slid her cell phone into his hand and made sure the curtain blocked off the room from the hallway.

"What do the police want?"

Stefani shook her head. "They want to arrest you. They had us take a tox screen, collected your clothes, everything. They think you may have been drinking and driving."

"No, I wasn't."

"I know you weren't. But the police are sure of it. Some eyewitness claims you were driving erratically, swerving in and out of traffic, you name it. Even said they saw you throw an empty bottle of beer out the window."

"That's BS."

Stefani continued to appear as if she were administering aid to him, checking his lines, his vitals, adjusting the bed, anything to keep her there longer and the police away longer. "I know. Your blood had nothing in it: no alcohol, no drugs, no nothing. I saw the report. It hasn't been released yet, but I saw it. What happened?"

"Someone ran me off the road: a white cargo van and a gray Ford Taurus. I had to swerve to miss getting crushed by a Kenworth and another pickup. It wasn't an accident," he said. "Someone tried to kill me."

Stefani stopped moving. "You're serious?"

"If you knew everything, you wouldn't doubt me for a second."

"What is it you do?"

Zack was about to answer when two policemen entered the room.

"Mr. Stack, we have some questions for you. It appears you're up to the task of answering."

Stefani mouthed "I'm sorry" to him and turned to the officers. "He is still coming off the pain medication. I don't feel asking him questions at this time would be appropriate."

"We think it will be fine."

"Officers, I'm sorry, but you'll need the doctor's permission." Stefani didn't know if that was true or not. All she knew was that she liked this guy. This was the second time Stefani cared for him at the hospital, and Stefani felt like she should protect him. "The patient has rights at the hospital, so, if you'll please exit the room and we can go find the doctor."

The police officers stared at her. "Ok, let's go find the doctor."

Stefani turned and winked at Zack. "Don't go anywhere. I'll shut the door."

Zack quickly looked at the phone and saw it was five in the afternoon. He dialed a number on the phone and prayed he would answer.

CHAPTER 24

Ted Barnes looked at the passenger side of the mangled car. "This may be white paint here. Looks like it, doesn't it?"

"I'd guess it is," Andre agreed. "This thing is a mess," Andre said. He looked over the car with a flashlight. "Jules is going to be pissed." He saw the keys still in the ignition and pulled them out.

Two hours had passed since Barnes received the phone call from Zack. Shortly afterward, Barnes learned of a car matching the description pulled from a river after an accident the day before. Conflicting reports from eyewitnesses led the police to consider criminal charges for Zack.

Barnes nodded. "He's lucky to be alive."

"I'll remind him to revisit his stance on religion," Andre smiled. "But, his version matches the damage on the car."

"It certainly may," Barnes said. "There's also some red paint here."

"From the truck that side-swiped him after he swerved left to avoid the semi the white van forced him into," Andre said. "Ted, come on, man, someone is setting him up. He wasn't drinking. I know Zack. Someone tried to kill him."

Barnes finished walking around the car. "On a Sunday afternoon, after Julie left town, you're telling me he wasn't drinking? That's one I have to see," Barnes said. "I can't keep covering for him. One of these times it's going to bite me in the ass."

"If he said he wasn't, he wasn't." Andre stared at Barnes who looked away. "The evidence supports Zack's story. Plus, with the other stuff going on," Andre trailed off. "He's clear here."

Barnes took pictures of the scrapes and paint on Julie's wrecked car. "I know."

Andre tried to shut the car door, but the bent hinges and the mangled door wouldn't swing back. "Jules is gonna be pissed."

"And so is Zack," Barnes said. "Someone is gonna pay."

They walked to Barnes' car and got inside. The two were silent for a long period until Barnes spoke. "Unless our Indiana friends are here, why would anyone want to kill him because he is investigating Ashley Blumenthal's death?"

"He isn't only investigating the death of Ashley, Ted."

Barnes shook his head. "So what's the connection?" He exhaled. "Let's go see our boy."

* * * * * *

Julie sent another text to Zack. *Why wasn't he answering? It's been over 24 hours!* She worried herself sick. What little food she ate she threw-up. She couldn't focus at whatever rally, town hall meeting or dog-and-pony show Rosler spoke at that evening. Julie couldn't find a better term for the events either. All show, pomp, and circumstance but nothing of value. Just rhetoric. She understood now that she, too, had fallen for the charisma and charm of Rosler. But that charm and charisma had vanished, and frankly, she didn't care. All her caring was on Zack.

The crowd erupted, Rosler waved and walked off stage. He saw Julie and smiled as his team surrounded him and ushered him to the campaign bus where they would head to the hotel for the night and settle in until the next day's events.

Julie followed and soon found her seat in the back of the bus. She sent yet another text but this time to Andre. *Someone HAS to know something!*

In front on the bus, two men stood with Rosler in a tight circle. Everyone guessed strategy meeting with the campaign manager and his head of security. After all, nothing could be taken for granted now that someone had tried to take Rosler's life.

"Where are we?"

"He's in the hospital. We had cops pin him with drunk driving, reckless endangerment; you name it. Unfortunately, the charges won't stick. It looks like his cop friend and partner investigated, and Stack is well enough to remember what happened. Corroboration."

Rosler nodded. "He'll be out tomorrow, then?"

The head of security nodded. "Well, now we go to plan B."

"Good. In the meantime, keep Fletcher busy. I don't want her on her phone or even thinking about Stack. Finish the damn job. She'll roll over like a trained puppy after that." Rosler winked and relaxed onto the couch inside the motor coach.

The two men looked at each, and each took a deep breath. The head of security knew one thing was for certain: the worst was yet to come.

* * *   * * *

At nine o'clock that night, Andre and Lieutenant Barnes entered Zack's hospital room. Zack had his head turned to look out the window as a nurse typed on the computer in the corner of the room. They hesitated inside the door.

"I'm not eating that crap, Stef," Zack said. "You try eating it."

"You need to eat something," she said, both still oblivious to the visitors. "Oh, I see, you're going to pout now and stare out the window until you get your way?"

"That's exactly what I'm doing," Zack said. Then they heard Andre burst out in laughter.

"That IS exactly what he's doing," Andre laughed as the two looked and saw the visitors.

Zack smiled. "Please tell me you brought something from the Bistro or something."

"Sorry, you didn't ask for food when you called," Andre said.

"I did bring your gun I retrieved from the police," Barnes said. He removed it from his coat and put it on the tray next to Zack.

"I can't eat that."

Stefani shook her head. "He's been whining about food all night."

"I'm starving. I thought this place was supposed to care for patients, not try to kill them with horrible food," Zack complained.

Barnes looked at Stefani. "He won't, so I'll apologize for him."

Stefani smiled. "I'm used to it."

"Haha," Zack said. "Did you prove me right yet?"

"You'll never stop owing me, Stack," Barnes said.

"For what? Doing your job and finding the truth?"

"Wow," Stefani said as she rubbed her hands with disinfectant. "He's on a roll. I'll be back." She left the room.

"You aren't out of the woods yet, Stack," Barnes said. "We're still waiting on the blood tests."

Zack rolled his eyes. "They're clear."

"I hope so," Barnes said.

Zack shook his head and exhaled. "I wasn't drinking, and before you ask, Ted, I wasn't using my phone. My phone records will prove that."

"Where is your phone?" Andre asked.

"Stef said it was in the front pocket of my pants, which the cops have in a bag somewhere after she cut them off of me. She said the phone was toast. The river killed it."

"She saw you naked?" Andre asked.

"Apparently," Zack said.

Andre laughed.

Barnes spoke. "How long are you going to be in here?"

"Ask Stef."

Barnes looked at Andre. "If someone did try to kill him," he hesitated.

"SOMEONE DID TRY TO KILL ME!" Zack interrupted.

Barnes nodded. "Then we have to prove it." He looked at Zack. "And you're in no kind of shape to do anything other than pretend you're a slug. I'm sure you're here tonight. That will be good."

"For whom? Not me! Did you try to eat the food here? It's criminal!"

Andre smiled. "Keep working the nurse. I bet she'll get you something good."

"Not from this place."

"Aww, come on, Zack. How bad can it be?"

"Dre, for crying out loud, they think Jell-O is a food group. Jell-O!"

Barnes waited for the two. "Are you two done? Good. Standard procedure, Stack. I have to do some things by the book when it comes to you and getting the police not to pursue charges against you was not easy."

"There's nothing to pursue. Someone tried to kill me. Charge those guys."

Barnes ignored Zack. "Well Dre, there's nothing more we can do here, and it's late. How about we get out of here and go have dinner?"

Andre nodded. "You bet."

"Oh, you guys can suck it!" Zack said.

"See you tomorrow, bro," Andre said, and he and Barnes left.

"Seriously?" Zack yelled. "You're leaving me here to starve?"

The two were down the hall when they saw Stefani. They stopped her. Barnes asked, "Did he say anything since he was here? Anything at all that would corroborate his story?"

"Nothing that would contradict what he told you," Stefani said.

Barnes nodded. "I know. Zack wouldn't lie to either of us about something like this. Are you on duty tonight?"

"Until tomorrow morning."

"Good. Can you do me a favor and keep a close eye on him?" Barnes looked at Andre. "He has been known to quote-unquote leave the reservation. Long story," he said to Stefani after seeing her quizzical look. "If he tries to leave, call me immediately at this number, Ok?"

Stefani pierced her lips and nodded. "Count on it." She smiled. "I'll be happy to do it."

"Good," Barnes said. "Oh, after he eats, he'll be in a better mood.

CHAPTER 25

Zack stared out the window from his bed in silence.

"Hey, you should eat something," Stefani chastised him as she rechecked his vitals.

"There's an amazing Italian place about fifteen minutes from here. They serve the best seafood fettuccine in the area. They usually serve until one because it's that busy. What do you say?"

She smiled at him. "No. Out of the question."

"Come on, Stef. Look, I'll make you a deal: I won't go anywhere if you run to get us dinner." He smiled. "I'll even buy."

She looked at her watch. "I can't."

"I promise you Stef; you won't be disappointed. Their crab ravioli is to die for."

She was hesitant. "No."

"I'm begging you. I need sustenance! I will be in your debt." He smiled at her, and she laughed. "I promise. I will owe you indefinitely. Anything you want!"

"Do they deliver?"

"If they don't, I'll crawl there to get it. Get me out of here and let's go there. This place has fantastic wines."

"I'll see if they deliver. Give me your card." He handed over his credit card, and she called in an order for delivery. She begged them to make it and lied about it being the last wish for a dying patient at the hospital. They promised it in thirty-five minutes. She left to check on her other patients.

A few minutes later Stefani reappeared. "It better be as good as you say."

Zack opened his eyes. He wasn't sleeping. He was thinking of Julie. *Jules has to be worried and pissed. I need to talk to her. But if she finds out what happened, she'll freak out.* "What?"

"Hey, you ok?" Stefani asked. "You look like something is wrong."

Something is. "No, just pain meds wearing off."

"I haven't given you pain meds all day."

Zack look surprised. "That explains the pain."

"You weren't complaining, or I had given you something."

She was silent as she sat on a chair beside him. He noticed she wasn't doing anything.

"Do you have a boyfriend or husband or even a girlfriend to go home to?"

She smiled. "Nope. Just me. I don't even have a cat."

"How did that happen? You're gorgeous, have a great body, smart and have a good job. You're a major catch."

She blushed. "Well thank you, that's very sweet."

Zack shrugged.

"Well, I guess I just haven't found the right guy."

"In this town, I'd be surprised if you could." *Julie is probably thinking that same thing about me right now.*

She laughed. "My mother tells me that all the time. My parents are so concerned with me getting married and having kids. It's all they talk about. It's like I'm not fulfilling my duty if I don't do either," she complained. "It's like, oh my God!"

He smiled. He had heard Julie's mother say the same thing. "Well ultimately you have to make yourself happy first," he told her.

"Aww, thank you! You are sweet!" She heard a beep in the hallway. "Back to work." She winked. "Don't go anywhere."

I'm sneaking out of here the second she leaves this room. I'll get to the office, call Jules, explain to her what happened and then, I don't know. But I can't stay here. If someone is trying to kill me, just being here is putting Stefani in danger. I can't do that to her.

* * * * * *

Stefani exited Zack's room and headed for the room that called her. *That lady probably can't figure out how to change the channel again.* She turned the corner of the hallway and walked into two men.

They looked lost. Both men wore black leather jackets, black jeans and black ankle high hiking boots. They had short cropped haircuts and an intense look about them.

"Can I help you?" She asked.

"Yes, we were told our friend is on this floor. We've been worried sick about him since the accident yesterday and want to make sure he's ok," one man said.

Stefani looked at her watch. The clock approached midnight. "Umm, maybe I can help. What is the name of your friend?"

"Zack Stack," the second man answered.

Stefani looked puzzled and looked towards the ceiling. "That name doesn't ring a bell. Let me check the computer. Follow me." She smiled and led them to the nursing station where she logged onto her laptop and looked through screens but made sure they couldn't see.

"We know he was here," one man said. "Can't imagine he got released already, not as bad as that accident was."

The other man shook his head. "After we saw it on the news, we thought for sure he was dead."

Stefani glanced at them with a smile. "How do you know him?"

"We went to college together. Same fraternity," the second one said. "Delta's for life."

"Ahh yes, I know what that's about," she lied. She shook her head as she scrolled through her emails and reduced the screen. "I'm sorry, but I don't see him here. He may have been transferred to another hospital." She opened another screen. "Oh, I see. He was transferred to John Hopkins earlier today."

"Really? That's odd. Wouldn't someone had said something?"

"Not to you unless you are immediate family," Stefani said. "Is there anything else I can do for you?"

The men looked at each other. "Maybe later. Thanks for your help."

Stefani watched them leave. Something was wrong. *Zack was right*.

The men disappeared on the elevator, but Stefani had to check a different patient. Several minutes later, Stefani returned to Zack's room. Zack sat on the edge of the bed. "What are you doing?"

"Preparing to get out of here."

"What? Why? Zack, you can't."

"When is our food arriving?"

"Any minute now. Why?"

"You just talked to two guys looking for me in the hallway."

"You heard that?"

"Yeah, I saw."

"Let me guess: you never belonged to a Delta fraternity?"

"No. Marine Corps. No frat guys there. Tell me what they wanted."

She told him everything.

"I need clothes."

Stefani stared at Zack.

"Go get our food, grab your stuff, find me some clothes. Do it quietly but do it fast. You bought us some time. But not that much. Maybe twenty minutes." She nodded and headed for the door. "Oh, Stef," he called. She looked at him. "If you hear shooting," he raised his gun, "don't come back."

She nodded. "You said us. What did you mean?"

"Sweetheart," Zack said, "you tricked them. They know you know me and they'll use you to find me. And you can ID them. At first, I wanted to ditch you safely away from me, but now I don't think that's a good idea. They don't like loose ends."

"Who are they?"

"I don't know. But we're going to find out. Now go."

What seemed like an eternity was only thirteen minutes. Zack finished tying the shoelace. "This is it? This is the best you can do?"

Stef eyed him up and down. "Maybe being dressed like a doctor in scrubs will help get you out of here."

"Well, at least the shoes fit," Zack said of the pair of Nike cross trainers Stef found in a doctor's locker.

"Are you sure you're alright?"

"No, but we need to get out of here."

"Are you in trouble? I mean, what is going on? I don't think I want to be a part of this."

Zack shook his head. "Too late. Look, I will explain everything and no, I'm not in trouble."

"Aside from people trying to kill you? Seriously?"

"Yeah, aside from that. Trust me, Stef, you need to come with me. Now."

* * * * * *

Two men entered the only unlocked entrance to the hospital: the emergency room. They went to the receptionist and flashed badges. "Ma'am, we're looking for Zack Stack. We know he's a patient here and we need to see him now," one of the men said.

The receptionist smiled. "I'm sorry. If he's a patient here, you'll have to come back during normal visiting hours tomorrow."

"You don't understand, we know he's here and we are going to see him now."

The lady behind the desk didn't budge. "Well unless you are the chief of staff or the President of the United States, and since I know you ain't either, you ain't seeing no one in this hospital no more tonight."

The men smiled and regrouped quickly. The first one put his badge on the desk again. "Ma'am, I'm not asking. We work for the government, we believe his life is in danger, and it is imperative we see him now. So please, tell us what room he's in." He stood straight. "I assure you: it is a matter of life or death."

The lady stared at the men and their badges again. She had seen fake badges before. They all look real until you examine them. The gun under their jackets worried her more. "Let me find him," she said. She clicked on her computer and instantly knew which nurse was assigned to the patient. She picked up her cell phone.

The men looked at her; their expressions told her they didn't approve.

She smiled. "Oh, it's quicker to text the nurse upstairs," she said. "The computers are really slow tonight. I'll have that room number in a moment."

* * * * * *

Stefani looked at her phone. "We have three minutes."

"I was wrong. Eighteen minutes. How many exits do we have?"

"Two elevators and stairwell at each end," Stefani replied.

Zack checked his gun. "Are there cameras in the stairwells?"

Stefani thought about it. "No."

"Which end did you park, east or west?"

"East."

"Then we head there." Zack stared at the delicious smelling food. "They'll track the smell. We'll use it as a decoy. Come on." They exited the room and turned west towards the nearest stairwell.

They walked past several rooms. Zack's mind worked fast. Fight or flight. Zack readied for both.

Zack found an empty room. He looked up and down the hallway. Still no one. "Put the food in the bathroom but don't close the door."

Stef took the food into the bathroom and put it on the sink. She came back out quickly and said ok.

Zack and Stef entered the stairwell and closed the door silently when two men stepped into the hallway. Zack ducked out of the window and waited. Moments later they found Zack's room.

"Zack, we should run right now. You can't fight anyone."

Stef was right. The men were there to finish the job. Zack was the job. "No, we have to deal with these two first. Thugs like this usually travel in packs."

Stefani didn't recognize Zack. He was different. "What *do* you do for a living?"

The men exited the room and looked each way but saw nothing. They followed the smell and entered the room with the food. Within seconds, they burst out of that room and sprinted west down the hallway towards the stairwell. Zack leaned against the wall, his breath heavy and heart pounded. He knew Feds when he saw them. These weren't Feds. Zack stepped back to the flight of stairs going up and sat down on the fourth step. "Hide there and do as I tell you, got it?"

"What are you going to do?"

"Draw their attention. Stay tight in the corner. It's dark, and you'll be behind the door. With luck, they won't see you. Then follow my lead." Zack remained on the step and waited.

"And if they see me?"

"Charge at one of them and shove him down the stairs."

"Oh, great plan."

The sarcasm was not lost on Zack. But it was a plan.

CHAPTER 26

The men burst through the doorway and stopped immediately. Zack sat on the steps and eyeballed the two men. He rested his arms on his knees and smiled.

"Looking for someone?"

The two men stared at Zack, briefly looked at each other and bulked up their shoulders to look more intimidating. "Not anymore. Come with us."

"I like sitting here."

"Get up." One of the men ordered. "We're taking you back to your room. It's time for your medication."

Has to look like an accident. That makes sense. "Well gentlemen I'd love to oblige you but uh," he paused and barely moved his body, "I like it here."

"Get up, Stack. We're not messing around."

Zack exhaled wearily. "Pardon the expression, gentlemen, but fuck off."

The men looked at each other. One pulled his gun and pointed it at Zack. "Get his ass off the steps," he said to his partner. "And where's the hot nurse looking after you?"

"Behind you," Zack said.

Stefani jumped at the man closest to her and kicked him in the chest. The man fell backward down the flight of stairs.

The other man looked at Stefani as Zack leaped to his feet, grabbed the man's jacket, spun him, launched a right cross into the man's jaw which knocked him over the railing. The man fell down the narrow open shaft between the stairs, he clunked and banged against the sides the whole way down three flights before hitting the floor hard. *Someone had to hear that.*

Zack looked surprised at Stefani, who stood with her fists clenched in a karate stance as if waiting to attack again.

"I'm a black belt," she said. "Daddy wanted me to be able to defend myself."

"Smart man," Zack said, removed his Sig from his waistline and rushed down the stairs at the man Stef kicked to the bottom.

The man grunted as Zack reached him eight stairs below. The man moved, opened his eyes and lunged, but Zack reared back and smashed the gun into the side of his head. The man dropped like a brick. Out cold or dead, Zack didn't care. Blood oozed across the man's face. Zack hesitated for a moment, to make sure the man wasn't playing opossum. No movement. Zack pulled the man's gun out of his coat, pulled his wallet out, saw no ID but $500 in cash, he took that, leaned against the wall and fought to subdue the pain that ravaged his body. He looked at Stefani. "Come on; we aren't out of this yet."

* * *   * * *

They reached the bottom of the stairwell. Zack checked the man sprawled in blood at the bottom level. He felt no pulse. Zack removed the dead man's gun and wallet, found another $500 in cash, returned the wallet and fought to stand straight.

"Zack, you're bleeding," Stef said. "You tore your stitches."

"Good thing I have you with me."

"We need to go back inside."

"Not an option. We're leaving," Zack answered.

"No!" Stefani objected. "You could bleed out."

"We have to leave, and we have to leave now," Zack said firmly. "There will be more. We can't stay here." He stared at her, and she stared back, but she knew he wouldn't budge.

"Ok, then we should exit here. If we enter the lobby, cameras will pick us up," Stef said.

Zack pushed open the exit door, and they stepped outside. The parking lot was sparse with cars scattered about it. "It's darker in the lot, harder to see us. Keep your eyes open. Ready?"

Stef nodded, and they scrambled through the few cars towards the far end. After a few minutes, they made it to Stef's car. Zack leaned against it.

"Zack," Stef began, "I need to go back in. I need the supplies to stitch you up."

If there are any more bad guys, they'll follow her to get to me. She should be safe going back. He pulled out his Sig. "Here, take this."

"Zack, no," Stef objected.

"Just do it." He grimaced and fought to control his breathing. "I'll stay here. You go in, get your stuff and get back here as fast as you can. It's ready to fire. Just squeeze the trigger."

Stef left, Zack slid to his butt, his back against the drivers' side rear door. He crossed his arms over his bleeding ribcage, took small breaths as his face dripped perspiration, his hands hidden inside the light coat Stef borrowed.

Zack waited. Time moved slow. Not being able to lead Stef back into the hospital bothered him. He felt guilty. Zack knew there would be more bad guys there. There always was. *Sometimes, the movies DO get it right!*

He heard footsteps approach. They weren't female steps. Stiff soles. Boots. Like the kind he saw on the feet of the men in the stairwell, they made a distinctive sound on the pavement. The two sets split. One went around the front of the car, the other behind. *Smart move. They know I'm here and now have me at a severe disadvantage.*

Zack saw the two men. Dressed in dark clothing, short cropped haircuts and weathered experienced seasoned faces, they looked intimidating and formidable. Zack looked slowly at each but didn't move. Both men carried a handgun at their side, but neither pointed it at Zack.

"Get up, Stack. You're coming with us," the one in the front of the car said.

"What, no proper introductions?"

"You shouldn't have survived the crash," the other man said. "Now get up."

140

"I'd love to gentlemen; I don't go anywhere with strangers. I told three of your buddies that the other day." Zack paused. "How are they, by the way?"

"Get up, or we'll shoot you here, leave you for dead then go find that pretty little bitch with you and do a number on her," the main one said.

Zack kept his hands still inside his jacket at his beltline. "I would advise you to not even think about her," he said. "I promise; you won't like the ending of that story."

The man laughed. "You think you're pretty tough. Now get up."

"Oh, not me," Zack said. "It's her. You should see what she did to one of your friends."

The man moved his arm forward, but Zack was faster. Zack pulled out the two stolen guns, extended his arms to each side and fired. Zack shot both men three times. The two men hit the ground dead. He crawled to each and did the same as he did before: remove the guns and wallets. None of the men had ID's, but each had a sum of cash. Zack didn't feel guilty for lifting the money: threatening a woman carried a price. He figured they paid in full.

Stef ran back and stopped cold at the sight of the two dead men. Zack took a deep breath. "I'll tell you later. Let's go."

Stefani was slow but unlocked her car doors. Zack opened the rear door, pulled himself onto the back seat and laid there. *Please let there only be four.*

"Where to?"

The safest place he could think of was his place. "Fells Point. In the meantime, I need your phone."

CHAPTER 27

"Oww! Are you intentionally trying to hurt me?"

"Quit whining, baby."

"OWW! You just picked at that same spot!"

Stefani rolled her eyes. "Just sit still and quit complaining. I'll get this over faster."

Zack laid on his couch while Stefani re-stitched the wounds on his side. He wanted to drink, but she didn't let him, so there was no pain medication. He grumbled as she sewed the last stitch.

"There. Let me bandage it," Stef said. "Now do you want to tell me what is going on?"

"I don't even know where to begin."

"Begin? How about at the beginning," Stef said, clearly upset with the situation.

Zack sat up after she finished with the last piece of tape over the gauze on his wounds. "Can I have a drink now?"

"No, you cannot," she snapped at him. "What is going on? Are you a criminal or something?"

"No, we covered that," Zack said.

The front door unlocked and someone rushed up the stairs. Stefani stopped and looked at Zack alarmed.

"It's ok; it's Andre."

Andre reached the top of the stairs and saw the two on the couch.

"You called me here to see your half-naked ass lying on a couch with the hot nurse? Seriously, Zack?"

"We're in a bit of a pickle if you haven't noticed," Zack said. "We're not in the hospital for a reason. You want to hear why?"

Andre looked at Zack, saw the distressed look on Stefani's face and went to Zack's kitchen. He returned with three glasses half filled with bourbon. He handed Zack and Stefani one. "You both look like you could use this. Now, why are you here and calling me in the middle of the night to get over here?"

"Four guys tried to kill me in the hospital," Zack said. He gulped the bourbon and enjoyed the warmth down his throat. Stef shook her head at him but then sipped from her glass.

"Who were they?"

"I don't know," Zack said. "Next time I'll ask."

"That doesn't help."

"I picked cash and their guns from them," Zack said.

"Why?"

"Figured we might be able to trace the guns, and I was short on cash. Figured they wouldn't need it anymore." Zack drank more of the bourbon. "At least three of them won't. Not sure about the fourth."

"You capped three?" Zack nodded.

"Anyone see?"

Stefani shook her head. "The place was pretty quiet tonight."

"We should call Barnes," Andre said. "Best to get in front of this just in case." He grabbed his cell phone and dialed. "Were either of you hurt?"

Zack shook his head. "Tore some stitches and I learned not to mess with Stef," he said. "Chick is a black belt," he said to Andre.

Andre smiled. "I may hire her to be your bodyguard because you look like hell."

That made Stefani smile. She looked at Zack and winked.

Lieutenant Barnes answered. "Lieutenant, I have Zack with me, along with the nurse we met earlier tonight."

"This sounds ominous," Barnes replied.

"Four guys went after Zack tonight at the hospital. Zack capped three of them for sure. Any reports on that?"

"Thankfully, my phone has been silent until you two called. My wife thanks you for waking us, by the way."

"Sorry, Lieutenant. This couldn't wait."

Barnes groaned. "I'll call you back."

Andre put his phone down. "We're on to something, partner," Andre said.

Zack sipped his bourbon. "It has to connect to Ashley Blumenthal."

"How?"

Zack finished the bourbon. "The pictures I pulled from her desk," Zack said. "Our favorite Senator."

"Terrific. A conspiracy." Andre slammed his drink. "You gonna be all right tonight? I want to get some sleep."

"Yeah, we'll be fine here," Zack said.

Stefani waited, but nothing was said, so she asked a question. "What DO you do for a living?"

"Andre and I are private investigators."

"Is it always this exciting?"

Andre smiled. Zack exhaled slowly and held his throbbing ribcage. "Not until lately."

"Are people always out to kill you?"

Zack slouched into the couch. "Not until lately."

"The worst part for you, though, Stefani," Andre said, "is that you are part of this now. You saw them. They saw you. You are now a loose end." Andre explained. "Your best bet now is to stay with us until this is over."

Stefani shook her head. "Part of what? Saw who? I didn't do anything!"

"You saved his ass," Andre said pointing at Zack. "And that makes you an accomplice."

Stefani finished her drink and grimaced. She let out a deep breath. "You drink this stuff? Wow. Do you have any more?"

Zack pointed to the kitchen when Andre's phone rang.

"Lieutenant, what do you have?"

"Nothing," Barnes said.

"What?"

"I'm saying I sent over Schmidt. There was nothing there. A patrol met him. There were no bodies, no blood or body in any stairwell and no signs of a struggle. The only thing the staff said has been odd all night is that someone left a fresh order of Italian food in the bathroom of a room on the fourth floor."

"You're sure Schmidt found nothing?" Andre asked.

"He said he looked everywhere. Drove all around the parking lot and there was nothing. It looked like nothing happened," Barnes replied.

"I saw him kill three people and bash another's face in with a gun. Something happened," Stefani burst out loud enough for Barnes to hear.

"It was self-defense," Zack said. "If I hadn't, we'd be dead."

"Ok," Barnes yelled. "Goddamnit. Well, I'm up now. I'll follow up on it. See you after the sun comes up."

* * *   * * *

Julie looked at her watch and wondered why her phone hadn't buzzed yet. She wasn't upset; she was worried. The campaigning kept her on the run at event after event and speech after speech, and in between, she had to do the book and take notes and make sure that she was wording his 'message' properly, so Jerry Pantalini was constantly asking her to verify this or that…she was exhausted. But still, Zack was supposed to text or call every morning. She said she would, and she did today, Tuesday, but no word from Zack since Sunday afternoon. She knew something was wrong.

"Oh, there you are," Rosler appeared from the front of the bus and smiled. "I've been looking for you."

Julie wasn't surprised. Rosler found her every chance he got and had been more hands-on than off lately. She was ready to get a restraining order. "I've been here the whole time since we left this morning. What town was that? Cornville or Soybeanville?"

Rosler laughed. "Trying to get away from Jerry and the campaign staff is next to impossible."

"Well, you are the main attraction." Julie sat next to the window with the seat next to her filled with her notebooks and papers. Her computer on her lap.

She had the food tray on the aisle seat pulled down with a plate of fruit and a cup of coffee on it. She planned the blockade to prevent unwanted visits.

"Yes, I am, and it is going well." He leaned as close as he could to her. "Look, I know being away has been hard on you. This pace can be quite frantic," he said.

Julie nodded.

He grabbed her hand and squeezed it. "I think I can get away from all this tonight after we discuss how today's events went. What do you say you and I have a nice dinner alone and away from all this hub-bub?"

"Senator, no," she objected. "I have to get this done, and I'm sure you have to prep for tomorrow's stops," she tried.

"Oh nonsense," he said with disgust. "I won't hear of it, and I told you to call me Mike."

Damnit. "Mike, I really would like to just crawl into bed as soon as we get to the hotel, call my fiancé and talk to him."

He smiled at her. "I haven't seen you on your phone. Has he called since you left?" He moved his hand up her arm but didn't give her a chance to answer. "Look, I insist. You are coming to dinner with me tonight. Besides, we both need a distraction from the campaign."

She knew there was no way out of it. "I already do." She pointed at her laptop. "I have a deadline to meet."

"It's a good thing I'm the boss around here then," he said.

Someone called for Rosler, he winked at her and disappeared into the front of the bus. She looked out the window and knew what Rosler had in mind for dinner. *Zack is going to be so mad at me! Damnit. I should never have agreed to this. Zack was right all along. But why hasn't he called or texted? Zack can't be mad at me. We talked about that, and he promised. Zack, call me!*

* * *   * * *

Zack sat in his bed that morning still in pain. He decided to lay in bed and process things. The legal pad in his lap and pen in hand, the notes he wrote filled a page.

Julie never left his mind, but without a phone, Zack couldn't text or call her. Plus, he didn't know what to say. A day rarely passed when Zack didn't fear

Julie leaving him because of his past and his occupation. She wanted something stable and safe. Julie deserved that.

He heard a person stir in the living room. A brunette with wild hair stuck her head in his bedroom. "Hey, do you mind if I shower?"

"Go ahead."

Stefani disappeared in the bathroom. He heard the water, the curtain close, and he returned to brainstorming. *Start at the beginning. What started this? Ashley Blumenthal. What do I have on her? The fact that she was pregnant. Find the father. Paternity test. Start there.*

He got out of bed and entered the spare bedroom and found Stefani's phone. He dialed a number and waited. He got an answer. "Doctor Patterson, please," he said. "I'll wait."

A few minutes later he hung up and frowned. *That was not the news I wanted but somehow expected. What's plan B?*

Zack left the bedroom, entered his bathroom and stuck his head inside the curtain. "Hey, I need your help."

"Zack! I'm in the shower!" Stefani yelled as she covered her parts as best she could.

"Yeah, my shower."

Stefani stared at him. "Can I finish?"

Zack looked up and down, winked and smiled. "Hurry up. I need your help."

Stefani exited the bathroom and entered the kitchen with a towel wrapped tightly around her body and her hair. Zack leaned against the counter when he heard her behind him.

"Do you always walk into the shower of a woman?"

"Exactly one hundred percent of the time before a few minutes ago, the only woman who has ever showered in here has been Julie. So, the answer is yes. Forget about that. You saw me naked, so we're even."

Stefani blushed. "Do you have any coffee around here?"

"Not allowed. Get dressed."

"Yes, you do. I see it right there," Stefani pointed at a bag of Julie's favorite coffee beans.

"Yeah, but I hate the smell and taste of coffee, so I don't allow it in my apartment."

"Well, you do today if you want my help. So make me some while I do my hair, or I'm outta here." She eyed him and pushed his shoulder as she walked past back to the bathroom.

He shook his head. *What is it with coffee? What's wrong with water?*

She returned with her hair dried and curled and grabbed the cup of coffee that awaited her. She clutched it with both hands, smelled it, smiled in delight and sipped it. "Umm, this is good. You should try it."

"As soon as pigs fly."

"What do you need me for? You do realize I am probably out of a job now, don't you?"

"I want to test your medical knowledge."

"Ok, shoot," she said.

"A medical examiner had a DB. Police said official cause of death was drowning. The doctor said it wasn't. No marks, bruises, she wasn't drunk, but she was found face down in a pond. How did she die?"

"What?" Stefani asked.

"The doc said he put a syringe in each lung. There was nothing in them. Nothing. So, Ashley didn't drown. She was dead before she hit the water."

"The police said she drowned, but the examiner didn't?"

"Not exactly," Zack said. "The cops pressed him for a COD, and he said at first glance it looked like drowning but that he'd have to do an autopsy. The parents wouldn't let him, so the cops just ran with the preliminary cause."

"But there was no water in the lungs?"

"No."

"And there were no other marks on the body to suggest foul play?"

"None at all. I saw the pictures. He's thorough even though he wasn't supposed to be thorough. He has frozen blood samples, a urine sample, hair samples and he even figured out she was pregnant," Zack said.

"Wow," Stefani said. "Too bad none of that will be admissible in court."

Zack opened then closed the refrigerator door. He was hungry but didn't feel like cooking. "I need to know how she died."

Stefani said, "Have the blood tested for SUX."

"What?"

"Succinylcholine," Stef said. "It's a paralytic that disappears from the body very quickly. Given the wrong dose, it would paralyze her and kill her. Throw her in the water, and it would look like a drowning. If there was no water in the lungs, maybe they gave her too much, and it stopped her breathing before she could take in any water." Stefani shrugged. "It might still be in the urine sample."

Zack said, "How do we do that?"

"You know anyone at the FBI Crime Lab in Virginia?"

"Yes, we do."

"It will take some time, but they have the equipment to do it."

"Ok. What I don't get is how did Barnes' men not see that? I mean, if she had drowned, her eyes would have been messed up or something, wouldn't they? They should have known something was off. There should have been more questions. And I found this out in six hours so how can three other private investigators not figure any of this out? It doesn't make sense."

"You'll have to tell me the whole story. None of it makes sense to me, either."

"I will. First, let's get you some normal clothes and eat. Plus, I need your phone again."

"Why?"

Zack exhaled. "I haven't talked to my fiancé in two days. She's going to be pissed. Plus the watch she gave me for Christmas was destroyed in the crash. She's not going to like that, either."

"I don't blame her. I'd be pissed, too."

"Yeah, then I have to tell her car is totaled. I suspect that might go over like a lead balloon."

"And you love this woman?" She snorted. "I can only imagine what you do to women you don't like."

CHAPTER 28

Her cell phone finally rang. Julie jumped and picked it off the seat next to her.

She didn't recognize the number. She hesitated to answer it when Jerry Pantalini, the campaign manager, appeared alongside her. Julie put her finger up and was going to respond when Jerry put his hand on the phone.

"Sorry, Julie. It will have to wait. We need you up front right now."

Julie stared at the number. *It's a Baltimore prefix. It could be about Zack.* "This will only take a minute, Jerry."

Jerry tugged at her arm. "It can wait. We're on a tight schedule," he said and continued to prevent her from answering.

She put the phone down on the seat and left it there. *Please let it be Zack!*

"I am sorry, Julie," Jerry said. "You need to hear what the Senator is saying; it's important for the book."

Julie nodded and followed him. *He's been saying the same thing for three days. I've heard everything he has to offer.*

* * * * * *

Zack sighed as Julie's phone went to voicemail. "Hey honey, it's me. No, this isn't my phone. It's a long story that involves my phone not working anymore. I'll get a new one today with the same number. Call me when you can. I'm sorry about the last couple of days. As I said, it's a long story. Don't worry. Everything is fine. I love you, call me later." He hung up and handed the phone back to Stefani.

"That's your message? Seriously?"

"What?"

"You straight up lied to her. Everything is not fine."

Zack shook his head as he headed down the stairs of his apartment. "I didn't lie. I'm fine now aren't I?"

Stefani laughed. "I don't even know how to respond to that."

* * * * * *

Though it was mid-afternoon, Zack didn't feel like entering the office the usual way and having to deal with an angry Michelle. But, he had to get to the office. So, like he was prone to do when he didn't want to be seen, he had Stefani park to the north of the square out of sight from the office, and they walked to the alley behind the building.

"What are we doing?"

He stopped her. "You are going to learn an entrance to my office only one other person knows about," he said. "If you tell anyone, I will be forced to kill you." He winked. "Well, not really, but seriously, don't tell anyone."

They stood atop a dumpster, reached the fire escape, climbed to the roof where Zack showed her an opening in a sloped shelter that covered an air conditioner. "Secret passage," he said. "It's coded."

He exposed a keypad that was hidden beneath the soffit, punched in a number and a small door popped open. Moments later, they were inside the walls of the building the Dre-Zack Detective Agency rented their space. Only Andre and Zack knew who owned the building: Zack and Andre.

After Zack helped Stef down a ladder, he opened a panel in the wall of the shower in his private office bathroom, and the two entered his office.

Stefani looked at him suspiciously, yet with an air of wonder. He nodded and walked out of his bathroom into his office. The door was shut though they could hear talking on the other side of the door. Zack sat behind his desk, saw a red light flashing on his office phone and picked up the receiver. He hit play.

The voice was female, but it was disguised with an electronic device. "Honestly, Mr. Stack, if that is your name, why have an answering machine if you never listen to your messages? Here's a message you will want to remember: Meg Chatwell. Find her. She is the key." The message ended.

Zack's stomach knotted. Stefani noticed.

"What's wrong? Everything all right? You just turned white."

Zack smiled and knew the blood had left his face. "Just remembered I forgot to take out my recycling," he said.

"You're a bad liar, Zack," Stef said.

The phone beeped, and another message played. It was left that morning. "Mr. Stack, you like to find dead women, don't you? Get this one right. Linda Polzinski doesn't drink. She never did. Tick, tock, tick, tock." The message ended.

Zack hung up the phone. *Get this one right. Donald Fairfax's wife. He has a helper.*

"Zack, what is it?"

He exhaled and slumped in his chair. "You want another cup of coffee?"

"Yeah, I'd love one."

"Stay here." Zack stood from his desk and walked to his door. He opened the door and walked past Michelle. Stefani heard Michelle scream in fright and then yell at Zack.

"What the hell are you doing? How did you get here? Where have you been? What happened to you? You look like hell! Zack, damnit, talk to me!"

Zack returned to the office with a mug of coffee and handed it to Stef. Her eyes were wide with shock and surprise as Michelle stormed into Zack's office. Zack grabbed a Pepsi from his mini-fridge and sat behind his desk.

Michelle stopped and looked confused. She raised her arm and pointed at Stef while she stared at Zack. "Who is this?"

"Michelle, meet Stefani. She's a nurse. Stefani, meet Michelle. She's," he paused, "well, she's Michelle."

Stefani smiled. "Hi."

"Why is she here and how did you get in?"

Zack wrote something on a sticky note and stood from his desk. "She saved my life last night, and now she's stuck with me until this is over, whatever this is," he said as nonchalant as he could. He walked to a closet by the bathroom, grabbed a light coat and put it on. "I need you to get Ronald the FBI Guy to do something for us."

Michelle shook her head. They always called her boyfriend that name. "That's it? You're not talking today?"

"I need a urine sample tested."

Michelle saw the look on his face. He wasn't talking. "Ok. Anything else?"

"Yeah. There is one thing noticeably missing from the Ashley Blumenthal file: phone records. Can you see if you can get me the list of numbers of calls and the text record of the people she talked to the night she died?"

Michelle put her hands on her hips and bit her lower lip. "Ok."

"Here," he handed her the sticky note. "I need to find this girl immediately. That's all I know about her. I was told Meg, could be Mary, I don't know."

"Ok. I'm on it. Anything else?" Michelle crossed her arms, disgusted at Zack but she knew he wasn't talking. She recognized his moods quicker than anyone and knew when to push and when to back off. This was a backoff time.

"Did you find anything yet on my other requests?"

"Not yet. There are two other investigators here that need things. Anything else?"

"Yeah, you look beautiful today. Thank you for everything," Zack said.

Michelle watched as Zack grabbed Stefani's arm and the two left the office the normal way.

* * *   * * *

The day was another never-ending circus. Julie was forced to sit in on strategy meetings, policy sessions, news and poll reviews, even rehearsals of speeches. The bus stopped, and she finally was left alone. She rushed back to where she typically sat and grabbed her phone. It was dead. She tried turning it on. Nothing.

Damnit! The battery died. They were rushing to an event, and she wouldn't have time to charge it. *I'm sorry Zack. I'll call you tonight, I promise.*

* * *   * * *

"Remember what life was like without these things?"

Stefani drove away from the cellular phone store and smiled.

153

Zack quickly sent a text to Julie. "What's your number, Stef?" She told him, and Zack typed it on his phone and sent her a text. "How did humans exist without them?"

Stef laughed. "Good question. Nowadays, people can't go a few minutes without checking to see what they missed. Back in the day, I guess we were happy being blissfully uninformed."

"Blissful is the right word. Ok, I'll try to get him to agree to give us a sample. If the ex-boyfriend refuses, make up an excuse to use his bathroom or something to steal a sample."

"Oh, good plan," she scoffed. "You are full of them, aren't you?"

"I try."

"How the hell did you make it this long as a private detective with plans like that?"

Zack shrugged. *This is my first time needing a DNA sample.* "I could always just punch him and then we could use his blood off my fist."

She turned the corner and entered the campus. "I'm not bailing you out of jail nor being an accomplice to any more crimes. I was able to lie my way into keeping my job and getting a few days off, but if I end up a felon, I doubt they'll be so understanding."

"Duly noted." Zack pointed out the frat house of Steve Moreland. "Julie hasn't called me or texted me back all day," he said. "You think she's mad at me?"

"Yes," Stef said. She stopped the car. "I told you I would be."

"You don't think she'd sleep with Senator Rosler, do you?"

She considered the thought. "He is cute and rich. So, there is that. But, no. You think she would?"

"No."

"Then don't worry about it. The woman loves you. Now let's go get some DNA," she laughed as she exited the car.

"I bet you've never said that before."

"If only this were a date. What a party story for the question, 'how did you meet?"

* * *   * * *

154

Julie Fletcher exited the limousine by the hand of Senator Michael Rosler. They were in Ames, Iowa at an upscale restaurant. She didn't like the dress that Jerry Pantalini got for her, but he insisted that the supper club was formal, so a formal dress was necessary. The strapless black Vera Wang showed off her curves very well. It cost more than her entire wardrobe, and if not, then it did with the shoes. Zack would love her in that dress, and she would love to wear it for him. But with Rosler this night, Julie was uncomfortable.

Rosler reserved a table in a dark corner, out of sight of nearly the entire restaurant. Secluded for impropriety, Julie suspected. She wondered how often he had this arrangement when his wife was back home working the family business.

He ordered a bottle of Bordeaux and said it was the best there. She didn't want to drink. She wanted to get into her warm pajamas and crawl into the bed with the man she loved. If only she could contact him. Her phone was in her room charging. *Zack, please don't be upset. I should leave in the morning. They don't need me here anymore.*

"You look lovely tonight, Julie," the Senator gushed over her. "You should dress like that more often."

"I haven't the budget or the reason to," Julie said.

"We should change that then," he held up his glass of wine. "To the future and all that it may entail."

She tapped her glass against his and sipped the wine.

"So, what do you think of the campaign trail?"

"It's exhausting," Julie answered. "I wouldn't want to have to do this every four or six years."

"It is exhausting," he replied. "But getting out here with the people, meeting them in the stores and coffee shops and school gymnasiums is the most exciting part of it."

Julie feigned interest. "Really? How so?"

"I think it's the adrenaline rush campaigning gives me. You know that every speech has to be on and you don't know how it is going to play out until election night. It must be a competition thing, like what professional athletes must experience when they play their seasons for the chance at the national title."

Julie nodded. "That's an interesting comparison."

"Ahh," he scoffed, "listen to me bore you with more politics. Forget about that. This night is about us, Julie. I want to get to know you and forget about all the campaigning. I have to admit; I've been watching you from afar. You are stunning. How have you managed to stay single?"

Julie knew a come on when she heard it, and this was full-court-press flirting. "I'm not," she answered and held up her hand and wiggled the finger with her engagement ring.

"Lucky man. Where is Zack tonight, do you know?"

"I'm sure he's at the office or home." She hoped it was one of those and not in another hospital.

"I can't believe he isn't following you everywhere. I know I would be. Has he called you since you left?"

That's a strange question. "We've both been busy."

"I'm sure he is, but I'd still be calling. He's probably jealous and trying to make you suffer," he said. "You don't need that."

"I'm sure he's just busy."

"Well, I can't wait to meet him."

"Perhaps we'll invite you to the wedding, and you can meet him then."

"We'll see. Zack's a lucky man to have your heart."

"He is. I remind him of that every day." *Wait. Did he say Zack's name?*

"Enough about him," he said and raised his glass again. He waited for Julie to raise hers and they both drank again. "Tell me, Julie, how did you become a journalist?"

CHAPTER 29

Zack opened the door with his lock-pick set, raised the yellow "Crime Scene Do Not Cross" tape so Stefani could enter below it and followed her. He shut the door behind him and turned on the lights.

"Are you sure it's ok we're here?" Stefani said. "It feels like we shouldn't be here."

Zack pulled a small but powerful flashlight out of his coat pocket. "I have friends in high places," he said. "And I may be forever in his debt."

Zack looked around the foyer of the Polzinski house. Stefani stayed close by his side.

"Whose debt?"

Zack shrugged. "A very nice Lieutenant on the Baltimore police force," he said. "Don't touch anything, be careful where you step and if you see anything that looks oddly out of place, let me know."

"What would that be?"

They entered the living room where Jules and Zack found Mrs. Polzinski dead. The furniture had not been moved, and Zack remembered seeing her lifeless body in the chair. An eerie feeling crept through him. "I don't know. You're a woman. Put yourself into the mindset of a woman who just lost her husband of over twenty years, and no one cares about him. How would you feel? What would you do?"

Stefani looked at the magazines on the tables. "Well, I sure as hell wouldn't be reading Tactical Weapons."

Zack smiled and looked on but then stopped. "What?"

"Tactical Weapons, the magazine," she said. "See it? On the table?"

Zack looked at it. He could tell it had been opened; a page in the middle had been folded as if left as a page marker. Zack removed two pairs of latex gloves from his coat pocket. "Here, put these on." He did as well and grabbed the magazine. "Odd," he said as he examined it. "There's no label on it."

"What do you mean?"

"I mean, there's no mailing label on it. Look at the other magazines: Good Housekeeping, Glamour, People, Sports Illustrated, they all have labels. This one doesn't."

"Yeah, and that one definitely doesn't go along with Glamour," Stefani said.

A plastic bag came out of his pocket next. He put the magazine in the bag. "Maybe Mr. Polzinski had a subscription. Good eyes. Keep looking."

Zack entered the formal dining room from the living room; a wide doorway on the other side opened to the kitchen. The bouquets of flowers still sat haphazardly about the room, but now most of the flowers had wilted and died. It seemed morosely apropos to Zack. He looked at a large hutch against the wall that displayed fine China the Polzinski's likely never ate off.

"Are we looking for anything specific?"

"Signs of a struggle," Zack replied. "Prescription drug bottles, a liquor cabinet, things like that," he said.

"Why?"

"Anything that might suggest she really did overdose on drugs and booze." Zack picked up a stack of mail on a corner of the table. It looked similar to the mail he usually let pile up: electric bill, cable bill, letters from insurance companies letting him know about savings for teenage drivers, fliers from local stores, and AARP solicitations. Zack set the mail down and headed into the kitchen.

Suddenly, glass shattered, a lamp exploded and hit the floor. Stefani screamed. Zack saw another piece of the window bust, and part of the cushion on a chair ripped apart. He ran towards Stefani and tackled her just as more glass shattered.

The flower bouquets exploded, bullets hit the hutch, the front windows disintegrated, down and stuffing from the furniture filled the air and pieces of glass, ceramics, furniture, and table rained on the two as Zack sheltered Stefani on the floor.

Then it stopped.

Zack grabbed his gun, hopped to his feet and ran to the door. The sound of a car squealing its tires sped away.

"What the hell was that?" Stefani yelled.

Zack holstered his gun and looked around the room. He knew where Stefani stood and where he had been. With the lights on inside, their positions were easily seen from the street.

"I think it was a warning." He walked to Stef and grabbed her hand. "Come on. We aren't finished."

"You want to stay here? We almost just got killed! What did you drag me into? This is insane." Stef's breath raced, she tried to pace but didn't know whether to leave Zack's side or not, her hands shook, and Zack saw perspiration on her forehead.

He grabbed her arms and squeezed them. "Hey! Stop," he ordered. "Just relax. You're going to be fine. Look for liquor. Five minutes and we'll be out of here."

"Five minutes? What if they come back? Are you nuts? What is going on, Zack?!"

Zack exhaled. "If they wanted us dead, they would have hit something closer to us. That was a warning." He walked into the kitchen with her in tow. "They are telling me to stop."

* * *   * * *

The limousine stopped outside the hotel in the back where the reporters and cameras were not. Rosler's security set up the perimeter so he could come and go when he wanted without the hassle of cameras and microphones being shoved in his face every time he was in the open. They said it was for security reasons. Rosler only used this setup at night.

The driver opened the door; Julie exited followed by the Senator, and the two walked inside a rear entrance. Julie walked towards the elevator, but Rosler stopped her.

"Let's take the stairs. I don't want to deal with the lobby tonight," Rosler said.

She didn't like it, but the two turned left and climbed the wide carpeted stairwell towards the third floor.

"I had a lovely time tonight, Julie. Thank you so much for accompanying me."

Julie watched the Senator have no problem climbing the stairs. No breathing issues or struggling. Like he had never been shot a week earlier. "You're welcome, Senator."

They turned the corner and climbed the last flight of stairs to the third floor. "I feel I'm a lot closer to you now. I'm so glad we did this. You're a wonderful woman."

"Thank you," she said. They entered the main hallway on the third floor.

"Would you like to come to my room for a nightcap? Perhaps talk about the ending of the book?" He moved closer than she liked.

Julie smiled. "I'm sorry, Senator, I can't. I'm exhausted and feeling a headache coming on. Plus, I have to call my fiancé," she added. "I miss him so much."

Rosler seemed put-off but regrouped and smiled. "Of course, you do."

"I'm sure you have work to do and should check in with your wife. Goodnight, Senator," she said as she held out her hand for him to shake. He did.

"Goodnight, Angel. I will see you in the morning."

Julie quickly disappeared into her room and locked it. She closed her eyes and thought. *How am I going to avoid him for another week??*

* * * * * *

He wanted to be at home with his wife and kids. Another long day and the clock approached ten at night. But, Andre Kitchell wanted this meeting. Said it was important. So, on the way home, a quick stop to find out what he wanted.

Lieutenant Ted Barnes walked into the pub and spotted Andre alone at the bar. Barnes dodged the patrons and sat next to Andre. "Hey, Dre. Shouldn't you be home taking care of your girl instead of meeting me?"

"She takes care of me," Andre corrected. "What about your wife? How did you get out?"

Barnes ordered an Oktoberfest and nodded. "I'm on my way home. She knows my hours suck." Barnes drink arrived. "This Rosler case is driving me to early retirement."

"That's what I wanted to talk to you about," Andre ordered another beer. "Did you tell me everything you had?" He looked at Barnes. "I mean everything?"

"Why?"

"The press thinks we found the shooter and they are tearing Axford's life apart. All of America knows about him. They think the case is closed. Even Rosler thanked the police and FBI for their handling and solving of the case. The only thing left is to speculate why he did it," Andre said.

Barnes thought for a moment. "I am thinking you aren't thinking the same."

Andre's drink arrived, and he drank from it after the customary 'Cheers' and glass clink with Barnes. "The why we'll figure out, Lieutenant," Andre paused. "But we know differently. Meaning, you, me, and Zack knows this isn't over. I understand why you want people to think that, but," he paused.

"But what, Dre?"

"We know there's a second shooter."

"Based on what Axford said? He could have been crying patsy."

"He may have been. But Jules recorded the event. And the video doesn't lie. The girl was killed first." He looked straight at Barnes. "She was shot twice. Polzinski was shot next, and then Rosler was hit. Four bullets but you only told me about testing two. Which means you lied about the ballistics test."

Barnes hesitated with his drink halfway to his mouth, slowly swigged from it and put the glass down. He turned his head and again nodded in agreement. "Technically, no, I didn't."

"Don't bullshit me."

"Sorry, I did lie." He looked at Andre. "I had to."

"Why? Why didn't you tell us?"

"I needed you two to have an open mind."

"So, you only tested the two bullets that killed Hannah?"

"No. All three. I kept the third under wraps. Only the tech and I know. Now you and Zack." Barnes sipped his drink. "This felt wrong from the beginning. Maybe I should have shown all the cards," he shrugged. "I just believed less was more in this case, you follow?"

Andre thought for a moment. "Yeah," he said, "I do."

"I hate to say this, Dre, but sometimes I know I can trust you and Zack more. So," Barnes paused, "I brought you two into this. This is big. I need this."

Andre processed what he heard. He wished Zack was with him since Zack knew Barnes better. Andre decided to go with his instinct. "No one is asking why."

"That's what I need you and Zack to figure out."

"What is wrong with Schmidt and O'Malley asking those questions?"

Ted was silent. It turned into an awkward silence before he spoke again. "Well, ask Zack this one: you two have been on the case for how long? What have you figured out?"

Andre knew Zack's answer. "I think he'd ask how are we getting reimbursed for this?"

Barnes chuckled.

"We think the Blumenthal case and this, they're related, Ted. This is all related."

"How do you know that? Look," Barnes turned to face Andre. "I need help, all right? I don't know who to trust other than you and Zack. I need proof. And it has to be rock solid, but you see what is going on around here. We can't afford any more scandals and negative press. If you and Zack find shit, you can't give it to Julie to put in a newspaper. I can't have that."

"So you're covering your ass."

"I'm trying to get this department respectable again. I'm trying to earn back the people's trust. Solving this would be a big first step."

They stared at each other until Andre nodded. "Ok. I'll buy that. But we need to know: do you have our back?"

Barnes drank from his beer. "I just gave your partner permission to search the house of Linda Polzinski, and if there are any calls about someone being in that house tonight, they go through me. What does that tell you?"

Andre raised his drink, Ted did the same, and they clinked glasses again. "Tells me we're good. Just don't lie to us." He stared at Barnes and then smiled.

Ted smiled and nodded. "Yeah, that goes both ways. By the way, tell Zack he is off the hook. Some guy had a dash cam and showed a white van pushing Zack into traffic. Confirms his story and enough eyewitnesses that the other police force dropped the charges. That guy will never stop owing me." Barnes finished his drink. "Thanks for the beer." He winked and left.

CHAPTER 30

Thunder from the remnants of a tropical storm rumbled and woke Zack early.

He looked at the clock: five in the morning. *Too early to call Jules. Where the hell was she last night? Why didn't she call me? Better not have been with that snake Rosler.*

He put his head on the pillow but knew sleep wasn't happening. Zack did his bathroom thing, got dressed and walked into the kitchen. He was hungry, but the food in his refrigerator didn't appeal to him. *I should have bought more bacon.* Zack saw fruit, but unless it was grapes in the form of wine, he wasn't interested nor did he care about the vegetables unless it was in a Bloody Mary. He left the kitchen and stared out the window.

The day before was fruitful. The ex-boyfriend gave a DNA sample. He was adamant he wasn't the father just like he didn't kill her. They took the sample to the lab, and Doctor Patterson said he'd run it immediately.

The search of the Polzinski house proved nothing other than there was no alcohol anywhere in the house, no other prescription medication and that Linda had joined a support group three days before her death to help her with the sudden loss of her husband.

It didn't make sense to Zack. *Why would she kill herself? She wouldn't. Who called me? I can't tell Michelle. If she finds out someone else knows about my real identity, she'll freak, and I don't need that. It's hard enough dealing with Jules' reaction to my past.*

Zack and Stef stopped by the BPD and dropped the magazine at Barnes' office. He left a note saying, "please have checked for prints." By the time they got back to his apartment, it was eleven at night. A long day. Sometimes they were inevitable. And the only message he had was there were no prints on the magazine.

His restlessness didn't dissipate. He felt the need to get out. The storm didn't dissuade him. He grabbed his keys, cell phone, and wallet and headed for the door.

"Hey, you're awake," Stef said in a gruff yet sexy morning voice. "Where are you going this early? Did you even sleep? It's still dark out."

"I dozed off for a little. I'm fine. I'm going to the office."

She exited the spare bedroom; a blanket clutched to her chest. "You're leaving me alone?"

He stared at her as another crack of thunder rumbled and bright lightning lit up the room. "You're safe here. Besides, you should sleep. I heard you rustling around late last night anyway."

"Shacking up with you makes me a little restless."

"Join the club."

Lightning preceded a crack of thunder as rain pelted the windows.

"Just wait, I'll come with," Stef said, but Zack walked to her and put his hands on her bare shoulders.

"No, go back to sleep," Zack said slowly. "Go in my bedroom; it's more comfortable. I appreciate you but stay here." After a quiet moment, she nodded and said ok. "Besides," the thunder and lightning continued its routine, "I only have one rain jacket, and I bet the rain would ruin your hair."

She laughed. "It would. You sure about this?"

"I'm sure." Zack put his arm around her shoulders and guided her to his bedroom then let go as she entered the room. *I don't want you to end up dead!!*

"You sure about me being in your bed? I know if I was your fiancé and came home and found another woman in your bed, I wouldn't understand. I would probably beat you with a rubber hose!"

Zack smiled. "Well, here's her number, you explain it to her."

He left the apartment, tightened the hood over his head and jogged in pain the short distance to his office. The rain poured and blew and soaked him from the waist down.

Once at the office, he hung his coat, walked into his office bathroom, disrobed and got into a hot shower. He soaked in it a long time. It cleared his mind. Exactly what he needed. Laying around reading files and asking questions that couldn't be answered while he was on his couch put fog in his head that only action would clear.

At long last, he exited and toweled off. He stared into the mirror at his discolored face and the multiple bruises, cuts, scars, and stitches all over his torso and took a deep breath.

"You do look good in a towel."

He jumped in surprise and turned to see Michelle in the doorway.

"Even with all the bruises, scars and cuts all over your body," she said. "You always have."

"Thanks. I should have been a towel model, huh?" He dropped the towel with his back to her and put on a pair of boxers followed by blue jeans. "What are you doing here?"

"I knew you'd be here before dawn and probably leave and not come back. I wanted to be here just in case."

Zack leaned against the wall. *She knows me well.* "Well, I'm here."

Michelle leaned against the opposite wall. "How ya' doing?"

He shook his head. No words sufficed. "I've been better."

She smiled. "I know. I see it in your eyes." She eyed him up and down. "Get dressed." She turned away but looked back. "Or not." She winked. "But, I have some stuff for you."

He wrapped his midsection, put on a white V-neck tee shirt and a black long sleeve dress shirt. He walked into the front buttoning the shirt and rolling the sleeves up to his elbows. "What do you have?"

"Let's start with the missing girl. I have no idea where Meg Chatwell is. By the way, her real name is Mary, but she goes by Meg. She has a credit card, but she hasn't used it for three days." Michelle swiveled a monitor so that Zack could see. "Look at these: transactions starting the day Hannah was killed. Meg filled her gas tank here in town and then headed west. The same day she uses it in Columbus, Ohio. Fills up with gas and gets some food looks like then stops in Indianapolis that night where she stays in a hotel. The next day she uses it in Merrillville, Indiana, close to your favorite city in the world," Michelle quipped, "but thankfully for you she kept heading west and used it again in Wisconsin." She pointed at the word Wauwatosa. "How do you say this city?"

"Wauwatosa," Zack said quickly. "Indian name. Have no idea what it means but it's pronounced just like it looks. Right by Milwaukee."

"How you know that is beyond me," Michelle said. "If she filled up with gas there, judging by her car and stops I'd guess she's in a 500-mile radius of there because she hasn't used it for gas since."

"Could she be there?"

"I don't know why. Her parents live in Illinois, down near Peoria," Michelle looked at a page she printed. "Her grandparents live in Florida most of the year."

"Probably not now. Hurricane season," Zack said. "Hear it raining out?"

"Yeah, I know," Michelle said. "She's only used it once since, and that was to withdrawal cash. She ended up getting a thousand total, took several transactions. What do you think that could mean?"

"It means she fell off the grid. She realized she could be traced via her cards and her phone. So, we have a smart girl. She could be anywhere right now."

"Well I'll keep searching, but you may have to go to Wisconsin."

"Great. I'll pick up some cheese," Zack said.

Michelle smiled. "Ok, next up for bids. The guy in the picture that you are suspicious about. His name is Pete Kilgas. He's the head of security for Rosler," she said as she exited one screen and went to another. "Here's the deal on this guy. He's only existed for the last ten years. He's worked for Rosler the last nine. Before that, well, whoever hid him isn't very good. Looks like he's pulling a Zack Stack." She turned another monitor as she worked a keyboard.

"Funny, 'Chelle. Real funny. What about this guy?"

"There's this thing called the deep web, you familiar with it?"

Zack shook his head. "Michelle, I can barely log onto Google."

She shook her head. "Yes, you can. You're just lazy."

Zack smiled. "That's why I have you, my dear."

Michelle rolled her eyes. "Well it took me a while, but I found out who he is."

Zack leaned in closer to the monitor to read the small type beneath the picture of a man he knew to be Pete Kilgas. "Mark Leary," he said. "Ok, so who is he and why would he change his name?"

"Former Army Ranger, two tours in Iraq and one in Afghanistan. General discharge," she said. "Sniper, expert sharpshooter, you know the drill," she added. "But I thought the good shooter part would interest you."

It did. "How good?"

"According to his file, one of the best," she pointed at the accreditations listed on the computer screen. "Wouldn't you say?"

"Ok, so why change his name? You can't find a rap sheet or a warrant for his arrest or that the FBI wants him for having bad taste in who to work for?"

Michelle chuckled. "Well, he came back and had trouble adjusting, got into a little trouble with the law, simple stuff: bar fights, drunken disorder, oh this one: sexual assault. That never went to trial. The alleged victim withdrew her statements and had charges dropped. Well, I guess he had enough and needed to make a little money, so he changed his name and disappeared. Mark Leary is no more," she looked at Zack. "He found work as a mercenary and maybe thought that changing his identity would protect the people he knew and family around him?"

"When I get to that point, I'll let you know," Zack said. "So, he's a mercenary just like Axford."

"Right. Leary found Rosler though, and you know the rest," she said.

Zack stared at the screen. "Anything else?"

"Yeah, the phone records for Ashley Blumenthal the day she died. Can't get them."

Zack looked surprised. "What do you mean?"

"I mean I can't get them. The records don't exist."

"That's impossible."

She spun on her chair. "Zack, no it isn't. Someone erased them. The last week of her life there isn't a single record of any calls or texts."

"Well now. Isn't that interesting?"

"So, if you want to know, give me the numbers of people in her life, and I can dig that way, but it looks to me like someone went through a whole lot of trouble to hide information."

"Well, that seems like a tremendous waste of time."

"It would be," Michelle said. "Ok, the next item up for bids? Dr. Frank Hewson doesn't exist."

"What?"

"The doctor you had me look for doesn't exist. There isn't a Doctor Frank Hewson within a thousand miles of here and nowhere in Linda Polzinski's history is there one." She swiveled on her chair to face him. "What I'm saying is that she never received a prescription for any anti-depressants, Zack. Those pills weren't hers, and the label was fake."

"I wonder if Barnes would be interested in that information?"

Michelle leaned back in her chair and twirled the ends of her hair in the fingers on her right hand. "You going to share it with him?"

Zack stood straight and rubbed his eyes. "Eventually. But not yet."

CHAPTER 31

The rain fell, but the darkness lifted as dawn arrived. Zack sat on the corner of Michelle's desk when the main door pushed open. Andre, water dripped from him, stepped inside and shook off.

"Man, it's a wet one out there this morning," Andre said.

Zack and Michelle stared at Andre as he shook water off his jacket and brushed it off his head. Andre fetched his coffee mug and filled it with the fresh hot brew. He let the scent flow up his nose, and he smiled. "Best coffee in town, Michelle."

"Thank you. I should order some more."

Zack shook his head. "Why can't you just buy beans off the shelf from the grocery store?"

"Not as good, bro," Andre said. "Come on, man. To do what we do you got to stay sharp, and bad coffee just means lack of focus, know what I mean?"

Michelle laughed. "Thanks, Dre. Any more questions, Zack?"

Zack lowered his head. "So what brings you here this early?"

"Couldn't sleep. You?"

"Same. Things aren't adding up, know what I mean?"

Andre nodded and sat on the couch. Zack walked around the desk and grabbed his ritual bottle of Pepsi out of the fridge behind Michelle.

Zack exhaled. "Tell me if I'm wrong here. I've been reading over the Blumenthal file and thinking about everything we've found in the last few days."

"Me, too," Dre added.

Zack took a deep breath. "I spent a few hours asking questions and learned more about Ashley Blumenthal's life than the cops and the three other PI's did in five months," Zack said.

Andre nodded. "Yeah, and in four days I found one of the shooters."

"And killed him," Zack added. "Which makes me question a lot of things."

"Me, too."

"We are being warned repeatedly, sometimes not so delicately, to stop investigating." He looked at Andre. "Why?"

Andre nodded and sipped his coffee.

Zack sat down, albeit slowly.

"It isn't going to get any better, partner," Andre said.

Zack nodded. "We could quit now. Walk away. Take what we know and file it in the trashcan. Never look back."

Andre was silent. He drank from his coffee and Zack drank from his Pepsi. Michelle stared at the two of them. The storm continued to make noise outside.

"It's up to you, partner," Zack said. "I'm not going to be the one who decides to put your life or anyone else's in danger. I can deal with them coming after me. But not you or anyone else. I'll tell Cheryl Blumenthal the same everyone else did."

Andre sipped his coffee, stood and walked to the window. "Could you live with yourself if you walked away right now, Zack?"

"Dre, I already told you, it's up to you now."

"Yeah, me neither. We're in too deep to quit now, partner." Andre looked at Michelle. "Mickey, I need you to do your thing," Andre paused, "on Detectives Schmidt and O'Malley."

Michelle stopped. "Whoa. Those are Barnes' men."

"We know," Andre said. "And we need you to do your thing."

"I'll tell Barnes later," Zack said. "We don't care about the normal stuff. We want bank stuff. Accounts, transactions, retirement accounts, everything you can find. Add Judge Blumenthal to that list."

"Ted is going to shoot you for investigating his men."

Andre and Zack looked at each other. Andre spoke next. "Do the same on Barnes, too. We need to know who the players are before we can figure out how to win this game," Andre said.

Zack stood from the couch. "Make it your top priority."

"Ok, it's your funeral," Michelle said, and she returned to behind her desk.

"That's what we're trying to avoid," Zack said.

"What is on for today, Zack?"

"I'm going to visit the home of Pete Kilgas."

Andre looked at him. "And what are you looking for?"

"A connection."

"I'll come with."

"No, you won't," Zack said. "I think we should limit our being together."

"Dude, you need another set of eyes."

"Kilgas should be out of town with the campaign. I'll take Stef. It will be fine."

*** ***

Stefani followed the directions supplied by Zack. He didn't say much else. She tried talking, but he was quiet.

Ten minutes later she turned into an older neighborhood but well kept. She drove down the street like she belonged, just like Zack said.

"There it is, 1654," Zack said. "Looks empty."

"Should I stop?"

Zack observed everything. "No, drive past and turn the corner. Don't slow down."

She did.

"Pull over here," he said, out of sight from the house. Stef did and stopped the car. "You sure you want to do this?"

"Whatever you need me to do."

Zack nodded and saw a car coming down the street. It looked like the car that had been behind him in the accident. "Kiss me."

"What?"

Before she could say anything else, Zack grabbed the back of her head, pulled her to him and the two kissed. Stef didn't resist. She put her hand on the back of his head.

Moments later, Zack pulled away. He looked up and down the street. "People are uncomfortable with public displays of affection. They look away."

She was speechless and nodded as she pierced her lips and wiped them with her tongue.

"You ready?"

"Are you going to kiss me again?"

Zack didn't pay attention. "Here's what I need you to do."

* * *   * * *

Michelle's computers worked hard that morning. Her fingers eased over the keys like an artist would play the piano. The coffee had kicked in, and her searches hit their mark.

She hacked through another firewall, and her program deduced the password. The account opened. "Bingo," she said.

She scrolled through and saw nothing out of the ordinary for the past few months but then came the month of May. Her heart stopped. It was too much of a coincidence. She was in the bank account of Judge Blumenthal, the father of the deceased Ashley Blumenthal. The same day as the death, a deposit appeared. Cheryl was not listed on the private account.

Michelle knew it was a wire transfer but wouldn't be able to trace its origin. It didn't matter. Now she had three done: the two cops and a judge. Next, she'd try to find the smoking gun. She doubted there would be an email trail. Bribes were usually done in person or worst case over the phone. But Michelle had seen dumber mistakes so while her one computer targeted the financial life of Lieutenant Ted Barnes, she used another to attack the firewall protecting Judge Blumenthal's email accounts. Zack could have made it easier and given her a place to start, but she was good. Google searches provided a starting point. And since he was a public official, he'd have contact info. And then it was a simple game of cat and mouse for Michelle. She smiled. This was turning into a very productive day. And it wasn't even nine in the morning.

* * *   * * *

On the outside of Baltimore in a quiet suburb, a dark-haired woman carrying a clipboard walked on the sidewalk despite the heavy rain and turned onto the front walk of the house numbered 1654. It was nine o'clock in the morning; she had seen other people leave for work.

She climbed three stairs and looked to see if anyone peered through the windows. She pressed the doorbell once. She waited and pushed again. After a few moments, she rang the bell again and knocked. Five hard wraps on the door produced no one so to be sure she did it again.

Fifteen seconds later she turned around and left the same way she approached. Once around the corner, she got back into her car. "No one. I pounded on that door. Either they don't want visitors, or no one is home, but it looked like no one was there."

Zack let out a deep breath. "All right. Park the car on the opposite side of the street at the end of the block and keep an eye out and if anyone or anything comes down the street and enters that driveway, you text me immediately. Then start the car and drive off the same way we came, you got it?"

"What about you?"

"Don't worry about me. I'll clear out the back and catch up. Keep your phone on, and I'll contact you," Zack said. "Just don't get caught playing whatever game you play on your phone and miss something, Ok?"

"No more gunfire, Ok?"

Zack exited the car and fastened the hood of his raincoat over his head. *Shouldn't look suspicious. It is raining after all.* Zack walked around the block to see the back of Kilgas' house.

Zack saw a fenced-in yard immediately behind Kilgas' house. Small trees lined the property and grew through the chain-linked fence. He continued around the block and headed back towards the home of Pete Kilgas, a.k.a., Mark Leary.

Zack illegally entered houses before, but usually, he had just cause. This time, he needed a break.

He acted like he was expected. Zack walked to the back of the house and disappeared in the backyard. There were no signs of an alarm system. No signs of a dog or video.

He manipulated the door lock easily and entered the kitchen. It was a small square room that had little counter space and too few cabinets. The room contained a stove, refrigerator, microwave, sink and a table big enough for two with one stool beside it. Zack concluded that was all one needed in a kitchen.

Zack opened the cabinets one by one, seeing the everyday kitchen essentials in bowls, plates, glasses, cups, pans, a rectangular glass dish, and a cheese grater but nothing special. Zack thought it was under-equipped. "No colander," he said. "Utensils suck, too. No pizza cutter."

Zack opened the refrigerator. It was as empty and unequipped as the cabinets and drawers with only three eggs, a box of baking soda, ketchup and mayonnaise, a half-empty half-gallon of milk, a 2-Liter bottle of Dr. Pepper and a twelve pack of Smithwick's bottles. "Let's leave a message," Zack said as he opened the box and removed two. He put one in each coat pocket.

Zack searched the first bedroom. It was devoid of anything other than a single size bed. The closets were empty, and dust bunnies lined the outside of the room. The closet in the main bedroom showed an extensive collection of blue, black and gray suits and a shelf filled with clothing that was all black.

Zack gave up on the closet and chest of drawers and looked for a wall-safe or hidden compartment. There was nothing. He left the bedroom, searched the bathroom, covered the living room and found nothing. Zack saw the basement door.

Zack hated searching basements. There typically was no way out once in the basement; if someone entered the house while down there, nothing good would happen.

He clicked on the light to the basement, his gun drawn, and slowly descended into the basement. Three single 60-watt bulbs hung from the ceiling barely giving enough illumination for the open space.

A water heater, furnace, washer/dryer, and sink sat in one corner. Nothing else was in the open floor, but a workbench along the side wall had separate lighting above it. Zack walked to the bench and smiled.

Pete Kilgas made his bullets. Long range bullets for rifles like the M24. And he made a lot of them. All the supplies, gunpowder, casings, and caps Kilgas would need to make those bullets along with .40 caliber shells for a handgun were there along with a box of latex gloves. *Smart man. No prints on the casings. Perfect for an assassination.*

Zack looked over the rest of the bench and scanned the room. Then, underneath the stairwell, Zack saw a black case. A large one. Large enough to hold several rifles.

Zack pulled the case out. There was no dust on it; Kilgas moved it often. The latch was locked, but it was a key lock. "Let's see what you're hiding in here," Zack said.

He used his pick-set to pick the lock. He turned the latch. It clicked, and Zack heard a winding sound. Zack lifted the lid and saw not only several guns but a device in the middle that had a timer attached to a small brick of C4 explosive. The digital time read 20 and ticked towards 0.

A voice recording started. "Goodbye, Asshole," it said followed by a maniacal laugh.

Zack's heart stopped then raced as he realized what he had done. He ran to the stairs, leaped them two by two, raced to the kitchen and ran through the door.

The bomb exploded. Zack ran, the explosion blew out windows and took out the house. The force of the blast caught Zack and forced him through the air and crashed to the ground. Debris littered down around him.

The fireball subsided; the house burnt even in the rain. The gas line blew. Cracks and pops of the bullets fired — the yard filled with burning pieces of wood and furniture. Zack groaned and rolled to his back and sat up. He rubbed his brow and forehead and stared at the blown apart house.

The rain stifled the inferno, but Zack knew he had to get out of there. His body ached even more, and his left side throbbed and burned. *I am lucky to be alive.* Zack felt the bottles of beer in his coat pocket. They survived. Twenty after nine in the morning? *Hell, it's five o'clock somewhere.* Zack opened a bottle and swigged it.

"Well, that escalated quickly."

CHAPTER 32

Stefani heard the explosion. She saw the fireball rise into the air. She stared straight ahead, her hands clutched to the steering wheel, and her mind raced. Leave, stay, leave, stay, played over and over in her mind. *What about Zack? How long do I wait? The cops and fire department will be here! Shit! Shit! Shit!*

She didn't know how long she sat there debating when the passenger door opened. Zack jumped inside.

"What are you still doing here?"

"I," she paused, "I, I, I," she stammered.

"Calm down and drive us out of here." He took a drink from the bottle of beer.

She started the car and drove away. "Where did you get the beer?"

"Just drive."

"Where to?"

"First get us out of here."

Stefani drove away from the burning house. Zack heard sirens.

"How do I look?"

She looked at him. "Like you've been in an explosion! You are always bleeding, Zack. I'd ask if you need a doctor, but I already know what you're going to say."

"That's why I have you."

"Not funny, Zack!" Stefani suddenly lost her cool. "How many more crimes are you going to have me a part of? I mean, murder, stealing, breaking and entering, harboring a criminal, what else is there?"

"Destruction of property for starters," Zack said.

"A joke? You're making a joke?" She drove faster with each sentence.

"Relax."

"Relax? You want me to relax? Are you serious?"

"Yes, I am serious," he said as calm as he could be.

"I'm a crook. That's it," Stef said matter-of-factly. "My life is over. I'm going to prison."

"You wanted excitement," he said. "Everyone is a crook out here, Stef. The key is to make sure you break the law for the right reasons."

"The right reasons? Seriously, Zack? You're rationalizing criminal activity?"

He looked at her. "We're an hour from DC. Where do you think I learned it? You're going to have to hide your car."

"What?"

"Take a left here. We should stay off the main roads."

"This can't be happening," Stef said. "I mean, I was only helping you out because I liked you. Then when I learned you have a fiancé, I helped you out because it was exciting. But now, now, Jesus Christ! Now you're telling me I have to hide my car? My life is over!"

Zack exhaled. "Nah, you'll be fine. Plus, look at the stories you'll be able to tell your kids someday."

"Tell my kids? Sweet Jesus! They'll need therapy!"

Zack finished the beer. "Probably."

* * *   * * *

Senator Michael Rosler sat in his hotel room. Nothing was planned until later that day. To him, it was perfect timing for a much-needed strategy session.

"Where are we?" Rosler said. "From what I've been hearing, I wouldn't say winning is a thing we can say."

Jerry Pantalini refilled his coffee from a pot on a wet bar across the room. "We've taken further steps to discourage any further activity as recently as this morning."

Rosler nodded. "Why didn't we just pay this guy off like the last ones?"

Pantalini shook his head. "We have to be a lot more careful now. Now that you're a candidate, the scrutiny over finances is worse. That money has to come from somewhere, and we have to report finances to the FEC. Scrutiny is the absolute last thing we need at this time."

Rosler exhaled. "Everyone has a price. Find this guy and end it."

The third man rose from his chair and also refilled his coffee mug. "I already told Jerry; this guy won't accept it."

"What is he, an idealist? I am tired of hearing his name."

"He has principles, Mike," the man said. "You remember what those are?" The man sat down. "Don't worry. We are applying pressure on him every chance we get. It will wear him down. We'll keep it up and then make him an offer. He'll realize he can't win and accept."

"I would appreciate it if you would speed things up, Pete."

"I'll do things my way. That's why you hired me."

"Well, your way is causing me consternation."

Pete Kilgas nodded and looked at Jerry Pantalini. "Consternation is the least of your problems, Mike. Do me a favor and leave the Fletcher girl alone. She isn't worth the repercussions."

Rosler smiled. "Let me worry about that. You just keep it so she can't talk with Stack."

Pete Kilgas put down his coffee. "It's like you didn't hear a word I just said."

"You do your job. Concentrate on that."

Kilgas shook his head.

Pantalini spoke. "What about their snooping around the death of the college girl?"

"Stack doesn't have anything but speculation. The girl worked on your campaign. Big deal. A lot of people do. She drowned — end of story. College kid partying too much got careless late one night. He won't find anything different." Pete said.

"And if he does?"

Pete shrugged. "Then we'll kill every one of them and make it look like a gang shooting."

"That easy?"

Pete laughed. "Stack capped three of my men the other night. Did you hear anything about it on the news? No," Kilgas smiled. "A building fire or car crash isn't that hard to pull off."

Jerry sat down. "He did kill three of your men and smashed another's face. Maybe you're taking him too lightly."

Pete looked at Jerry again and was about to open his mouth when his phone rang. He looked at the screen. "Don't worry about it. I don't worry about your gerrymandering or rigging elections so don't worry about me tying up loose ends to keep him safe." He pointed at Rosler. "I have to take this phone call." He left the room.

Rosler looked at Jerry. "Keep the girl on the run. Keep me informed with Stack and for God's sake, clean up this mess."

* * *   * * *

Zack looked at his broken watch. It broke when the explosion blew him across the yard. Not even ticking. The second favorite wristwatch down. He looked at his phone instead. Time could not have moved slower that evening. He laid on his couch as Stefani again re-stitched the wounds to his side.

"I'm getting pretty good at these," she said.

"You're not any better at doing it without causing me pain," Zack said.

"That isn't my intention."

"Then you are getting better." He looked at his phone again. "Why won't she return a text? I've sent at least a dozen the last day and a half, and I've called."

"Maybe her phone is dead."

Zack rolled his eyes in disgust. "Right. I'll send an email."

"You never know. You didn't have a phone for a while."

Zack accessed his email site, typed in Julie's email and sent a quick email just asking for her to email, text, call, message, Skype, anything. He said he missed her and loved her.

"You need to do nothing for a few days, Zack," Stefani said.

"The weather will make sure of that." The rain continued to fall outside, and flash flood warnings filled the airwaves. His cell phone rang. *Please be Julie!* "Stack here," he answered.

"Zack Stack, Private Investigator," the voice said.

Zack paused. "I am at a disadvantage," Zack said. "You know me, but I don't know you."

"You do, Stack. After all, you blew up my house today."

Zack let out a deep breath. "Yeah, you shouldn't have rigged your gun case."

"You shouldn't have been in my house."

"I think we could go back and forth with what we shouldn't have done recently, Mark."

There was silence. "That name doesn't exist anymore. Wouldn't you agree that forgetting the past is best right now?"

Zack closed his eyes. *Subtle.* "What do you want?"

"Simple. For you to do as I ask."

"Which is?"

"To stop doing what you're doing."

"I'm about to eat the best wings in Baltimore. Why don't you stop by? I'll buy you a plate."

Mark Leary, a.k.a., Pete Kilgas, laughed. "Dry rub or sauce?"

"Sauce," Zack answered. "Cooked in just right, perfect."

"Ahh, see, I prefer dry rub. So, we have a problem."

"I don't. You do."

"I like you Stack. You remind me of me. But the problem isn't me. It's you. So, do me a favor and stop what you and your partner are doing."

"Is this the part where you offer me a suitcase full of cash?"

"Would you accept?"

"No."

"I knew you wouldn't. So we are not wasting each other's time with that."

Zack stared at Stefani. Stefani had an idea this phone call wasn't one Zack wanted. She stared back.

"Stack, I have a job to do, and I am good at it. I suggest you play ball."

"And this is where the veiled threat comes in?"

Mark Leary laughed. "Oh, I'm not going to veil anything. The most difficult part for me would be where to start? Your fiancé, the hot chick that works for you, the girl you've been spending your nights with or the two guys you have working with you? Or maybe I'd start with you. Either way, people get hurt, or worse. And all because of you."

"Well, that would be a shame now, wouldn't it?"

"Honestly, Stack, did you think I'd have anything in my house that could incriminate me?" Leary paused. "I'm impressed you found it, but I'm not stupid. I am, however, upset that I had an unopened twelve pack of beer."

Zack smiled. "Only ten. I needed to get the smoke taste out of my mouth."

"A lot can happen, and you can't be everywhere, Stack."

The line went dead.

"You ok? Who was that?" Stefani said.

Zack faked a smile. "A fan wanting an autograph."

"What now?"

"How soon before we get the results back on the paternity test?"

"I'll check today. You think the results will help anything?"

"No. But there is one other possible father. And before I go into the wolf's den to get a sample, I want to be sure it's necessary."

CHAPTER 33

"Are you sure this is Ok? I mean, if you are video chatting with Julie and she sees me in the background this late at night, she may have questions," Stefani said.

Zack put his glass of wine and bottle by his computer on the table facing his couch. "We've been emailing all day. I told her all about you, and she already knows you're here."

"Yeah, but you two haven't talked, and you know, you might want to," Stef trailed off.

Zack looked at her. "What? You mean video sext?" He laughed. "Trust me, that isn't even a consideration. Just relax." He took a deep breath. "Besides, after our latest negative paternity test, I doubt anything good will happen. Just go into the bedroom and shut the door."

"Sure, you bet. I don't want you to get in trouble, that's all."

Trouble? Our lives were threatened again today. Trouble is already here. "It will be fine, Stef." Zack exhaled.

Stef disappeared into Zack's bedroom and shut the door as he asked. Finally, some face time with Julie. Zack had been waiting since Julie emailed and told him about her phone. He couldn't believe how excited he was to see her. He wanted to hear her voice and see her face and her smile and those eyes of hers. Zack needed to hold her, smell her scent and feel all of her. But, that was still several days away. This was the best he was going to get.

He sipped from the Duckhorn cabernet sauvignon. Julie said the bottle cost too much, but Zack realized that the you-get-what-you-pay-for adage generally held with wine as well. Zack promised he would open it with her on a special occasion. To Zack, that night seeing Julie was a special occasion. Then, his mind considered the possibility of video sex.

He sipped the wine again. Zack found it at a wine shop and was told it supposedly had lower residual sugars and didn't have chemicals like arsenic some reportedly had. Zack said if he was going to drink he might as well try to drink healthy. Julie and Andre both told him that the phrase 'drink healthy' had an oxymoron hidden in there somewhere but it sounded good to Zack.

Another drink and he refilled the glass. *This tastes a lot like more. Hurry up, Jules!*

* * *   * * *

Julie rushed back to her hotel room after another painful day on the campaign trail. The candidate repeated the same things, the same repetitive nothing-filled speeches and with each passing second, she just wanted to leave. She wondered if elections were simply manipulation contests to see who had the most uninformed voters show up at the polls because Rosler talked a lot but said nothing, yet everyone loved it. Rosler's speeches consisted of making shallow, non-specific promises and bad-mouthing his opponents. It was painful and excruciating.

Julie wanted to be with Zack. Something about him made her feel safe. And loved and wanted and needed but Zack also made her smile and laugh and feel comfortable with herself. And the sex with him was phenomenal!

His touch, where he touched her, how softly he touched her or hard when appropriate, and his lips. Oh, how Julie loved his lips! Best kisser she ever had, and she had a lot of guys during her high school and college years. None like Zack though. She imagined his arms around her, and a warm, tingly feeling swept over her.

She had her computer on her lap and dialed his number. The ordeal with her phone infuriated her. Julie told Jerry she had to get a new cell phone, that hers had died. Jerry promised they would find time to stop at a cellular store, but instead he kept her busy at meetings, taking notes, checking pages and references and facts for the book. Even Kilgas, the security guy, got involved and advised against it. He said it was too dangerous as long as there were concerns about the Senator being attacked again. She angrily decided it was a conspiracy until she got the email from Zack.

She had to sneak sending them all day. She wanted to be back in Baltimore with Zack after she learned what he had been through. And the picture of the stitches and bruising on his side looked horrifying. Julie needed to be there.

Seconds later, there he was: his face on her computer, smiling. It was still swollen and black and blue in spots with what looked like more cuts and scrapes than before.

"I missed you. I'm so sorry. It seems like they don't want me to talk to you," Julie said.

Zack smiled. "I'm sure they don't, but they can't stop us, can they?"

Julie stared at his face on her screen. "I want to come home, babe."

"I'll leave right now to come and get you," Zack said. "I'll be there before lunch tomorrow."

"Don't tempt me," she said. "I've thought about nothing but that for the last three days." She leaned closer. "Baby, you look pretty bad. Are you ok? Did something happen?"

You mean blowing up Pete Kilgas' house? Nope, nothing else happened today worth mentioning. "Oh, nothing. The morning kind of blew up on me," he said. "But other than that, nothing explosive going on here. I'm fine. You have too many clothes on, by the way."

She smiled. "Did you want to talk to me, or is something better on your mind?"

"Originally I wanted to talk. But seeing you now, I want to talk you through exactly what I would do to you if I were in bed with you." *This took a turn I didn't expect. I'll have to thank Stef for planting the idea in my head!*

Julie giggled, and she unbuttoned the top button of her blouse. And then the second button. "It is getting warm in here." She adjusted her shirt, so her cleavage was clear for him to see. "See anything you like?"

"Oh, my!" Zack said. He felt the blood surging through his veins. "You know how I like to start by kissing that magnificent neckline of yours."

185

"I know. I love that. What's next?"

Just then, they both heard a loud rapping on her hotel door. "Who is that?"

Julie turned to look at the door, frustrated. "Damn it! Not now!"

The pounding on the door continued and grew louder. "Julie! It's me, open up!"

Zack could hear the voice. "Who the hell is me and why the hell is he knocking at your hotel room door now?"

"Zack, honey, I don't know!" Julie was frantic. "Please! Just hold on, I'll get rid of him."

She jumped off the bed and went to the door while re-buttoning her shirt. Julie opened the door. Senator Michael Rosler stood at the door with a bottle of wine and two glasses. "Senator, what are you doing here?"

Rosler stepped inside the doorway without an invitation and smiled at Julie. "I wanted to see you."

"I'm sorry, but this is not a good time."

Rosler cut her off before she could say more. "Yes, it is, we need to talk about the book. I have meetings lined up all day tomorrow, so it has to be now."

"Senator, no, this is not a good time,"

"Oh, nonsense. You'll see Stack soon enough. Just one quick drink and I'll be on my way. I'm your boss right now, and I insist. Besides, I miss you. You are just so damn beautiful."

Julie knew she was stuck. *Zack is going to be furious!* "Just give me a minute," she said. Julie ran back to the bed to tell Zack she'd only be a minute, but Zack was already gone.

* * * * * *

Zack looked at his watch, Julie had bought this one for him, ripped it off his wrist and threw it across the room. It slammed into a wall and the crystal shattered.

Stefani rushed out of the bedroom and saw the furious Zack stare out the window. "What happened?"

Zack fought his emotions. After a long pause, he said, "the Prince of Darkness is trying to sleep with my fiancé."

CHAPTER 34

Zack laid in bed and stared at the ceiling. His head hurt as did most of his body. Restless, Zack swung his feet from under the covers onto his wood floors.

He wiggled his toes and stretched his calves before he stood and stretched his lower back and arms. Zack didn't want to do much that day. Rest seemed like the better alternative to doing something. He exited the bedroom, headed for the bathroom, opened the door without thinking and walked into a completely naked Stefani. She had just showered.

"Whoa," Zack said as he stared at her.

"Well get out and close the door! JESUS!" Stef yelled. "Don't you knock?"

Zack shut the door, leaned against the wall. *Why would I knock? It's my house.* He shook his head, walked into the kitchen and heard his phone ring. That early, a little after eight, it had to be Andre or Michelle. He rushed back into the bedroom and got it.

"Stack, here."

"You have been busy," the sultry, deep, female voice said.

"Ok," Zack sounded exasperated. "Yeah well, so I have been. What of it?"

"You are missing something."

Zack exhaled. "I've heard that before. Who is this?"

"Someone you should have talked to three years ago."

"That doesn't help. What do you want?"

"An innocent man is a prisoner at the BCCC because of you. A woman was killed because of you. And things are only going to get worse for you. Do I have your attention?"

"I'm really tired of threats and vague suggestions. Give me something concrete or quit wasting my time."

"Linda Polzinski doesn't drink. She didn't commit suicide."

"Yeah, well, that seems meaningless, doesn't it?"

"Donald Fairfax didn't kill his wife."

Zack's heart stopped and felt a pit in his stomach. "The evidence said otherwise," he said calmly.

"What evidence? Mr. Stack, or David, whatever your name is, connect the dots and do your job. Find Meg Chatwell. She has what you need. Time is ticking. Tick tock," the woman said and then hung up.

The line went dead. Zack saw nothing and put the phone in his pocket. The ramifications of that phone call made the pit turn into knots. *This is never going to be over.*

Stefani exited the bathroom dressed but with her hair still wet and curly. "Ok, peeping Tom, anything you wanted from me, or just sneaking a peak?"

Zack rolled his eyes. "I'm sorry, Stef. I forgot I have company."

She stared at him and smiled. "That's ok. What are your plans today?"

"I thought you ordered me to rest?"

"Since when do you listen to your nurse's advice?"

"How about if I start today?"

*** ***

Alone in his apartment, after Stef left to run errands, Zack stared at a blank computer screen while his mind raced. The phone call from the anonymous woman told him one thing: Donald Fairfax was somehow involved. That part made sense suddenly. *But how did he know about my past and who is the woman?*

And then it clicked. Right under Zack's nose the entire time. *Sonofabitch. Played like a chump.*

Staying in his apartment was no longer an option. He stood, waited for the pain to subside and went to the shower. The water streamed hot, and the ceiling fan purred but couldn't keep up with the steam. It didn't matter to Zack; it was therapy to his aching body.

The green light appeared by Julie's icon on his computer. He couldn't hear the sound of her calling him. The light disappeared. Julie's time ran out, and she had to go.

Zack finally exited the shower, dressed, put his shoulder holster on and slid his Sig into it. A jacket over that completed the ensemble, and he headed to the office. He never looked at his computer to see he missed Julie.

Halfway to the office, his phone rang. "Stack here."

"Hey, it's me. I'm at the hospital."

"Uh, visiting and not a patient I hope?"

She laughed. "Yeah, dummy." Stef changed her tone. "Zack be honest with me. Were you drinking the day of the car crash?"

"No."

"Don't lie to me, Zack. I saw you drink two beers yesterday before ten in the morning."

"Well, in my defense a block of C4 almost blew me to bits yesterday, so I was under a little stress. As for the crash day, no, I was not drinking."

"Your tox screen says you had a BAC of .26%. That's over three times the legal limit."

"That's impossible," Zack said. "You said you saw it and it said nothing."

"I did. But this one says differently. You're telling me the truth?"

"Stef, I don't know you well enough to lie to you. I did not drink that day."

Stef paused. "Ok. I know the lab tech. I'll go talk to him." She hung up.

Zack shook his head. *Three times the legal limit? I know I drink too much but not that much!*

He reached the office, entered but saw no one. Zack hesitated, then went to his desk and clicked on his computer. He found the file he compiled on Donald Fairfax and read it.

No matter how many times he went over it, nothing changed: all the evidence said Fairfax killed his wife. *So if he didn't do it, what did I miss? The Mistress. Was it her, or was he with her? If he was with her, then who killed Donald's wife?*

Zack found the pictures Julie showed him before of Rosler, Fairfax, Polzinski, and Pantalini in college. There she was: the slender, sleek, dark-haired beauty that married Rosler. But with Donald Fairfax's arm around her waist and her head resting on Donald's shoulder while Rosler looked a different direction oblivious to the obvious affection between the two beside him.

"Hey, when did you get here?" The familiar voice of Michelle called out as she stuck her head inside his office.

"A few minutes ago. Where is everyone?"

Michelle shrugged. "Working I assume," she said. "You're staring intently at your computer. Should I be worried?"

"Yes," he said and stood from the desk. "Any luck on finding Meg Chatwell?"

"No. You'll want to see what else I've found though."

Zack looked at the time. He exhaled. "Ok. What?"

* * * * * *

Zack hung up the phone. The sun had passed his window and the day vanished in front of him. Where the afternoon went, he wasn't sure. The information Michelle uncovered was not a surprise but was both disheartening and enlightening. He tried to explain to Michelle which took a lot of time for her to only say, "Barnes is going to be pissed at you."

That didn't help, but the pieces started to fall together. The most significant part, however, Zack needed to find. That was Meg Chatwell. He stared at the sheet of information Michelle garnered on Meg. He wasn't traveling to Wisconsin. That left the winery in St. Michael's.

"Hey," Michelle said from the doorway. "I'm heading home. You need anything else?"

"Did you hear from Julie today?"

"No. Was I supposed to?"

Zack frowned. "No. See you tomorrow." Michelle left, and he logged off his computer.

There is no way she can be mad at me for hanging up last night. And my phone works so I know she hasn't tried to call or text. No messages on my

190

computer either so why the hell is she avoiding me? Nothing happened. Get it out of your mind, Zack!

Zack locked up the office and stood in the square enjoying the quality of the air. It smelled fresh of the ocean not far away. The temperature was comfortable, and the humidity wasn't high. A perfect night for a stroll.

Not wanting to cook, Zack headed to the pub he liked with the thought of a simple dinner of crab cakes and wine and would then head home and rest. His mind settled into a happy place: he was sitting on a beach watching birds fly past. Julie was beside him taking in the sun holding his hand in a state of bliss. *Our honeymoon. St. Lucia, the white beaches of Florida, Hawaii, or a resort in Mexico?*

Zack walked down a street, his mind elsewhere but pseudo-aware of the few people he encountered on the streets. *No threats here. I don't want to go to Mexico. Probably can talk her out of that one. Hawaii would be beautiful, but that is forever on a plane from here and likely not cheap in first class, which leaves St. Lucia or the Gulf. Only going to honeymoon once. I say St. Lucia.*

Happy in his decision, Zack stepped off a curb to cross the street. The lighting was dim as the sunset settled into the evening. *I'll run it past Jules tonight.*

He heard a car accelerate. Zack turned his head.

The Taurus crossed the center line and swerved at him. Zack leaped onto the hood of a parked car; the vehicle sideswiped it, Zack bounced off the hit parked car and slammed into the sidewalk on the other side. The car sped to the end of the street and spun around.

The thump on the ground jarred him; pain surged through him, and he froze. His mind ordered him to get up. He knew he couldn't stay there.

The Taurus waited for him to move and accelerated. Zack stayed on the sidewalk until the car sped over the curb and charged towards Zack.

He waited and at the last moment jumped onto the parked car and rolled over the hood. He hit the street again with a thud. The vehicle broke hard and spun onto the road. Its tires squealed. Zack eyed the Taurus as it accelerated again. Zack couldn't run away, and there was no place to hide. He grabbed his Sig, but it was too late. Zack dove onto the hood of the parked car. The Taurus slammed into it and knocked Zack off the vehicle. He flew across the sidewalk and slammed into a fence. He hit the concrete hard.

The car spun and squealed and sped down the street again. Zack went to the car. His ribs ached; he felt the stitches rip. His body defied what Zack felt. The car charged, he pointed his Sig but then gunfire rang out, and bullets tore up the car.

Gunfire ripped through the air and glass shattered. Zack dove to the ground. Broken pieces of glass fell on him. The car sped down the street and turned the corner.

The car disappeared. Winded, sweating, bleeding, and anxious, he waited. Zack looked around, but no one saw. Nothing but dark windows and shadows. He felt his hands shake as his heart beat out of his chest. The dark alleys and walkways between buildings seemed threats. He took a deep breath and exhaled slowly.

His cell phone rang. Zack couldn't read the number on the broken face nor could he see the green slide button. He touched it several times where he thought the answer key should have been and it stopped ringing.

"Stack here."

"Hey, it's me," said the female voice.

"Ok." He paused. "Me who?"

The female laughed. "Stefani," she said. "What are you doing?"

"Oh, you know, the usual," he walked along the sidewalk cautious and aware. "Just staying alive."

"I have some news for you."

Zack looked at the sunset. Dark purple hues of the clouds hid the sun on the horizon which made it darker with each passing moment. "I'd say shoot, but that isn't appropriate right now."

"You ok?"

"Just peachy." *If peaches ever get run down and shot at.* "I'm heading to dinner. I'll be at the Abbey Burger Bistro in about fifteen. Meet me there if you want to talk." He hung up. He looked at the phone. *At least my watch isn't broke.*

CHAPTER 35

Zack limped into the burger bistro, saw Stef smile at him from a booth and hid his pain to get to it. He sat down.

"You're late."

Zack took a deep breath. "I'm pacing myself."

She eyed him closely. "You look terrible."

He looked at her and hesitated. "I actually don't have a comeback for that."

Zack leaned back as a waiter came to the table, did his spiel and asked if they wanted a drink. Zack ordered a Coors Light. She ordered a vodka and club soda.

Stefani cocked her head, was about to say something then closed her mouth. "I'm worried about you. Your clothes are ripped, you've been sweating, you look frazzled as hell, and you're bleeding again. You're hiding something from me."

"Am I?" He wiped his face with a napkin. "You have some news for me?"

She stared at him; an expectant look on her face.

"Just one of those days," he said.

She frowned, discouraged, and handed Zack two pieces of paper. Zack looked at the sheets. Stefani was silent, and the waiter brought the drinks.

"Are you ready to order?" The waiter asked.

Stefani's big brown eyes looked at Zack with a blank help-me-out look.

He smiled. Stef had her hair pulled back in a pony-tail with the tail coming out the back of a Baltimore Ravens cap. "Are you a chicken or beef person?"

"Chicken," she smiled. "But I can adapt. You know, that whole when in Rome thing."

He nodded. "Well, we're in Baltimore, not Rome. She'll have the chicken burger, and I'll have Harry's Bistro Burger. And don't let the bottom of these glasses get dry," he pointed at the drinks.

The waiter left. "Will I like it?"

"Who cares? Like you said: when in Rome." Zack looked back at the paper. "What am I looking at here? I missed this class in basic training."

"Your blood tests."

"Tests?"

"Yeah." She leaned forward. "The one in your right hand is the one that says your blood alcohol content is .26%. The one on the left says it's 0."

"Ok, so why two tests? I know I wasn't drinking."

"That's just it; there weren't two tests. Zack, look at the time stamps."

Zack looked then looked back at Stefani.

"This one," she grabbed the left, "I took when you arrived. See my initials? This one," the one in Zack's right hand, "was stamped two hours later. See any difference in the initials?"

"They're different."

"That's because someone forged them. And the second test isn't your blood. It's fake."

Zack looked at Stefani, her brown eyes full of excitement.

"Someone snuck in and planted this test to make it look like you were drunk. The police wanted you arrested."

I know.

"Zack, who can do that? Who can make that happen? We have protocols and security locks and everything. Joe Schmoe off the street can't walk into our lab and switch blood samples."

"How did you figure it out?"

"The same tech was on duty today during that day." She shivered. "I can be persuasive, and he wants to go out with me."

Zack smiled. "You promised him a date to get the truth?"

"Worse. I need a shower by the way."

Zack scrunched his face. "Gross. But thank you."

"Yeah. You owe me. If the police got this report, you'd be in jail right now."

I wonder if being in jail would be safer?

"Anyway, he told me two guys came in, flashed badges and handed him a vial of blood and said it was yours. He was ordered to test them first and give the report directly to them. I beat them to it."

"I wonder what the guys looked like." *Schmidt and O'Malley perhaps? Or two of the thugs I capped the next night? That might explain why no one came back for the tests.*

"I didn't ask him. I was already ready to vomit. Scary if you ask me."

Zack nodded. "Thank you."

She shook her head. "I really need a shower. And a drink!" She made a face as if she were going to vomit. "Ok, back to business. So, how do we find the father?"

Zack finished his beer. "We visit the Wolf's Den. Not tonight though. I need another beer." He looked at his hand: full of blood. "And a Band-Aid."

CHAPTER 36

Another gray, overcast, dreary day. Zack and Stefani drove to West Friendship, an upscale neighborhood just outside of Baltimore. Even where the money lived, it was still gloomy, gray and overcast. Zack needed sunshine.

Zack stopped the car and stared at a house. "Nice house."

Stef smiled. "Yeah, that it is. Too far from downtown for me though."

Zack nodded. "I concur."

They walked across the grass, onto a sidewalk and turned onto a long walkway. Leaves swirled about their feet. They climbed four steps, and Zack pressed the doorbell alongside the large dark green entry door. Zack felt it: steel and thick decorated to look aesthetic but functional. Small thick windows about eye height arched in the middle of the door, and Zack saw a person walk towards the door through the windows.

He looked at Stefani. "You're a pretty good kisser, by the way."

She blushed. "You aren't too bad yourself."

Zack winked at her as he shut his jacket to hide the gun under his left arm.

The door opened, and a tall, slender dark-haired woman stood in the doorway wearing black yoga pants with a thick knit gray baggy turtleneck sweater that went below her buttocks. Sleek was the first word that came to Zack's head.

"Mrs. Rosler?"

She feigned a smile. "We can dispense with the introductions. You're late."

Stefani looked at Zack. "Was she expecting you?"

"Yes," Zack responded quickly. "Three years ago."

The woman eyed him up and down and crossed her arms. Even her hands and fingers were sleek. She had an attractive yet intimidating look about her. She wore her hair pulled back tight, and it tightened her face. He suspected with her hair down she would be more attractive and sexier. But she needed to be professional and fearsome in her world. Her look succeeded.

"Better late than never," she said in her sultry, deep voice. "Won't you come in?"

They sat in the living room in a triangle. Mrs. Rosler perched on the edge of her chair directly across from Zack and Stefani sat to Zack's left. Mrs. Rosler stared at Zack and almost ignored Stefani.

"I apologize for popping in like this, but somehow I felt safer without announcing my plans over a phone," he said. *And I know we weren't followed here. I couldn't even retrace the route I took here. Should be safe.*

She almost broke a smile.

"Well, Erin, can I call you Erin?"

She did smile this time. "You may. Likewise, I'll call you Zack. That is your name isn't it?"

"Today it is," he quipped.

"What happened to you?" Erin asked. "You look terrible."

"I get that a lot lately."

"I'm sorry," she said.

"Not as much as the person responsible for this is going to be," he said. "But, that is why I'm here."

She took a deep breath. "And what does that have to do with me?"

"You've called me three times in the last few days."

Erin Rosler let out a long exhale. "I'm listening."

"I want answers. I'm tired and sore and can't even enjoy the football season because of this," Zack tried to joke. Stefani smiled, but Erin did not.

"I hate football. It's barbaric," Erin finally said.

Zack shrugged. "That's why it's so popular. Not difficult to understand." Still no smile. "I'm more of a baseball fan, though."

"Really? What team do you root for?"

"The Cubs."

She nodded her head. "So, you're a fan of special torture." Finally, she smiled. "At least the curse is over."

"Well, according to Chad and Jeremy they say that all good things will stand someday, and autumn leaves must fall," he said. Her expression didn't change. "It's a line from a song back in the '60s." Still no expression but he saw Stefani with a confused grin on her face. "I wouldn't have pegged you a baseball fan, but it makes sense now that I think about it," he shifted gears. They stared at each other. "Let me guess: you're a Yankees fan?"

She showed a hint of a smile. "Yes. How did you guess?"

"Intuition, I suppose," he said though it was a lie. He remembered that Fairfax had bought season tickets to the Yankees a year before Zack got hired by Fairfax's wife. His wife hated baseball she had told him and refused to go to any games, but he had two tickets.

"Can I get you a drink?"

"Yes, you can."

Erin looked at Stefani and back to Zack. "Can your babysitter have a drink, too?"

"Oh, no," Zack jumped in. "It's too early for her. I'll have hers, too." He smiled at Stefani.

Erin left the room and returned with three drinks. She handed Stefani one. "I take it he's a smartass. I was kidding about the babysitter remark. I am curious why you are here with him, though?"

"Oh no, he really needs a babysitter. But drinking makes him more tolerable," Stefani said and took the drink. She stuck her tongue out at Zack.

Erin sat on the chair. "You are terrible at checking your messages."

"You told me already. What else do you want to tell me?"

"What else do you want to know?"

Zack leaned forward in his seat. "Why didn't you come forward and say you were with Fairfax the day he allegedly killed his wife? I mean, I understand why he never gave up you: he was protecting you. But your husband knew. So why not say something and keep Donald out of jail?"

She crossed her long shapely legs, legs of an athlete: curvy and tight. She kept herself in top physical form so that her body and mind would be stronger for her job and her marriage. "As I said, you should have been here three years ago."

* * *   * * *

"We had no choice," Erin explained as she looked out a kitchen window holding a steaming cup of coffee. Stefani cradled it in both of her hands, and Zack wondered yet again why did everyone love coffee? He preferred the Mimosa's, but that had disappeared. He declined coffee.

"We didn't know he was going to kill Donald's wife. I figured he'd divorce me or kill Donald. We were shocked when we found out about it. Terrified and horrified all at once. I knew Michael was capable of bad things, but I never suspected he'd have Donald's wife mutilated like that," she explained.

"And you know it wasn't Donald?"

She scoffed. "Of course, I know." She turned to look at Zack. "You just made it sound like you knew for sure he and I were together."

"I guessed."

"Good guess, Zack. He and I were together in the uptown Marriott that afternoon."

"Can you prove that?"

"Of course, I can. I have a recorded voicemail, texts and best of all video footage of Donald and me together in the elevator when we arrived and four hours later when we left and from the hallway entering and leaving our room. It's an hour drive to that hotel from the office, a half hour from his house to the office and he stopped at the office on the way to the hotel. His code scan showed he was there thirty minutes and add another hour to get back to his house from the hotel which means he was gone over seven hours that day. You saw the file. The suspected time of death is between eleven and noon. He left his house at eight thirty." Zack found the dead body at twelve thirty.

She sipped her coffee and leaned against the counter. Stefani sat silent and watched Zack figure things out.

"And you're sure Donald had nothing to do with hiring the killer? I mean you must watch TV. Killing the spouse to be with the lover is the oldest cliché in the book."

"Do you want to see the divorce papers? His wife was being served that day. What a coincidence, huh?" Erin shook her head. "He had nothing to do with it just like I'm certain he had nothing to do with the attempts on your life."

"Erin," Stefani spoke, "you have all this evidence. How did you get it? How did the cops not get it? Why didn't you use it to get your lover free?"

Erin looked at Zack. "I think you know, don't you?"

Zack processed and nodded. He looked at Stef. "She's smart and resourceful and has money, that's how she got the information. As for the cops, I have a feeling I know why they didn't bother looking. She didn't use it because it would have ruined her, too," Zack said looking right into Erin's green eyes. "When did your husband find out?"

"I wasn't sure he knew until he killed Donald's wife," Erin said.

"And the embezzling? We found that at least three million had vanished from Valentino Industries. What happened to that? Why didn't Rosler want that back?"

"Zack Stack, if that is your name," Erin said which made Stefani look confused at Zack, "you need to learn that if you are playing a game of life or death, you better hold something on your opponent."

Jesus Christ. Everybody has something on someone. And they all know about me.

Zack nodded. "I get it. So, you and Donald figured you'd get caught. But instead of stopping like most people would have, knowing your husband is a monster, you two found dirt on him and threatened to use it if he hurt either of you. Is that it?"

"Yes."

Zack waited, but she said nothing. Disgusted, Zack said, "well? Are you going to tell me what you have on the Dark Lord of the Underworld?"

Erin smiled. "Michael decided he wanted to run for Senate. But there was a problem."

"No one liked him?" Zack injected.

Erin snorted. "Actually, yes. No donors would back him. He needed a large sum of cash to get his campaign off the ground. Even that spineless weasel Pantalini couldn't help him with that. Michael needed about seven million to get the party to put his name on the ballot. He didn't have it. Mommy and Daddy wouldn't give it to him. The only way to get it was to embezzle. Donald and I knew. Make sense?"

Zack nodded. "So, after Rosler killed Fairfax's wife, he threatened the two of you. But you and Donald turned around and told him that if either of you is hurt, or if he goes after the nest egg I'm assuming you and Donald will live on after I get him out of jail and you disappear, that you'll turn over the proof that he embezzled from his own company. He'd end up in jail."

"Correct."

"And in return, Rosler said if you try to get Fairfax off the murder charge, he'll tie you to the embezzling, and you'd end up in jail. Which also would have damaged his image of being the perfect husband family man, right? So you get to play wife while he plays husband meanwhile he continues to bang any college girl that will say yes and keeps a close eye on you to keep you under wraps. So far so good?"

"I'm impressed."

Zack nodded. "You were dating Donald in college. How did Rosler get you away then?"

"You'll have to ask Donald that. I don't know the whole story. I know Michael tricked Donald into something bad and extorted him to get me. I was young, naïve, and heartbroken. And," she lowered her gaze to the floor, "no one says no to Michael Rosler."

Zack walked to the window and stood next to Erin. "And now you and Donald have decided to use me to ruin his presidential run and get Donald out of jail."

"That's part of it."

"There's more?"

"Well, Mr. Stack, you have a fascinating past, don't you?" Erin stared into his eyes. "You can't use the embezzling information." She looked at Stefani. "Nor can your babysitter."

Zack knew what she meant. *Subtle. Include me on the crime and if I talk, ruin me.*

"And I'm supposed to trust your word that all this goes away as soon as Donald is out of prison and Rosler ruined?"

"Yes."

Zack shook his head and looked at Stefani who still had a confused look on her face. "Why didn't Donald call me earlier? I would have helped without all this cloak and dagger bullshit."

"We needed leverage. And after we got it, Donald did call. You don't open your mail or listen to your voicemails, and you've been in Europe for several weeks."

"You have all the information needed to get Donald free. Why do you need me?"

Erin smiled at him. "Darling, think about it."

Zack leaned on the counter and rubbed his forehead. "Because you'd end up in jail for obstructing justice among other charges." He faced Erin. "And with knowing my past," Zack stopped. "How many laws am I supposed to break?" *I said myself the key to breaking the law is to do it for the right reasons.*

Erin smiled. "It's up to you. How much do you love the people around you?"

Zack was furious with himself. He was caught again. He clenched his fists and felt the gentle touch of Stefani's hand on his back.

"I am sorry." Erin touched Zack's arm. "There is no other way. I'll give you all the information you need to get Donald out. You will hide who it came from so I won't be in danger. Michael won't know about Donald's release until after we disappear."

Zack let out a long, slow breath. "Well, that's a good plan. Except they'll see your face in the video. The police will want to know why you didn't come forward. That's obstruction, sweetheart." Zack hoped this was the hole in the plan.

Erin rubbed his forearm, then leaned back and crossed her arms. "Dear, I've thought of that, too. I distorted my face on the video. All they'll see is Donald clearly with another woman at the precise time his wife was murdered."

Zack chuckled. "You aren't stupid. It looks like I am your pawn. What do you have?"

Erin put her hand on his arm again. "I'm sorry it has to be this way. We just needed you to have the proper incentive."

Incentive? That's a joke. It's extortion. "I suppose you're right about the proper incentive."

"I'm sorry. Donald and I needed to be sure you'd do your job this time."

Zack stood straight and faced Erin Rosler. "You know Linda Polzinski was killed, don't you?"

"Of course she was. She agreed to talk to you. And if they find out I'm talking to you, they'll kill me, too. That's why you need to hurry. And to keep this meeting a secret."

Zack felt worse. "You know about Meg Chatwell. How does she fit into all of this?"

"Find her. That will make it all clear. Linda Polzinski was spirited in college. She loved to protest, to fight unjust causes, to put together rallies and groups to fight against whatever she deemed evil. It all started there. She started it, and Sam helped the group mature. Somehow, someone in the group messed up, and Michael found out about it. That was six years ago. I don't need to tell you about the eight girls who died since then. Your fiancé did a lovely piece on it. She was close to tying all the girls to Michael then. She stopped too soon. That's why Michael picked your fiancé to write his book." Erin grabbed Zack's hands with hers. "And sweetheart, as bad as I feel for what Donald convinced me to do to you, that's not as bad as what Michael will do. You need to get to the bottom of this now. Find Meg Chatwell."

Zack's lungs felt light, his stomach empty; he felt guilty but didn't know why. Despite the cool, dry touch of Erin's hands, his hands sweated heavily and shook. She squeezed.

"The Presidency is nothing more than a throne for Michael. He is purchasing it. And once he gets it, he won't relinquish it. You have to stop him, and you know exactly how to do it."

Zack's mind raced. "How?"

She grabbed his hand then motioned her head. "Follow me," she said as she pulled him from the room. "You're about to earn your money."

Stefani remained in the kitchen confused about everything she had just heard. She waited for several minutes before Zack returned behind Erin Rosler. He carried a shoebox. They both looked at Stefani until Erin smiled and held out her hand.

"It has been nice meeting you," Erin said to Stefani. "You should be going now."

Zack motioned his head for Stefani to head for the door. Erin turned to Zack, kissed him on the lips, and held his arms. "Good luck."

Zack stared at Erin a moment longer, then he and Stefani left the house. Zack was silent on the ride away. Stefani finally had enough of the silence. She needed answers.

"She made two references to your name. What did she mean by that?"

Zack closed the lid on the shoebox of information. "It's complicated."

"I like complicated things. What is it? Is your name not Zack?"

Zack exhaled. "I'll tell you what, Stef, when this is all over if you still want to know and I'm still capable of telling you, I'll fill you in."

"On what? It sounds very cloak and dagger. Like secret identities and double agent stuff," she joked. She looked briefly at Zack and noticed his expression didn't change. "Should I be worried?"

"Probably." He frowned. "Can we talk about it later?"

Stefani nodded. She lost to his stubbornness before. "Ok. So, what now? What are you going to do with that stuff?"

"Hopefully use it to dig out of a deep, deep hole."

CHAPTER 37

The two hours plus ride on his motorcycle didn't bother Zack early that morning.

With his binoculars and spotting scope safely in the storage compartments, a day in the field clearing his mind birding was precisely what the doctor ordered. And Prime Hook National Wildlife Refuge in Delaware along the coast during fall migration was as good a spot as any.

Not hearing from Julie wore on his nerves. Zack's mind didn't slow down, and the possibilities no matter how hard he fought them raced across like a Nascar race: round and round repeat and repeat. Getting out of his apartment, away from Stefani and the office and work, was necessary. Necessary for his mental health, and for his physical health.

Birding on a motorcycle was not as easy as from a car, but Zack had done it before and figured it out. So, he made his way around the refuge, hiking, sitting, standing and peering through his spotting scope, staring through his binoculars at migrating hawks overhead, studying flocks of geese in the salt marshes and identifying various shorebirds about the marshes and beaches. And his mind cleared.

He picked a good day, and the birds were in full force. The storms passing through stalled the migration but packed the birds tight and kept Zack busy with the different flocks of birds in the trees, shrubs, beaches, marshes, waterways, and sky. His new cell phone remained quiet.

Zack only wanted to hear from Julie. They hadn't exchanged as much as a message since the unscheduled visitor to her hotel room the other night. It did upset him. Zack heard Stefani's voice telling him how stubborn he was and how he needed to talk to Julie about it. *Thinking about it will only make it worse. You know she isn't doing anything with that guy, so why worry about it and get all upset about it?*

A small flock of American Oystercatchers flew past followed by a noisy incoming flock of Snow Geese. Meanwhile, a kettle of hawks soared above interested only in the updrafts as they headed south. This was when he wished he had a birding partner. One pair of eyes couldn't keep up with all the activity.

Zack looked at the time. Still plenty of daylight. He saw a distant flock of shorebirds land. He packed up his scope and headed that direction.

* * *   * * *

By mid-day, the air had changed, and yet another fall storm approached. Clouds blocked the sun, and the winds switched. The east wind into Zack's face made his eyes water as he stared over the ocean to view whatever birds he could see. As sore as he was, the day invigorated him.

His cell phone rang. It was Stefani worried about where he was. Easy phone call. Just stay put and relax. Michelle called wondering where he was a few minutes later. Zack said he was out, but he was safe.

A dark bird flew barely above the crests of the waves a couple hundred yards from shore. Zack knew loon species and quickly caught the bird in the view of his scope. *Red-throated Loon! Awesome!* Zack smiled and switched to his binoculars to scan the horizon then saw a Northern Gannet. *This is shaping up to be a great birding day!*

His phone rang again. It was Andre. "Hey, what's up?"

"You man," Dre said. "Where the hell are you?"

"Birding," Zack said. Andre was silent. "Don't worry. I didn't leave the reservation."

"I'm getting swamped with calls. Even Darnell is worried. You sure you're alright?"

"Yeah, I'm fine," Zack said. "Birds are great today."

"One of these days I should tag along to see what you see out there," Andre said.

"As soon as I get to taste your mom's fried chicken. Look, I'm overnighting out here," Zack said but was specific to not say where. "I'm following a gut instinct. Maybe help wrap this up quicker," he said.

"You're ambiguous. Any reason why?"

"Yeah, we've been one step behind the whole time and on the radar of whoever is behind all of this. I want to get ahead for a change."

"I hear ya," Andre said. "I would still prefer to know where you're at and what you're up to."

"Let me put it this way, I'm not going to whine about it, but I can taste this thing coming to a head soon." Zack smiled. If anyone could figure out Zack's intentions from that sentence, Andre could. "By the way, Rosler insisted Jules call him Michael like he's some sort of Saint. Pisses me off. Anyway, I'll see you at about eleven tomorrow. You know where." Zack hung up.

Five hours later, he left the national wildlife refuge, rode south, and checked into a hotel called the Dogfish Inn. He and Julie stayed there before and loved it. Zack still hadn't heard from Julie. *Wrap this up, and I'm flying to Iowa for her. This is ridiculous.*

Zack had dinner, enjoyed several samples of the craft beers, settled on one he really liked, went back to his room and sent an email to Jules. There was nothing more he could do that night. Sleep seemed a good idea.

* * * * * *

The next morning, Zack rode his motorcycle into the small parking lot and looked at the white building with blue trim. The shiplap style gave it a very East-coast coastal vibe. Three other cars already parked in the lot and though it was just eleven in the morning, the exact time the place opened, people lined up outside the tasting room entrance.

Zack locked his bike, attached the helmet to the bike and stretched. He looked at his watch and walked inside. Zack stepped inside and paused. The long narrow well-lit room already had a couple tasting different wines. Zack smiled as they looked at him and walked to the solid wood bar that was a wide plank of dark stained wood set atop oak barrels.

Zack stood away from the couple as a tall, blonde-haired female on the other side of the bar approached him.

"Good day, sir, welcome to the St. Michael's Winery. Are you here for tasting?"

Zack smiled and nodded. "Yes, I would love to try your reds."

"They're delicious," she said. "Here is our list and each sample is one dollar. What would you like to start with?"

Zack opened his wallet and slid a twenty-dollar bill on the bar. "The Island Beauty Reserve," Zack said.

The cute girl smiled, poured a little into a glass and put it on the bar in front of Zack. She explained the origin of the grapes and how it got its flavor. Zack let it sit a moment and stared into the large blue eyes of the girl as she talked. She wore a blue baseball cap with the winery logo on it and a green Get Wobbly tee shirt untucked that flowed over the waistline of a pair of tight designer blue jeans. She stood six-feet tall, and Zack guessed she was around 21 years old.

He lifted the glass, swirled it, put it to his nose and sniffed. He looked back at the girl. "I was also hoping you could provide me with some information," he said. He sipped the wine, let it linger in his mouth, swallowed and nodded. "I'm new around here."

She smiled. "How was the wine?"

"Very good."

"What else would you like to try?"

"Just give me a glass of the Reserve," Zack said. She filled the glass.

"What can I help you with?"

Zack reached inside his coat pocket and removed a photograph. He placed it on the bar and slid it forward. "I'm looking for her."

The girl's smile disappeared. The color in her face evaporated, and her hands on the bar clenched as she hid the tremble of fear in her body. Her eyes slowly lifted from the picture to Zack.

"It's ok," Zack said. "I'm the good guys," he said. The couple at the other end of the bar looked down at the girl, anxious for another sample. Zack pointed at the money in front of him. "Go get them their samples and take it out of this. I'll wait."

The girl, a petrified look on her face, barely nodded and moved down the bar to the other couple. She served the couple who finished their samples and left to a different area of the winery. The girl returned to Zack.

"How did you find me?"

"Well, Meg, or do you prefer Mary?"

"Either is fine."

"I likely wouldn't have except you left a check stub in your desk. Pretty smart having your credit card tracked to Wisconsin. You never left Maryland, did you?"

She frowned. "No. A friend of mine took it. I mapped out where for her to go and where to use it and as soon as she got to Wisconsin, she cut it up and threw it out." Meg Chatwell looked at Zack. "Who are you?"

"My name is Zack. I was hired to find out what really happened to Ashley. I'm not here to hurt you," he said. "I'm here to protect you. You're in danger. Do you know that?"

"I do. Claire said you're one of the good guys and that I can trust you."

Zack nodded. "You can, but look, Meg, before you start thinking I'm some super sleuth or anything like that, let me tell you I'm not. So if I found you, it's safe to assume the bad guys will, too."

Tears filled Meg's eyes. She knew she was trapped. "Claire said two guys stopped at my dorm last night. They searched my room, and they weren't police. They said they were feds and investigating the assassination attempt of Rosler. She told me as soon as they left."

Zack drank the wine. "Did she call you?"

"Yes. I'm staying at a friend's house. She called there. I got rid of my cell phone."

They likely traced Claire's call. Where are you, Andre? This would be an excellent time to show up. "Has she called here before?"

"No."

Zack finished his wine. "Meg, I don't want to alarm you, but we need to leave here now and get you someplace safe."

"There is no place safe from them," she said. "You don't know what you're up against."

"I've heard that before." He grabbed her arm and lead her around the bar. "I'll take my chances. Come on. We're leaving."

On the way outside, Zack sent a text and his phone immediately rang. Zack answered. He listened for a minute and then hung up. Zack kept a firm grasp on Meg's arm.

"Who was that?"

Zack looked around. He saw his motorcycle but then saw a black Taurus down the road. "Let's go for a walk. And in the meantime, you're going to tell me everything you know."

CHAPTER 38

They reached the end of the street and after a few turns crossed a nature trail. Zack looked around but still saw nothing. "Let's walk on this," he said. A place called Waterfront Park was in front of them, but it was too open. *Perfect for a sniper. Keep walking.*

They walked down the trail and over a bridge. "Talk to me and keep close."

"Ash, Hannah, Claire, myself and a few others along with Sam are part of a secret group. Sam's wife started it a long time ago when she went to college. In short, we believe it's up to the people to keep the politicians honest, and the way to do that is to expose what they do behind the scenes. If people really knew," Meg shook her head, "we could change the world for the better."

"Ok but save the platitudes and ideology for another time. Tell me what you know right now."

"Six other girls in the last eight years have been killed too. The reports made them look like accidents, but they weren't," Meg said.

Zack nodded. "I know. Can you prove it?"

"They were killed because they all had affairs with Senator Rosler and he made sure they would never talk," she said.

Zack sighed. "I can guess that. But I need proof. The only way to stop all of this is to prove it. Understand?"

Meg stared at Zack. "I got it. I have everything you need." She put her hands on her hips. "We have Rosler on tape promising favors for his donors, discussing gerrymandering and voter suppression, eliminating polling sites, creating discriminatory voter identification laws. We have it all." Meg said as they walked again and crossed over a walking bridge.

"Sam hated Rosler," she went on. "Sam knew what they were up to and it is all about maintaining power and suppressing the voters' voices. They don't want us to vote. They want us to follow blindly," she said. "We have the corrupt bastards on tape discussing it. We knew it was just a matter of time. Manipulating information out of him was easy. He will do anything to get in a girl's pants. Disgusting pig. Makes me want to puke."

And right now the pig is with my fiancé! I have to get Meg safe and then get to Iowa.

"How did he find out about your group?"

"We don't know. I know Ash didn't tell him anything. Neither did Hannah. Maybe he found out from one of the earlier girls, or maybe from Sam. I just don't know. But I know they are after me now."

"And me, too," Zack said. "I don't look like this because I choose to." He pointed to the bruising and cuts on his face.

Meg stopped and stared at Zack. "Then stop it. We have Rosler on tape bribing judges, paying off judges, officials, and cops. We have emails from private servers promising laws that directly aid large donors. We have them discussing developing new voting machines they can hack to make sure they win the election. His own company was developing the voting machines. Rosler was using technology from his company to design voting machines his party could hack, and no one would know it. We found out and have it on tape."

Zack looked around. Still no sign of Dre. "Where do you have it?"

"It's hidden," Meg said.

"What about the day Sam and Hannah were killed? Do you have any information on that day?"

"Enough. Initially, it was only supposed to be a botched assassination attempt to boost Rosler's name across the country. They must have caught Hannah and connected her to Sam. I don't know how, but by the time Claire and

I figured it out, it was too late. They don't know that Claire is involved. That was part of the plan all along. One of us would never get mentioned over the phone, via text, email, at a meeting, anything. We planned it so one of us would be alive with all the information in case Rosler found out. So far," she looked at Zack with tears in her eyes, "it's worked."

"What about the first six girls? Why were they killed?"

"Three were pregnant. You can't have an anti-abortion candidate paying for abortions, can you?"

Zack shook his head at the irony. *Doesn't anyone use birth control anymore? Or is that against his fake moral code?* "And the other three?"

"He gets tired of them," Meg said. "Rosler always wants the new shiny object. Pigs like him always do. But when you're planning on ruling the world, you can't be married and have a mistress half your age telling everyone she slept with you. When you're rich like him, people disappear or die, and no one asks questions."

A girl's voice called out. Zack looked and saw a familiar girl run towards them.

Oh no. Not Claire. I don't need this right now. Andre, where, in the name of a flying frog, are you?

"There's Claire," Meg said but realized Zack knew that. "We're leaving town. We have to go hide," she said.

"I know. I'm already on that. Keep walking," Zack said as he looked around. No signs of anyone else. The cloudy, gray day kept many of the visitors away and the locals inside. That worked both ways, Zack realized. Claire finally caught up to them, but Meg kept speaking.

"We have the tests to prove he was the father for Brittany and Annika, two of the first killed and a conversation where he ordered Lisa Dutton killed, in his words, 'just like we did the other one.' We have enough to prove he killed the others." Claire heard enough to stand united with Meg, both looked fierce and determined to end the terror of Michael Rosler.

Zack felt it. *The swamp has suddenly deepened. This is bad, Zack.* Eight girls, a state senator, and his wife already lost their lives. "Why did you keep going if you knew other girls were killed?" He looked at Claire. "You told me your dad thought the college was cursed, you found out why the other girls died, but you still got involved with this whole thing?"

"You were in the Marines, weren't you?" Claire said. Zack nodded. "You stood for something. So are we."

Zack understood. *If you believe that firmly, some things are worth dying for.* "That's fine and dandy, Claire, but people are dying. Do you get that?"

"Yeah, people have died at the hands of Michael Rosler, and he's set to become the most powerful man in the world. How many more will die because of him? One death is too many, and that piece of garbage is responsible for eight deaths that we know of. He has to be stopped."

Zack shook his head. "And you two think you're going to get in your car and disappear?" The two girls looked at each other as if that plan would work. "Not today, girls. You're coming with me instead. Stay close."

CHAPTER 39

A man hid in the forest behind a knoll and watched Stack and the girl. The phone call from the other girl Claire led them right to St. Michael's. The detective got there first, but now, all the loose ends walked in a tight bunch in the middle of a remote, quiet, wooded part of the remote village. Thanks to the wet and gloomy fall weather, the town was quiet. Perfect.

This was redemption day. Kilgas will be pleased. The man lined up his rifle. Meg Chatwell's head squarely in the site. He smiled and let out a long, slow, calming breath.

The man felt the barrel of a .45 press against the back of his head.

*** ***

"Uh-uh, don't do it," Andre said. He pressed the handgun harder.

The man looked back at Andre.

"Take your hand off that trigger. You don't want to die today." Andre slid his hand along the man's belt and removed the Glock pistol. Andre pressed the gun harder to the man's head. "I'm not messing around."

The man held both hands to his side while he lied flat on his stomach. "You have no idea what you're up against."

"I know enough," Andre said. "Now where's your partner?"

Andre saw Zack and the two girls through the trees ahead. The man had a perfect shot. No one was around. The rain was imminent. "Come on, where is he? I'm running out of patience."

Andre heard a twig snap behind him. A barrel of a gun hit his back. "I'm right behind you ready to blow your head off if you don't drop your gun," the man behind Andre said. "I'm not messing around either."

Andre stood straight slowly and closed his eyes. The plan worked right up until they pulled a split-and-juke on him. *Shit. How do I get out of this?* The man on the ground had his Glock back and readied the rifle again. Andre put his hands out to his sides and set down his gun. *Zack needs a warning.*

"ZACK! RUN! RUN!" Andre yelled and spun towards the man behind him.

Zack didn't hesitate. He heard the shots. Zack grabbed Meg, spun her away from the gunmen and dove at Claire. Claire screamed. Zack reached Claire right as a bullet ripped through Claire's back and exited through Zack's arm. Another round slammed into Zack. They hit the ground. The girls were silent.

The second man looked at Zack long enough for Andre to catch him in the midsection with a kick, but the man fired his gun. The bullet grazed Andre's upper shoulder. Andre grabbed the wrist with the pistol and spun it away from himself, but it shot again towards the ground. The bullet hit the shooter on the ground. Andre heard the rifle pop three times. Andre raised the gun as high as he could with the man still holding onto it and kneed him in the crotch. Andre spun and flipped the man over his back and slammed him to the ground. The man yelled; his fingers broke as he twisted in the air, the gun ripped out of his hand.

The rifle guy spun to shoot Andre, but the gun from his partner already pointed at his head. The sound of a bullet fired from the gun was the last thing the man heard.

Dre looked back at thug number two but didn't fire. Dre pointed the gun at him. "Don't move." Andre looked back at Zack and the girls. No movement and a quick scan of the area resulted empty: no other person was around. *No witnesses.*

"What are you going to do now?" The unarmed man said. "Looks like they are dead."

"Start talking. Who the hell are you guys?"

The man laughed. "There's nothing to say to you."

Andre looked out at his partner. The man made a move for a hidden gun. Andre squeezed the trigger. The bullet entered in the middle of the man's forehead and left his brains scattered in the forest behind him. Andre turned to Zack and ran out to the group.

"Zack! Zack!" Andre reached him and knelt beside Zack. He rolled Zack off Meg and saw Claire beside them, her eyes wide open and lifeless. Dead. "Zack!"

Zack grumbled as he opened his eyes and fell to his back, horrific pain throughout his body. He groaned.

"You OK?"

"No, I'm not alright," Zack answered. "Tell me that mother..."

Andre smiled. "Watch your language, Zack."

"Tell me you killed them and if you didn't, drag me over there so I can put a bullet in their skulls."

"Sorry. Couldn't wait for you. Brains are all over the place. You're bleeding dude," Andre noticed.

"Yeah, that happens when you get shot." Zack tried to sit up. "What happened?"

"They did a split-and-juke on me. I never saw them split. Sorry man. Once they got to the trail, I lost them for a moment. Long enough for them to find me after them." Andre let out a deep sigh. "I'm sorry. This one's on me. Damnit!"

"No, it's not. It's on me," Zack said. He looked at Meg who remained motionless on the ground.

"What do we do?"

Zack looked around. No one else had seen or heard. They could have disappeared. He looked back at the two girls. "We use this to our advantage." He found his cell phone with his right hand and dialed a number. "Go get the car and fast." Andre ran after the car as Zack waited for the other end to pick up.

"Stack, what now?"

"Ted," Zack said with heavy breath, "I need your help, and I need it fast."

"What is it?"

"Get to St. Michael's fast and on the way figure out how to make a person disappear."

* * *   * * *

217

Exhausted and sick of everything, Julie's mood hit bottom. Pantalini kept her involved with more than she felt was necessary, and she suspected that there was more to the dog and pony show. Julie told him she had everything she needed and just needed to be left alone so she could finish the book. At nine o'clock that night after not hearing from Zack, she got back to her room, leaned against the door and turned the deadbolt.

She planned to shower, forego eating and go straight to bed. Julie knew Zack was furious. She understood why. Letting Rosler into the room was a mistake. Next time, she would keep the lights out and pretend she isn't there. Until then, her priority was talking to Zack. Then all would be better.

She walked across her king suite, disrobed, and was in the shower in seconds. She didn't even wait for the stream to warm; the cold water didn't bother her and felt good. It heated quickly, and she turned the knob to get it as hot as she could stand it. She kept it that way for a few minutes and set the temperature back down to her comfort level. The steam billowed from the shower, and she smiled. The thought of Zack wrapping his arms around her in the shower warmed her more.

Zack will come to get me. I'll call him or Dre or Michelle or whoever I need to as soon as I'm out of the shower. He'll be here by morning. There is absolutely no reason for me to be here any longer.

She smiled as she washed her hair knowing that this was her last night in Iowa. Fifteen minutes later she exited the bathroom with a white towel wrapped in her hair and nothing else on until she found her pajamas and slid into those. She flopped on the bed, turned on the television to the movie channel Zack liked because there were no commercials. It drove her crazy how his habits were becoming hers. But, Julie realized, as she laid there watching a black and white movie, she didn't know the name, but she recognized Cary Grant in it and knew Zack probably loved that movie, that it was relaxing not being interrupted by commercials.

As soon as she grabbed the room's phone since her cell still didn't work, she heard persistent knocking on the door. She cringed and rolled her eyes. Julie knew it was Rosler. *He won't take no for an answer. I can't wait to talk to his wife!*

She went to the door and looked through the peephole. Rosler stood in the middle of the hall with two bottles and two glasses. "Who is it?"

"Oh, come on, Julie, you know who it is! Open up, I have something for you," Rosler replied sounding festive.

"Senator, it's late, I just want to go to sleep."

"Don't be a party pooper," he said. "Come on, open up. I brought us some wine and some news about the book."

Julie knew he wouldn't go away. She took a deep breath and grabbed her robe. Julie wore flannel pants and a baggy matching flannel top, but she still didn't want to be around him without extra protection. Julie unlocked the door. She only opened it a little and saw him smiling wide at her.

"Senator, it is late. Can't this wait until tomorrow?"

"We'll have no time together tomorrow I'm afraid," Rosler said as he walked inside past her and put the bottles of wine down on the table and began the opening process. "Has to be tonight. We have to celebrate."

She hid her disgust. "Celebrate what?"

"The book! Jerry tells me you have all you need, and you only need to finish it, so we set a release date earlier, and pre-sales are going through the roof."

"What? How could you do that so quickly?" She was confused. "I don't even have it done. Then it has to be proof-read, edited, the cover designed, sent to a printer and," she knew there was more, but it was overwhelming, "I don't even have it done yet. You don't even know what it says."

Rosler laughed as he poured his glass of red wine and then opened her bottle of white wine. "I know what it says. It's about me! I'm living what it says every day," he laughed. He filled her glass. "And besides," Rosler said softer as he brought the glass to her and stared into her eyes. "I trust you, Julie. As I've gotten to know you, I've realized that you are a special person and I can't wait to spend more time with you."

Julie smiled surprised. "Well, I don't see how that is going to happen. As soon as I finish the book, I'm done. I have another life I want to get back to." She took the glass but didn't drink from it and realized what she just said. She was proud of herself for not succumbing to him.

"I thought you might say that. But that doesn't discourage me," Rosler said. "And we aren't going to talk about such things tonight." He put down his wine glass. "I have this for you. You have earned it and based on the pre-sales there will be more coming your way. You drove a hard bargain, but it was smart on your part." He pulled a check out of his pants pocket and handed it to her. "You've earned every penny. This is your reward."

She put down her glass and unfolded the check. It was made out to Julie Fletcher to the amount of $50,000.

"What do you think?"

"Wow. I wasn't expecting this. You already gave me an advance. This is more than we agreed," Julie objected.

"Oh, nonsense. You have earned it and like I said, the pre-sale is unexpectedly high, so it's only fair that you get your fair share." He picked up his wine glass and held it in front of him. "So, a toast."

She picked up her wine glass.

"To a successful book by a terrific writer."

She smiled; the joy of the money finally set in. "Here, here!" They drank their wines.

"Julie, this is going to be a good night."

She knew he was hitting on her; Julie was always good at spotting a flirter, especially one as aggressive as Rosler. He wouldn't leave, and she didn't want to ask him to leave after he gave her the check. He wanted to talk about her. The wine was good, but it was going to her head. Maybe it was the empty stomach? She could handle her wine. Something was wrong. She felt woozy, but she couldn't explain it. She heard herself talking. She was telling him she needed to get to bed. She only had one glass.

She tried to get out of her chair and issue him to the door, and inside her head, she knew she said it. But then she felt his hands on her. His body pressed against hers and he tried to kiss her.

"No, Mike!" She said, and she heard it. "Mike, stop, please, this isn't going to happen." She was sure she said that too, but he didn't stop. Her world spun. His hands were inside her robe and on her bare skin. She said stop again, but then she went black.

Julie woke the next morning on her bed, naked but under the covers. The bed was messy. Her head hurt, and she tried to remember what had happened. The wine bottles and glasses were gone. She knew she had wine but where was it? She recalled saying no. That was the last thing she remembered and realized Senator Rosler made a move on her.

She sat up in a panic. Her hands shook, and as the fog escaped her mind, she felt other things in other places of her body. She then knew. She was sore. Tears came to her eyes, and she rushed to the bathroom and threw up. She knew for sure: Rosler raped her.

CHAPTER 40

Julie clutched her legs to her chest and cried. The hot water did nothing to soothe her. She wished it was a nightmare, and she'd wake and that it hadn't happened. But it did. She wanted to disappear. Julie at once wanted Zack but didn't want him to know. It hurt too much. She couldn't let him know. Julie wanted no one to know. She exited the shower and dressed.

The knock on her door scared her. She didn't want to answer. The knocking didn't go away and then she heard Rosler's voice.

"Julie, open up. It's me. I brought breakfast. I thought you might be hungry."

She curled on the bed.

"Julie, open up. I know you're in there. If you don't open, I'll use a key. Come on," he urged.

She didn't move. She sat on the edge of the bed, she shook and wanted to run. The door opened and in walked Rosler carrying a tray of food with a big smile on his face. "Hey, darling, how are you feeling this morning?"

Julie wanted to scream, to run, to attack him and make him suffer; to hurt, to feel violated. But she was scared. He put the tray down.

"Hey, are you all right?" Rosler sat next to her, and she instinctively moved away. "Hey," he said softly, "what's wrong? You look like you've been crying." He tried to touch her face, but she swiped his hand away.

"Don't you touch me!"

"Julie," he said surprised, "Julie, what's wrong? After the night we had, I thought you'd be happy to see me. You don't know how happy I am because we finally let go of the conventions and let our chemistry finally meld."

"Are you insane?"

"What are you talking about? I thought we had a wonderful night."

She looked away, disgusted at his sight and not wanting him anywhere near her.

"Come on, Julie," he said softly and tried to move closer. "We belong together." He moved closer and tried to kiss her, but she leaped off the bed.

"What the hell did you put in my drink? You RAPED ME!" She screamed. "Get out of my room!"

He got off the bed with a smile. "I don't know what you're talking about."

"You drugged my wine and raped me after I passed out. Don't deny it, you bastard. You are going to pay for this if it is the last thing I do!"

His laugh made Julie's skin crawl. "It will be the last thing you do," he said. "Let me spell it out for you: you are stuck. There is no win for you with this. You can't cry rape. You'll only look like a whore who didn't get her way. No one will believe you. My team will put a spin on this and crush you. I will destroy you. No one will hire you. You'll be a laughingstock. Just look at it, Julie," he laughed.

She shook with rage and anger.

"You took a check from me last night for the book. That's it. What wine? I don't see it. Who will believe you? After all, I'm a married man running to be the next President of the United States. Why would I jeopardize that and my reputation by hooking up with someone like you?"

Julie clenched her fists. She wanted to pummel him.

"So, here's how it's going to play out, sweetheart," Rosler said as he stepped forward and she jumped away from him. "You're not going to say anything. You're going to play along. Oh, you'll get more money from the book,"

"I don't want your payoff. All your other flings might have gone along with your games, but I'm not."

"Oh yes you are, naïve little girl," he said. "You don't have a choice."

She didn't want to believe it. She wanted Rosler gone.

He walked closer to her, and she stood defiantly. "And your boyfriend Stack isn't going to help you out of this one. You tell him I'll have him killed. Do you want that?"

"How do you know his name? I never told you."

He smiled an evil smile. "You think I didn't do my homework on you before I hired you?" He laughed. "I knew exactly what I was getting when I picked you." He shook his head. "You won't say a word, Julie. Not if you know what's best for you."

She stared at him. Hatred radiated from her eyes.

"I'll tell you what; you need some time to think about it. Take today off. Don't worry about the book. Have some food," Rosler said. "Come to my suite tonight. We can talk about us," he winked at Julie. "You will realize that you are better off with me than without me. I promise you that."

Julie wanted to tell him to go to hell. She wanted to smash a lamp over his head. Instead, she watched him leave the room and as soon as the door shut she rushed to it, hit the deadbolt and latched it. Then Julie leaned her back against it and slid to the floor in tears.

* * * * * *

Zack entered his apartment tired, dirty and worn out. The day before drained him. He ignored his bedroom, threw his damaged Kevlar vest on the floor and sat on the couch. His back had two large contusions and a bandaged arm. But he didn't care. He watched Claire die, and that gnawed on his conscious.

Zack had been with Barnes and the police all day. First at the scene, then at the police station all night. He hadn't slept or eaten. Michelle and their lawyer managed to keep Zack and Andre's name out of the paper, but the story was on the front page of the newspaper: KILLINGS IN COASTAL TOWN SHOCK RESIDENTS. It didn't name the people killed, or any facts other than two men and two girls were shot dead, and that police had leads and were investigating.

Those girls should not be dead. Zack had been warned. *Is this all my fault? Is Claire dead because I wouldn't back down?* He looked at the bloody hastily wrapped bandages around his left arm, felt the throbbing pain and didn't care that he refused the paramedics to look at it. *Claire wasn't supposed to be there! Just Meg. God fig and noodles! I deserve whatever happens to this arm.*

He looked at his wristwatch. His fourth favorite. It, too, broke. Four down. It was eight in the morning, but a glass of bourbon sounded like a decent breakfast. He went to the kitchen, poured a glass of Woodford Reserve and gulped it down. Zack poured another drink when he heard footsteps behind him.

"Hey, I thought I heard someone out here," the sleepy female voice said.

Stefani in baggy pajamas, wild dark hair, black-rimmed glasses, and a smile, walked past him, grabbed the glass out of his hand, set it down and grabbed a separate glass and poured orange juice into it. "Drink this instead. You'll thank me later."

"No, I won't." He found the bourbon again and drank from it. "I'm fine, Stef."

"OH, MY GOD! LOOK AT YOUR ARM!"

"It's fine," he tried, but she was already unwrapping it.

"Sit down and shut up!" Stef ordered him. "You refused treatment, didn't you?"

"It's fine."

"NO, IT'S NOT!" Stef snapped. "I've seen enough GSW's to know! Jesus," she said. "This doesn't look good."

He mumbled something inaudible and sipped the bourbon as a trance overtook him. He didn't hear Stefani talk or feel anything as she sterilized and examined the wound.

"Zack?" She knelt before him, her hands on his knees. "Zack?" No response. "ZACK!"

His eyes came back to life, and he focused on her.

"You need stitches. You need to see a doctor. Please, trust me."

"I'm not seeing a doctor. In the bathroom, in the closet, top shelf, there is a first aid kit specifically for gunshot wounds."

"Why would you have that?" She shook her head. "Never mind. I've only known you for a week and know why. Look, hon, you need to see a doctor. I can take you now."

He looked at her. The look said it all.

She stared at him. "You are so stubborn. When you lose your arm, don't blame me."

CHAPTER 41

Stefani did what she could with his arm and hoped for the best. The bullet didn't appear to hit anything serious. She wrapped his arm.

"I'd buy a lottery ticket quick if I were you," Stef said softly. He looked at her. "As lucky as you've been with gunfire lately, you'd be crazy not to. No one is this lucky."

"I don't feel lucky," Zack said and sipped more bourbon.

"You ok?"

He raised his bourbon to his lips. Stef stopped him and took the glass from him.

"Honey, come on, let's go to the kitchen. I'll make you a veggie omelet."

He shook his head. "Now I know why you're still single."

She smiled. "Men do eat veggie omelets," she said.

"This one doesn't." He stood from the couch. "Can I get this wet?"

"I already told you no. You want an infection?"

"I'm taking a shower. You can clean it after I'm done."

"Why are you so damn stubborn?"

"I don't know," he said from his bedroom.

She followed him into the bathroom. "What happened yesterday?"

He slid his shirt off and tossed it to the floor. He looked at Stef and took a deep breath. Zack didn't want to hear it. He couldn't make himself say it: *A girl died because of me.*

Frustrated with his silence, Stefani lashed out. "Jesus Christ, Zack! How does Julie put up with you? Maybe if you talked, you wouldn't feel the need to drown your emotions in alcohol."

His pants joined the pile of clothes as he turned on the shower. "Drown is a strong word." He stepped into the hot stream of water. "Saturate maybe, but not drown."

She shook her head at him. "That woman is a saint. She truly is."

* * *   * * *

Julie wasn't staying there. She couldn't. She packed her bags, walked to the door but hesitated. *What if someone sees me?* Julie fought back the tears and fear and quietly unlocked the door. She heard nothing and peeked in the hallway. No one.

She stepped out, shut the door without a peep and tip-toed to the nearest exit sign as fast as she could. She reached the exit door for the stairs, looked one last time down the hallway and disappeared down the stairs.

The door shut and a man dressed in black with black sunglasses atop his head and a scruffy beard stepped from one of the doorways down the hall. He moved fast down the hallway and opened the door as quietly as the girl had.

Light on her feet, Julie didn't make a sound on the stairs. She hesitated at the exit door, looked into the parking lot, saw nothing, and exited the hotel. *Walk normally but quick. Keep it together, Jules.* Two blocks away she ducked inside a flower shop. Julie shut the door and looked through the window down the street.

A store clerk approached Julie. "Good afternoon, ma'am. Can I help you?" The appearance of bags did give the clerk pause, but she persevered.

Julie jumped, startled and turned to the clerk. "Oh, I'm sorry," she said, suddenly aware she startled the store clerk. "I didn't see you there."

The clerk paused and looked at Julie's appearance. She cocked her head. "Is everything ok?"

Julie frowned but realized she needed help. "No. It isn't." She let out a sigh. "I need to get out of town," she said. "Can you help me?"

The female clerk let out a deep breath. "Of course I can. What do you need?"

Julie smiled while a tear trickled down her cheek. "I need to reach my fiancé and to get out of here. My cell phone is dead and won't charge. This week has sucked!"

"Here, you can use mine," she handed Julie her cell phone.

"Thank you so much," Julie said. "This has been the worst week of my life."

"Where do you need to go? I'll close up shop and drive you someplace safe."

Julie smiled at her compassion. "Thank you. I appreciate this."

* * *   * * *

Zack sat on the edge of the bed, a towel around him and his head held in his hands. "I don't know what else we could have done."

Stefani put her hand on his black and blue back. "Those men were going to kill her no matter what as soon as they found her. You can't blame yourself, Zack. What you need to do is stop it from happening again."

Stefani wore him down. She didn't leave the bathroom and harped at him the whole time he was in the shower. Without Julie, Zack needed to talk to someone.

"I don't know. It just feels like," Zack stopped, the words not forming.

"Like what?"

Like we're fighting a battle we can't win. "How long before we get Rosler's paternity test back?"

"Shifting gears I see," Stefani said. She shook her head. "You do that a lot. Is that a coping mechanism?"

"You want me to drink instead?"

"Could be any day now." Stefani shook her head. "And no, I don't want that. I want you to open up to me. I can't help if you hide everything from me."

Zack looked at her. "Stef, I'm sorry. I, uh, don't like communicating at times."

She laughed. "I've noticed. Come on," she said and patted Zack's bare leg. "Get dressed. You don't want veggies, so let's get some meat and potatoes. I'll be ready in ten minutes." She entered the bathroom and shut the door. His cell phone rang, and he jumped with hopes it was Julie.

"Stack here."

"Zack Stack, Private Investigator."

Zack exhaled. "Yes, that is what I do."

"You should change your occupation. Immediately."

Zack recognized the voice. "Mark Leary, mercenary-for-hire." Zack hesitated, but there was no response. "I think you should change your occupation."

"I don't know who that is," Kilgas said.

"I know how you feel," Zack said. "What do you want?"

"I thought we had an agreement."

Zack rubbed his forehead. "I said I would think about it."

"Well, Stack, I presumed you were just saying that because you are smart enough to understand there is no way you can win here."

That had occurred to me. "What do you want?"

"I want to get through to you. To make you realize you can walk away from this unscathed. As can your friends."

"No strings attached?"

"No. I don't like strings. Those are loose ends. Loose ends need to be tied off."

Zack nodded. "We both know I am now a loose end."

"All you have to do, Stack, is walk away. Pretty easy don't you think? I mean, yeah, I'll have to overlook you killing two more of my men. But the girl is dead. Just give me what she gave you, I'll give you a bunch of cash, and it's over."

"She gave me nothing."

"Don't treat me like I'm stupid. It's insulting."

"Your thugs-for-hire killed her before I could get anything," Zack said. "I have an idea. You seem like a decent guy, well, you know," Zack shrugged, "apart from trying to kill me and being Rosler's assassin. How about you tell me what you know and let's send Rosler to prison where he belongs?"

"Somehow I don't think that would bode well for me."

"Ahh," Zack said, "you're a clever guy. You're well trained and have a nice nest egg hidden somewhere. I have no doubt you could disappear and have a nice life somewhere far away from here."

"You're right. I could do all that. But you see Stack: I'd have a problem with that: I just couldn't live with myself. There is honor in what we do. We have a code, loyalty, and pride. You must remember what those things are; you served in the military."

Zack smiled. "Then we see eye to eye on something because I can't walk away for the same reasons. I couldn't live with myself if I let your boss walk."

"That saddens me, Stack. I was hoping we could come to an agreement."

"We still can," Zack said. "Agree to walk away now. Forget about Rosler because he is going down. I'll forget about you, and we'll be good."

Kilgas was silent for a moment. "This is your last warning. You cannot win. You can't be that stupid."

"Duly noted."

Kilgas exhaled, dissatisfaction and disgust in the sound. "Take care, Stack. You'll need to."

The line went dead. Zack put down the cell phone. *He's scared. Scared animals are dangerous, Zack. Don't forget that.*

CHAPTER 42

Before they left his apartment, his cell phone rang. He didn't recognize the number.

He answered. "Hello?" Zack heard a sob.

"Zack?" The timid voice rang out to Zack.

"Jules, honey? What's wrong?"

"Come get me," Julie said at long last.

Zack paused. His body tensed. "Where are you?"

"Iowa. Ankeny," she said. "Just hurry." She hung up and broke down. She needed to hear his voice, but she couldn't hear his voice. It tore her apart.

Zack put the phone down. "She wants me to go get her." He looked at Stefani.

"Then you need to go get her," Stef said.

"Shit," Zack said. The possibilities raced through his head. *I'm going to kill Rosler!*

Stefani grabbed his arm. "You have to call Andre; in your condition you want him with you at all times now. I'll call Michelle, and she'll do what she does."

Zack stared at the phone.

"Zachary," Stef said as Zack settled into silence, "Zack, are you with me? What's going on up there?"

Zack just shook his head as he pressed a button on his phone and waited for Andre to answer. *Jules, this is all my fault!*

"Zack, hello?" Stef asked again.

Zack snapped out of his trance. "After you drop me at the airport, come straight here.   Lock the doors. In my bedroom in the bottom drawer of the nightstand on the window side of the bed, there is a gun. Keep it near you. And whatever you do, don't leave. You understand me?'

"Hon, you're scaring me," Stef said.

"Just do as I say. I promise you'll be ok." But that was a promise Zack knew he should not have made.

* * * * * *

Michael Rosler stood in the suite of his hotel and stared out at the grey sky and brown landscape beyond the parking lot. Rosler could see the dark wall of clouds approach from the west. The storm would be there soon. Rosler swirled a whiskey and water in his hand and let his mind wander. He had no talks later, so it was almost a day off. *Almost.*

Jerry Pantalini entered the room. Rosler's longtime Chief of Staff and right-hand man, Pantalini knew how to get things done for Rosler and how to win elections, and the next one so far was shaping up in their favor. The assassination attempt bolstered Rosler's national recognition and manufactured the amount of free press he needed. The other candidates struggled to be heard. Rosler was comfortably ahead in the polls, and his donors wrote sizable checks. Everything was almost going perfectly. *Almost.*

Rosler turned from the window. "Jerry," he greeted and walked to a table to top off his whiskey.

"Kilgas is on his way here now, Mike. Should be here any minute." Pantalini helped himself to the wet bar with a vodka and tonic.

Rosler returned to the window and sipped his drink again. "Stack is more of a problem than we thought. Why hasn't Kilgas taken care of him? Does he understand what's at stake?"

"He does."

"Then why the hell am I still hearing his name? And what about the girl? Where the hell did she go?"

The black skies opened. Rain pounded the window, wind rocked the building, and thunder shook the ground. Water quickly covered the parking lot.

232

Rosler liked the symbolism of the storm: he had nearly completed a blitz of a storm on his party to all but wrap up the nomination for President. It cost him money and a nasty bruise on his ribs. But instant recognition, check that: instant free recognition was worth every penny and calculated risk. Now it was time to put that all behind them.

"Where the hell is Pete?"

Pete Kilgas didn't knock; he entered and shut the door behind him. His dark suit gave the appearance of Secret Service, but he was private security as was all Rosler's security team. All hired by Kilgas. He had been with Rosler since before his first Senate term.

"Good afternoon, everyone." Pete helped himself to the wet bar. He poured a glass of bourbon on the rocks.

"Pete, I brought you on to solve problems. Not create them," Rosler said.

Kilgas sat and smiled. "Don't worry."

"Don't worry?" Rosler said. "Stack has killed eight of your men. Plus, two more girls from the same college that can be tied to me are dead. How long before the press snoops into that and ties them all to me? I think I have good reason to worry!"

"If you would keep your dick in your pants and not bang every co-ed that crosses your path we wouldn't have all these problems," Kilgas replied calmly.

Pantalini hid his smile. "That doesn't help us right now, does it?"

"They won't find anything on our men," Kilgas said. "No ties to us at all. They'll spend months trying to find something on them but will find nothing. That's how I work, that's who I get." Kilgas drank his bourbon.

"And I'm supposed to be reassured by your confidence?"

Kilgas stared at Rosler and Pantalini. Kilgas had no respect for the two; in another world, Kilgas would have already joined forces with Stack and buried the two monsters in front of him. But they paid well, and Kilgas had to maintain his reputation. Fulfilling his duties with Rosler would go a long way toward big paychecks. "Yes," he said. "You are."

"Well we have one more problem to fix," Jerry said. "Fletcher, the girl writing the book has to be silenced. And we don't know where she is."

Pete Kilgas smiled and finished his bourbon in a gulp. "Yes, we do. I have a guy on her. Followed her since I heard about your night with her," Kilgas looked disgusted at Rosler. "I knew she'd bolt."

"Good, let's go grab her then," Rosler said.

Kilgas shook his head. "That would be a colossal mistake. The last thing you need is her face anywhere near you right now." Kilgas stood and walked to the bar to refresh his drink. "She'll call Stack to come to get her which brings all our problems to one place. Let me do my job, and you keep talking the bullshit you keep talking. That's your job," Kilgas said. Kilgas loved the power he had. Rosler and Pantalini would be in jail without him. And dead if they turned on Kilgas. The irony. Kilgas smiled.

"All our problems are not going away," Rosler said. "You said Stack wouldn't be a problem."

"NO, I specifically told you to NOT fuck around with his fiancé. What do you think he's going to do when he finds out you raped her? Do you understand that? He's going to hurt you, Mike," Kilgas rose his voice.

"Then kill him before he does," Rosler said.

Kilgas rubbed his brow. "I had a plan. It was working. We wear him down. Wage a war of attrition. That was the safest for you, Mike."

"Safe? He is still sniffing around my affairs. You call that safe? If I go down, we all go down. Do you understand that?"

Kilgas stared at Rosler. He nodded his head and set down his drink.

"Look, Pete, we have the money. We have backers. Just get it done." Rosler turned to the window and stared out at the storm. "God, I hate this state. I can't wait to get the hell out of here."

Kilgas's phone beeped. "I have business to take care of. Mike, do me a favor and quit raping women." He gulped his drink and set down the glass. "Eventually, not even I will be able to save you from yourself." He eyed him with disdain. "Nor will I want to."

Kilgas turned and left the room.

"He's right, you know, Mike," Jerry said. "Everything is going to intensify after you win the nomination. Half the press will be parading you around like a king and the other half will be digging to find every little thing they can to discredit you."

Rosler hated to be lectured, but he knew Jerry was right. "Just help Pete clean this up. Make sure none of what happened comes back on me. We'll be good after that."

CHAPTER 43

The rain continued. The front stalled, storms erupted and soaked the area. Zack and Andre shook off water from the heavy rain. Zack looked at his last watch. From the time Jules called him until he and Andre set foot in the hotel took only four hours. They got off the elevator and walked down the hallway.

"Is this it?" Andre asked.

Zack nodded. "Yeah, she said 504."

"And you have no idea why she wants out of here?"

"Wouldn't you?" Zack knocked on the door. "I hope we can catch the return flight. Be home by dinner. I'm starving." He took a deep breath.

"You and me both."

Zack knocked on the door again. "Jules, it's me."

Zack looked at Andre, went to knock on the door again but the door unlatched and opened.

"Jules," he began, but she shook her head no.

She walked back into the room, her eyes never leaving Zack.

They followed Julie inside. "Jules, honey, what's wrong?" Zack sensed something wrong. In her eyes, her breathing, her movements. She was tense, afraid. "Sweetheart, are you ok?"

Julie stopped. Zack saw a figure in the corner of his eye: a man with a gun pointed at them.

The man shook his head. "Don't do anything stupid," he said. The gun, silencer attached to the barrel, pointed at Zack's head. "Keep your hands up."

Zack knew the man was part of the Kilgas psycho-squad. He wore all black, including leather gloves.

The man kept the gun pointed while he put his cell phone to his ear. "Yeah, they are all here." He listened. "Will do. I got this." He put the phone in his pocket.

"You going to kill us right here?" Zack asked. "Housecleaning will hate that."

"Shut up and do as I say. You," the man pointed at Andre as the man dug something out of his pocket. "Move over there."

Andre hesitated.

"Come on, I don't have all day," the man said.

Andre walked towards the window as instructed. The man stepped closer, raised a device and fired it. The taser probes attached to Andre and 50,000 volts of electricity knocked Andre to the floor.

The man dropped the taser and pointed the gun at Zack. "We only want you two. Let's go. Out in the hall and to the stairs."

Julie looked at Zack with pale skin, teary eyes, she trembled, and sweat covered her forehead. Zack saw that look before. At the zoo in Michigan City, Indiana with a gun held to her head. It broke his heart.

"Woman grab your bags. You help her. And don't think I won't shoot you both so don't try it."

Julie grabbed her backpack and purse. Zack picked up her two suitcases. The man kept his distance. Zack looked back at the man.

"I know what you're thinking, Stack. Start walking to the stairs. Turn right," the man ordered as they exited the room into the empty hallway.

Zack followed Julie. She reached the door to the stairwell, turned to see the man and slowly pushed it open.

"Don't try anything," the man snapped. "Keep walking. Real slow. As you said, house cleaning won't like cleaning up your splattered brains off the carpet."

"Actually I never mentioned anything about splattered brains," Zack said.

"Shut up," the man barked.

Zack entered the stairwell, but instead of following Julie to the stairs on the right, he walked to the left staircase to the upper floor.

"Stop. Where are you going? We are heading down."

"Oh," Zack said as he stopped and faced the man, "I figured you'd take us to the roof and throw us off."

"My orders were specific," he said. "Now, down the stairs."

Zack stopped. The man took his eyes off Julie. "You were told not to kill us. Why?"

"Goddamnit," the man stepped closer to Zack. "I was never told I couldn't shoot you." He raised the gun just as Julie jumped on his back and knocked his arm away. The weapon fired harmlessly. The man flung Julie into the wall.

She hit the wall and floor with a thud. Zack dropped the suitcases, deflected the gun hand and connected with a right cross on the man's jaw. The sudden movement tore at Zack's midsection.

The man fell backward, and Zack attacked. He followed with another right cross. Zack grabbed the wrist with the gun, but the man punched Zack's ribcage with his left fist and knocked Zack to the floor with a knee to his midsection and a quick kick to Zack's chest.

Zack landed on his back on the stairs. The man came at him, Zack kicked him, and jumped at the man. The man grabbed Zack, slammed him into the wall and threw him down the half flight of stairs.

Zack landed on his back; the wind knocked out of him and in immense pain. He lied motionless.

"Accidents happen, Stack. You are about to have one."

Zack groaned and tried to move, but his body didn't respond. The man reached the last stair above the sprawled Zack and raised his gun.

"I told you not to try anything."

Suddenly, Julie slammed into the man, the gun fired, the bullet ricocheted off the metal railings. Julie tried to kick the man as she held onto his arm, but the man grabbed a handful of her hair, yanked her head back, punched her in the face and tossed her down the stairs.

The man turned to Zack and took a fist to his face. The man hit the wall hard. Zack charged and landed a left fist into the man's stomach. The man hunched, grabbed Zack's arm, twisted it and forced Zack's face into the wall. The man punched Zack in the back and hit his ribs. Zack winced and folded. The man straightened Zack, grabbed his shoulders, slammed him into the wall, and tossed Zack down the next flight of eight stairs.

The man looked at Zack and Julie. Neither moved. The man wiped his mouth and grabbed his gun. The man stepped down each stair slow with a cocksure grin on his face. He cocked the gun.

The man heard something from above. Andre tackled him. The man staggered while Andre got to his knees and punched the man's face twice with vicious right crosses. The man blocked the third punch and jabbed Andre in the throat. Andre slumped long enough for the man to knock Andre off him, kick him in the stomach and reach for the gun again.

Julie kicked the man from behind, from the floor, he lost his balance. Zack tackled him, and the two tumbled down the next flight of stairs. They got to their feet; the man swung at Zack who deflected it with his bandaged arm, screamed in pain but counter-punched the man's stomach. The man grabbed and squeezed Zack's injured arm; Zack yelled as a fist landed on his torn stitches. The man tossed Zack down the fourth flight of stairs.

Andre attacked again. He tackled the man from behind; they hit the wall, Andre moved his leg fast enough to miss a knee from the man and returned with a knee to the thigh. Andre freed his right arm and tried to jam his forearm against the man's neck, but the man deflected with a swipe and punched Andre, knocking Andre to his butt. The man stepped forward, but Julie raised her leg, the man tripped forwards, and Andre kicked him backward.

The man fell down the stairs and landed near Zack. Zack kicked the man in the head and scrambled to wrap his legs around the man's neck. Zack locked his ankles and squeezed as hard as he could. The man flailed at Zack; his legs kicked. He tried to lift and free Zack's grip and pounded on Zack's legs with his elbows. Andre raced down the stairs and jumped on the man.

The man lost his breath, and his fight slowed. Moments later, with bulging eyes and blood trickling from the corner of his mouth, the man lost consciousness.

Zack let go of his clutch; his breath labored; blood flowed from all over his body. Andre rolled off the man, beat up and bloodied and picked up the gun.

Zack's body shook and covered in sweat. He closed his eyes and focused.

Andre stood straight. "Get up, Zack. Jules, you ok?"

She nodded. She grabbed a railing and pulled herself to her feet.

Andre watched Zack struggle to move. "Jules, help him up. Reinforcements can't be far behind."

Zack stepped forward but wanted to collapse. Andre retrieved Julie's bags and rushed them down the remaining flight of stairs.

"We have to go now."

Zack nodded and arm-in-arm with Julie; the three exited the hotel side door.

The rain poured and soaked the three quickly, but they reached the car. Andre opened the driver's door and entered. The car started immediately. Julie opened the rear door, and Zack leaned against the car.

"Get in, Zack," Andre said.

Zack nearly fell over, Julie caught him and helped slide him into the rear seat. She plopped into the car seat beside him and leaned back so she couldn't be seen. Andre stepped on the accelerator, headed for the exit to the parking lot.

A black Escalade appeared from the north and turned left into the parking lot. Andre turned quickly into a parking stall between two cars and ducked. The Escalade raced past and headed for the rear of the hotel. It disappeared, and Andre drove out of the lot. He turned onto the main street, saw a sign for the Interstate and hit the on-ramp for the Interstate.

"Uhh, just so you know, we are heading East," Andre said. He heard nothing from the rear seat. "Get comfortable. It's a long drive to Baltimore."

CHAPTER 44

Andre closed the car door and watched the other cars at a gas station along the interstate somewhere in Illinois. "Don't draw any attention to yourselves," he told Zack. "The quicker we get back on the road, the better."

"Ok. We'll get into the bathroom and clean up. You do the shopping."

Andre nodded and stuck the gas dispenser into the car. "Hurry up."

Zack disappeared with Julie inside, and the two went straight to the men's room. "Less traffic," he said. "And men generally don't care. We'll be fine."

The two cleaned their faces at a sink and Zack was right: only one other man entered, and he didn't even look at the two. Moments later they walked out and saw Andre at the checkout.

"Straight to the car," he whispered to Julie.

Andre paid for some food, drinks, and frozen items for their bruised faces and met them at the car. Zack sat in the back seat with Jules. "There's some tape in the bag," Andre said. "Use it where your stitches tore. We can't stop at a hospital."

"Triage, 101," Zack said. The next thing he did was rip his shirt off. He held pieces of it over the wounds while Julie pressed pieces of the Duct tape over them.

"That should help," she said. "You're a freaking mess."

Zack smiled and closed his eyes. "You should see the other guy."

"They're going to come after each and every one of us until we stop, Zack. You know that, don't you?"

Zack's eyes opened. "Stefani."

* ** * **

Stefani knew she was told to not leave his apartment. But she was hungry and didn't want anything in Zack's apartment. Whole Foods wasn't too far of a walk, and it was a beautiful day. She decided to go out. "Besides," she told herself, "Zack isn't around, and they are after him."

She walked down the street in black yoga pants, white running shoes, and a light blue jacket over a grey tee-shirt. Comfortable and stylish. The sun shone bright, and it felt good on her face. There hadn't been much sun lately. People on the streets walked and biked and jogged; enjoying a brief respite from crappy weather.

Her phone beeped. It was a text from Zack. She smiled and unlocked her phone to read it when she spotted two men on the opposite side of the street. They stared at her as she passed them then crossed the street behind her. They reminded her of the two men at the hospital: same clothes, black jackets, same boots. There was no mistake. The hair raised on her arms and she trembled. *They are after me!*

She turned the corner and broke out into a full run.

They reached the corner and stopped. Stefani was gone.

The two men passed the Whole Foods Market and saw the young brunette run across the open parking lot beside the market. They ran after her.

On the other side of the parking lot, Stefani allowed herself to look behind her. Zack told her one night to never do that. He said "in the movies in a chase, the person being chased always looks behind them and then trips. It's cliché as hell, but there is an increased chance that happens so never look behind you when you're running away. Just run as fast as you can."

She had to know and looked. She was right. The men pursued her. And they gained on her. Stef knew she couldn't run faster than the two men, but she knew she wouldn't tire. She ran long distances all the time. But they closed. *Don't look behind you! Run. Run as fast as you can.* She crossed streets, turned corners, ran down another road. The men gained but were still sixty feet behind. Stefani ran into a parking garage. Middle of the day. Plenty of cars.

She ducked and dodged from car to car.

Stefani ran to the third level, further from the street. Cars drove past; a horn blew, a businessman closed his car door and headed for an exit, another car screeched past, all distractions Stefani needed. She reached the southeast corner of the floor, dashed into the stairwell and leaped down the stairs three and four at a time. Her heart pounded.

She heard them yell, "Down the stairs!"

Stefani burst out the door on the ground level and ran east. The street ended, and she saw the men behind her. She ran towards two buildings, wedged herself through the narrow walkway between the buildings and made her way to the other side. The nearest man behind her reached the opening and followed. Stef stepped aside and stumbled on a garbage can. Stefani caught her balance and picked up the metal lid. The man's face appeared, she swung as hard as she could, the lid edge smashed into the man's nose. He let out a noise and fell to the ground. Stef turned and ran.

The second raced past his partner who struggled to his feet with his face bloodied and nose broke. They saw Stefani dodge between more buildings across the street. Bushes and trees blocked their view.

Stefani was winded but found another gear. This was not how she was going to go. Stef passed the Fells Point Tavern and raced up Thames Street. She was close to Zack's apartment and his office, but she knew she couldn't go to either. She needed to hide.

She turned the corner and entered the Admiral Fell Inn. She pretended she belonged there though her lungs wanted to explode and sweat ran down her face. She wiped her face, smiled at the counter person and kept an eye on the windows. The men raced past but stopped to look around.

Stefani knew concealment was her friend. She walked the hallways and through doorways and soon was on the other end of the building. She peeked through a window but saw no one. Stefani fought with herself. *Patience? Bolt? What do I do?* She finally looked at Zack's text: "Stay inside with the doors locked. They are coming after you!"

She shook her head. *Why did I say I'd help him??*

She caught her breath and saw one of the men run past. She saw the sign for Max's Taphouse across the square. He ran the opposite direction of Max's. He must have thought she backtracked to throw them off. Stef found a doorway on the north side of the building, took a deep breath and peeked outside. She saw neither.

She knew Max's was Zack's favorite pub. Zack was there probably three times a week. If Zack was right, she could get in there, and they would hide her. She just needed to remain unseen. Confident the men disappeared, Stefani burst out of the doorway and sprinted. Her legs burned, but it was close. She dodged the people in the square. She crossed the street, reached the door, looked behind her, saw no one running after her and went inside.

She went straight to the bar, waited for the bartender and smiled.

"What can I get for you?"

"I'm a close friend of Zack Stack. He told me to come here and that you could hide me until he gets here."

The bartender looked her up and down. "You know Zack, huh?"

She nodded. "Please."

"You aren't his fiancé. I don't want to get in the middle of that."

"Please, Julie and I are friends. Two men are after me. I need a place to hide."

The bartender stared at her. She looked too frazzled to be lying. "Come on. There's a place upstairs."

Ten minutes later, the men entered the bar. "Hey, did a pretty girl about five-foot-eight, dark brown hair, black yoga pants, white shoes, blue coat come in here?"

The bartender hesitated and shook his head. "Nah, people come in here pretty steady. I'd remember a pretty girl with dark brown hair — just my type. But feel free to look around," he said. Two minutes later, the men left.

Meanwhile, in a locked upstairs storage room, Stefani crouched on the floor with her phone in her hand. She texted Zack: I'm at Max's hiding. Two men chased me. I'm staying here until you arrive. PLEASE HURRY!

CHAPTER 45

The skyline of Baltimore with the sun rising behind it was a pleasant and beautiful sight the next morning for Andre, Zack, and Julie. The thousand-mile trip went quicker than expected thanks to good weather, fast drivers, and no cops. Still, almost a full day had passed since Julie called Zack. The first stop was to collect Stefani from the confines of Max's.

Then, Zack decided it was time to let Michelle and Darnell know the full extent of what had transpired. Once he determined they were safe, he'd talk to Barnes. The plan made sense.

But something gnawed at his conscience. He had to talk to Jules.

"Dre, I'm going to drop Jules and me at my place. I need you to go to Max's and get Stefani."

"Ok, then what?" Andre sat in the front passenger seat as Julie slept in the back.

"I have to do some things." The traffic tightened but still traveled at seventy miles per hour.

"I hate that exclusionary tone you use sometimes," Dre said. "Makes me feel like you haven't told me everything."

"I have to get Donald Fairfax out of prison," Zack said.

"WHAT?"

"I think he's innocent."

"What brought this on?"

Zack shrugged. "The evidence Erin Rosler gave me the other day." Zack's look darted from the road to Dre back to the road. "He knows."

"How did he find out?"

"I don't know. Fairfax said he'd tell me once he's out."

Andre scoffed. "You believe him?"

"I have no choice. Look, bring Stef back to my place. Then I'm going out. I need you to make sure they stay safe."

"Who's going to make sure you stay safe?"

"You better check on Alysha. I think Kilgas planned to beat us up until we couldn't take any more." Zack turned the car off the interstate at their exit. "And I think they are about to change the rules of the game."

"Why is that?"

Zack glanced back at Jules then to Andre. "Cuz I think Rosler changed them."

* * * * * *

Julie exited the shower and slid under the covers of Zack's bed, towel still wrapped in her hair and around her body. She clinched the sheet and comforter tight around her and turned on the television. Zack entered the bedroom, pulled clean clothes out of his closet, tossed them on the bed and disappeared in the bathroom.

He hadn't eaten much other than gas station snacks in the last day, and he stunk, and his body was a mess. Stefani yet again stitched his sides and stayed in the spare bedroom upon Zack's request. The two girls talked while Julie watched Stef stitch Zack's wounds. The girls bonded quickly. They had spoken to Zack's surprise. He still wasn't sure how Julie would feel about another single, beautiful woman in his apartment.

The shower revitalized Zack, despite the sting and burn when the water hit his many open cuts. *At least I don't smell anymore.* He exited the shower, dried, entered the bedroom and dressed.

"Honey, I have to leave for a little," Zack said. He slid a black tee over his head slowly. Pain emanated through his body with every movement. "Are you going to be Ok?"

She didn't reply.

246

He buckled the belt on his blue jeans, grabbed his shoulder holster from the closet and checked the Sig in it. He set that on the end of the bed and walked to her side.

"Jules, honey, I'm sorry for being a jerk and hanging up on you. I overreacted. I know that. I should have talked to you after that instead of acting like an immature teenage boy." He frowned. "I'm sorry."

She finally looked at him; the tears streamed down her cheeks. "That's not it, you idiot," she said with a sad smile, and she jumped to him. Her arms clung tight around his neck. "I think they broke my phone and kept me from you intentionally."

"Of course they did," he said as he held her tight. "Who wouldn't want you all to themselves?"

She smiled but closed her eyes as the tears flowed faster. "Zack," she began but couldn't get anything else out.

She pulled away slightly, their eyes met. Zack moved his hands to her cheeks and wiped away the tears with his thumbs. "It will be all right. I promise." He offered a smile, his own eyes tearing up.

She let out a breath, smiled, her eyes darted between his eyes and to his lips. "I love you," she said and quickly kissed him deeply. The kind of kiss filled with passion and love. She left him at the airport in Europe with a similar kiss. One to remember. "Come back to me. I mean it."

* * * * * *

Zack opted to ride his motorcycle rather than the car despite the pain it caused to ride it. Once on it, he called Barnes. "We need to meet," Zack said after Barnes answered.

"Ok. I'm heading home for lunch. Meet me there."

"On my way."

Fifteen minutes later, Zack knocked on the door of Lieutenant Ted Barnes' house and waited. Ted's wife answered and smiled, but her smile quickly dissipated into a look of horror and astonishment at Zack.

"Zack, are you ok?"

Zack smiled. "Becki, I've never been better. Is the good Lieutenant here?"

She shook her head, used to Zack's sarcasm and opened the door. "He's in the basement."

"Thank you. I won't be long."

Zack had been in the house before. Barnes owned an 80-year old Colonial which he updated. The basement was refinished, and one of the best Man-Caves Zack had ever seen. Large flat screen televisions on one wall to watch multiple games, a cherry-wood bar complete with a tapper, wine fridge, a liquor rack that most bars would envy and leather recliners that oozed comfort. A full-size pool table, dart board, two pinball machines, and an electric race car set and HO-scale train set at the far end of the basement for the kids complimented the area. It even had a full bathroom with a walk-in shower. If Barnes's wife didn't work as an attorney, Zack would have wondered how he afforded it all.

Zack saw Barnes sitting in a chair eating a ham sandwich with a cup of coffee beside him. Barnes heard Zack and met him at the base of the stairs. "Jesus, you look like shit. Who the hell beat the crap out of you now? How are you even upright?"

"Smoke and mirrors."

"I have Pepsi for you, but your fiancé has been telling me not to encourage your onset of diabetes."

"Real funny, Lieutenant," Zack remarked. "That joke just never gets old, does it?"

"Here," he handed Zack a bottle of Pepsi from his fridge.

"Where is she?"

"Right there," Barnes said. "On the couch."

Zack walked around the couch and saw the quiet Meg Chatwell. She was enjoying a ham sandwich along with Barnes. "Hi," he said.

She smiled at him.

"You ok?"

"Thanks to you I am," Meg answered. "How long do I have to stay here?"

Zack sat beside her. "We have to talk about that." He took a deep breath. "Your life is about to become very different."

She frowned and nodded. "I was afraid of that." Meg looked at him.

He swigged the Pepsi and hoped the acidic, sugary kick down his throat would give him another burst of energy. "Meg, I need what you have on Rosler."

She looked at her hands. "How do I know I can trust him?" She pointed right at Ted. "Rosler has people bought in high places. He owns some police. Maybe even him."

Zack looked at Barnes and frowned. "Because I know he isn't on the take," Zack said. "Michelle proved that for me." Ted looked angry and surprised. "Sorry, Ted." Zack looked at Meg. "If he were one of them, you'd be dead already."

"I guess there is that."

"Once you give us the goods on Rosler, you'll have to go into protective custody until we are sure you are safe. There's no debate on that."

"Great. How is that even fair?"

"Hidden or dead, Meg," Zack said. "Your choice."

Meg frowned. "Fine, it's hidden."

"Protective custody is your choice?"

"No, what I have against Rosler is hidden." She looked at Zack. "You better make sure I don't have to go into protective custody."

Zack looked at Barnes who still looked angry at Zack. "Now where is it?"

* * * * * *

Zack walked upstairs with Barnes behind him. Meg remained on the couch in the basement. Zack stopped when he reached the backpack he left by the door. He picked it up and turned to Barnes.

"You investigated me?"

"Ted, I'm sorry," Zack began, "but I had to be sure."

"Be sure? I've been covering your ass for how long now, and you don't trust me?" Barnes stepped forward, only a few feet away from Zack. Zack saw Barnes this angry before and got punched in the jaw that time.

"Yes!" Zack snapped back. "You would have done the same damn thing if you were me."

"You thought I was bought? You thought I was on the Rosler payroll? That's how you repay me for all that I've done for you? You sonofabitch," Barnes snapped. "Are you sure you can trust me now? Because of what Michelle found on her computer?"

Zack just stared back at the furious Ted Barnes. "Here," Zack said. He pulled out his Sig, placed it in his hand and extended it to Ted. "Here's your chance. Take my gun and shoot me. If Rosler owns you, I'll know the second you pull the trigger, and all this shit will be over for you," Zack said.

Ted took the gun but held it at his side.

"Go ahead, Ted. If you shoot me with my gun, just put in my hand and tell whatever story you want. Call it a robbery gone bad. Who won't believe you? You're a goddamn rock star right now. Prove me wrong." Zack said. "Prove to me you aren't one of the good guys."

They stared at each other in silence until a creak in the hallway behind them broke it.

"Ted?" It was his wife. "Is everything ok?"

Ted looked at his wife and nodded. "It's fine, honey. Zack was just inviting you and me to dinner at The Charleston, his treat. He even said he'd pay for the babysitter."

Becki looked confused at the two men and shook her head. "I will never understand you two." Zack watched her turn and disappear. He looked back at Barnes. Ted extended his hand and offered the handle of the gun back to Zack.

"You know damn well I'm not going to shoot you," Ted said. "Though I should." Barnes flashed a brief smile. "What else did you learn about me?"

Zack took the gun back. "I'm sorry, Ted. I had to know for sure." Zack holstered the weapon. "Your 401K sucks, by the way. You need a promotion."

"Screw you."

Zack pulled three files out of the backpack. "You won't like this." He handed two to Barnes. "You had to be suspicious to ask us for help."

Barnes leaned on the back of the couch as he flipped through the files. "This is legit?"

"It's from Michelle."

"Great," Ted answered. He nodded his head. "I was afraid of this. I'll take care of it."

"Sooner rather than later would be appreciated."

Ted put down the files. "There will be extra units in your neighborhood starting as soon as I make the phone call. And trust me, no one will know why."

"I appreciate that."

"I can't keep the girl here, Zack." Barnes shook his head. "My wife and kids, man."

Zack understood. "Give me until nightfall. I'll sneak her out after dark. Does that work?"

Barnes nodded. "Anything else?"

Zack pulled out a small box and a videotape. He handed them and the third file to Barnes. "Over three years ago, we imprisoned the wrong man." Zack waited as Barnes leafed through the file. "Donald Fairfax didn't kill his wife. He was screwing Erin Rosler in a hotel uptown when Donald's wife was murdered. There is all the proof you need to get him out without another trial or any circumstance."

Barnes shook his head. "Are you sure this stuff isn't manufactured?"

Zack shrugged. "I'd almost bet my life on it, but I need you to get me in front of Fairfax where I can talk to him and see for myself. If it's true, I'll let you know, and then I need you to do your magic and get him out quickly."

"Sonofabitch. Just what this force doesn't need," Barnes groaned. "It could take some time."

"We don't have time, Ted." Zack's tone told Ted everything: forewarning.

"Should I guess, or will you just tell me how bad it is?"

"He knows everything, and he's threatened to use it if we don't get him out."

"Goddamn it all to hell. I freaking knew associating with you is going to land me in jail."

"Not yet it hasn't, Ted. Just get me a meeting with him quick. I'm going to the spot Meg said and then to see Fairfax. Text me with the details."

"Jesus. You're full of good news today. I don't even want to ask if there's more."

Zack slung the backpack over his shoulder. "The Charleston? Really? I haven't even taken Jules there."

Barnes smiled. "I'm in the mood for a nice six-course meal with their finest wine. I'll try to keep it under two-fifty a plate."

"If I survive this, make the reservation."

CHAPTER 46

He crouched low, shifted gears and cranked his right wrist. In seconds he hit over eighty miles an hour. Stefani's voice rang in his head, *"I'm going to start sending you pics of motorcycle crash victims!"*

Zack slowed to a slightly above average speed and soon reached his destination: the college chateau where Meg Chatwell shared the room with Hannah Davison.

It took convincing, but a girl finally allowed Zack inside the chateau. She took him to the room in question. He stepped inside. The place hadn't changed much, but his feelings did. His stomach knotted. Zack hated being there. The sense of loss, tragedy, sadness, and death filled the room, and the damp, musky air made it worse. *Why would Jules want kids if this could happen? How do you deal with that?*

Zack knew where to look. He walked to the side of the room, knelt, moved his head to the floor, turned it and looked across the floor. There it was.

Zack rose and took six steps to the wall and saw the floor vent. He lifted off the metal grate and got to his knees. Zack stuck his hand and forearm in as far as it would go. He felt a lump under a piece of Duct tape and pulled it off. Zack removed his arm, smiled at the jump drive and stood. Meg's hiding place choice was either genius or lucky. Zack couldn't decide. The girl stood behind him with her arms crossed.

"Are you a cage fighter or something?"

Zack smiled. His face must have looked like it. "No, cat owner," he said. The girl looked oddly at him. "Enormous cats," Zack moved his hands to suggest large, large cats.

"What is that?" She pointed at the drive in Zack's hand.

Zack smiled. "Hopefully a means to an end." He put it in his pocket. Leaving didn't seem quite right. "Look, I need a favor, ok?"

"What?"

Zack opened his wallet, leafed through a few bills and pulled out two fifty-dollar bills. "I was never here. You never saw me, you have no idea who I am, ok?"

"Ok. Fine by me."

Zack winked and left with the small silver zip drive in his front pocket. Next stop: Donald Fairfax.

An hour later Zack walked into the Baltimore County Correctional Center and asked to see a prisoner. He entered a visiting room that movies had made famous: several metal chairs lined against a small metal ledge with dividers from the shelf to the ceiling for privacy that created a stall. Separated by the bullet-proof glass was an identical room on the other side of the glass with one metal door at the far end. A phone on each side of the glass in each stall allowed the visitor to talk to the prisoner, but that was it.

Zack stared at the faded, yellowing paint that peeled in places and the fluorescent lighting that tried to make it bright, but it was a dismal place to be. For both the visitor and the prisoner.

The metal door creaked open, and a man in an orange jumpsuit entered. The man saw Zack waiting and smiled as he sat down. He picked up the phone.

"I thought you'd never figure it out. It's about damn time."

Zack hated the feeling that he was the last to know. "I was pacing myself."

"You seem pretty cocky considering what I know about you."

"I'm here now, aren't I?"

"Why am I still in here?"

Zack let out a slow breath. "Because I need to be sure. I need to know everything."

"Erin gave you what you needed to get me out of here."

"Yeah, she did," Zack leaned forward, "but not everything. What does he have on you?"

"Look, Stack; I'm not safe in here."

"Should I make an inappropriate prison sex joke here or do you want to tell me? After all, you're acting as if I owe you a favor and Erin acted like I'm the only person you two can trust right after you threaten to ruin my life and people try to kill me. What am I supposed to believe?"

Fairfax frowned. "The truth and you have it. You didn't do your job very well, but neither did the police. The two detectives I understand, but not you. Not after I learned about you. And no, I didn't orchestrate any of the attempts on your life. Erin told me you were concerned so let me put those fears to rest."

Zack said, "how did you do that? Find out about me? Because that little tidbit of information is important to me."

"Stack, here's the deal: if I were a pedophile or rapist or woman abuser, I'd probably be dead in here. That's the way it works. But murder, even if it's a woman, is considered with a little more respect in here," Fairfax explained. "And having a boatload of money gave me power and protection. With the money, I was able to hire someone to follow you. To investigate you and find out everything about you and I hit the jackpot. Sure, it's been three plus long years, but it's about to pay off."

"Once you're out of here what guarantee do I have that your information never is seen by anyone else?"

"You have my guarantee," Fairfax said. "I can't speak for the guy who I hired. You'll have to take that up with him."

"Give me the name."

"I'll tell you after I'm out, safe with Erin."

Zack made a note to make sure to find out who. "Ok, start talking."

"I knew Rosler would want to get at me. I took precautions to make sure that wouldn't happen. I know Mike. Even though I am locked away in here and the deal we have, I knew it wouldn't be good enough for him. I know too much. A couple of weeks ago some guys I didn't know started a fight with the guys that protect me. One tried to kill me. My men stopped them before the guards got in here to break it up. I can't prove it, but I know Rosler is tying up loose ends as he makes his way towards the presidency."

They do hate loose ends. "How did Rosler end up with Erin?"

Fairfax exhaled. "Junior year at Harvard, we thought we were on top of the world. Mike, I, Sam, and Jerry did what we wanted whenever we wanted, and no one bothered us or questioned us," Fairfax began.

Zack pierced his lips. His education was in the Marine Corps. *Money has its advantages.*

"Well, Mike had urges, for lack of a better term," Fairfax continued. "And these urges usually involved women. He'd see one, and he'd have to have her." Fairfax frowned. "I managed to keep him away from Erin but as it turns out that was his plan all along: to get her from me."

"Yeah, I got that, too," Zack sounded frustrated. "Tell me something new."

"Well, towards the end of the school year we had a party. It was epic. Girls everywhere, pretty girls too. Erin wasn't there, though. She went home to see her parents, and in hindsight, I wish I had gone with her."

Zack saw Fairfax hide a tear. *Don't fall for it, Zack. This guy is still a jackass.*

"There was this one girl; I'll never forget her name, Amy Morris. A gorgeous girl from head to toe. She was dating some jock, but Mike didn't care. He moved in on her and tried as hard as he could to get her, but she was tough. Nice but tough. She was there with all her sorority friends, or I suspect she would have left. But Mike kept giving her drinks and was hanging all over her and eventually they disappeared. About a half hour later he came down with a big smile on his face and told me I had to get a piece of that action, so he took me upstairs to my room where he took her and there she was unconscious, naked and spread out on my bed."

Zack spoke next. "Why did he use your room?"

"Because he had another girl passed out in his room already," Fairfax's disgust showed. "Jerry was taking advantage of whoever she was. He wanted Sam and me to have Amy, too. I liked Mike, but Mike was a pig. I didn't know how big a pig he was until that night. And how evil he is."

"What happened?"

"I wouldn't. Sam said he'd be right back. He was smart. He got out of there. I didn't. I went to her side on my bed and tried to get some clothes on her. Well, she woke, went nuts, frantic and started screaming rape. She thought I did it because she couldn't remember if I was there or not before whatever Mike gave her kicked in. I tried to keep her quiet, and she bit me and scratched me. I bled, and it got on her and the sheets, and then Mike came behind her and jammed a syringe into her neck. She died a few seconds later in my arms."

We should know soon what he used on Ashley Blumenthal. "Then what?"

"I panicked," Fairfax said. "I wanted to call the cops even though I just watched Mike kill a girl. And I knew he raped her before that. But I freaked out because my fingerprints and blood were on her. She was in my room."

Zack shook his head. "But he raped her. There would have been semen that wasn't yours."

Fairfax dropped his head. "I was 21 and drunk. Would you have thought of that? All I knew was that I just was all over this naked woman, my sweat, my prints, my blood and she had scratched and bit me."

"You never violated her in any way?"

"Other than by enabling Mike, no."

"Ok, so then what?"

"Well after she was dead I realized my DNA was all over this woman. Mike said we had to get rid of the body and make it look like she drank herself to death or else I'd end up in prison the rest of my life."

Fairfax shook his head. "Mike showed me an open condom wrapper. He said there was no trace of him on her; not even sweat or saliva. He wiped her clean after he finished. He had thought of everything."

"Including how to get rid of the body?"

"He said he'd help me out of it. All I had to do was keep my mouth shut and not get in the way if he wanted to date Erin."

"And you agreed to give up your girlfriend that quickly?"

"If the police investigated I was going to jail and losing her anyway. Mike pointed that out. He said he'd take care of me. All I had to do was," he paused.

"Be his bitch forever."

Donald Fairfax lowered his head. "Basically."

"What happened to the girl?"

"I don't know. Mike got Jerry and told me to leave. Mike told me to remember everything he said, and everything would be ok. As best as I could tell, they got her back into her room and made it look like she drank herself to death. He even typed a suicide note on her computer to make it a better sale." Fairfax took a deep breath. "I'm not sure if his dad paid off the police or not, but they closed the case rather quickly, and several of them were driving brand new cars shortly after that."

Zack interrupted. "So, you hid a murder to save your ass."

"Don't judge me. I know you'd do the same."

Michael Rosler touching Jules crossed Zack's mind. *Maybe.*

"He didn't kill anymore after Amy that I know of, but he did rape a couple. My biggest fear though was that he'd kill Erin. I know he had my wife killed. You saw the scene. Erin and I figured we were safe until Sam was killed."

Zack nodded. "Ok, about your wife's murder. Why was your blood at the scene?"

"Simple," Fairfax said. "We gave blood earlier that week. It was part of a blood drive he set up to make his name into the community. He kept a vial and placed my blood conveniently at the crime scene."

Zack nodded. "And the cut on your hand where most novices cut themselves when stabbing someone?"

"Complete and utterly stupid pure coincidence," Fairfax confessed. "I cut it while moving the bed at the hotel that day when I was with Erin." He shook his head. "She didn't like the way the headboard knocked against the wall when we made love, so I moved it and pinched my hand." He shook his head again. "After I was arrested, Erin and I threatened Mike with what we have on him. He leaves us alone, and we stay silent. I die, or Erin dies, or both, and the information gets released. After that, I told Erin I'd find her and me a way out. And then you went to Indiana, and I found a way out. I knew Mike would be Mike. I just had to get you to find out about it."

Zack moved the phone away from his ear and rested the back of his hand against his mouth as he stared at Fairfax. "Were you and Sam working together to bring Rosler down?"

Fairfax nodded. "Yes, we hatched a plan about two years ago. His wife was killed, you know that, right?"

Zack nodded.

"She was afraid to tell anyone, just like Erin is afraid now that you talked to her. Rosler won't stop until he has won, and he doesn't care who he has to get rid of to get his way."

Zack listened but said nothing.

"Listen, Stack, you don't think Sam was killed by an errant shot, do you?"

"I never did."

"Sam was the target, and Rosler was smart. Mike was lagging in the polls. He needed free press. A lightning rod to bring energy to his campaign. What better way than by surviving a fake assassination attempt?"

"So Rosler set it up to kill Sam because he knew about you two collaborating."

"And to get rid of another girl he impregnated."

"I get you out, you give me what I want."

"I promise. Get me out of here, Stack. And do it fast. He's tying up loose ends before he becomes President. We are all in danger."

Zack exited the facility with his cell phone in one hand, and the motorcycle keys in the other. He sent a text to Barnes reading, *"Get Fairfax out. He's innocent."* Barnes replied, 'On it.'

A text from Stefani waited. He read it: 'call me.' Zack hit the number and waited. She answered. "Hey, what's up? Everything ok?"

"Hi, Zack," Stef answered. "Yeah, everything is fine. Julie just fell asleep. Hey, can you talk?"

"Yeah, but I'm about to get on my bike, so hurry."

"Where are you?"

Zack shook his head. "I am outside the BCCC. Just left. When Jules wakes up, tell her I have one hell of a story for her. What's up?"

"I got results today."

Zack stood still. "What are they? Please give me good news." He pointed his remote at his motorcycle.

259

Stefani smiled. "We have a match," her voice rose in excitement. "We have him, Zack! We have proof Ashley Blumenthal had succinylcholine in her system, and that Rosler was her baby's father! Zack," she squealed as she tried not to yell to wake up Julie, "we have the sonofabitch!"

"It's about time," he said and pushed the button to deactivate the alarm system on the motorcycle.

KA-BOOM!!!!

The explosion slammed Zack into the wall. The phone flew from his hand. He landed hard and fell to the ground dazed, his ears buzzed, his eyesight blurred.

"ZACK!" Stefani heard the explosion and yelled into the phone, but the line went dead after the sound. Stefani knew only one thing to do as her nurse training kicked in: find Zack.

*** ***

Zack felt hands on him. He felt a hand in his pocket. The buzz in his ears turned to a ringing. He heard muffled voices. He struggled to open his eyes.

"Stack! Wake up! Stack!"

Zack felt a hand on his arm pull him. Zack resisted and got his arm free. His eyesight blurred.

"Come on, Stack! We need to get you to the hospital. Stack, can you hear me?"

Zack struggled to focus. He moved his head one way, saw pieces of metal and tire burn. The wind pushed a plume of smoke into Zack's face. He coughed. His hearing cleared some.

Two men stood over him, bent forward, each attempted to grab Zack's resisting arms.

"STACK!"

He looked again at the two men with a clearer vision: Detective's Schmidt and O'Malley.

"Stack, we have to get you to a hospital," Schmidt said. "Come on; you're coming with us."

"No," Zack forced out. He heard sirens in the distance and the screech of tires from a car nearby.

"Yes, Stack, you're injured. We can get you to a hospital," O'Malley said. "Come on," he reached for Zack's arm again.

"NO," Zack forced out.

He saw someone run towards him. A female raced at him. Zack blinked several times; the fog lifted from his eyes. Stefani.

She forced herself between Zack and the detectives and immediately grabbed his wrist.

"Ma'am," Schmidt said, "we're police. We have this. We're taking him to the hospital."

She never took her eyes off Zack or stopped her inspection. "No, officer, you're not!" She snapped. "I'm a nurse; we need an ambulance!" The sirens neared.

"We're wasting time, lady," O'Malley said. "We have to move him now."

Stefani wedged herself closer to Zack. People gathered on the street. "Do you understand anything about trauma injuries?" She paused. "I didn't think so. Let me do my job!"

Schmidt looked around. A police car arrived with a fire truck and an ambulance right behind it. Schmidt looked at O'Malley and nodded. "Ok, all you people move back, give them some room," he barked.

Stef leaned over closer to Zack. "Are you ok?"

"The disk," he said. "My pocket. The disk."

"What disk? Zack, slow down. What are you talking about?"

But it didn't matter. Zack passed out.

CHAPTER 47

Zack slid on his shoulder holster, checked his Sig, placed it in the holster and put on a jacket.

"You sure you're ready? I mean, it's only been three days," Julie said as she handed him a new cell phone and his wallet. "Thought you'd stay longer since you have three women in your house."

Zack smiled. "Yeah, a real treasure chest."

"How long are you going to keep Meg here? You can't hide her forever."

Zack looked at his bare left wrist. His last watch shattered in the explosion. "They took the disk," he said at length. "Meg is the only one who can talk now. Just keep everyone here, ok?"

"It isn't them I'm worried about, Zachary."

"Honey, I'm fine," he said. "Besides, I was hired to do a job, and I have answers."

"I know, babe, but you're a mess."

Zack smiled. "Only on the outside. I'll be fine. I got Dre. Just stay here and rest, ok?"

She grabbed him and looked him in the eye. "Be careful. Come back to me, ok?"

Zack smiled, heard the door open, Andre looked inside, Zack hugged and kissed Julie. "I will."

Julie watched him leave, heard the door lock and returned to the couch. She sat, turned on some soap opera and curled under a blanket.

* * *   * * *

Zack pounded on the door of the large house; a colonial, big and beautiful. He looked at Andre. "Would you ever live in a house like this?"

"And give up living near downtown? Not a chance," Andre said. "You?"

"I'll never be able to afford it. Even if I could, I'm not sure if I'd want something this big."

"What if you and Jules have lots of little Zack's running around? Your apartment isn't going to cut it," he joked.

"You sound like Jules. You two conspiring against me now?"

Andre laughed. "Maybe. You need all the help you can get."

Zack shook his head and knocked on the door again. "So, it seems."

The door unlocked and opened. The woman's shocked expression didn't faze Zack.

"Cheryl," Zack said. "We need to talk." Zack walked through the door past Cheryl into a sitting room where Mr. Blumenthal sat with a surprised look on his face.

"Mr. Stack, I have to insist that you leave this instant," Cheryl said as Zack passed her.

"Who are you? What are you doing in my house?" Mr. Blumenthal stood firm.

"Sit down, Albert," Zack said. "You have some explaining to do." He looked at Cheryl. "You better sit down too. You don't want to hear this standing."

"Cheryl, who are these men? What is going on here?"

"My name is Zack Stack," Zack said. "This is Andre Kitchell. We are private investigators, and your wife hired me to find out how your daughter died."

Albert's eyes widened as he looked at his wife. "Cheryl? We agreed not to pursue it any further. You betrayed me!"

"Sit down and relax, Albert," Zack said. "I'm here to share what I've learned. You want to hear it or not?"

"She drowned, Mr. Stack! We already know that. We've been through enough already so don't put us through anymore and leave, or I will be forced to call the police. I'm a federal courts judge. No one does this to me!"

"I do so shut up. After you hear me out, I'll call the police for you, though I think you'll be singing a different tune." Zack sat on the edge of a chair across from Mr. Blumenthal. The room went silent. "Good. Let's begin. We found an account of yours, Albert and in it a large sum of cash was deposited the same day your daughter died." Zack handed Albert a sheet of paper. "Two hundred and fifty thousand dollars wired to that account that I bet your wife doesn't know about. Coincidence? I doubt it." Zack paused. "The cops called it an accident at the same time." Another pause. "The two investigating cops were wired large amounts of money the same day. Now since I usually deal in speculation, I will tell you what I think. You ready?"

"I think you should leave," Albert said as his wife glared with a white face at her husband.

"In due time, now shut up. Your daughter was involved with Senator Rosler. They were having an affair and ten days before she drowned she found out she was pregnant." Zack watched their faces. The expression change in Albert's face was subtle, but he noticed it. Cheryl was flabbergasted. "I don't know if you knew, but the father, Senator Michael Rosler did know. You demanding no autopsy suggests you knew and didn't want anyone to find out. We know Rosler didn't want anyone to find out. This test here proves Rosler is the father." Zack said and handed him another piece of paper. "Now we've all seen enough TV to know how scandalous that would be for who many believe will be our next President. That would ruin him. Especially with everything else your daughter and her clandestine group of friends working under the tutelage of Sam Polzinski found out." Zack stared at them both.

Cheryl Blumenthal stared at her husband with a terrified look on her face.

"That doesn't matter here. What matters is that Ash was killed. She didn't drown. She was killed. She was poisoned and thrown into the pond. This test here shows what was found in her system." He handed Albert that paper. "Someone, I'm assuming Rosler or his toady, got to you before you got to the medical examiner's lab and convinced you not to allow an autopsy because that could have told you what your wife believed from day one: that it was murder."

Zack looked at Cheryl whose icy glare never left her husband. He looked back to Albert, and Albert's look betrayed him: he shook with guilt buried beneath anger and hatred toward Zack for exposing his terrible deed.

"You see, the examiner knows his stuff. There were red flags so even though you told him no autopsy he checked the lungs. No water which means she didn't drown. He also took blood, hair and urine samples immediately and froze them. Ingenious if you ask me. That's how we know she was pregnant and how we matched the paternity test with Rosler. They overdosed her, unintentionally, with the drug. It was supposed to paralyze her so when they threw her into the pond she would not have been able to swim, but she'd inhale water and drown. Instead, the dosage stopped her breathing before they threw her into the pond. I am curious, Albert. How much did you know?"

He was silent at first. "I will not have you come to my house and impugn me."

Zack stood. "Oh, I'm impugning, dude. And according to what we found we know for your silence in addition to the cash you were promised a federal judge appointment after Rosler gets elected." He stepped closer to Albert. "So that's what your daughter's life was worth to you, you bastard?"

"How dare you! You can't prove any of that. That money had nothing to do with my daughter."

Zack wanted to beat the life out of Albert. "The DA might not take up the case. I know the information we have wasn't obtained through a legal search warrant and some of the evidence may be circumstantial. I doubt anyone in this town would take a highly reputable judge to task on this. But you have to live with yourself." He looked at Cheryl and then back to Albert. "And with her and I think that will be worse than any prison." He stared at the man's eyes which strayed from Zack and trembled. "Rosler is going down," Zack said softly. "Maybe not for murdering your daughter, but he is going down." Zack stood above the man. "Enjoy your money."

Zack turned to Cheryl. "I'm sorry," he said and walked out. Andre stared for a moment longer and followed Zack out.

The two got back into Andre's car and drove off. They were silent as they headed back to Fells Point. Andre broke the silence.

"You think she's going to kill her husband?"

"Yep," Zack said stoically.

"Me, too. You want to get a drink?"

"Yep."

* * *   * * *

Stefani sat next to Julie and watched television. She brought Julie a cup of coffee and one for herself. They were silent despite Stefani's attempts to talk.

The show ended, they watched the news in silence, and the next soap began. Finally, Stefani had enough and turned to Julie.

"Julie, Zack said you wanted me here, and I'm here. I didn't say anything because I figured you'd tell me why. You aren't talking much, but there has to be a reason you wanted me here."

Julie, knees to her chest with a blanket on her, looked at her and offered a half smile. "I just didn't want to be alone and to be honest: you're the only other girl I know enough to hang out with."

"What about Michelle?"

Julie grimaced. "Too much history."

Stefani nodded. "Ok, I don't want to know about that. What is wrong?"

Julie looked towards the floor. She exhaled and slowly raised her morose gaze to meet Stefani's watchful eyes. "Zack can't ever find out." She paused and took a breath.

"What can't he find out?"

Julie looked away. She struggled for the words, the courage. "I need your help," she said.

"With what?"

Julie glossed over, and tears streamed down her cheek. "Last week," she began, but the words choked on the way out of her mouth. She didn't want to hear herself say it. "I was in my hotel room." She wiped tears from her cheeks, and Stefani squeezed her hand in support. "He drugged me," she sobbed. Her breath caught in her throat and a panic attack overwhelmed her.

266

Stefani held Julie while she cried uncontrollably. Stefani knew what happened. "Hey, it's ok, Jules," she said softly. "I'm here for you. Just take a deep breath and tell me what happened."

"Zack can never find out," Julie cried.

"Julie, look at me." She raised Julie's face so she could see her eyes. "Were you raped?"

Julie closed her eyes, anguish all over her face and she nodded yes.

Stefani's heart fell even further into the pit of her stomach. She hugged Julie tight, and tears fell from her own eyes. "I'm sorry, Julie," she whispered. "I'm so sorry."

"There was nothing I could do. I said no, I tried to fight, but the drug, he put it in my wine," Julie cried.

"That bastard."

"You can't tell Zack."

Stefani shook her head and wondered why not. "We have to go to the police."

"NO! We can't," Julie shot back. She shook her head, tears still falling from her eyes. "We can't; you have to believe me."

Julie leaned back. She wiped her eyes with the sleeves of her hooded sweatshirt and fought to compose herself. Julie took a deep breath and felt like a weight had been lifted. She fought off the feelings of guilt and despair and self-doubt. Julie had been telling herself since the morning after it wasn't her fault.

"Julie, who did it?"

"Rosler."

Stefani added things up in her mind. The meeting with his wife, the affair she had with the man in jail, what Zack said happened in college: Rosler was a sexual predator. A rapist. And he was set to become the most powerful man in the country.

"He brought two bottles of wine but only drank from one and made me drink from the other. By the time I felt the effects, his hands were all over me. He forced himself on me, and I was too drugged to do anything about it. I remember telling him no several times. Then nothing. I woke up alone," Julie said. "Naked and alone and I knew right away something didn't feel right."

Stefani wanted to harm Rosler. "He threatened you, didn't he? Told you not to say anything or he'd destroy you?"

"He promised he'd ruin me and Zack and everyone around me."

"Why did you tell me?"

"Because I need your help. I need to make sure," Julie trailed off, and Stefani knew what she meant.

"Julie, I can't get that for you. I have to take you to the hospital."

"NO!" Julie yelled suddenly. "They'd have to report it. Stef, this can't get out. You're the only person who I am ever going to tell. Please, I need your help. Please tell me you can help me."

Stefani had used so many favors already; she didn't think she had any left. "I could get in big trouble," she said and saw the look in Julie's eyes and knew that potential trouble paled in comparison to Julie's trouble. "Ok, just let me take you to where I work. I know the people, and I'll do the exam," she paused, "get you what you need."

"We can't stay here?" The pleading in Julie's voice made Stefani nearly cry.

"No. We can't. It will be Ok. Ok?"

Julie hesitated. "Ok. Just promise me you will never tell Zack."

Stefani frowned. "You need to tell him."

"No, you don't understand. You don't know Zack. He can never find out. Now promise me."

"Ok, I promise," Stef agreed. "But, Jules," she added softly, "you need to tell him."

Julie lowered her eyes. She knew Stefani was right. Only Julie knew she couldn't tell Zack.

CHAPTER 48

The people on the plane buzzed with activity. Senator Rosler's staff hurried with preparations for his next event, his next speech, opposing the rival party's agenda and supporting his own party's views. Rosler sat on the plane quiet. He rested his eyelids and thought while his campaign manager/Chief of Staff Jerry Pantalini sat beside him and either Ok'd or nixed what the staff presented him. Pantalini loved the power.

Rosler opened his eyes. "God, I am so glad to finally get out of that state." He looked around to make sure no press was around. He looked at Pantalini. "How the hell did that place become the place to 'decide' who is President?" He shook his head. "Makes no sense. No one lives there anyway. I hope we don't have to go back. I'm tired of looking at cornfields."

Pantalini laughed. "Better keep those sentiments to yourself, Mike."

"Jerry, you know, I've been thinking." He looked at the man that has been his loyal servant since college. "We've been going about it all wrong."

"How so?"

"When you want to eliminate an enemy, you don't apply pressure on the enemy's support. It's like if you want to get rid of snakes, you don't kill all the mice. You cut the head off the snake, right?"

"If you're talking about other candidates, they are like mice, and we've eliminated the scraps for them to eat," Jerry said.

"No. I'm talking about our other problem," Rosler said, the vagueness deliberate. "The problem Kilgas has with a potential loose end, follow?"

Jerry's eyes widened with acknowledgment. "Oh. So what are you suggesting?"

"Cut the head off the snake. Forget about everyone else. Get rid of the leader, the rest will disappear," Rosler said. "Look, the female reporter said something to me once when she was interviewing me in my office. It was storming outside. I made a comment about how it was a great morning to stay in bed and cuddle with my wife. She made a comment on how her boyfriend always goes to the office early when it storms. It stuck with me for some odd reason," Rosler said.

"Ok, so what's your point, Mike?"

"Did you see the weather for Baltimore?" Rosler smiled. "Cut the head off the snake."

* * *   * * *

Zack and Julie laid on his bed, watching television but not watching television. The news started and the first story like every night was of the charming and attractive Senator Rosler. Back in Baltimore for a rally and then headed to DC. His every move made the news since the assassination attempt. Zack switched the channel immediately. He stopped at the Weather Channel and thought of being a weatherman again. Wrong all the time but still gainfully employed. Seemed like the best job in the world to Zack.

"How long are we living like this?" Julie asked, breaking the silence.

"You mean you and I together? Hopefully forever," Zack said.

"That's not what I mean," Julie said with a smile. She elbowed him. "I mean afraid to go out alone, Stef and Meg holed up here like they're seeking asylum. It's like we're just waiting for the worst."

Zack knew precisely what she meant. "I don't know. I'll think of something."

Julie bit her lip. "You can't do this alone." She found courage and turned to him. "Zack, we have to do something. We have to expose the sonofabitch, or they'll keep going until all of us are dead. You know that."

"Yeah, I do," he said. "But without the disk from Meg, we have nothing but he-said-she-said. What evidence we do have we got illegally, and no one we talked to will testify against him."

Julie spoke. "Look, honey, I can do this! I'll write a story. I have enough connections that will run with it. Proof or not people will ask questions. Connections will be made, and Rosler will have to answer questions. Even if he denies it, his image will be tainted. He'll have to pull off the dogs on us. We'll be safe then."

"No, we won't," Zack said at length. "They have mastered the art of administering accidental deaths." He looked into her eyes. "Jules, he'll discredit you and attack you. We both know what he'll do: lawyers, bullying, threats, denials, lies," Zack shook his head. "He has power, and he'll use it. That's what people like him do." He looked into her blue eyes. "I'm not letting him hurt you again."

Zack looked into her eyes, but she looked away.

She thinks I know but is afraid to ask. Probably wants to blame Stefani. Just tell me, Jules. We can survive this.

Julie took a deep breath and squeezed his hand. "We have to end this."

"I know," he said. "We'll come up with something. We always do." He squeezed her hand tight. "Sweetheart, we'll make it through this. I promise." He kissed her. "This will be over soon." *They won't waste time eliminating us.*

Julie smiled at him but said nothing.

Zack stared into her eyes and saw her internal struggle. He felt the tension within her and between them. He didn't know what to say. Her silence told him she didn't know either.

"I love you, Zack Stack," she said.

"I love you too, Julie Fletcher."

* * * * * *

The thunder woke Zack. He looked at the clock: 5 AM. He flopped on his pillow and reached across the bed for Jules. She was curled in the fetal position, her back to him, as far away on the bed as she could which wasn't unusual but it created a dilemma for Zack.

As much as he wanted to scoot across the bed and cuddle with her, he'd have to leave his pillow. Hers was much softer and spooning with her for only a few minutes would make his shoulder and neck hurt.

Zack also knew to lie in bed that morning would create problems as well. For one, the rain kept him awake. The occasional thunder and lightning and wind stirred his mind, and now his thoughts raced. Also, his body ached all over and now that he was awake, getting back to sleep would require a fair amount of tossing and turning as well as a trip to the bathroom which would likely wake Julie which would upset her and then she'd be crabby and take it out on him all day.

Much to Zack's dismay, he understood that his best course of action was to sneak out of bed, dress, turn her coffee pot timer on so it would brew when she woke in two hours, then go to the office and start his day. Maybe he could figure a way out of the mess that embroiled their lives.

He slid out of bed, tip-toed into the bathroom, shut the door, did his thing, snuck back into his bedroom, grabbed some jeans, shoes, socks, vest and a long sleeve shirt and left the bedroom. Zack closed the door behind him and went to the kitchen to dress.

Zack pulled his blue jeans up then grabbed Julie's favorite coffee maker. Despite his protests and comments, he knew the coffee made Julie happy. And that made him feel good about prepping it to have fresh brew for her when she stammered out of bed. He knew one thing about Jules: she would be ready for coffee at 7AM. So it would be done.

"Hey."

Zack jumped around and saw the wild-haired brunette with the black-rimmed glasses and flannel pajamas smile at him.

Zack realized he was shirtless and his pants were unzipped. He zipped and buttoned his pants. "What are you doing up?"

"Thought you knew I can't sleep in storms," Stef said.

Zack looked around her and saw Meg wake on the couch. "No one can around here apparently except for Jules."

Stef smiled. "They don't bother her?"

"She sleeps like a rock through these things."

Meg exited the couch and walked into the kitchen. "You making coffee?"

Stef noticed it. "Wait, you told me it isn't allowed here." She reached out and nudged him. "So you know me well enough now to lie to me?" She smiled and cocked her head.

"It's for Jules," he said as he slid on his tee-shirt. "In two hours. And coffee still isn't allowed here. It's just that I won't be here."

"Where are you going?"

"To the office," Zack said.

"Want me to come with?" Stef asked. "You said we shouldn't go anywhere alone."

"No," Zack said. "I'll be fine." He put on the dress shirt.

"You're still a mess," Stef said. "I can't believe you're even upright."

"Why does everyone keep saying that?" Zack asked. He slipped on his socks.

"Mr. Stack," Meg said.

Zack stood straight. "Mr. Stack?" He chuckled. "Wow. I've finally made it."

"You don't look like a Mr. Stack to me," Stef said.

"Hey, you aren't paying rent to stay here so I'd show more respect." Zack winked at Stef then looked at Meg. "Call me Zack. What?"

"We need to talk."

"What about?"

"You aren't going to be happy with me when I tell you," Meg hedged. She fiddled with her hands.

"I'm going to be even less happy if you make me guess," Zack said. He slid on his shoes. "What is it?"

"I haven't been completely honest with you." Both Zack and Stef stared at Meg. "You have to understand I wasn't sure I could trust you." Stef stood beside Zack. "The disk that you got in my room the other day?"

"What about it?"

"It was fake."

"What?"

"I'm sorry, Zack. It was fake."

"I almost died because of it!" Zack tensed and his hands clenched as the anger in him swelled quickly. Stef recognized his demeanor and squeezed his hand. "What was on it?"

"Term papers about European history during the Renaissance Era and the French Revolution," Meg said. "We bought them from last year's seniors who bought them from the class before them." She shrugged. "Why try to re-invent the wheel, right?"

"Are you kidding me?" Zack covered his face with both hands and drug them down as if to pull away his frustration. "Ok, let's move on now. So do you even have the real disk you talked about?"

Meg scrunched her face and blushed. She reached inside her pajama top, inside her bra and pulled out a flash-drive about the size of her thumb. "Right here."

Zack remembered meeting her at the winery and seeing her since then. "Wait, I know it wasn't there the whole time. Where did you keep it?"

The blush transformed into a deep red embarrassment. "The only place I knew no one would search me."

Stef looked at Zack, her eyes wide and a broad smile on her face. "Ingenious, if you ask me."

Zack finally got it. "OH." He nodded. "You're right, I would never have checked there."

"This is what you need."

Zack thought. "Ok. You're coming to the office with me. You're going to show me what is on it." He looked at his bare wrist. "I need a watch. Get dressed. You're coming with me."

Stefani grabbed Zack. "Zack, not alone. You need backup."

He stared at her and knew she was right. "Ok. I need you to do something for me."

CHAPTER 49

Zack unlocked the office door and led Meg up the stairs into the office. He unlocked and opened the glass doors atop the landing and entered the office. He turned on the lights and pulled Meg into his office.

"Sit behind the desk. Work on my computer," Zack said.

Meg went to take off her coat.

"NO!" Zack said. "Keep it on."

"But it's bulky and warm."

"Keep it on," he said. His computer booted on, and he slid the drive into the USB port. "Ok, show me what you have."

"I need some coffee. Is it banned here, too?"

Zack shook his head. "What is with you coffee drinkers?" He left the office and started the coffee maker in the front office by Michelle's desk. He waited to make sure it was brewing and remembered what Stefani was insistent about before he and Meg left his apartment.

"It will be ready soon," Zack told Meg as he disappeared into the closet and bathroom in his office. He returned a few minutes later.

"Your computer is slow," Meg complained.

"I forgot," Zack remarked, "you are part of the instant gratification generation. Another ten seconds isn't going to kill you."

Meg sneered at him. "Haha, old man. I'm surprised you even have a computer being as old as you are." Her sarcastic mocking put a smile on his face, and then he laughed.

"We just had the tin cans with a string attached phone system upgraded last week."

The two stared at the computer screen as it readied and Meg finally was able to access the drive. "Is my coffee ready yet? I need it," Meg said.

"I'll go check."

"I like it with sugar and a little cream," Meg called out as Zack left the room.

He shook his head and poured the coffee into Michelle's giant mug, added sugar and cream and stirred it. Zack brought it back to his desk and set it beside Meg.

She sipped it. "Umm, good. You could be a barista if you apply yourself."

"And after you get your college degree, you can ask me if I want fries with my order."

"You're funny," Meg said. "Ok, here we go. What do you want to see first? Let's start with the bribes." Meg paused and looked at Zack. "I really want to thank you for saving my life by the way and apologize for almost costing you yours."

Zack took a deep breath. "You're welcome, and I forgive you provided this information ruins Rosler."

"It will," Meg said. "Whatever it is you drink in the morning I suggest you get it now because once we get started, you won't leave for a while."

Zack nodded. Pepsi sounded like a good idea. It was only half past five in the morning, still raining heavily outside and dark. It was going to be a long day. "Hold on, I'll be right back."

Zack left the office and turned the corner to get to the fridge behind Michelle's desk. He pulled out a bottle of Pepsi, opened it and drank from it. He screwed the top back on when suddenly two men burst through the door.

The shotgun pointed right at Zack; the man pulled the trigger.

The blast lifted Zack off his feet, slammed him into the wall, and he dropped to the floor on his stomach. The men walked over to him, one cocked the shotgun again and stopped over Zack. He saw blood trickle from his legs, arms, and neck. Zack didn't move.

"What do we have here?" The other man said.

Meg didn't scream. She sat behind Zack's desk and trembled, but she didn't move.

"That's her! Meg Chatwell," the shooter said. "Call Kilgas."

The man got Kilgas on the phone and told him what they found. He listened and nodded. At long last, he hung up and smiled. "Bonus points for us."

"What do we do now?"

"Continue with the plan. Tear the place up, make it look like a robbery and bring the girl with us. We'll drop her with the guys on the northwest corner behind the square," he said. "I'll take her out of here. You take care of this place. I'll send in backup."

The man yanked Meg from behind the desk by the wrist and dragged her outside. Meg didn't scream but resisted and pulled back. The man pulled her through the door. She looked and saw the motionless Zack on the floor behind Michelle's desk.

The other man smiled at the office and knocked everything off Zack's desk, turned over the desk and chair, kicked over the fridge and went to work on the couch with a knife.

A third man rushed up the stairs, he grabbed the door and stepped inside. He heard the commotion in the back office and looked for the target. He carried a shotgun as well.

He saw the feet of Zack from behind the desk. He walked towards it and raised his weapon. Then, his eyes got huge, shock overwhelmed him, and he fumbled for his trigger.

Zack, on his back, fired the Mossberg that Michelle had hidden under her desk and pointed at the front door. The blast exploded the man's chest, killed him instantly and flew him through the air into the wall. Zack struggled to his feet.

The man in his office ran to the doorway and pointed his gun at Zack. Zack dove over Michelle's desk as the man's shotgun blew apart her computers and part of the desk. Zack hit the floor and cocked the gun, but it was empty.

Only ONE SHOT? JESUS CHRIST, MICHELLE!!

He grabbed the Sig around his ankle, grabbed the bloody grip, rolled across the floor as another shotgun blast eliminated the desk between the two men and fired the Sig repeatedly. The man stood as if suspended by puppet strings and his body reacted to all seven shots that tore into his body. Blood sprayed behind him, his eyes in shock and horror until he collapsed to the floor dead.

Zack struggled to his feet with one thought only: *Save Meg!*

He knew a shortcut. Zack limped to his office, grabbed a new clip of ammunition for his Sig and rushed out his hidden passageway. *Just don't let me die until Meg is safe.*

* * * * * *

Zack landed in the alley behind his building in a puddle amidst the pouring rain. The wind howled, and darkness was only interrupted by the flash of lightning and the dim light from streetlights, muted by the storm. He struggled to his feet and rushed up the alley as fast as he could.

A crack of thunder shook the ground, the rain blinded him, but Zack endured and forced his way to the end of the alley. He rested against a trash dumpster, moved forward and leaned against the side of the building at the end of the alley, hidden by the dark.

Then, a man turned the corner with the struggling Meg in one hand; she fought each step, and the man dragged her. Zack realized this bought him time. They would have been long gone by now had it not been for Meg's resistance.

A car came forward. Zack didn't wait. "STOP!" He yelled and stepped onto the sidewalk, away from the building. He raised his Sig and pointed it at the man. The man stopped, saw Zack and pulled Meg close. He wrapped an arm around her but pointed his gun at Zack.

Zack aimed and fired. The man yelled and dropped his arm, Meg let out an 'ugh' and dropped to the ground. The man hesitated, and Zack shot three times. The man fell to the ground dead.

The car screeched to a stop. Zack rushed to Meg, a severe limp in his gait and leaned to her. The car door opened, a man popped out, and from behind the open car, door fired his handgun. Zack returned fire.

Several shots rang out, smoke rose from the barrel of Zack's Sig as the clip emptied. The man behind the door hit the street dead. Zack waited, but it was silent. Water ran down his face and diluted the blood from his wounds. He looked at Meg.

She opened her eyes in relief. Zack helped her sit. "You shot me!" She said.

"I know. Damn good shot, wasn't it?"

"YOU SHOT ME!"

"Indirectly," Zack said. "He let go of you, didn't he?"

"My chest hurts. I can barely breathe," Meg said.

"Yeah, I feel really bad about that." He looked around and knew he had to get her out of there. "Don't worry. I'll get over it."

"YOU'LL get over it? What about me?"

Zack checked under the Kevlar vest he made her wear. "You're going to have a bruise there for a while. I wouldn't plan any swimsuit photo shoots."

"Is that a joke?"

Thunder rumbled softer. Lightning flashed a few seconds later, but the rain didn't slow. Zack couldn't hear anything beyond the rain pelting the street and building beside him. "Help me up, we have to get out of here."

Meg stood, grabbed Zack under the shoulders and helped him to his feet. He grunted and hunched over. Zack took a deep breath, put an arm around Meg and the two walked towards the square. Zack figured back to his apartment would be the smartest...if Stef did what he asked.

They walked about fifteen feet when suddenly two gunshots rang out. Zack heard them clearly.

He felt both.

Zack hit the ground, face first, two bullets in his back.

Meg screamed and stood in disbelief. She stared at Zack as two men rushed at her. She looked at the two men as they neared and recognized them.

Then she saw a man and woman appear from the corner of her eye from the alley. She saw the muzzle flash once, twice, three times. The two men that charged her fell to the ground. One splashed in a puddle at her feet. The other groaned and reached for his dropped weapon.

The man from the alley was there fast. He stepped on the wounded man's hand before he reached his gun. The man from the alley leaned over to the man on the ground.

"O'Malley, you dirty piece of garbage, this is way too easy for you."

Lieutenant Ted Barnes kicked O'Malley's gun away and watched O'Malley take his last breath and die. Stefani ran past Meg to Zack.

"CALL AN AMBULANCE!" Stef screamed. "PLEASE HURRY!"

Barnes was on his phone fast and made the call. He made several. He covered Meg in his raincoat and huddled with her and Stefani as Stefani did what she could to stop the bleeding from the unconscious Zack.

Meg shook uncontrollably. Tears flowed from her eyes as rainwater streamed down her head. She glanced at the four men dead on the sidewalk and street. Two were bad cops. She knew they were on the payroll of Rosler. Only the man in front of her, Zack Stack, saved her again. And now, he lied in a pool of water and his own blood while another woman clutched him tight and yelled to him to keep fighting, to please keep fighting.

CHAPTER 50

Julie Fletcher held her arms tight across her chest. Her bloodshot eyes hadn't dried in hours. Nor would they as she stared at her fiancé as he fought for his life, tubes stuck in his body all over, on a hospital bed in an ICU room.

Andre and Darnell flanked her and Michelle stood in the corner of the room with Ronald, her boyfriend. Michelle's face streaked with tears. Stefani sat by the window and stared at Zack and watched the monitor attached to him.

It was nighttime. Dark long arrived and the storm long gone. Only hours in surgery kept Zack alive, but that thread of life in him was still tenuous. Lieutenant Ted Barnes entered the room quietly. A nurse checked the drip of antibiotics attached to Zack's arm.

He nudged Andre and motioned for him to step outside. The two left the room and stood in the hallway.

"I got two uniforms in this hallway and increased patrols around this place. I can't stay long though," Barnes told Andre.

Andre nodded. "We aren't leaving tonight."

"You know he'll be fine," Barnes said. "He still owes me. Zack knows better than to stiff me."

Andre smiled. "Where's Meg?"

"In deep hiding. We'll try to connect the dead guys, but I bet they're like everyone else and are ghosts. If this was Rosler's doing, we won't make a link. You know that."

Andre nodded. "Then what the hell are we going to do? Wait until he kills us all?"

Barnes exhaled through his nose with his hands on his hips. He shook his head. "Something tells me Rosler only wants Zack dead. Where is what he found on Ashley Blumenthal? I want to know everything you two know."

"In his office."

"Ok. In the morning I'll get someone up here I know I can trust. Then you and I are going to your office and looking at all of this stuff. Until then, stay safe my friend."

* * * * * *

The clock struck midnight. Julie had enough. She knew why it happened, and she felt guilt, anger, rage, sorrow, remorse, and fury all at once. The conversation with Zack the night before went through her mind. He was wrong then. Zack couldn't fix this on his own. But she could.

She looked at Stefani and then to Michelle. "Stef," Julie said. Stef's gaze snapped off Zack and looked at her. Julie walked across the room and held Stef's hands. "I need you to stay here with Zack tonight. Will you do that for me?"

Stef looked surprised and confused. "Of course. Why? Where are you going?"

"I have something I need to do."

"What? Jules, no, you should be here. He needs you."

Jules looked back at Zack. Her religious upbringing instantly made her pray for Zack. "He does need me. But not here. Please stay here with him, ok? If anything changes with him, call me," Julie said. She smiled a soft, compassionate smile and let go of her hands and walked over to Michelle. "Michelle, I need your help with something."

Michelle looked into Julie's eyes. "Ok. What do you need?"

"Not here. Can we go to your place? You have computers there?"

"Of course."

Julie turned to look at Zack. "Let me talk to him quickly, then let's go." She walked to Zack, leaned close to his ear, whispered how much she loved and needed him, kissed his lips softly, then her, Michelle and Ronald left.

* * * * * *

282

Michelle watched the emails disappear into cyberspace and exhaled. "You have about three seconds for me to bring that back if you have any doubts about what you just did," she said to Julie.

Julie stood beside her; arms crossed as she chewed the nails on her right hand. She exhaled. "No, I have to do this."

"There is no turning back now," Michelle said. "How about another cup of coffee?" She rose from the desk, and Julie nodded yes. "You think it will work?"

Julie shook her head. "The pen is mightier than the sword." Julie smiled. "I think the contacts I've made over the years will trust me. This has to work."

Michelle raised her eyebrows as she poured the coffee into two mugs. The clock struck five in the morning. The two had been up all night composing articles and stories based on what they knew.

"We'll know soon enough." Michelle sat at the chair behind her desk in her apartment. The spare bedroom in her apartment served as her home office. Julie sat on a loveseat against the wall perpendicular to the desk. "Sometimes, the waiting game is the hardest part."

"I could have prevented all of this," Julie said.

"How so?"

Julie scoffed in self-disgust and shook her head. "Rosler knew of Zack's history with Donald Fairfax. Rosler knew Cheryl Blumenthal was going to hire Zack when we were still in Europe. That's why he hired me. He wanted to keep me close so that he could keep an eye on Zack," Julie said. "I should have picked up on it sooner. He and Kilgas said Zack's name several times, and I never told them his name. They wanted me to watch Zack."

"It isn't Zack's fault nor is it your fault," Michelle said. "Everyone fell for Rosler's charm and good looks."

"Everyone but Zack."

Michelle sipped the hot coffee. She eyed Julie. "Are you going to tell him?"

Julie shook her head. "I tried," she confessed. "I didn't even want to tell you."

"You did because you have to talk about it, Jules." Michelle smiled, swiveled her chair to face Julie straight-on and put her hand on Julie's knee. "Even if it is to me."

Julie looked at Michelle and eventually hinted a smile. "I guess we really aren't adversaries when it comes to Zack, are we?"

"No, we aren't. I love Zack, you know that. But not like that. Not like you. I want him happy, and he's happy with you. And when he's happy with you, he's not such a pain in my ass," Michelle laughed.

Julie set down her coffee and leaned forward. "Come here," she said, and the two hugged. Julie hid crying, and Michelle knew why: for Zack. After a moment, she pulled away. "I tried to tell him. I really did." She shook her head. "But I know him, and I'm afraid of what he'll do."

"Well that's easy: he's going to kill him." Michelle leaned back in her chair. "He'll never hurt you. But Rosler? I don't feel sorry for him though. Zack may not kill him, but Rosler won't be the same after Zack gets through with him. Rosler will get what he deserves."

Julie looked at Michelle. "I know. And he'll get taken away from me, and that scares me."

* * *   * * *

The lights brightened. At first, it was dim and shady, but it slowly widened and built. Then, the light shone strong. Voices suddenly were audible. Like he had woken from a deep sleep. Zack opened his eyes. The clouds and fog remained but cleared slowly.

After several blinks he stared into the beautiful cerulean eyes he fell in love with years ago. He smiled. Julie smiled. Her wet eyes smiled, and she wiped a tear off her cheek.

"Hi," she said softly. "I missed you."

Zack wanted to talk, but the effort made him tired, so he laid there and stared into her eyes while she clutched his hands.

"I love you," she said softly.

He smiled and mouthed the same thing with no sound. It was enough for him. Her eyes, her love, her close: Zack figured he may have died but knew if he were looking at Jules, he was in heaven. That was good enough.

* * *   * * *

The day went fast. Zack learned of his fate. He wasn't in heaven, and he hadn't died. But he was stuck in a hospital for another few days. Multiple wounds, two bullets in the back narrowly missed killing him. Shotgun blast wounds narrowly missed killing him. The vest he put on the morning at his office, though it wasn't plated like the one he had Meg wore, did enough of a job to prevent holes being blown through his chest. But he got lucky. No open heart surgery. No ripping open his chest.

Julie sat in the room with him along with Stefani and Andre. It was his last night in the hospital. Zack stared at the television while Julie flipped through a magazine. Andre texted on his phone and answered emails while Stefani bounced between watching the TV and playing a game on her phone.

The restlessness got to Zack already. He hated being stuck to a bed. He flipped a channel and stopped briefly on a national nightly news program. The anchor talked, but Zack didn't hear what was said. Zack changed the channel.

"Wait, wait!" Stefani said, breaking the silence in the room. "Turn back."

"Why?"

"Just turn back. It was about Rosler."

Zack turned back, and the anchor was mid-sentence.

"...alleged improprieties with college-aged female interns. A spokesman for the Senator vehemently denies the allegations, calling them false, unfounded and a partisan smear-attack attempting to derail the Senator's Presidential run. For more on the story, we'll send it to our DC correspondent..."

Zack sat up in bed and looked at Julie. "Honey, is there anything you want to tell me?"

CHAPTER 51

Zack sat inside his office alone a week later. After the shooting, Zack's phone was silent. The news covered the incident, and unfortunately, his agency made the news again, but Barnes convinced the press it was a robbery attempt gone wrong. The local media covered it. Five men were killed, another seriously wounded and two were cops. But then, the news of Rosler hit the airwaves, and suddenly everyone forgot.

Julie told him what she and Michelle did. The press was all over Rosler. Eight dead girls and allegedly staging his own assassination attempt while taking out an adversary were serious accusations. This time, the media didn't let it go.

The only thing that stood between Rosler and jail was the jump drive in the desk drawer to Zack's left. That was the final nail, and Zack waited to use it.

He looked at his bare wrist, wished he had a wristwatch, saw the clock on the partially rebuilt wall said four thirty in the afternoon and wanted a drink. Zack hadn't had alcohol since before he was shot and the sound of bourbon or a beer or even popping the cork out of a bottle of wine sounded good.

Zack watched the construction crew close shop for the day on the repairs to the office and leave. The bottle called his name, but the sound of female heels on the floor stopped that. He looked. "Mrs. Blumenthal, what are you doing here?"

She smiled a tired yet warm smile as Zack stood.

"Won't you sit down?" Zack offered her a chair, helped her sit and limped behind his desk. He looked at her and opened his mouth to end the awkward silence when she spoke.

"Mr. Stack, my husband died last night."

Zack leaned forward in surprise.

"I found him this morning. He passed away in his sleep."

"I'm sorry," Zack offered.

"It's ok, Mr. Stack. I wanted to tell you in person in case you didn't see it on the news." She took a deep breath. "He had a heart attack."

Zack still didn't know what to say but immediately shifted into detective mode and his ears perked.

"There was no funny business if that is what you are thinking."

"I wasn't actually." *The hell I'm not. But this will keep the press on Rosler.*

"Shortly after you found out what you did about my Ashley, we fought, naturally," she confessed. "He tried to apologize, but you caught him, and he confessed. He said he didn't know Ashley was pregnant and that they came to him only after she was dead. By then he reasoned nothing good would come out of pursuing why or how Ashley died and deep down he hoped if Rosler became President and appointed him higher in the courts, he could do some good is what he said. But it was too much for me, and I couldn't stand to be with him or even look at him," she said.

"Cheryl, you don't have to explain."

"Yes, I do. I need you to believe that I had nothing to do with any of this. And I need to thank you for following up where everyone else failed."

"Everyone else stopped, Cheryl. They were intimidated or paid off to stop investigating." *Well, I just blew her thinking I'm a super detective.*

"I left him. I was staying in an uptown apartment with my sister. I went home this morning and found him dead. I called 911 immediately, but they determined he had a heart attack in his sleep and died."

She stared at Zack. Zack's mind raced, and questions lined up one after the other. He took a deep breath. "Was there any reason to think he had any visitors last night?" *Like my good friend, Pete Kilgas and his gang of psychos?*

"I know what you're thinking, Zack and I thought the same thing." She reached into her purse and removed a small vial of a liquid and a syringe, both in a sandwich bag. "These were on his nightstand."

She handed them to Zack. He read the vial label. "Potassium chloride," he said and leaned back in his chair. "I'll be damned."

"I hid them from the paramedics and police."

"Why? That proves he was either killed or more likely committed suicide." And then he understood. "Oh. I get it."

"Exactly. Life insurance benefits aren't always paid in cases of suicide."

Zack reached his limit and opened his desk drawer. He pulled out two glasses and the bourbon and poured some in both. "Would you like a drink?"

"No, thank you."

He took a large gulp off the bourbon and put down the glass. "Cheryl," he said softly, "you do realize that you are admitting a crime to me. I'm not even sure where to start, but insurance fraud is a good start."

"That's why I'm telling only you. I know you'll do the right thing. I don't trust anyone else," Cheryl said.

"Cheryl, I wish you hadn't told me. You are putting me in a very precarious position."

"I'm aware of that," she said. "Please allow me to explain. Well, first, let me give you your payment." She handed him an envelope and instructed him to open it. Zack's eyes bulged.

"Holy," he caught himself before the profanity left his lips. "Cheryl, I can't accept this. It's not only way too much, but it's way too much. I wouldn't even charge you a fraction of this." He looked at the number again. "Well, maybe a fraction."

"Let me explain, Zack. I know he committed suicide. He couldn't live with himself for what he did and, to be honest, I couldn't live with him either. A part of me feels like Albert got what he deserved."

He still got off way too easy.

"When I found him dead I decided I could turn the evil he did into something good," she explained. "You have no idea how much life insurance he has, and I was afraid it wouldn't have paid out had I not hidden the drug he used to kill himself. Nor could I afford his name to be ruined. With that money, I decided to start a memorial scholarship in Ashley's name to help many students every year. And what I gave you," she shrugged and offered a sheepish smile, "I feel you deserve it for what you went through." She paused. "And looking at your office, it looks like you could use the money for some much-needed repairs."

"Yeah, we're renovating," he said. "Cheryl, several other girls died in addition to Ashley and Hannah." He sipped his bourbon. "It was much deeper than we thought."

"And that's why I'm only telling you. You can use that money however you want, or you can tell the police although after how the police investigated Ashley's death I doubt they'd solve anything."

Zack stared at the check and put it down. "This kind of feels like a bribe."

Cheryl stood. "It's a payment for your services, Mr. Stack. You did a job, and I paid you a fee for doing it. The fee entirely was my decision." She walked to the door, stopped and looked at Zack again. "Thank you for Ashley. She deserved a better fate, and I don't know if the men responsible will receive justice, but I believe you won't let that go either. Just think about that when you're mulling everything else. Good day, Mr. Stack."

Let that go either? He shook his head. *I just got paid to hide a crime.* Then he remembered what he said in jest to Stefani not long ago: *the key is to break the law for the right reasons.*

He put the check down, looked at his phone and thought of Jules. He missed her and missed being with her. Zack dialed a number and waited for the answer. "Hey, what are you doing?" He smiled at the answer. "Can you meet me at the pub in about thirty minutes?" He listened. "Dinner is on me. Just pay attention, Ok? See you in thirty." Zack hung up and sent a text. He didn't expect a return. Julie was at her mother's. She spent a lot of time there the last week since he was released from the hospital. Zack finished both glasses of bourbon, checked the Sig in his shoulder holster and left the office.

CHAPTER 52

Stefani walked through the door and saw Zack alone near the end of the bar. He stared at the glass in front of him.

She sat next to him. "I walked fast and paid attention," she said. "Last time I was here I didn't get to enjoy it."

"This time you can," Zack said. "Here, I bought us shots."

"Oh, no. Zack, are you nuts? You shouldn't be drinking alcohol."

"You're like a parrot; you know that?"

"Because I repeat myself?" She laughed. "Well, you never do what is best for you and for some stupid reason I care about you."

He lifted the shot glass. "Then let's toast: To a solid future."

She shook her head at him but slammed the shot. Her face scrunched as the liquor burned down her throat. "Ugh! Not bad," she laughed again with a cough.

Zack ordered two more. "And get her a glass of merlot."

She laughed. "What are you trying to do, Zack? Get me drunk and sleep with me?"

"I don't need to get you drunk for that," Zack said. He lifted the shot glass, and they slammed the second shot.

After the shots, he went back to his beer. He sipped it, and Stef sipped her wine.

"You really shouldn't be drinking. Not after what you went through."

He looked at her. "Polly want a cracker?"

She laughed and hit his arm. "Shut up. I just don't want you to die. Ok?"

"I'll be fine."

She rolled her eyes. "What's up?"

"I know you know. Jules told you. I know it. So now my dear, you are going to tell me."

Stef's face lost its color. "What do you mean? Tell you about what?"

Zack grabbed her knee with his hand and squeezed it gently. "Stef, honey, I like you. You've helped me when you had no reason to, and you've turned out to be a great friend and a valuable asset. But don't buffalo me, sweetheart." His stare burned holes through her.

"I don't know what you're talking about."

Zack slouched back and scoffed loudly. "Now we're hiding things from each other. We could be a real-life couple!" He leaned close and stared into her eyes. "Let's bypass the lying to each other stage of this relationship and get right to the part where we swear on our lives to never keep any secrets from each other ever again. Ok?"

She sighed. "I need another shot."

Zack put up two fingers to the bartender.

Stefani downed her shot. "I promised her, Zack."

Zack stared at her but said nothing. *Next one to talk loses.*

She dropped her head and shook it. "UGH!" She leaned back and almost yelled. "Zack! Why are you doing this to me?"

She lost. Now she'll play her last few cards. "Because I know you're not going to lie to me."

She stared at him torn. "What do you think happened?"

"She slept with Rosler," he said plainly. "I need you to tell me if she did it willingly or if he raped her."

Her head dropped. Zack knew she had no cards left. "Ok. Two things first: one, you have to tell me about your past. You said you would, and I have to know. Second, you have to promise me Julie will never find out I told you. I like her, and she'll hate me."

"Trust me. Now talk."

"You first."

Zack nodded and frowned. *Ok, now she has no cards left.* "Ok, you want to know. Here it is. About sixteen years ago, I was a senior in high school. Long story short, I went home and found my father dead, with a bullet hole in his head."

"Oh my God! Zack, I'm sorry," she said.

Zack continued. "Even longer story short, a dirty cop framed Darnell for it and then after Darnell was sentenced, the cop threatened to kill me if I didn't leave town. Naturally, I left town. I came east on my motorcycle with a few hundred dollars to my name. Somehow I found Michelle. Her uncle made a living at making fake documents." He drank from his beer and looked at Stefani. "The person I was ceased to exist, and a few months later, Zachary Ulysses Stack joined the Marines where I met Andre. I am leaving out a lot of details, but fast forward, and here I am with a past only a handful of people know about."

She stared at him; her mouth open, speechless.

"Yeah, exactly."

"So," she paused, "Zack isn't your real name?"

Zack finished his beer and ordered another. "No."

Stefani computed what she heard. "Wait, that means that no one,"

Zack nodded. "No one can know. If it gets out," he folded his hands in front of his face, "nothing good happens."

"Wow. That is not what I expected. Your motto 'break the law for the right reasons' makes sense now though. You committed a federal offense when you entered the Marines. So Erin Rosler and that Fairfax guy knew and were extorting you."

Zack nodded.

"Zack, I don't know what to say," she said at length. "Ok, so tell me the long and longer story now. Wait, how did Darnell end up here? Did you get him out of jail, too?"

Zack nodded. "I had to."

"And then what? Spill it, Zachary Ulysses. Come on, I feel like the wall finally came down so let's keep going."

"Another time. Your turn."

"There it is, the Zack I know. There's that wall," she said and rolled her eyes. "Why do you do that?"

"I'm the one changing the subjects here, not you, sweetheart. Now talk."

She smiled. "After what you just told me, I don't see how you think you can keep control of this conversation." She sipped her wine, her eyes never leaving Zack's. "Who else knows?"

"Jules, Dre, Barnes, obviously Michelle and Darnell, and now you. The list keeps getting larger which it can't."

"Wow," Stefani drank her wine. "I guess I have the upper hand on you now."

Zack stared at her.

"Just out of curiosity, how can you live like that? I mean, how can it ever end?"

"I can die," Zack said plainly. "Now tell me the truth about Jules and Rosler.

CHAPTER 53

Four Weeks Later

"Good morning, and Happy Thanksgiving. We have delicious turkey tips for you but first on Today, the trouble for Presidential Candidate Senator Michael Rosler keeps building as more information surfaces surrounding his affairs with interns and their subsequent mysterious deaths.

Plus, his wife Erin Rosler, the CEO of the family-owned Valentino Industries has filed for divorce further casting a dark shadow on the Senator. A press conference is planned by the Rosler camp later today. We switch to our DC correspondent..."

Zack turned off the television and smiled. He turned back to prepping the turkey on his counter. Alone in his apartment, he enjoyed the silence. It had been silent since Julie's news reports hit all airwaves. Zack realized that Julie was right: that made them safe. *The pen indeed is mightier than the sword.*

Zack invited everyone over: Jules, Dre and his girl Alysha, Darnell and his new girlfriend Leigh Ann, Michelle and her boyfriend, Ronald the FBI Guy, and Stefani who had become important to all of them. He expected them to arrive around noon, though he hoped Jules would come earlier. He missed her terribly, and she still hadn't talked to him about what happened.

Things smoothed out at the agency though Zack was loads of paperwork behind. Erin Rosler sent an obscenely large check as a thank you before she disappeared with Donald Fairfax. He'd tackle that issue after the weekend. Today, almost entirely pain-free and looking healthy, he just wanted fun, relaxation and to move forward.

By noon, all arrived except Stefani. She came at one o'clock. She entered, and Julie saw her first. She called out a warm greeting, walked to Stefani, and the two hugged.

"Zack didn't tell me to bring anything so on the safe side I brought some wine."

"You know how to get to my heart. Who cares about Zack?" The two laughed as Zack approached.

"You're supposed to plot against me after you eat my food," Zack joked and hugged Stefani. She held him tighter and longer than he expected and caught his eye with a warm smile after they pulled away. "You're late, so grab a glass, help yourself to anything and pretend you're having fun."

"This is his first attempt at a meal like this so definitely have fun now," Julie laughed.

"Good idea." She looked at Julie. "What are you drinking?"

"Moscow Mule. You want one?" Then Julie winked. "We'll have the wine later."

Stefani looked relieved. "Oh my God! Now you're after my heart. Serve it up."

The two walked across the room to the drink table. Everyone greeted Stef. Andre stopped in front of the television, it was halftime of the football game, and it cut away to a special report.

"HEY! Quiet down!" He yelled out. Zack saw the TV and moved closer to him.

The anchor said they had a special report at a press conference from Senator Rosler's camp concerning the mounting investigation of improprieties with Rosler's college-aged female interns, eight of whom have ended up dead.

They cut to the conference where police stood by, and the Chief of Staff Jerry Pantalini stood behind the podium. He was in his speech already and listed off the things he did adding that Rosler did not know anything. Pantalini claimed he had the help of Pete Kilgas, the head of security and members of the security staff that Kilgas formed, not Rosler or Pantalini.

"That sonofabitch," Zack said.

"He's taking all of the blame." Andre shook his head.

Pantalini confessed that it was he who impregnated the dead girl Ashley Blumenthal and after he had found out she was pregnant, she threatened to use her pregnancy to blackmail Rosler as Jerry found out she was in love with Rosler and was sleeping with Pantalini to get closer to Rosler. Pantalini confessed he ordered his security staff to use the anesthesia SUX not to kill her but to threaten her. Only they used too high of a dose, and it killed her. He reiterated that Rosler had no knowledge of any of this and said the authorities already have his computer and cell phone and that a search would exonerate the Senator of any wrongdoing.

"That sonofabitch," Zack repeated slower this time.

"This guy is going to get the death penalty, and Rosler is going to let him." Andre shook his head slower this time.

"And they're buying this bullshit hook, line, and sinker. Rosler is going to walk away clean. He's going to get away with all of it. Sonofabitch."

Andre looked at Zack. "Looks like it's over, dude. Everything we did and what we went through, none of that matters now."

Zack picked up a drink and gulped it. "That sonofabitch," he said softly.

Michelle grabbed the remote from Andre and turned the television off. "Enough work you two!" She turned them both away from it. "We're here to celebrate and have some fun and not talk about work, so that is what we are going to do."

"You're right," Andre said. "Michelle, it's cornhole time. Your reign is about to end."

"Bring it on, big man," Michelle said. "Beating you two is so much fun."

Zack smiled and tried to pretend like the news didn't bother him. But it did. And when everyone else went outside to play the bean bag game that Zack despised, his cell phone rang.

"Stack here."

"Interesting development, huh?" It was Kilgas.

"Deep down I knew someone else would take the fall for that piece of shit."

"Come on, Stack, is the name calling necessary?"

"Yes. Why are you calling me? Don't you have some puppies to go kill or something?"

Kilgas laughed. "You're funny, Stack. I like you. You have skills. You should consider coming to my side and working with me. You'd be surprised how well good mercenaries get paid these days."

"I probably would. But I couldn't dream of giving all of this up." Zack looked, but no one was inside with him.

"Bring that partner of yours with," Kilgas said. "We could be one hell of a team."

"Well with all due respect I think I'll pass on your offer."

"I knew you would," Kilgas replied. "I wanted to congratulate you and your fiancé."

Zack was silent.

"I have to admit; I didn't see her writing those articles and never expected the press would run with them. Rosler won't be president and Pantalini the weasel is going to prison. It pains me to say it, but you win after all."

"I assume you're going to walk away?"

"I go where the money is," Kilgas said. "It's not here anymore. Pantalini threw me under the bus. I stay around here any longer I'll end up in prison next to him."

"And you don't think you deserve that? How many people did you kill?"

Kilgas laughed. "Come on, Stack, I didn't kill a single person. I did what I was told. I delegate, that's my job. Now, it's time to move on. If it helps, I can't stand Rosler either. I wanted to put a bullet in his skull after he did what he did to your fiancé."

Zack was silent.

"Keep my offer in mind. If you ever get bored finding lost dogs, have that secretary of yours find me. Bring her along too. She is skilled."

Zack was silent.

"Stack, you still there?"

"Oh, I'm sorry. I dozed off there for a moment. You were saying something?"

"Funny. Trust me, Stack: it wasn't personal. It was just a job."

"That won't make Hannah Davison or Ashley Blumenthal's parents feel any better."

Kilgas paused, and Zack heard a sigh. "Take it out on Rosler. Sayonara."

Zack took the phone away from his ear and pressed end. *Until we meet again, Kilgas.* He turned and saw Stefani.

She smiled. "Hey, you ok?"

"I'm fine."

Stefani shook her head. "I know you better than that. Julie sent me to drag you outside. Alysha and Michelle are beating Andre and Darnell pretty bad, and you and I are to take on Ronald the FBI Guy and Julie next."

Zack nodded.

"Who called?"

Zack let out a deep breath. "Andre sucks at the bag in the hole or whatever the hell that game is called. Michelle always wins."

Stefani smiled. "I will break down those walls of yours, Zachary Ulysses." She stared at him. "Don't count us out. I spent a lot of time tailgating. Call me your ringer," she winked at him. "You coming out?" She grabbed his hand. "Come on, Zack. You shouldn't be in here alone. It's Thanksgiving. Come on. For Jules?"

He forced a smile despite the conversation with Kilgas replaying in his head. "I'm fine. Really," he nodded. "Besides, I have to peel some potatoes. Go back out and tell them I'll be out as soon as I can." They stared at each other until Stefani frowned, nodded, and let go of his hand.

Zack's phone rang again. He didn't recognize the number but answered while he stared into Stefani's brown eyes. "Stack here."

"I never got a chance to say thank you."

Zack knew the voice: Donald Fairfax. "I'll gladly accept the information you have that I want instead of one."

"Yeah, I was thinking about that," Fairfax said. "You see, I still have a problem. You know who it is. So, I've decided that as long as he is a threat, I need a bargaining chip."

"What the?" Zack snapped. "That is not my problem. I got you out of jail. That was the deal."

"I know. But I changed it."

Zack's hands shook, and he looked away from Stefani. "You better hope I don't find you before he does."

Fairfax chuckled. "That would be extraordinarily bad for you. If something happens to me, the information gets released. You lose. Everyone you know does. Get it? I know he has his thugs looking for me. When that threat ends, you'll get the information."

"Something tells me you like extortion too much to quit this gig."

"Just make sure he doesn't hurt Erin or me." The line went dead.

Zack closed his eyes and struggled but lost control and threw his phone across the apartment. It smashed against the wall, and he clutched a side table. Zack squeezed it; the veins bulged out of his arms. Suddenly he felt the hands of Stefani on his shoulders.

"Zack! Please!"

Zack took a deep breath and let go of the table.

"What's wrong?"

He stared at the table, his rage about to burst again.

"Zack. Talk to me. What's wrong?"

I'm going to find him and kill him myself.

"Zack!" Stefani rose her voice. "Talk to me."

He looked at her finally and took a deep breath. He smiled. "I broke my phone. That's five phones and five watches in the last month." He leaned forward and kissed her cheek. "Costing me a fortune. Tell Jules I'll be out real soon."

She stared at him and shook her head. "Stubborn, but consistent. Jules is more than a saint!"

CHAPTER 54

Senator Michael Rosler parked his Lexus SUV in the driveway of his house in West Friendship. He was relieved no media were there. He was still in full damage control mode. Christmas Eve was in three days, and his presidential campaign ruined, but that seemed to be the end of it.

Pantalini was going to prison for a very long time. He and Kilgas did their jobs, and the FBI couldn't find anything linking Rosler to Ashley Blumenthal's death or the deaths of Hannah Davison and Sam Polzinski. That was a tough sell. He had repeatedly been grilled, and impeachment proceedings began before it was declared Rosler did not know about the actions. That saved his job, but the Presidency was lost.

He entered an empty house. Damage control was necessary for his wife leaving him. Erin didn't help him, but she could have hurt him worse. Rosler had dodged that bullet, too. The sudden divorce hurt his likability factor. It was another nail in the coffin to kill his Presidency campaign. Erin resigned from Valentino Industries, left the country with Donald Fairfax and the two disappeared. What pissed him off most was that they were living off his money — a lot of it. To complete his losses, Kilgas resigned and left him. "I go where the money is," Kilgas said. "And your well has dried." *For now, it has. But I'll be back.*

He locked the front door behind him, dropped the keys on a table along the wall of the entranceway and headed for the kitchen. The refrigerator revealed nothing appealing, so he went to his den to review more papers, reports, press releases and what else his new campaign manager spun to get the focus off of Rosler's shattered personal life and the debris of atrocities that blocked his pathway to the Presidency.

He poured a glass of whiskey with two ice cubes and sat down in the luxurious, brown leather chair behind a large mahogany desk. Suddenly a light turned on in the corner of the room.

Startled, he looked up and saw a man in all black clothing seated on the edge of the large black leather couch against the dark wood wall. He wore paper booties over his shoes.

"Surprised?"

Rosler recognized him. "What the hell are you doing here? How did you get inside? I have an alarm system."

"Not a very good one."

Rosler sat back. He didn't feel threatened. After all, he was still a United States Senator. And there was a Glock nine millimeter in the desk drawer in front of him. "I was wondering how long before you decided to meet face to face."

"I was pacing myself."

Rosler let out a smug sound. "So, you want to gloat?"

Many thoughts swirled in Zack's mind. "I have something much different in mind."

Rosler stared at the intruder. "We'll see about that after my new head of security gets here."

"I hope he hurries. I'm bored with you already."

Rosler had a drink. "I bet you were sitting in your shitty little office with your detective wannabe friends thinking you won, weren't you?"

Zack was silent.

"I have to say I'm impressed. Most people would have quit."

"I'm not most people."

Rosler laughed. "HA! You know Stack, the real world has evolved and isn't like you. Not in this town. Morals, values and ethics?" Rosler laughed. "Wake up and open your eyes. There isn't as much gloom and doom and depression in a world where you play ball. You and your girlfriend didn't win. The people of Maryland will re-elect me. It's all about patience now."

"Is it?" Zack lost patience already, and he felt the fire ignite. *Stay calm. Stick to the plan.*

Rosler laughed. "You are so naïve. It isn't about votes. That's what idiots like you believe. But it isn't. It's about money, and I have the donors behind me. Now more than ever they know I'll do what is necessary. As for the public? Oh sure, my image took a few hits. But Pantalini took the fall for everything. People forget. They're ignorant. You'll see. They don't want any of it to be true. That's called gullibility. I'll be back."

Zack was silent.

Rosler sipped his whiskey, his smile ever widened. "This is just a minor inconvenience."

Zack reached his left hand into his coat pocket and showed Rosler the flash drive Meg placed in his hand so many weeks ago. "This here will be a little more than a minor inconvenience I'd say."

Rosler hesitated then scoffed. "Bullshit. You're bluffing."

Zack was silent.

"You would have used it already if that were of any value."

"Like I said, I was pacing myself."

"You're a liar, Stack. That is nothing. It won't work. There's nothing to confess. I didn't know what Pantalini was doing. No one will remember Erin. No one cares," Rosler explained. "I had no idea. I was fighting for the people." He smiled. "In three years, the people will forget and eat it all up. Because there's no proof that I did anything wrong."

Zack put his right hand inside his coat pocket. "Egomaniacal narcissist." He got off the couch and walked to the desk. "That will be your undoing: always thinking you are smarter than the other guy." Zack smiled. "Bet you never counted on a group of college kids playing you to get the details of your sordid affairs. They played you like a fiddle at a Mississippi hoe-down." Zack sat on the edge of the desk. "Out of curiosity, how did you find out about them?'

Rosler smiled. "A girl named Darcy two years ago told me she was pregnant. I didn't believe it. I had her followed, and one night she went to a late meeting in an obscure place. It was a secret meeting. I texted her, and she told me she was home studying. That's when my guys spotted her leaving with Sam and some other girls. From there, it was just a matter of time until I learned all about it."

"And had them all killed," Zack added. "You must be proud."

"Stick the condescension up your ass, Stack. I did what I had to. I did this for the country! People like you weaken it. I make it stronger."

Zack shook his head. "I envisioned all these things I wanted to say to you and ask you, but now that I am sitting in front of you, all I want to do is vomit." He paused. "All you care about is power and money. I can't believe people were stupid enough to vote for you. At least you won't be President."

Rosler laughed. "It may be four years, maybe eight, but I will be President. No matter what you think. It's over, Private Dick. And that's why I win." He drank his whiskey. "Again."

Rosler smiled. "I have to tell you, though, that Julie of yours. Wow!" He leaned back in his chair and smiled as smug as he could. "Man, did we share one beautiful night. I'll tell ya; she can do a lot better than you. That book is going to help me dig out from this inconvenience."

Patience lost. Zack unloaded a solid right hook into Rosler's jaw. Zack could feel the jaw dislocated. Rosler looked shocked. Not done, Zack squared Rosler in the chair and straight punched him in the nose. Blood gushed over Rosler's face.

Zack stepped away. "Inconvenience? You call getting caught killing innocent people, bribing people, raping women, attempting to rig the election an inconvenience?" Zack felt the fire roaring inside of him. Rosler shouldn't have brought up Julie. Andre warned him not to leave the reservation. He didn't want Zack to do this. But Andre agreed, as long as Zack stuck with the plan. *I'm changing the plan!*

"Yeah, that's what I'd call it." Rosler wiped his face and saw blood cover his hands. "You idiot! I'll be back." Rosler held a handkerchief to his face. "It's all about money. Not truth or facts. People only care about themselves but aren't smart enough to vote for their best interests because I tell them what their interests are. So in a few years, I make a few promises, prey upon their fears, exacerbate their woes, and I'm golden again."

Zack stared at him.

"You, on the other hand, won't have a second chance. Breaking into my house was your last interference in my affairs. Hoping that flash drive in your hand would coax me into spilling anything was clever but you don't send amateurs to do a professional job."

"Which is why I'm here and not dead," Zack said. "Amateurs." Zack reached inside his coat and withdrew one of the guns he had taken off the men he killed at the hospital. Zack pointed at Rosler's head when the door opened and in walked three men dressed in black.

"My new security team, hotshot. What are you gonna do now?"

"This." Zack shot Rosler in the shoulder. Rosler yelled and slumped, exasperated and silent. The three men reached inside their coat pockets, but Zack quickly pulled a Glock from behind his back and pointed it at the men. "Ahh, ahh, ahh," he said. "Don't do it."

The men stopped.

"Now shut up and don't go anywhere," Zack said to Rosler and smacked the gun into the side of Rosler's head.

Zack looked at the men. "I'm in a good mood. I'll let you three turn and leave and forget all about this. Find a new job and forget what you saw. Best option," he said.

"KILL HIM!" Rosler yelled.

Zack dropped the gun he shot Rosler with but kept the Glock pointed at the men.

"I said KILL HIM! I have a million dollars upstairs in a safe. Kill him, and it's yours!" Rosler screamed.

Zack kept his eye on the men. He pointed at a black case on the couch. "There it is," he said. "His wife told me about it." Zack looked at Rosler. "Erin has been helpful. I like her," he said.

Zack looked back at the three men. They went for their guns. Zack took out the two behind the lead man with two quick shots. The third man stopped as Zack smiled and pointed the gun right at him.

"KILL HIM!" Rosler yelled again.

Zack looked back, leaned over and shot a rear kick into Rosler's face. It knocked him from the chair. "I said shut up."

304

He turned back, and the lead man charged at Zack.

BANG! BANG!

The man dropped dead on the floor in front of Zack. Zack stared at the dead men and heard Rosler scramble for his desk. Rosler opened the drawer, but the Glock was not there. He saw the gun Zack dropped on the floor and dove for that. He clutched it in his hands, aimed at Zack and pulled the trigger.

It clicked. Empty.

Zack turned back to Rosler. "Dumbass. Get up." Zack grabbed the top of Rosler's head, lifted him off the floor and punched him in the face. Rosler fell back into the chair. "You should be more careful about where you hide your gun." Zack held out the Glock. "Found it in four seconds. Now, where were we?" Zack stepped forward and punched Rosler in the face again.

Rosler gurgled. Blood poured from his face. "You think you're going to kill me? I'm a United States Senator. You kill me, and you're as good as dead. No one will believe your story," he said.

"I don't care," he said and punched him in the face again. Rosler lurched forward, but Zack kneed his head; Rosler snapped back into the chair, and Zack hit him again.

Rosler leaned back in the chair. His legs spread. Zack lifted his foot and drove the heel into Rosler's scrotum. Rosler coughed blood onto himself.

It wasn't enough pain yet. Zack thought of Julie and what Rosler had done to her and how it had hurt his relationship with Jules and wondered if they would ever recover.

"You can't kill me, Stack."

Zack took a deep breath and let it out slowly through his nose. "I never was going to."

* * * * * *

Zack crossed the lawn of the backyard, disappeared over a fence, dodged alongside a row of thick hedges and reached a sidewalk, walked for a few minutes, turned into a park and vanished into the darkness. On the other side of the park, he walked into a parking lot. He walked up to a BMW 550. The window rolled down.

"Problem solved?"

Zack exhaled and looked around. "Yup."

"And Kilgas?"

"He's gone. We don't have to worry about him."

"You sure?"

Zack nodded. "Unless he's getting paid, he doesn't care." Zack reached behind him, pulled out a bag and handed it to Dre.

"What's this?"

"A bag of money. You earned it. Merry Christmas." Zack saw the look. "Don't worry. It's a gift from the former Mrs. Rosler. Do me a favor and make sure Michelle, Darnell, and Stefani get some. Do that quietly, ok? Advise them to not be stupid about it, too."

Andre nodded and stuck the bag under his seat. "Jules is going to be pissed when she finds out you have that thing."

Zack nodded and waited as the silver car slipped away in the night. He grabbed his helmet, put it on and climbed aboard his new BMW motorcycle. Seconds later, he disappeared into the night.

CHAPTER 55

One PM on Christmas Eve; alone at the bar. The bells on the door dinged. A patron entered. The bartender saw Zack's empty mug and filled another.

A man sat beside him. Zack paid no attention. The bartender placed the filled mug in front of Zack and asked the man beside him what he'd have.

"Whatever he's having."

Zack turned to see Barnes beside him. "Merry Christmas," he greeted.

The bartender put a Sam Adams Winter Ale in front of Barnes and left them.

"Merry Christmas, Stack," Barnes said with a sullenness in his voice. He drank from his pint glass. "Been busy lately? I haven't heard from you."

"Holiday vacation," Zack said.

Barnes sighed again. "I don't want to ask you where you were three nights ago. I suspect with Julie, right?"

"Julie was at her mother's. You know how I am not exactly welcome there."

"Is there any wonder why?"

"No," Zack said. "So instead I went birding. Why?"

"Birding? Really? At night?"

"Owling. I participated in a Christmas Bird Count and wanted to add a couple of owls to the list."

Barnes nodded. "Were you alone?"

"It was dark. I couldn't see," Zack said. "What are you getting at?"

"Ok, if you want to play dumb. Senator Rosler was found dead at his house a couple of days ago. T.O.D. was three nights ago. Three men with no ID were also found dead."

Zack nodded and drank his beer. "That's a shame." He looked at Barnes. "What happened?"

"Rosler bled to death. Someone beat him half to death and put two bullets in him. The other three died via bullets from Rosler's Glock."

Zack picked at a small bowl of bar peanuts, pretzels and some cheesy piece of crunchy something that kept him reaching into the mix. "That's tragic."

"Do you know what's odd? They think," Barnes turned to Zack and smiled, "they think it was a robbery gone bad. They found a briefcase with two hundred grand in cash inside. It looks like three guys broke in and beat the shit out of him. He must have told them about a safe and the cash, they got it, but somehow Rosler managed to get his gun and shoot all three. He took two bullets from their guns. Forensics even backs them up. I mean, it couldn't have been staged any more perfectly to draw that conclusion." He stared at Zack.

Zack nodded. "Can't argue with science."

Barnes turned back. "Anyway, they found a flash drive. Looks like a journal of all the bad stuff Rosler was doing. Recordings, payments, meeting times and dates, lots of names, everything. If Rosler weren't dead, he would be getting the chair soon. But, Rosler is dead."

"Damn," Zack said. "I will need to vote for someone else next election."

"The fallout is going to last a while. A lot of people are in trouble."

"Shouldn't have got in bed with the devil."

"Yeah," Barnes nodded and drank from his glass. "Anyway, the press ate it up; the investigation is over. There were no signs of anyone else in that house. Just seems odd to me." Barnes drank again.

Zack shrugged. "Shit happens."

"We went through the information on that jump drive," Barnes said.

"Yeah?"

"Funny thing, there was no mention of Schmidt or O'Malley or Judge Blumenthal on Rosler's payroll."

Zack sipped his beer. "That's good."

Barnes stared at Zack in silence.

Zack sat silent for a long minute. "So, it's over?"

"Yep." He stared at Zack's hands, saw some discoloration and bruising. "Are you going to tell me what happened?"

Zack looked at Barnes, and the two held their fixed position. Zack exhaled. "You already know Lieutenant."

Barnes turned back to the television. The two finished their beers and got another. "It's Captain now, thanks to you and Dre."

"Congratulations, Captain Barnes," Zack said. "That should improve your 401k."

Barnes smiled. "Merry Christmas, Zack," he said at length.

"What now?"

"Well, Meg Chatwell will be pleased to know that since all the bad guys are dead, she can come out of hiding. I'll take care of that," Barnes said.

"Let me know where she is," Zack said. "I owe her some food."

"Will do. What are you doing next?"

Zack thought of Julie. He shrugged.

"You're supposed to get married this spring. I haven't received my invitation yet."

Zack stared at his glass and wondered if that would happen. "We haven't sent them out."

Barnes chuckled. "You delayed it, didn't you?"

No, I didn't. This time it was Jules. "I guess I just want to make sure everything is right, you know?"

Barnes laughed. "I'll bet you a hundred right now that she'll never get your scared butt down the aisle."

Zack smiled. "Never? You're on." They shook hands.

"I'll let you heal and then make reservations for four at the Charleston. Sound good? Mid-January time frame should work," Barnes smiled.

"Is there a saying about no good deed goes unpunished or something like that?"

Barnes swigged beer. "You going to be alone all day?"

Zack shook his head. "Probably." He drank. "I'm thinking of a trip to Europe." He looked at Barnes. "There is some unfinished business there to attend to."

Barnes nodded. "I was afraid of that." They each drank. "Anything else?"

"I'm planning a vacation for this spring."

Barnes laughed. "Just don't get involved with anything you shouldn't and please, for the love of God, stay clear of Indiana."

"What? Are you kidding? During spring migration, a front comes through at the right time, and the Dunes National Lakeshore is the perfect bottleneck for migrants. Hell, you can get 30 species of warblers in a few hours."

Barnes shook his head. "You can be such a nerd." He finished his beer and stood from the stool. He stared at Zack with a smile. "Merry Christmas." The two shook hands firmly. "And thank you, Zack. But you still owe me." He winked and turned away.

Zack watched him leave and turned back to the television. He didn't know what he was watching and didn't care. Zack thought about Andre, Michelle, Darnell, and Stefani. He thought of Julie. He remembered what Darnell told him repeatedly back in Michigan City, Indiana. *"If you ain't got family, you ain't got nothing!" They are my family. This is it for me.*

He finished the pint in front of him and sent Julie a text.

"Want a refill, Zack? It's on the house."

His phone buzzed. It was from Julie. *"I love you,"* it said. *"I'll be over sometime tomorrow. Staying at home tonight."*

Zack stared at the message and exhaled. *Alone on Christmas Eve. Merry Christmas to me, Zack.* "I might as well, Buck," he said to the bartender. "Nothing to go home to anyway."

THE END

ANDREW GRUSE

Acknowledgements

I remember being told that a political book, or a subject that has political overtones, may not be wise this day in age considering the divisiveness of the current situation. It was said that some will think I am attacking one side or whatever and that may lose future readers.

Well, to that I say tough shit. Please recall that this book is FICTION. And if that is not enough, I encourage those offended to look up fiction in the dictionary. (Any similarities between current or known politicians is purely coincidental and it is not my fault if there are politicians out there that may have participated in behavior that is in anyway equivalent to the scumbag senator in this story.)

This book was in the works long before now and long before the current administration (which will be true forever actually) and in the works before "Stacked Case" was released. So, to borrow a line from a quarterback in the NFL, "R-e-l-a-x."

Now, onto the acknowledgements. Thanks go to:
 My wife, Heidi, deserves the biggest thank you for supporting me even if she in the back of her mind doesn't think I'll ever sell enough books to support us. (Which I'm not sure of either her thinking that or me selling a lot of books.) To that, well, let's fifty shades this MF'er and prove 'em all wrong!

My mother, while in the hospital before she passed away told me that all of her favorite authors were dying. I asked why did she bring that up? Her reply was "because you're as good as any of them and now that they are gone, there's room for you." So I have to thank her, posthumously, for believing in me. If her belief in me turns out to be warranted, I know she'll see it.

312

To my brother Joe for letting me use one of the computers that was in his possession. The phrasing of that is key and he'll understand what I mean. By the way, Joe, the battery doesn't hold a charge any longer. I'd buy a new one, but I haven't gotten that far yet and as long as I'm within three feet of an outlet, it works just fine.

And I cannot write an acknowledgement page without mentioning our two sons, Benjamin and Matthew. From seeing Benjamin's first steps at seven months, three weeks old to seeing Matthew's last college baseball home run, and everything in between and since, you two are two of the reasons I write. As a side note, selling a lot of books is key so that if your mother and I ever have grandkids, we can be there to babysit. 😉

I also need to shout out to my uncle Tom Retseck. He was the first person to arrive at my very first book signing for "Stacked Case." I don't know if he liked the book or not, but that's not important here. It was great to see him again, and after talking a bit he told me that a couple of the sayings my mother told me were sayings he and his siblings heard from their mother. Tommy, you will be pleased to know that my kids are very familiar with them as well. (Neither will ever tell me they are bored!)

To my dad: keep fighting. You have all of our love and support.

And last but certainly not least, as the cliché goes, to you, the readers. Without you there would be no authors. There would be no writers like me striving to write a novel that entertains you, makes you think, question, smile, cry, laugh, get angry, or feel any of the bevy of emotions possible with books. Not saying mine will have you do any of them. I hope so. At least the entertaining part. And I hope you enjoyed it enough to post on social media about it and tell your family and friends to buy a copy. (I know, not very subtle, but a guy has to eat!). In all seriousness, though, thank you.

I sincerely hope you did enjoy this Zack Stack novel and are looking forward to the third installment in the series, "Smoke Stacks." I promise it won't take so long to be released.

Thank you all again and keep on reading!

Zack Stack and his fiancé Julie Fletcher wanted a vacation to get away, reconnect and start their relationship fresh. Now, in Andrew Gruse's explosive new thriller, a stop in a rural midwestern town tests the limits of their relationship, the boundaries of loyalty and turns Zack's world upside down...

SMOKE STACKS

Coming soon
A preview follows.

Chapter 1

Zack Stack slowed the car on the rural two-lane highway. "Look at that smoke," Zack said. "Looks like someone is having one hell of a bonfire."

"Swearing," Julie Fletcher said as a reminder. It was her goal to eliminate Zack's swearing by their wedding. "Remember what my mother says."

Screw your mother. "Sorry," Zack said. They drove around a slight bend in the state highway and saw flashing lights ahead. Lots of flashing lights.

"Oh my God," Julie said. "That's not a bonfire. The whole house and barn are on fire!"

A large farmhouse and its surrounding buildings burned out of control. Several fire trucks faced the buildings and poured as much water on the fire as they could.

Zack slowed the car further with the county sheriff's car in the middle of the road ahead. Zack looked at the house: it was completely engulfed in flames. Two barns burned out of control. He saw five horses running in the back field and hoped there were no more animals inside the barns. The fire crept closer to a silo behind the barns. Black smoke billowed miles into the air.

"Oh my God," Julie repeated slower and softer as the realization of what unfolded only a quarter mile in front of them hit her.

Zack saw the sheriff wave at Zack's car and pointed to the far side of the road. Mid-morning on a Saturday in the middle of farm country in the Midwest. It was quiet except for the wild blaze.

Zack slowed further and stopped as the sheriff approached. Zack rolled down the window.

"Folks, I need you to turn around and head back."

Zack looked at the house. Part of the roof collapsed. The barn toppled, swallowed by the orange and yellow flames. The roar of the fire could be heard clearly even over a hundred yards away where they sat.

Zack frowned and nodded. "No chance we can just sneak around on the shoulder?" Zack looked and noticed it was wide and clear. All the fire trucks were on the north side of the road. Zack and Julie were headed west and the south side was clear.

"Sir, it's dangerous up there."

Suddenly, an explosion filled the air and sent a large cloud of smoke and debris into the air. The cop flinched as did Zack and Julie. The silo disappeared in the shockwave, obliterated by the explosion. The barns disappeared with it. There was nothing left of the farm buildings. The explosion wave subsided and to the cops surprise, the flames lessened.

"What the hell?" The cop said as he stood and watched the fire.

"The explosion took all the oxygen," Zack said. "Is that orange smoke?"

"It sure is," the cop said. "Why?"

Zack shook his head. "No reason. Sir, I didn't see a road to turn off on the way here," Zack said. "I don't want to go back to the interstate. I promise I'll be careful and get around this quickly."

The sheriff looked both ways. Still no other traffic. "Go ahead. Don't stop and film it on your phones or anything or I'll arrest you both."

Zack smiled. "Thank you, officer. We won't."

The cop waved him along and spoke into the mic on his shoulder. Zack drove to the far shoulder as far over as he could and drove past the dying inferno. He saw the emblems on the fire trucks scattered about the front of the property. "There must be four or five different departments there. Probably every volunteer department in fifty miles!"

"Oh my God," Julie said softly again. "I feel so bad for that family. They just lost everything."

Zack looked again over his shoulder as he passed the county sheriff on the opposite side of the property blocking eastbound traffic. Zack knew he saw orange smoke but quickly focused on the sheriff, nodded, got back into the proper lane and slowly accelerated away from the catastrophe.

A sign listed the next two towns along the highway. Clyde was 9 miles away, Hobby followed at 22 miles. The two were silent.

Julie stared out the window before she put her left hand on top of Zack's right hand which he rested on the center counsel.

"I've never seen a fire like that before," Julie said.

Zack had in the military while serving overseas. He watched as the US airpower leveled towns and scorched the earth. Intentional. *Like when you want to make something disappear.* "How the hell does the house, barn, garage and another barn all catch fire at once and what would make the silo explode like that?"

"I don't know, babe," Julie said and squeezed his hand. "Let's focus on us today. We can't do anything about that fire. What about your birds? What are we looking for?"

He shrugged. "Horned larks, kestrel's, maybe we'll get lucky and see pipits or longspurs," Zack said turning his attention back to birds. "When we get closer to the river, that's when we're looking for Eurasian Tree Sparrows."

"And what are those?"

Zack looked at her. "They look like House Sparrows, only prettier. Remember? I showed you the difference when we were in Europe?"

Julie looked out the window. "Oh yeah, how could I forget?"

The sarcasm wasn't lost on Zack. He let out a deep breath. "Here comes Clyde. I am sure there's a Ma and Pa's Diner here. Should we stop?"

"Hey, you're the one that insists that this is how you see the real America."

Zack smiled. "What's this on the left?"

They saw from the distance a group of kids marching in formation in a giant empty parking lot. In the rear view mirror, nine miles down the road, Zack could see the black clouds in the sky but from that distance understood why no one knew why.

"Looks like a high school band practicing. Let's stop, honey. It will be fun!"

Zack saw the welcome sign to the town and read it aloud: "Welcome to the town of Clyde. Where it all begins," he finished. "I don't like the sound of that. We should keep going."

Julie laughed. "A new beginning? What's wrong with that? Pull in, honey. I want to watch."

Zack pulled the car into the parking lot and parked near the marching band. They stepped out of the car and listened to the band play Michael Jackson's 'Thriller.'

"I think every high school band ever has to learn that song," Zack said but his attention was drawn to the school a few hundred yards away.

The school was L-shaped. The center looked like the original building with a giant smokestack behind the three-story building. A new addition, new being a relative term Zack figured, branched off the original building. One went to the east and looked like a gymnasium was most of it while the other side had an addition that faced north-south. It was above that part that caught Zack's attention.

"Is that smoke?"

"What? Where?" Julie shifted her focus that late morning to the high school.

"Just to the right of the smokestack. See it?" Zack looked through his binoculars.

"Probably just a vent or something," Julie said.

Zack recognized it wasn't just a vent. Black smoke increased and as he focused on the smoke he could see flames. "Sonofabitch, Jules! There's a fire!"

"What?"

Zack tossed the binoculars inside the car and headed for the building.

"Zack! What are you doing?"

"Getting anyone out of there. Call the fire department," Zack yelled as he broke into a run towards the building.

"No, Zack! Don't!" Julie called but it was too late.

Seconds later, one of the students yelled "FIRE!" The kids stood there, not knowing what to do as the flames intensified, windows shattered on the top floor and a couple of girls screamed. "MISS LOCKETT IS INSIDE!"

Julie turned to the kids. The band leader stared in awe as the flames shot from the roof and then ran towards the building. Julie turned again, but Zack disappeared inside the building.

Chapter 2

Zack raced through the front entrance and looked for a fire alarm. He saw one on the wall near a door with 'Office' above it. Zack grabbed the handle and pulled it down, but nothing happened. He spun around, saw no one and hesitated. *There were cars parked out front. Someone must be here.*

The main door opened and the male bandleader entered. He stopped when he saw Zack.

"Sara Lockett is inside," he said

"Where is she?"

"Probably in her room. Second floor. Room 222."

Zack shook his head. "WHICH WAY?"

The bandleader, an older gentleman who looked like he had taught at that school for several decades pointed to his left, towards the fire. "Down the hall is the stairs. She's near the end of the hall to the left of the stairs."

"Ok, I'll get her. You get out of here and keep everyone as far away as possible."

Zack ran down the hallway. Though the middle of the day, there was little light in the hall. He reached the stairs and sprint up three at a time. He smelled smoke, saw another fire alarm and pulled that one. Nothing. *Why the HELL doesn't the fire alarm not work? It has one purpose!*

Zack looked both ways, saw no movement and ran towards Room 222. He saw the number on the closed door as smoke filled the hallway. Flames crackled and popped and the heat made Zack sweat. A ceiling tile fell only feet away from Zack and fire, smoke, and heat belched from the ceiling. *This is not good! Where is she?*

Zack couldn't see through the tempered glass on the door and touched the handle. He tried to turn it, but it wouldn't budge. He tried again with both hands. The handle would not turn. *Why is it locked? WTF?*

Zack didn't think about it again and kicked the door handle with the base of his foot. The door jamb splintered and the door burst open. The sudden gust of fresh air enraged the fire as Zack jumped into the room to avoid the ball of flames. He scrambled to the desk, checked the closet. Nothing. "SARA LOCKETT!" He yelled. No reply. He ran to the back of the classroom and found another locked door. He ripped it open but it was empty except for the containers of flammable liquids. One quick take and Zack realized what the room was for: Sara Lockett used the room to develop pictures. *Oh this keeps getting better and better!*

Where is she? The conflagration closed in on the room. Zack hunched over and held his shirt over his mouth and nose. He heard more of the building crumble in the hallway. Zack knew he was moments from being trapped inside. Then, he saw a large coffee container on the desk. *The bathroom!*

Zack raced back to the hallway, looked both ways and saw the restroom sign on the wall closer to the fire. The smoke thickened; Zack coughed and his eyes watered. He reached the door and pushed it open. The room was dark but not filled with smoke yet. Zack coughed but saw no one.

"Sara Lockett!" No answer. He walked to the first stall and pushed open the door. "Sara? Are you in here?"

He heard a noise two stalls down. He leaned over but there were no feet visible. "SARA!" He screamed and he heard a voice make a small yelp. Zack reached the door, pushed it, it was locked, and then rammed his shoulder through it.

The woman screamed as she sat crouched on the seat, her feet on the lid.

"Come on," Zack said. "We have to get out of here."

She stared at him, fear in her eyes. Zack saw her hands shake; her face white.

"Sara Lockett?" Zack breathed fast. She nodded. "We have to get out of here. The place is on fire."

"Who are you? Are you alone? Is there anyone else out there?"

Zack grabbed her hand. "We don't have time. Come on."

Just then, a small explosion rocked the floor. A wall caved and crashed to the floor. Zack, with her hand in his, pulled the restroom door, but the explosion wedged it shut. He pulled it again, it didn't budge, he grabbed with both hands and yanked it as hard as he could. Finally, with a loud yell and one foot against the wall for leverage, the door let loose and flung open. Zack fell to the ground with Sara behind him.

"Come on!" Zack pulled her into the hallway.

The hallway filled with smoke and flames choked each end of the hallway. Lockers had blown off the hall and cluttered the hallway. Room 226 was the nearest doorway and the only exit from the inferno as it spread closer.

The fire spread fast. Faster than Zack thought it would in a building of mostly brick. The ceiling sagged and buckled. More smoke and flames then it dropped to the floor. The deafening sound suddenly silenced and the air sucked out. Zack knew what was next. He kicked open the door on Room 226 and leapt inside, pulling the woman with him.

A fireball exploded, engulfed the hallway and filled the room. Black and gray smoke blinded them and red-hot flames chased them. Sweat covered Zack's body and he felt like his clothes were on fire. The woman beside him crawled away from the doorway as the fire incinerated everything in its path.

Zack rushed to the windows in the back of the classroom, looked out with his burning eyes. Though on the second floor, the fire trapped them. Through the window was the only way out.

He grabbed a desk with both hands, spun and released it towards the windows. The desk burst through and fell to the ground. The added oxygen however added to the woes of the fire.

Zack looked out; his eyesight blurred. He blinked and wiped them to see what was below. He thought he saw something yellow or orange move along the school headed towards the back but a plume of smoke blocked his vision. "This way, it's our way out," he said.

The woman coughed and covered her mouth with her shirt as she crawled to Zack.

More of the ceiling above them crackled and sagged. Small explosions ripped through the building. The fire engulfed a classroom and another explosion ripped a huge hole in the wall of the building. *Sara's room. The flammables just blew.* He grabbed another desk and launched it through the window in the front of the classroom. Zack fell to his knees and coughed. His mind fought off the panic mode; *Stay calm! You only have moments before the smoke wins. Get out that window now, Zack!*

The fresh air from the second broken window vented some but offered little relief. Zack stood and got to the window. "Come on." Zack put his hand on the sill, a remaining piece of glass cut him. He ripped off his shirt and put it on the sill. "Get up, you first. Go for the roof of the school bus below," he instructed.

"What?"

Zack grabbed her by the waist, lifted her to the window and pushed her legs out. "JUMP!" He pushed her towards the roof top of the school bus below then got himself through the window and jumped behind her.

Sara landed awkwardly on the roof and fell off. Zack tried to be graceful but the roof bounced him off. They landed hard on the pavement below just as another window exploded. Flames shot out of the window and debris fell about the driveway behind the school. The row of buses lined up along the school burned.

They heard more small explosions. Zack saw the tall smokestack beside the boiler room: the heat supply for the entire school complete with a large storage for fuel oil. The fire swallowed it.

"We have to get out of here," Zack said amidst a steady cough and hack.

Zack pulled her off the ground. A part of a wall crumbled onto the drive to the north of them. They ran south, past the boiler room, towards the rear of the school and the forested fields behind them. Away from the main fire.

Zack grabbed her hand and the two ran. The heat didn't dissipate as they ran past the boiler room, through a large parking lot and towards the fence line. They ran through the gate, across a small field. Fifty yards away. Still running. Zack saw a large pond ahead and ran towards that. Then he heard it. An explosion he heard before; the pitch was different from an oil drum or gasoline explosion.

Where's the shockwave? Why aren't we dead or flying through the air?

He kept running and then heard the secondary explosion. The oil tank exploded. The fireball expanded. Zack kept her hand in his and dove headfirst into the pond. The fireball overwhelmed the pond.

Zack opened his eyes as they propelled across the pond beneath the water surface. The orange, red, and black fireball heated up the surface. Zack could feel the temperature change and it brightened the depths of the pond. The two swam further, holding their breath.

The flames dissipated. The two swam further and out of breath, lungs burned and hearts pounded, they burst to the surface near the far shoreline and gasped for fresh air.

He pulled her ashore and the two sat for a moment when Zack saw the smokestack teeter and lean. It crackled and popped, then started its freefall.

"No, no, no, no, no!" Zack grabbed her hand again and yanked her away from the collapsing stack. It hurdled towards the ground and the two ran. The smokestack slammed into the ground. Bricks, mortar, smoke, and ash billowed into the air and rained upon the two as they fell to the ground.

Zack coughed and pushed debris off him. The two crawled out of the smoke plume. They coughed, expelled the dirty smoke and ash from their lungs and nose and remained seated on the ground in long grass behind the pond as the school burned to the ground.

He caught his breath, looked at the woman beside him. She coughed and coughed before finally looking at Zack. He smiled and said, "Welcome to Clyde, where it all begins, huh?"

Chapter 3

She stared at him, coughed and nodded. "Did you see anyone else leave the building?"

"No. Was there someone else inside?"

Sara Lockett stared at the building but didn't answer. They both coughed and hacked.

Zack looked at her. He wasn't sure if it was shock or fear but there was something on her face. "Are you ok?"

She coughed and nodded. "Thank you. You saved my life."

Zack coughed and spit a gob of dark saliva from his mouth. "Now we'll just die of lung cancer," he said softly between coughs.

"You didn't see anyone else inside?"

Zack shook his head. "I didn't see anyone else." Zack got to his knees, rested his hands on his thighs and forced several coughs to expel what was in his lungs. "Why was your classroom door locked?"

"What?" She coughed and spit out dark gunk. "It wasn't."

Yes, it was. "Why were you hiding in the restroom?"

"I," she hesitated, "I guess I was scared when I heard you come in."

Zack looked at her and watched her face. She shifted her eyes away from him and her shoulders slouched. If he had to guess, and he was, she lied.

"When I entered the restroom?" He coughed. "Did you even know the building was burning?"

"I," she hesitated again and shook her head. "You didn't see anyone leave?"

He stood slowly, stretched his back and coughed. "Only the desks I threw out the window. Come on," he said and helped her to her feet. "My girlfriend is going to be worried about me and your students worried about you."

They both coughed again, hands on their knees, faces red and expelling whatever they could.

"Now what am I going to do?" Sara asked.

"Sara, I think school's been permanently dismissed."

* * * *

Julie Fletcher crouched near the fence at the far edge of the school parking lot on the northeast corner of the school campus. She watched in horror as flames ate the school and swallowed sections at an alarming rate. The kids around her, high school age, watched in awe. Some cried, some were silent, many were on their cell phones letting their parents know they were ok. It was just a simple band practice. That was all.

Members in the band had seen at least two people enter the school. Julie had since seen one exit, a man. She was told that was the principal. He got in his car and moved it far away from the inferno but came nowhere near the group of students and Julie.

She heard the explosions. She saw the fireballs and watched helplessly as the tall single smokestack at the rear corner of the complex tumbled and fell, surrounded by flames and smoke. Julie heard screams, but she could only fight off the tears: her fiancé was still inside the building.

At long last, the fire trucks roared into the parking lot. Firemen scrambled, hoses unraveled and hooked to hydrants and water streamed into the conflagration but to little effect: the damage was done. It was complete. Julie watched walls crumble and disappear, smoke, ash, dust and debris rise into the air in plumes that vanished into the air over the small town. The crowd assembled and grew. She guessed the entire town was along the street to the northwest of the school grounds, behind the police cars that stopped traffic and held the masses at a safe distance.

Still, all Julie thought about was the man she loved, Zack Stack. It was supposed to be a vacation for the two of them. A time to heal and get away from everything that had ruined their holidays. A re-birth of their relationship. She cried silently. Where was he?

* * * *

The two walked slowly around the outside of the six-foot chain link fence along a mowed four-foot wide path along the fence perimeter. Though the sun shone brightly and the song of an Eastern Meadowlark filled the meadow to the east of them, it didn't feel like a beautiful spring day. Zack and Sara coughed, though less frequently and trudged across the yellowish-green grass. Zack saw the group of the band huddled along the fence and knew Julie would be there.

The students dispersed from the tight gathering near the fence as parents arrived and the fire extinguished. The smoke plumes filled the air, but they turned color to white as the school smoldered and the water reacted with the coals. Zack saw Julie hunched on the ground, her knees pulled to her chest, arms tight around her knees and her head sunk into her forearms.

"Come on, climb over," he said to Sara from the other side of the fence.

She didn't hesitate. She secretly declared to herself she was going to do anything and everything this man asked her to do because she knew she would be dead inside the heap of ruins that used to be the school she taught if he had not risked his life to find her.

Sara grabbed the top of the fence and Zack helped her over. He stuck his foot against the link, raised up, foot to the top and hopped over to the ground. The thud raised Julie's head. She bolted off the ground, ran to him and leapt into his arms. Only then did she realize he was shirtless and completely covered in soot, ash, dirt, and blood.

"OH MY GOD!" She cried. "Are you ok?"

He nodded and fell to his butt on the grass. "I'm fine," he said. He looked at Julie who looked at Sara Lockett. "Jules, this is Sara. Sara, this is Jules." He took a deep breath.

Julie looked at the equally disturbingly filthy Sara. "Are you ok?"

She nodded and smiled. "Thanks to him I am."

"Oh my God," Julie said. "Are you sure? You two look awful."

Zack smiled. *I'm really getting tired of hearing that.*

Sara nodded again. "I've been better, but I'm fine," she said. "Did you see anyone else leave the building?"

* * * *

Zack sat at the rear of the ambulance while a paramedic cleaned and bandaged his many scrapes and cuts. Julie sat by his side and watched the events around them. Evening set in and the spring air cooled though not much. The sky remained mostly clear as the sun set, and the air smelled of smoke, ash, burnt rubber, wood, metal, and plastic.

The crowd dissipated but the fire personnel continued to soak hot spots. The police opened the road again and only the local force, all three of them remained on the scene. One approached the rear of the ambulance with a notepad open. Zack had seen him earlier; this one was in charge.

"Excuse me, you're," the policeman trailed off as he stopped in front of Zack.

"Zack Stack," he said. The paramedic finished.

"Stack, I'm Sheriff Barney Orbison. Sheriff of Clyde," he said. He looked at Julie. "Who are you?"

"Julie Fletcher," she answered.

"What brings you two to my town?"

"Just passing through, Sheriff," Zack replied. "We are on vacation."

"Vacation? Where you headed?"

Zack smiled. "West until we hit the Mississippi River, then north. Site seeing mostly."

"Not much of a vacation. Most people would head to Florida or Hawaii or somewhere with a nice beach," the sheriff quipped.

"That's what I said," Julie added.

"Well, Mr. Stack, I have to ask you some questions, routine you know."

"I know."

"So why don't you tell me how you ended up here and inside that school today before it burnt down."

Zack let out a deflating breath. *Barney Fife thinks I'm an arsonist.* "Actually, sheriff, I didn't go into the school until I saw that it was on fire. I saw the cars parked out front and assumed someone was inside."

The cop nodded and took notes. "Why didn't you pull the fire alarm? Maybe that would have gotten the fire department here sooner."

"I did," Zack said plainly. "It didn't work."

"What? How can it not work?"

"I know, right? That's exactly what I said. I mean, a fire alarm literally has only one job."

"Ok, what else happened inside?"

Zack told the sheriff exactly what he did inside the school and answered questions for the next ten minutes. Finally, the sheriff shut his notepad and slid it in his shirt chest pocket.

"Well, you both look tired. Why don't you get yourself a room at the motel in town right on Main Street and spend the night."

Zack smiled. "Sheriff, are we being accused of something? Are you holding us here?"

"No, folks, I am not. You just look like you could use a shower, a hot meal and a warm bed. And this town is as good as it gets around here."

Zack nodded. *He's probably right about that.*

"I know you didn't do it. Timeline is all off, but maybe you saw something. And you said you're a private investigator so maybe I'll see if you're any good at it," the sheriff smiled.

"He's supposed to be on vacation," Julie said.

"The high school wasn't supposed to burn down when you showed up either," the sheriff winked. "Just make life easier for me and stick around tonight, ok?"

Zack nodded. "I don't feel like driving anyway, Sheriff."

They watched the sheriff disappear. Zack and Julie stood and headed to their car. There was no more reason to be there that day. It would be dark quickly and though it was a middle-of-nowhere sleepy farm town, a hot meal and a warm bed sounded good to both.

"I'll cancel our reservations," Julie said. "You OK to drive?"

"It's only a mile into town. I'm sure I can make it." They opened the doors, got inside and Zack started the Honda Accord.

"This has been one hell of a day." She looked at him. "You know, Zack, I don't like seeing you seated at the end of an ambulance being bandaged. It seems to happen far too often."

"I know," he said. "I swear, honey, this trip was just supposed to be all about you and me and seeing some birds during spring migration."

She laughed. "Birds." She shook her head. "I don't think we're gonna see that Eurasian thing you wanted to see today."

He smiled. "Eurasian Tree Sparrow."

She stared at him with wet cerulean eyes and a sorrowful smile. She put a hand on his cheek, leaned forward and lightly kissed his lips. "Well, hopefully we can find them tomorrow."

Zack smiled. "I hope so, too." But something told him that they were not leaving the town of Clyde anytime soon.

www.ingramcontent.com/pod-product-compliance
Lightning Source LLC
Chambersburg PA
CBHW021530250626
47154CB00006BA/2056